Strangers with the Same Dream

ALISON PICK

ALFRED A. KNOPF CANADA

PUBLISHED BY ALFRED A. KNOPF CANADA

Copyright © 2017 Alison Pick

www.penguinrandomhouse.ca

Library and Archives Canada Cataloguing in Publication

Pick, Alison, 1975–,
Strangers with the same dream / Alison Pick.

Issued in print and electronic formats.

ISBN 978-0-345-81045-8
eBook ISBN 978-0-345-81047-2

I. Title.

PS8581.I2563S77 2017   C813'.6   C2017-900802-1

Book design by Five Seventeen

Cover image: © Marta Orlowska / Arcangel Images

Printed and bound in the United States of America

2 4 6 8 9 7 5 3 1

Penguin
Random House
KNOPF CANADA

For Eric

And surely your blood of your lives will I require; at the hand
of every beast will I require it, and at the hand of man; at the
hand of every man's brother will I require the life of man.
—Genesis 9:5

Spilled blood is not the roots of trees
but it's the closest thing to roots
we have.
—Yehuda Amichai

This story begins with a lie.

I killed myself. That's what they said. They made me pay with that particular shame. When our descendants spoke of me, I was not named but instead called "the suicide," or sometimes "the first suicide." A cautionary tale.

Committing suicide meant no burial, no mourning rites. No Kaddish, no winding sheets, no shiva. No final consolations, just as, for me, there had been no daughterhood or motherhood, no group of people who could stand in for the family I never had. Alone in death as I had been in life.

Back then, to kill yourself was a sin. It brought great disgrace. Which, of course, is what they wanted. Well. Maybe I deserved it after all the damage I had done.

We lived that whole year pushed up against death—illness, accident, things more sinister still. There was a gun, and we argued over it like the children that we were—who could touch it, who could hold it, who would be the first to discharge the verdict of its bullets. The first time I saw it I knew, somehow, that it would be the instrument of my death. I could not have guessed the story that would come first.

Now I am dead and that story is all I know.

I revisit it, questioning my judgment, my motivation. And mostly, I am graced now with compassion for myself I did not have in life. I understand why I did what I did, and why I sometimes kept silent. I can forgive my mistakes.

Still, it is small consolation to be alone in forgiving oneself; I would like for you to understand me too.

What does a ghost want? Redemption. To tell her story. And you are the ones I have chosen to tell. You are my own chosen people.

Now that I have been snipped free from linear time I can drift back and forth as I wish. Far in the future lies the terrible bloom of what we planted. It is your bloom now. The future is a tangle I prefer not to visit.

Instead, I go backward as ghosts love to do. I want to take you with me, to that first year when we were living only for each moment, and each moment contained the whole of time, a kind of perpetual present that we grew to take for granted. That first year, when the swamps were drained, when the land was readied and the fields were sewn, when the crops first faltered and then thrived. The year when, despite our failures, something bigger grew up all around us. How proud we were. How satisfied. How could we have known what was coming?

When the story of the first year is told—and it is, in poems and songs and books—our descendants gloss over the sickness, the long months of near starvation, the mix of Jews and Arabs whose backs they stood upon. Is truth revealed over time? In your time? I wish I could say so. But nobody knows the full scope of what happened—to all of us. And to me. I wish it didn't matter, but my honour is at stake.

I would like my truth to stand so my name might be spoken, if not in the hushed tones of reverence given to the founding members, then at least with respect. I did my best. I came up short. Can any of you claim otherwise?

PART ONE

Ida

CHAPTER 1

_W_ HEN IDA ARRIVED IN the new place and saw the hot sun broken over the mountain's crust and the sky above it an impossible ravaged blue, she felt that she had been dead up until that moment. Her real life was about to begin.

If she could have seen what was coming she might have felt differently. But only I could see it. And of course I couldn't tell her.

Ahead of her was a scraggly line of settlers, halutzim, winding its way toward the mountain.

"Smotri," someone said in Russian.

"Was?" someone else asked in German.

"Speak Hebrew!" a third halutz reminded them. This was the rule, along with equality, shared property, and communal living. It was 1921 . . . 5681, Ida corrected herself; she must force herself to use the Hebrew year, not the secular one. Theirs would be the first generation in two thousand years to raise children in the language pulled from the ashes of history. Still, when the halutz behind Ida muttered a curse, it was in Yiddish.

The line slowed; something was happening up ahead. Ida stopped, and someone bumped into her back. She turned, and the man blushed. He looked like he had stepped directly out of a Zionist recruitment poster. The peaked worker's cap. The loose white singlet. He was already tanned, as though he had spent many hours labouring under Eretz Yisrael's relentless sun.

"Sorry," he said. "I was dreaming."

Ida shrugged.

The man considered her, a half-smile on his smooth face. "All the deeds of men are dreams at first, and become dreams at the end."

"Quoting Herzl," Ida said, and laughed. "I feel like I know you already."

"Levi," he said. "You do."

She touched her ear.

"Shabbat Shalom," he said.

"Is it Friday?" she asked.

"Saturday," he said.

And at this, Ida knew that she and Levi came from the same kind of homes: religious fathers with beards and tefillim. Cholent on the stove so their mothers would not have to cook— to work—on the Sabbath. But Ida was also thinking of Levi's bravery at admitting his religious observance. The new kibbutz would be secular. Another rule.

Levi took his cap off and stuffed it in his back pocket, revealing straight chocolate-brown hair, a cropped cut that was growing out and stood up from his head at all angles. Without his hat, she saw he was not a man but a boy. Eighteen or nineteen. Not twenty. His eyes were green. He peered at her, as though looking for something.

"Your eyes are green," he said.

Nobody ever mentioned her eyes, so hidden behind her glasses. Ida laughed again.

"What's funny?"

"I was noticing the same about you."

Levi's face split into a grin; she saw his front tooth was chipped.

"We have something in common," he said.

"We have several things in common," Ida said, and returned his smile. Here they were, she thought, in this remote land of Palestine, far from their homes and families. They had left their lives as they knew them to turn the Balfour Declaration, and the idea of a homeland for the Jews, into truth. They were strangers with the same dream. Ida was a mild girl who had never felt strongly about an idea in her life. But this was the thing: Zionism was not just an idea. It was something that was happening, now and now and now. It was something *she* could make happen.

And after what had been done to her father, she had no other choice.

Somebody sneezed; somebody blessed them. A single tuft of cloud changed shape against the wide blue sky. The arid land went on forever, with only an occasional scrabbly shrub or struggling tuft of grass. The air smelled of baked mud and sweat and a dense kind of emptiness. The mosquitoes clotted in clouds, and beside her Levi swatted the air in front of his face.

"There must be a word for this many bugs," she said.

"A plague?"

"Next the cows will die."

They laughed; there were no cows—not yet—only the two spindly donkeys the Agency had given them.

"And the firstborn sons."

"There are so many men . . ." Ida gestured at the line ahead of them. Then she wished she hadn't said this.

"Four for every woman."

But Levi, too, looked like he had said the wrong thing.

"I don't know anyone," he added, gesturing at the halutzim in hobnail boots and kerchiefs.

"You know *me*," she said. And she reached over and touched his shoulder.

She was astonished by her response to this boy. He was pulling something out of her she had not known existed.

The sun beat down like a lunatic.

"It's so hot," Ida said. Sweat on her forehead, on her cheeks under her glasses, trickling down between her breasts. Levi fumbled in his canvas pack, then came out with a battered canteen.

"Here," he said, holding it out to her, a circle of hammered metal with a nozzle attached to the top. She looked at it in his hand. It had taken on, magically, the properties of something more than a water container, of something of great symbolic weight.

She froze, her hands against her shoulders beneath the straps of her own pack, so Levi was forced to ask, "Would you like a drink?"

A flush rose up his face. Ida knew he was asking if he could give her something, and he was also asking if he could take something. The answer came from some unknown depth inside her, rising like a bubble.

"Yes," she said.

He repeated the word, as if to underline it. "Yes."

Several long moments passed. Then he smiled, and the small chip in his front tooth extracted a tenderness from her that made her gut wrench. She wanted to get closer to him.

Levi was still holding out the bottle; she reached for it. The hammered tin was not cool, but it was cooler than the air. Their hands didn't touch, but they both rested on the canteen, scarcely any space between their fingertips.

When Ida drank, the water tasted sharp, metallic.

Later, she would think back to this moment. She hadn't longed for him unrequited. She hadn't wished for him, and then had her wish granted. Instead, he had arrived fully formed, filling a hole inside her she had been entirely unaware of. At the same time that her desire had arisen, its fulfillment was provided.

Later, it was her own blissful ignorance she would grieve for. She didn't yet know what damage love could wreak.

"Stop!" a voice shouted in Russian, the language most of them spoke despite the Hebrew they were rapidly trying to learn.

"Says who?" someone shouted back.

"Danger up ahead," said someone else.

Several other voices began to sing "Hatikvah," but the song petered out after the first two or three lines. Ida pushed her glasses up on her nose, straining to see what was happening. They were passing the homes of the Arab tenant farmers, a village of perhaps twenty families. The Arabs had come out of their houses and were gaping at the line of halutzim inching through the valley. Soon, the line stopped and two figures stepped forward. The first, the village mukhtar, wore his white jalabiya with the traditional black and white checked keffiyeh on his head. David, the halutzim's leader, was dressed in a simple settler's costume of a loose white shirt and short pants. The two men faced each other like kings on a chessboard.

The day was perfectly still, and Ida and Levi, near the back of the procession, could hear every word the others said.

"Salam!" David raised his hand. "The Hebrew tribe is here to settle this valley."

There was a long moment, and the old Arab nodded. It could have been acceptance, or a challenge: *We'll see about that.*

A hawk cried out from Mount Gilboa. The light changed, and Ida saw a scar bisecting the old man's cheek. The kind of scar that only a knife could have inflicted.

Behind him, his people had gathered. Ida spotted a young mother about her own age, maybe eighteen, with a gaggle of children clinging to her. Ida was toward the rear of her own group, but the woman stood on her tiptoes, as though looking for Ida specifically; as though she had been waiting for her. Her eyes, now locked on Ida's, were bright green in her hijab. The same colour as Levi's, and close to Ida's own. Something passed between the two women, a shiver of energy. Ida felt a tingling at the base of her spine, a cool breath against the back of her neck.

Ida briefly thought to point the woman out to Levi, but something made her change her mind. At the front of the line, the two leaders had lowered their voices, bending toward each other like wrestlers squaring off. Their negotiation went on for some time. After a while the halutzim around Ida lost interest and talked among themselves.

"You can't trust an Arab," one said.

"We're all sons of Abraham," came the answer.

"I myself am a daughter of Rebecca," a girl's voice said, indignant.

"Didn't you hear about the Nebi Musa attacks?" the first speaker asked. But they had all heard about the killings.

"No different from the Cossacks," someone said.

"Arabs were killed too," Levi said to the group, but this was ignored.

Ida did not want to think about murders—she had come here to get away from that—and she began to step away from the conversation. But just as she did there was movement, an uptake of dust. The line began to straggle forward again, followed by the wagons loaded with gardening supplies, canvas, barbed wire, water barrels. Ida glanced back at the provisions. Where was the food? It was high noon. She was hot and thirsty. They were all hot and thirsty. She thought about the clandestine meetings in the back of the bakery at home, all the fundraising, the scheming to get here to Eretz Yisrael. Had anyone addressed the question of what they would eat?

Still, she was here, and she did not take it for granted. She had been living out of her trunk in the port of Jaffa this past month, in Mother Lobinsky's boarding house. Longing for her mother, for little Eva, to be able to tell them she had arrived and would do her father justice. She had the feeling that she was experiencing something monumental, but having nobody to share it diminished it. Now here was Levi. The person she could talk to.

Ida opened her mouth to tell him this, and with a sharp intake of breath she swallowed a mosquito. She covered her mouth, trying not to draw attention to herself. The more she tried to stifle the coughing, the louder the sounds that came out of her.

"Are you okay? Do you want me to hit your back?" Levi asked.

Ida shook her head no. She stepped out of line and bent over, trying to clear her throat. The bug seemed to be blocking her airway entirely. She had the sudden thought that she might choke to death; that all the toil and hardship to get herself to Eretz Yisrael, all the long Youth Movement meetings, the raising of kopeks, the departure from Eva and her mother at their time of greatest need, would only result in her limp body, lifeless on the earth. But finally she expelled the bug; the coughing slowly ceased. She straightened and wiped tears from the corners of her eyes. Then she rejoined the procession beside Levi, as though she belonged there.

Mount Gilboa loomed ahead of them. They could see the northern side of the spring where they were headed. A single quinine tree, the sun blazing behind it, casting a shallow pool of shade. How could she have known then that quinine would come to mean the line between life and death, between birth and not existing at all?

The Jewish community should have known after the Kishinev pogroms in 1903, when they were accused of killing a Christian child and using his blood to bake matzah. The blood libel meant hundreds of Jews were killed or wounded in retaliation. They should have known, Ida's mother had said, after Bialystok in 1906, when first marauders and then the Czarist army itself filled their bodies with bullets and ruined their homes. But there is a moment when an idea becomes more than itself, when the balance tips away from the theoretical and toward lived experience, and this must happen in its own time. Ida had grown up feeling passionate about Zionism the way one feels passionate about an unreachable goal. Precisely because of its unattainability, you long for it, never expecting it to be fulfilled. And then the pogrom in her own town happened, in Kiev, and Eretz Yisrael turned from an idea into a necessity. Something they must do if they were to survive as a people. As Herzl had long been saying, the Jews would not be safe until they had somewhere to live in peace.

For her father, it had been too late.

"It's a new life," she had tried to tell him, and he had answered, "What do old people need with a new life?"

He reminded her that Mashiach had not appeared, as it was written, to lead them back to the Holy Land.

Still, he hadn't liked the way things were going, being told where a Jew could live, that he needed a permit, that false papers were prudent, and after Kishinev . . .

Her father had owned a store that was attached to their home. He sold buttons, needles and thimbles, bolts of fabric, nails and screws, jars of peppermint, shoe polish, floor polish, ribbon and string. He had been sitting behind the cash register in the storefront. It was Friday, late morning. Ida sometimes took her reading out to keep him company; they were working in amiable silence when they heard a sound down the street. Shouting. One voice, distinct, then more voices, individual at first and then joining together into a single stream of sound. Her father's eyes looked over at her from above his white beard. There was a quizzical expression on his face, like he had just heard the call of an animal that belonged in another season. It was that look Ida remembered, the one of innocent confusion. The other looks she tried to forget.

At night now, though, when she tried to fall asleep, the scene replayed on the backs of her eyes. The sound had been a mob of people looting the grocers'. It made its way down the street; everyone knew which were the Jewish stores. Ida saw men; she saw that they had been drinking. She saw, in the middle of the group, the father of Katya from school.

It was he who swung the bat at the window. The lines spread out on the glass and hung there, suspended, like a beautiful design etched into the frost. Time stopped, if only for a moment. Then all at once the whole wall fell, the shattering of the glass making a sound that filled everything, and the front of the building was open and exposed, like a dollhouse.

The men were holding pieces of jagged wood, and broken chairs, and one a rusty saw. There was a moment when they seemed to pause, the place where the glass had been still holding the memory of the barrier. And then it filled with people.

Immediately, her father was knocked to the ground. A ring of men encircled him, kicking with their boots. Katya's father—Ida knew him as mild mannered and boring—had been at the centre of the group.

"Die, pig!" someone shouted.

Eva, thank God, had been at school.

Ida saw—could still see, despite how she tried not to—the bats rising and falling. Behind the counter, several of the lesser hooligans were sweeping the shelves with the sides of their forearms, pushing goods into open burlap sacks. Her mother must have heard the noise; she came out from the rear room, her hair tied back in a kerchief with wisps of grey escaping around her face. She had been polishing the Sabbath candlesticks, and held one in each hand like a pair of exclamation points. They had belonged to Ida's great-great-great maternal grandmother, and had been passed down generations of women—all the way back, Ida sometimes imagined, from the Matriarch Sarah in the tent of Abraham.

There was a glass armoire at the back of the store where they kept their Seder plate, their kiddish cup; Ida's mother had been coming to put the polished candlesticks back in their place beside the other heirlooms. But Ida caught her mother's eye; they each saw, at the same time, a man with gold rings and a goatee noticing the shelf. While he turned toward it, her mother thrust the candlesticks at Ida, and Ida thrust them into a carton of old rags her father had used to polish his faucets and doorknobs. She shoved the crate under the counter with the toe of her shoe. She looked at her mother, who gestured at Ida with her chin. Ida dropped to her knees, briefly unnoticed in the chaos, and crawled under the counter as well.

When everything was over, she and the candlesticks were the only things that had been spared.

Another knot of men had noticed her mother; Ida watched their boots as they swarmed around her. Her mother had come out to the store through a small door that led to the rest of the house. She was pushed back through that entrance; Ida heard a slam. She never asked what had happened behind those doors. But after, her mother wanted her to go to Eretz Yisrael. Now. As quickly as possible. Theory had turned to reality in her mind too.

She and Eva would join Ida when they were able, her mother said. But even then, Ida knew this might be never. She knew she had to make good on her family's behalf.

She thought of her mother as she walked beside Levi. Had her own mother strolled beside Ida's father like this when they had met as children in the synagogue? Had her mother felt, as a teenager, what Ida was feeling now? The dizzying certainty that her life was about to change? The day grew, impossibly, hotter, the clouds of mosquitoes thicker. She arranged the brim of her hat to try and keep the bugs away. Some of the halutzim had netting over their faces, and pieces of cloth at their necks to protect them from the sun. Ida had nothing in her backpack save for a clean pair of underwear, a sweater that she would clearly never need in this blistering heat, and her mother's beloved Sabbath candlesticks. They had been a parting gift, laden with love and crippling responsibility. Eva had watched wide-eyed as their mother gave them to Ida, like she was witnessing a Torah scroll being passed from one great Rabbi to another.

The dusty earth gave way to marshes, and the stink of mud filled her nostrils. The pioneers' sandals squelched; every few steps someone lost one altogether and the procession had to halt while the shoe was fished out of the muck. Soon the sandals were abandoned, and the halutzim with long trousers pulled the fabric up over their knees. Some of the men took their trousers off entirely and navigated the marsh in their bare legs and under-clothes. Ida tried not to look at the curved backsides ahead of her, the buttocks visible through the thin white cotton underthings.

Levi kept his pants on, for which she was grateful.

The men jostled each other.

"Better here than frozen Siberia," she heard one say to another.

"Or Uganda," someone else laughed. "Can you believe they tried to give us Uganda?"

"At least the Turks let us land!"

"My cousins have gone to America. They say it's the future."

Someone coughed. "Wherever a Jew goes, he is on his way to the Holy Land."

"Rabbi Nachman was just an old Hassid."

Ida knew there was no greater insult among the Jews of tomorrow.

The slope of the hill grew steeper and returned from marsh back to parched earth, a thousand tiny lines criss-crossing its back. Again, the line slowed and stopped: first the skinny donkeys; then the wagons loaded down with hoes and rakes, burlap, jars of seed, scythes. Then the halutzim themselves.

"The foot of Mount Gilboa," Levi said, gesturing at what lay ahead. "The Spring of Harod."

The light in the sky was blinding, no clouds, no shadows. A terrifying clarity, Ida thought.

"And now, we will lap," she answered.

She was referring to the Biblical passage in Judges where Gideon's men were chosen by a divinely prescribed test.

As those around her set down packs and baskets, removed shoes and rubbed sore feet, Ida took off her glasses and wiped the sweat from her face with the back of her arm. She unbuckled her sandal and pushed tentatively with her fingertip at a blister bulging on her heel. The liquid moved around inside it.

Some of the pioneers moved toward the stream to drink but David called out to them, "Wait."

As though they were one collective body—as though this great goal had already been accomplished—the young people turned their heads in unison. Their leader climbed onto the back of one of the wagons, onto a heap of folded canvas. His hair was black with tight curls. Ida could see how fair his skin was, imagined how it would burn and peel and burn again. He stood, unmoving, his hands loose at his sides, waiting until the group was silent. When they were all facing him, he lifted his palms to the heavens. "Today is yom ha aliya ha karka. The day of the ascent to the land."

David did not raise his voice. His tone was calm and measured. As though he was their host—as though the standoff with the Arabs had never happened—he welcomed them with his blessing. "Beruchim haba'im."

And then he said, "I don't believe we are God's chosen people."

Someone behind Ida whispered, "I've been reading Klatzkin too."

"On nationalism," she heard someone else reply. "Land and language are the critical ingredients of nationhood. Forget religion!"

But Ida felt the blasphemy implicit in David's words, felt her body tighten against them. What else was a Jew if not chosen?

She imagined she could feel Levi tense beside her, too.

"I don't believe we are God's chosen ones," David said. "But I *do* believe we have been called here. It is up to us to make the dream of Zionist Socialism a reality. We have been summoned to create a new world based on justice, equality, and action."

His speech sounded polished, practised; his head was bare under God's judgment. He touched the slight bump at the top of his nose.

Ida craned her neck. To David's left, sitting with her legs dangling off the back of the wagon, was a woman. Brown wavy hair and freckles; thin arms and small, apple-like breasts. There was a child on her lap, a black-haired girl, younger than Eva but with something about her that reminded Ida of her sister. The child clutched a doll that was nothing more than a pillow with eyes drawn on it and a scrap of black material attached to the head. She whispered into the place where the doll's ear would have been, holding it up to her own ear to hear its answer. She made a face of astonishment, then held it up again so the doll could whisper the same thing into her mother's ear. Her mother smiled, and put a finger up to her lips. She would keep the girl's secret, and the doll's.

Ida looked around at the barren rockscape, the vast sky. To have a doll in this emptiness must feel like a miracle to the girl. Something rare and precious in a place where they had almost nothing.

David was rhapsodizing about Gideon's spring, gesturing to it expansively, sweeping his hand like he was casting a spell. The spring looked small to Ida, and muddy. A large rock blocked the place where it exited the mountain. But David extracted a bent and creased leather-bound notebook from his back pocket, and a stubby pencil from over his ear.

"You know this passage," he said to the group, magnanimous. He raised the book in front of his face, cleared his throat, and began to read from Judges. When he finished, he said, "You are the three hundred who will accomplish this task. We are the three hundred."

Ida knew that there were, in fact, seventy-five of them. Two companies of the Work Brigade: one had come from Judea where they had built railway tracks from Petah Tikva, the first Jewish moshava in Ottoman Palestine, the other from the Galilee where they had been paving a road. But she took David's point. Her new life was coming into view, in the same way that Eretz Yisrael itself had appeared to her from the boat on the horizon, bit by bit, vague and clouded, then suddenly, all at once, there: the beach, the silhouette of the new city of Tel Aviv, the Gymnasia Herzlia, the wide-trousered boatman swarming over the deck of the ship—speaking Turkish? Arabic?—grabbing bags indiscriminately and ferrying them to shore.

She once again had the almost violent feeling that life as she had known it was over.

She saw, in her mind's eye, the settlement they would build. She saw workers in the field and cooks in the kitchen and mechanics in the machine shed. She saw a nursery full of babies. Perhaps even one of her own.

She looked at Levi, trying to catch his eye, but he had replaced his workers' cap and was watching David, rapt. There was a confidence to David that she could see Levi wanted to get close to. He, like her and all of the others, had grown up with blue tin boxes to raise the kopeks needed to buy this land. They had grown up with framed portraits of Theodor Herzl in their dining rooms, his great beard and moustache presiding over every Sabbath meal. They had grown up at clandestine Youth Movement gatherings in the back rooms of grocery stores and gymnasiums, quoting Tolstoy and A.D. Gordon, debating the best way to take Eretz Yisrael. But while they had dreams, David had done it. He had immigrated to this land in the Second Aliyah, in 1910; he had helped establish the moshava at Kinneret, planting eucalyptus trees along the muddy banks, negotiating with the fellaheen. Ida heard he had travelled the entire length of Eretz Yisrael on horse-back, meeting the Arabs in every tent and marketplace, learning their various customs so as to help in the purchase of land.

While the rest of this group had been back in Poland and Russia, debating and discussing, David had claimed this place as his home.

"In a year from now," David was saying, "we will eat bread we baked here ourselves, and vegetables grown in our own fields. We will celebrate May Day, the holiday of the worker, together under the roof of our community house."

He pulled at his chin, a gesture a man with a beard might make, although David had none.

"The work will be gruelling," he continued. "But with each small task you will be completing something larger. *We* will be completing something larger," he corrected himself. "Something unprecedented in the history of the Jews."

Behind Ida, someone whispered, "Either that or we'll starve."

"We will seize the moment," David said.

To what end remained to be seen.

The first task was to dig security trenches and put up barbed wire. They wouldn't sleep before it was done; the Arab village was close and there could be no taking chances.

Ida had heard a rumour that this first camp would be tempo-rary. They would start here, but later they would seize the Arab houses and move up higher on the hill. The Agency, she had heard, had purchased this land from a mortgage holder in Beirut, who had promised that when it was time the Arabs would go eas-ily. But Ida wondered about this. Why would they go? Wasn't this their home too?

The halutzim fell asleep, finally, when the barbed wire had been erected, in a haphazard pile of bodies, their bedrolls laid directly on the earth. No roof above them. A thousand stars sparkling in welcome. Or so it seemed to those who wanted to see it that way.

In the morning, before dawn, Ida gathered with the others at the base of the mountain, rubbing her eyes. Everyone's clothes, which they had slept in, were crusted in dirt and sweat. Ida was glad when she recognized someone from home, a girl she knew from the meetings, just a little. A beautiful outspoken girl with wide eyes and a body bent toward a fight. Sarah. Her hair was even curlier than Ida remembered, as though already the new land had lifted her, shaken her, and put her back down in a different form.

Sarah nodded to Ida, a brief acknowledgement. Her eyes were still half closed in sleep.

"I can't stop yawning," she said, covering her mouth with her fist.

Ida, too, had slept as though she was dead.

"Hello to you too," Ida said, smiling.

"We made it," Sarah said, conspiratorially.

"It feels like we've always been here," Ida replied.

The sun was rising over the peak of the mountain. A dart of gold pierced the grey clouds, and the next moment the field was bathed in light, the tips of the marshy grasses shining with a dewy glow.

"Look," Ida said, gesturing with her elbow.

Sarah nodded, only mildly impressed. Already, Ida thought, they were beginning to take the beauty for granted.

Breakfast was gruel. There was no other word for it. Some unlucky schmuck had been awake for hours, building a fire, boiling water, muscling a wooden spoon through a massive vat. There was no honey to go with it, only a few figs. Ida ate hers hurriedly, as though someone else might take her portion, someone more deserving. It was true that the men were bigger and required more calories to sustain them. But here equality reigned.

From the direction of the cooking fire came snippets of talk. "The Baron Rothschild . . ." someone began, but was interrupted. "Where is the good baron now?"

After breakfast, shovels were passed out, and the group set to work clearing the earth. Before they could plough, or plant their crops, they needed to remove a million stones. Stones of all sizes, from pebbles to massive boulders. This would take days, Ida saw. Weeks. She didn't let herself think beyond that.

Without speaking, Ida and Sarah formed a team and worked beside each other for several hours, until the mist had burned away entirely and the sun baked the last of the dew into dryness. Heat rose in waves off the earth. For lunch there was a tiny ration of pita and a handful of olives they devoured instantly, without tasting them. Ida shook the pits in her palm like dice.

In the evening, it was not David but his wife Hannah who climbed up onto the back of the wagon. She bent at the waist to hoist herself up, showing her ample behind, but there were no murmurs from the men; women would not be objectified in the new society. Hannah, like David, had arrived in the Second Aliyah, which meant the halutzim instantly respected her.

In the group behind Ida, somebody began to recite one of Bialik's poems.

"All the word is a slaughtering-block / And I'm just one more Jew."

Somebody else corrected the first speaker's Hebrew.

Hannah smiled at the young halutzim; one by one they

smiled back, like a row of lamps being lit along a city avenue. The things Hannah told them were about the proper way to scrape one's tin plate before depositing it at the washing basin; where to put food scraps so the jackals wouldn't get at them. She and David had been at Kinneret, she said, the precursor to this new big kibbutz, and knew how daily details of communal life could inform the greater project. The historic speeches fell to David; Hannah was left with the logistics.

"Some of you have valuables," she was saying. "Let's collect these so they can best serve us all."

Her language suggested this thought had just occurred to her now, or that it had occurred to them collectively and she was simply the mouthpiece for the group. Hannah looked into the crowd spread out cross-legged on the earth. "You," she said, pointing to a peevish-looking man wearing lederhosen.

Lederhosen! thought Ida. In the heat!

"And you," she said, pointing to someone Ida could not see through the jumble of backs and heads.

"Could you please be responsible for the gathering of people's valuables?" Hannah asked.

But then a look crossed Hannah's face; she was reconsidering. "Perhaps it's more efficient to have everyone deliver the items themselves," she said, less decisively.

Hannah, Ida could see, did not want to appear to be an authority figure. To set the correct tone, the belongings needed to be surrendered willingly, enthusiastic offerings to the enterprise they were building together. She did not want strangers circulating like policemen to take each other's belongings. Especially not after what so many of them had been through in Czarist Russia.

Hannah was, Ida thought, the perfect replacement mother for all the real mothers they had left back home. How old was she? Maybe twenty-eight. But she would gather them all up in her wide lap; she would rub their backs and sing them to sleep.

"Before noon tomorrow," Hannah said, "please bring your valuables up to the wagon."

She smiled out at her husband, who held their little daughter in his lap. The perfect family—and Ida thought: maybe I can have that too. Maybe it's really within reach.

A slip of a moon was making itself visible in the east. The promise of night was like silk, or cool water. It made Ida want to lie down. She wanted to rest in someone's arms, to have someone—Levi?—push the hair from her face and kiss the line of her collarbones all the way to the base of her throat. She was overcome with melancholy and this hurt and pleased her in equal measure; she longed for something she had never had, and could not properly imagine, and yet a space inside her was calling out for it plaintively.

She saw again the railing of the ship pushing off from the dock in Russia; she saw her old life retreating not just symbolically but literally. Yes. It was gone.

"I have a pair of dirty socks," Sarah said beside her.

Ida turned, blank.

"I have nothing valuable from home," Sarah clarified.

"Oh. Neither do I," Ida said absently. But as she leaned back into her satchel she felt one of her mother's candlesticks dig into her low back.

She swallowed.

Surely candlesticks did not count. What good could they be to the group?

What good indeed. They could be sold.

The stars began to show their faces.

"Does someone tell us where we sleep?" Sarah asked.

But Ida didn't register that the question was directed at her. The full complexity of her dilemma was slowing dawning on her.

"Should we find a tent?" Sarah asked more pointedly.

"Oh! Yes," Ida answered. She pushed the candlesticks from her mind. Sarah wanted to be her friend.

Hannah's speech was over, and so they hoisted their things onto their backs and went out into the field to stake their ground. While Ida and Sarah and their group had been clearing stones, a second contingent of workers had raised the tents. These were simply designed, a pole in the centre, each sheet of white canvas raised into a single peak. Their crisp triangles looked like sailboats spread across a vast sea.

The girls chose one near the outside of the circumference of the rough circle. "For privacy," Ida said.

Sarah laughed. "You're in the wrong place."

Inside, two straw mats had been laid down along with two rough wool blankets from the Agency. One had been eaten through by moths. Ida took the holey one and gave Sarah the other. They set to work unpacking their few belongings. It was extraordinarily hot inside the canvas tent. Still, Ida felt pleasure in the making of a home.

"It's like playing house," she said. She was thinking of her family preparing for the evening meal.

"Wouldn't it be wonderful to have a child?" Sarah asked.

Ida nodded. "I miss my mother," she said, tentatively, testing whether she could trust Sarah with her feelings.

The other girl was examining a fingernail. She looked up. "I never had a mother," she said.

"Everyone had a mother," Ida answered, too quickly.

"Mine died," Sarah said. "Giving birth to me."

Ida could not think what to say, so she ventured, "My father died. In a pogrom."

Sarah gave her a sympathetic look, but said only, "Here, give me a hand."

They tied back the heavy tent flap to let some air in.

Later, after they had hung the lamp and lit it, Sarah wandered out into the evening. From where I am now I watch her go. There is something she is drawn to, something unnamed that she cannot resist. She doesn't know what it is. But I know; oh, I know. And I wish it were otherwise.

Sarah left and Ida was alone. The silence felt alive, animated. Her inner world was palpable again, like a spotlight illuminating a dark corner. She had been surrounded by people every moment for days now, and had forgotten herself.

The life of the group, she saw, was not designed for introspection.

She lowered herself gingerly onto her straw mat, wincing, her thighs and buttocks sore after the long hike to the mountain and the first day's labour. She felt around in the bottom of her bag where she had left her candlesticks. She drew them out, ran her fingers over the elaborate carving, the Hebrew inscription of the blessing. The dried wax from her last Shabbos at home was still crusted in rivulets. She pictured her mother, gathering the light around her head, and reciting the bracha. She knew, without having to ask, that the prayer—that any prayer—had no place here on the new kibbutz. But she heard again Levi's Sabbath greeting, his refusal to forsake his own truth. She saw, in her mind's eye, her father's body in a pile on the perfectly polished floor.

There was a scratching at the tent flap. Someone wanted to

enter, and Ida thought for a moment it must be Levi. He had heard her longing; he was coming for her. But when she looked up she saw someone else. He didn't wait to be invited, but entered the tent as though it was his own. Which, in a way, she supposed it was.

She recognized this man from earlier: the black hair, the lederhosen. She thought again how unbearable they must be in this heat.

"I'm Ida," she said, and her guest answered back German. "Grüsse."

He didn't offer his own name. In the lengthening shadows of the paraffin lamp, Ida saw that his skin was pale as milk. He had strange spots of pigment on his lips, as if God had marked him for some blasphemy he had let slip from his mouth. His eyes fell on the candlesticks that rested on top of her mattress. A long moment of silence passed between them.

"I was charged with collecting valuables," the German said at last, sweeping his eyes up to meet her own.

They were to turn in their belongings themselves; Ida, along with everyone else, had heard Hannah say so. But there was something in this man's tone that made Ida afraid to not comply.

"Thank you," she said. "I was just finishing in here."

She hoped this implied she would turn the candlesticks in later.

The German looked at her. "Those are beautiful pamotim," he said, now using the Hebrew word. A mosquito buzzed around his head but he made no move to swat it away. "Valuable," he said.

"I don't think so," she said, lying instinctively. But the German made a scoffing noise. For a long moment they held eyes.

"I know worth when I see it," he said.

Something turned over in her stomach. The hairs on the back of her arms stood on end. She searched for something to say that would make him leave.

"Where are you off to next?" she asked finally.

He lifted his eyebrows.

"The future," he said.

It was a strange answer, but Ida found she understood.

"Good evening, comrade," he said, speaking again in German, and turned to leave. Ida watched his retreating back—he was tallish, his shoulders narrow. One of his blue suspenders was twisted. There was something vulnerable about it. Or rather, on someone else it would appear vulnerable, like a child who had attempted to dress himself, but on the German it appeared vaguely threatening—the elastic with its tight cinch.

Ida lay on her pallet for an hour trying to sleep. The rough Agency blanket chafed at her skin. Eventually she kicked it off, got up and went outside. The sky was full of stars, exquisitely sharp and covering every bit of the blackness. They did nothing to alleviate the heat. She walked slowly, winding her way between the tents. Here and there the young pioneers were laughing, stretching their sore muscles, lying on their backs looking up at the astral spectacle. A woman with a long braid was massaging a boy's shoulder. Despite the temperature, someone had lit a bonfire to keep the mosquitoes away and a circle had gathered loosely around it, someone with a flute, someone else with another stringed instrument Ida could not identify. The fiddler had bright red hair and orange freckles.

The words of Rabbi Hillel floated up with the smoke, words turned into song:

Im ayn ani li, mi li?
If I am not for me, who will be?
And if not now, then when, then when!
Ay ma-tay!

Ida wove her way to the edge of the river. Several boys were dangling their feet in the cool mud at the edge of the water. One was eating a lemon, sucking the bitter juice straight from the rind; where had he found it? Her stomach growled. She bent to remove her shoes, thinking she would wade into the river, immerse herself entirely. An image came to her: her father going to the mikveh before synagogue. This river would be as sacred as any ritual bath. She wondered if Levi would see it this way as well.

But as she began to undo her buckles, she glimpsed the German out of the corner of her eye. He must have come here directly from her tent. He was a few metres away, where the mudflats extended into rushes. Ida smiled at him, raising her hand to the side of her face, but the German gazed beyond her toward the shadow of the mountain. His face remained impassive, as if he had never seen her before.

Ida squinted. She took off her glasses and rubbed the dirty lenses with her sleeve and put them back on. She recalled the sight of his back as he'd left her tent. His white shirt, the twist in his suspenders. The suspenders he had been wearing minutes before were blue, but these ones were red.

The next morning, work started early, before the sun rose. The blister on Ida's foot had popped. She covered it in medical tape and heel-walked beside Sarah out to the field where they resumed the removal of boulders. They bent and lifted, bent and lifted. Time became immeasurable; there was no way to mark its passage beyond the bell that rang for their noonday meal, and Ida could not gauge whether an hour had passed, or three.

By mid-morning her right hand had begun to take on the claw-shaped grip of the handle of her shovel.

At last the bell rang and a food-wagon came around, pulled by the donkeys someone had dubbed Trotsky and Lenin. The red-headed fiddler Zeruvabel drove them; a moon-faced halutza named Shoshanna, with dark eyebrows and bushy armpit hair, doled out tin plates of eggplant and pita from the back of the wagon. A group beside the river had the thought to make a shelter from the sun using a big roll of corrugated metal they would eventually use for irrigation ditches. The pioneers crammed in together, setting up picnic style in whatever portion of shade they could get.

Ida looked across to the wagon and saw two men deep in conversation: the German with his lederhosen and beard; and someone—she looked a second time to make sure it wasn't some trick of the shimmering heat—someone who looked exactly like him.

She nudged Sarah, who raised her head from the plate she was scraping with the side of her finger.

"Look," Ida said.

"What?"

She pointed to the men.

"Oh, that," Sarah said, turning back to her plate. "Do you think there are seconds?"

"Pardon?"

"I'm so hungry."

"Are they . . ." Ida started.

Sarah laughed. "Haven't you seen identical twins before?"

Ida considered. Cohen and Saul Janovitch from synagogue

were twins, but they didn't even look as if they were related, whereas these twins were truly identical. Despite herself, she felt a visceral fear of them—akin to the fear of the contortionist she had seen when the circus came to Kiev, or the tightrope walker with no pigment in her skin. She knew it was a natural occurrence, that the human body was far more versatile than had once been understood. But understanding and feeling were two different things, and she shivered.

Sarah brought her plate to her face and licked it.

"You really were hungry," Ida said, instead of commenting on the bad table manners.

Sarah made a face that said *I told you so*; she wiped her face with her sleeve and looked out at the field of boulders. To the east of them the pioneers had resumed working after their meal. "The men have cleared more than we have," she said.

"We'll show them," Ida said.

"Will we?" Sarah asked.

They laughed, and Ida followed Sarah's gaze, taking in the rockscape before them. It was best to focus on the small square of earth right in front of you, she decided—two metres by two metres, say. To raise your eyes was to see boulders all the way to the horizon, and the accompanying labour this implied.

Sarah was wiggling at the earth with her toe. She had dislodged a rock and was peering beneath it.

"Come here," she said to Ida.

Ida leaned over; there was a worm, fat and ridged, close to a foot long. It was wriggling madly, in some kind of frenzy. Flipping its tail the way a snake would.

Ida shuddered.

"How long do you think it is?" Sarah asked.

"Leave it alone."

But Sarah had drawn the worm up by its tip—its tail? its head?—and laid it on top of the boulder. "If you cut a worm in half it turns into two worms," she said. A look crossed her face. She gestured to the wagon where the Germans were now saddling Trotsky. "Same concept," Sarah said. "One egg, divided. It shouldn't work. But look how they thrive."

"Creepy."

"The worm?"

"The Germans," Ida said.

Her face must have shown a feeling that Sarah misinterpreted. "You don't believe me?" Sarah asked.

She held a hand out for the shovel. Ida passed it to her. Sarah lifted the serrated edge and cut the worm neatly into two.

There was no blood. But neither did either piece resume the terrible writhing. The severed halves lay limp on the rock.

"It's dead," Ida said, matter-of-factly.

Sarah laughed. "I guess I was wrong."

Across the field someone shouted, "Kol hakavod!"

Ida looked over to the wagon; the Germans had disappeared.

The rest of the week was spent establishing protocols. A meeting was convened to develop a system for night watch. David, who had been at Kinneret, had an idea about how the system should work. The idea was that he would keep their one gun.

Dov, a blank-faced boy who had volunteered for the first shift, had a different idea. What if the Arabs came? Wasn't that the point of a night guard?

"The Arabs mean us no harm," a girl named Leah said.

"Are you joking?" someone asked.

"You can't really blame them," someone else said. "I'd hate us too."

"You will have a whistle to blow," David said to Dov.

Dov's face did not change. But he muttered, "I'll kill them with my whistle."

It was no surprise to Ida who won the argument.

The next morning, at breakfast, Dov reported that the Arabs had indeed appeared. Five of them, or perhaps more; the moon had been obscured by the clouds. The Arabs stood on horseback in a row at the edge of the encampment, their posture erect, not speaking, but not taking their eyes off Dov either. As if to say, there are more of us. We will be back.

CHAPTER 2

*S*OON, NEW TASKS WERE assigned on the basis of gender. This was not stated explicitly, but what else could explain Leah, Sarah and Hannah being assigned kitchen duty while the men continued clearing the fields.

"I came here to work the land!" a halutza named Yana complained.

"Women's work is women's work wherever you go," said Sarah.

The Agency sent twenty bolts of white cotton. The girl named Shoshanna with the bushy eyebrows and armpit hair set about making shirts in various sizes. These were simple, with open necks and billowing sleeves to protect the wearer's arms from the broiling sun. At first, Shoshanna would add a flourish on each cuff, a bluebell or a Mogen David in needlepoint, once even a whole pattern of red roses on a sleeve. She was talented, Ida thought, her handiwork meticulous. But David came across her doing this and put a stop to it.

Perhaps because her sewing had been halted, Shoshanna initiated a group meeting about the principles behind the assignment of tasks. But the men were not interested in this dis-cussion, on balance, or if they were they did not speak up, and the talk morphed quickly into a debate about how—and if—they would celebrate the High Holy Days that were coming so quickly.

"Are we not Jews?" Dov asked. His voice was tight, but his face stayed blunt, like a block of wood that had been set down in the middle of the proceedings.

"We're *new* Jews," said Zeruvabel the fiddler, his red hair flaming in the light of the gas lamp.

Dov was silent.

"You're free to go back to the shtetl," Zeruvabel said.

Leah jumped in then with a diatribe about the difference between pro-Zionist and anti-Zionist social revolutionaries. The latter, she said, were really only self-hating anti-Semites. The goyim Winston Churchill and Lord Balfour were better Zionists.

Shoshanna said, "Karl Marx created the internationalist uto-pia as a replacement for the Jewish Messiah. If ever there was a self-hating—"

But David interrupted, drawing the debate back to the matter at hand. It was a tricky business, he conceded to the group. Here on the kibbutz they did not believe in organized religion, in archaic tradition, or even—especially—in God. But they believed in the Jews' need for a homeland, and what could be more fit-ting, he asked rhetorically, than marking the New Year within the first days of their arrival?

Zeruvabel moved his fingers aggressively up and down an imaginary fingerboard.

In the week that followed, the Germans and Dov set to work hammering nails into planks to make a rough approximation of tables. Until now the settlers had been sitting cross-legged on the earth to eat, and although there was something fitting about this, their skin touching the skin of the Promised Land, the coming holiday gave them motivation to scrape together some furniture. There were rickety old stacking chairs the Agency had provided, but not enough to go around, so Levi upended some old orange crates to use for seats. Ida watched him from a distance, his muscles moving smoothly under his tanned skin. It gave her a feeling she could only describe as a bellyache, although that was inadequate. Something gnawed at her now, a kind of happy sadness that filled all her days with meaning.

For her part, Ida was relieved to be freed from clearing rocks and placed in charge of the primitive laundry. This entailed building fires under enormous cauldrons of water. After only one morning, her arms were flecked with tiny blisters where sparks had flown up and burned her. Her glasses were continually fogged up from the heat. But she felt necessary, productive. Once the water was roiling, soap flakes were added. The dirty shirts were the final ingredient. She was not so much washing them as she was boiling the life out of them, sterilizing them down to their basic components. Laundry back home was to make a garment shine. Laundry here was to remove all possible contaminants.

Shirts were worn by a halutz for several days—and when they came to Ida they were filthy. After she washed them, they were reassigned. One shirt was as good as any other and they all belonged to everyone. When Ida hung the shirts on the line, they dried instantly in the blistering heat. As though they had never been wet at all.

On the eighth afternoon she saw Hannah crossing the field toward her. The older woman's hips stretched the material of her cotton skirt; her blouse was tied in a knot at her waist, and her hair was knotted on the top of her head. They were all equals here, Ida knew, but some were more equal than others. Hannah was

David's wife, and a vision of calm and competence. Ida pulled on her braids to straighten them and brushed down her own plain skirt.

"Shalom, Ida," Hannah said. "Ma shlomech?"

But something about Hannah's question seemed shrouded; Ida could not discern the level of reply that was requested. Was she asking about Ida's emotional wellbeing or was she asking whether there was enough soap for tomorrow's laundry?

Ida smiled vaguely and made a murmur in the back of her throat.

"Did you sleep well?" Hannah asked, trying again.

Ida nodded, the smile still plastered on her face. And when Hannah said "Can I ask you a favour?" Ida didn't hesitate.

"I'd be honoured," she said.

The words, once uttered, sounded ridiculous, but it was too late to take them back.

Hannah flushed and handed over a bundle. It was a pile of rags, wrapped and tied in more rags. The inner knot of fabric was soaked in blood.

The thought came to Ida that Hannah had killed someone. But that, of course, was ridiculous. Hannah stood there with her eyes lowered, and when Ida didn't speak Hannah nodded with her chin toward Ida's vat of water.

"Oh," Ida said dumbly. "Of course."

Hannah wanted the rags washed. She was ashamed about the private nature of the blood that had stained them.

"Is that the favour?" she asked.

Hannah's cheeks were pink, her jaw set. But now she looked up with a forced smile on her face. "Well, there's another one. It's nothing very exciting, I'm afraid. I'm organizing the Rosh Hashanah table. We have nothing, as you know."

Her smile turned genuine, as if this was a great blessing.

"I've been charged with cooking a feast out of air," Hannah added.

Ida laughed. "As Jews have been doing since the beginning of time!"

Her memories of home reconstituted themselves in her mind, like a latent sourdough starter coaxed into becoming bread. Back in Kiev her mother would be baking challah, not loaf-shaped but round as was tradition for the holiday. Little Eva would be dipping apples in honey.

There would be no apples and honey on the kibbutz, although David said they had kept bees at Kinneret, and one day they would have them here as well.

Eva and her mother would be preparing for their first High Holy Days without her father. He had been a holy man, entirely genuine in his piety. He loved his family, but his inner life turned around the synagogue like a planet circling the sun. Had he been alive, he would be busy repenting, for after Rosh Hashanah came Yom Kippur, the great Day of Atonement, when God decided who would be inscribed in the Book of Life for another year. What had he done wrong to not be included?

Hannah cleared her throat and Ida looked up.

"I need tablecloths," Hannah said. "For the meal. Or something to use as tablecloths. Just a bolt of fabric maybe? And I need a kiddish cup." Hannah paused. She touched the hair around her face that had come free of the knot.

"Could you try to drum those things up?"

Ida nodded.

"And pamotim," Hannah said.

Ida was quiet.

"Candlesticks," Hannah translated into Russian, in case Ida

didn't know the Hebrew. "Although I have no idea where you'll find them," she added, her face apologetic.

Still Ida was silent, her jaw clenched. Then she said, "I don't have any candlesticks!"

Hannah looked surprised at the vehemence of Ida's reply.

"That's okay, achoti," she said kindly.

Later, Ida would wish she'd remembered this moment.

Later still, Ida would look back and wonder why she had acted as she did. She could equally have taken the opposite path, and everything would have turned out entirely differently.

As it was, Ida wasted no time. She watched Hannah retreating, hips swinging, gait relaxed as though she belonged exactly where she had found herself. When Hannah was out of view, she went straight to her tent and felt around under her straw mattress. Dust rose from beneath it. She let out three fast sneezes and wiped her nose on her arm. Then she pulled out her candlesticks; they seemed heavier than she remembered, more substantial. She folded them quickly into her old blue and green flowered kerchief. The other tents were deserted, the rest of the pioneers clearing boulders from the fields, and she walked quickly away from the encampment toward the river without thinking where she was going.

She continued along the riverbank. A sudden movement in the corner of her eye made her flinch, but it was only a fat bullfrog saving itself from the heat. Soon, the Arab village came into view. There were flowers planted beside the mud houses and children playing a game with a knobby stick and a ball in the dirt. Two men wearing long robes were bent over a broken plough. She averted her gaze and continued down their donkey path until eventually a stone well appeared. It held a kind of allure, a magnetism, made greater by the oppressive heat: the promise of water. When she reached it, though, she saw that its old, rusted bucket was almost buried in sand, just the top of the handle sticking out. Nobody had used this well for years.

In the distance, she saw the silhouettes of four girls walking single file with jars balanced on their heads. She waited until they were out of sight, then looked in all directions. Yes, she was far enough; she would not be observed. There was a clump of prickly shrubs a few metres away. Ida dropped to her knees and began digging, automatically, frantically. She had forgotten to bring a shovel so she scraped the dry earth with the heel of her sandal, and then used her hands. She thought of her mother's clean white apron and the early morning smell of bread rising. She thought of the shattered storefront window with lines spread out across the glass. She thought of Katya's father, of the look of shame and defiance on his face when he had seen Ida watching what he was about to do. She heard again the short cry that her father had released when his body first hit the ground. And the sound of her mother crying from behind her closed bedroom door after. Ida dug faster. The earth was full of stones and her fingernails broke. Soon, though, she had a shallow hole. The candlesticks were nestled in the soft cotton of her kerchief. She would bury the whole package, and with it what had happened at home. It would be a burial with the idea of preservation at its core. Saving something for later, when it was safe to come back to. Ida smoothed the dirt in the hollow and turned to reach for the bundle; a woman stood, a metre away, watching her.

The sound Ida made was half scream and half sob. She drew up from her knees, the flat of her palm against her heart. She took a big step backward, then squinted. There was something familiar about this woman, her eyes sharp like emeralds in her hijab, and the visible part of her face brown from the wind and the sun. Ida remembered her from the day of arrival, remembered the freighted look that had passed between them.

For a moment, they regarded each other cautiously.

Then, suddenly, there was a blur of motion and the woman lunged for the candlesticks in Ida's hands.

Instinctively, Ida pushed forward, knocking her off balance. There was a tussle of limbs and hands. For a moment, each woman held separate ends of the bundle. Ida pulled hard before wresting it back. She cradled it to her chest. Her breathing was ragged.

The other woman had taken a step away.

They eyed each other warily. Then, suddenly and decisively, Ida turned her back. She no longer cared if she was putting herself in danger; her indignation had become bigger than the instinct to protect herself. She began to walk away. The woman shouted, though, an indescribable cry, and Ida spun back toward her. She was nodding and nodding, as if her head was attached to some kind of spring. "No," the woman said. "No."

"No indeed," Ida said hotly, mostly to herself. She didn't expect an answer.

The woman was gesturing behind them, toward her village. It occurred to Ida that these were the buildings the halutzim would eventually inhabit if David got his way. But would the Arabs really go as easily as the man in Beirut had promised? This, Ida understood newly, looking at the village, was their home. The Jews needed a homeland, yes, but what right did they have to make the Arabs leave?

It took Ida a few moments to register that her opponent had willingly surrendered the prize; there was something else she was trying to communicate. The woman ran a finger under the fabric of her hijab, easing it back to reveal another bit of her face, and then hastily tugging it back down again. She said something in rapid Arabic.

Ida caught the scent of a verdant kind of sweetness, some kind of flowering shrub perhaps, its smell aloft in the heat. From somewhere behind her came the violent caw of a vulture. Again the woman spoke, this time a long stream of words, going on until Ida thought she would somehow have to stop her. She shrugged and lifted her hands to show she did not understand Arabic, had no way of translating.

"Fatima," the woman said, and pointed at her chest.

Ida told the woman her own name.

Fatima began to speak again, and looked to see if Ida was following. Ida shook her head.

Fatima changed her approach. She nodded at the candlesticks and reached her hands out for them, but kept her eyes on Ida's face, to show that she was not going to take them but only mimic doing so. Then she acted out walking a few steps away, cradling the pile of air in her arms. Fatima pointed again toward her village.

"Beit," she said, and Ida understood the Arabic word for home, so similar to the Hebrew "bayit." Fatima was showing Ida the mud house she must share with her husband and children.

Perhaps there were other wives, Ida thought. Dov had told her Arab women were forced to marry young, some of them into harems.

Now Fatima pretended to hide the candlesticks under an invisible piece of furniture. When she mimicked lifting it, Ida could almost feel the weight. Fatima was an actress of some talent.

"Ida," Fatima said, pointing to her own chest. Fatima was Ida, now, come to retrieve her valuables. Then she was herself, giving them back to Ida willingly. And all at once Ida understood. Fatima would hide the candlesticks. She would keep them safe for Ida.

Fatima pointed to the dirty hole. "No," she said, wrinkling her face.

Ida stood still, holding one of her braids. Then she pushed her sweaty glasses up on her nose. Her heart was still racing. She looked at Fatima's bare feet, the dry cracks webbing her heels. She could take the bundle and find a new place to hide it, but in Fatima's gaze she had seen a kind of recognition. The women were from different worlds, but they both understood the preciousness of an heirloom. And they both understood the need to conceal certain things.

She wrapped the kerchief more tightly around the pamotim, thinking of them in her mother's hands when her mother had come out to the storefront to see what all the noise was about. She pictured her mother thrusting the candlesticks at her to keep them safe. Ida took a long breath and let it out slowly. Then she handed the bundle to Fatima. From her mother to her to this Arab stranger. An image flashed into her mind: a chain of women passing along a baby to keep it safe during wartime.

Fatima patted the bundle like she would pat a baby's bottom— she had understood—and said something in Arabic that Ida did not understand. But Fatima clearly understood this too. There were no more words that could be shared between them.

Fatima pointed again to her house, jabbing with her forefinger. *This is where you can find me,* her gesture said.

Ida nodded. She lifted her hand goodbye.

She hesitated.

"Ma'sallam," she said finally.

She turned to leave, both relieved and bereft.

Later, when the halutzim were gathering for dinner, they heard the sound of hoofbeats. The galloping grew louder and a wagon drew into the yard, a cloud of dust trailing behind it for almost a kilometre. "The right horse is pulling harder than the left," Zeruvabel commented.

Shoshanna said, "The rider is leaning toward the left."

The rider was a man of maybe thirty-five—an old man, thought Ida. He had a wide face and broad nostrils; he wore a straw hat. A woman and child sat upright beside him, staring straight ahead, their hands folded in their laps. The woman's face was thin and pinched. The man tied the horses and hopped down from the wagon. His face was red with the effort of riding so quickly. Word spread through the crowd that he had come from Kinneret. He was looking for Hannah.

A few moments later, Hannah came speed-walking from the kitchen, one hand making little flapping motions while the other held a bundle. Even from across the yard, Ida could see the rapid blinking that must have been the holding back of tears. Hannah hoisted her bundle onto the back of the wagon, then the old man extended his hand and helped her up. Ida waited for David to appear, for their little girl to come running for her mother. But neither did, and the man hopped up himself behind the horses. He slapped the reins. They were gone.

The preparations for the High Holy Days were miraculously completed on time. Before she left, Hannah had succeeded in finding tablecloths. It was not Ida who had provided them in the end, but Shoshanna, who had stitched together leftover scraps of the shirt material.

The candlesticks on the table—Ida didn't know where they had come from—were cheap and made out of tin.

The halutzim arrived slowly for the meal, some with grass in their hair, the knees of their pants stained bronze from the day's labour. Shoshanna passed a rag to one of the twins and scolded him like a mother, "Wipe the shmutz off your face."

The eggplant was the same as at every other meal, but a wagon had been sent to Tiberias for flour and out of it an enormous braided challah had been made. It was brushed with a precious egg, David told them, traded from a Sephardim in a flowing blue gown who spoke a strange Judaeo-Spanish called Ladino. Leah had received a package from her family, who lived near the Dead Sea: it contained newspaper twists of the region's famous rough salt. She distributed these along the length of the table for the halutzim to dip their challah into.

David, as patriarch, recited the prayers, but Ida could see he was doing so out of obligation rather than reverence.

In the morning, chores resumed as usual. Yom Kippur was coming, when work was forbidden, but the fields needed to be cleared of rocks so that ploughing and planting could begin. Ida was worried they would work instead of observing the Day of Atonement. The Agency had finally delivered on their promise of a tractor, and a large crowd of Arab villagers arrived to observe how it worked, an iron horse with a blade that cut into the land in the place of human hands. Ida scanned the gathering for Fatima but did not see her.

The next day, at lunch, Levi brought his plate over and sat down beside her. "Eggplant," he said.

"Is it?" she asked.

"Isn't it?" he asked.

"It's chicken," she answered.

It was a joke they all made use of, a joke that ran like a golden thread through the whole camp. It encompassed both longing for what they'd left behind, and collective belief in the ability of willpower to create something new. Eggplant? Imagine it's a chicken. Soon enough it will be walking around clucking and you'll have to cut its head off to eat it.

"I prefer eggplant anyway," Levi said. He pushed up his shirt-sleeves and rested his elbows on his knees.

Ida cocked her head, weighing his statement.

"Not really?" she asked.

"Vegetarian," he explained.

She lifted her eyebrows. "A real idealist," she said.

"Is that a compliment?"

They both laughed.

"The biggest compliment I know," she said.

Levi lifted his fork and looked at her, waiting for her to start first. As she ate, she soaked in the presence of his body beside her. He smelled of sweat, which in the old world made her think of stale old men, trudging through the snow to synagogue in their fur-lined coats and hats. Here it made her think of action. Levi was a good worker. An idealist. A vegetarian! They didn't speak, but their eyes both fell on her plate—chicken! They smiled, and then Levi turned his gaze to the tiny blisters on the back of Ida's hand from the laundry.

Levi put his fork down. He held his hand above hers in the air. Tentatively, as if he was about to touch something that might burn him too, he ran his finger over the raised bumps on her skin.

This felt both abstract, like something happening to some other girl, and extraordinarily sensitive, like he was touching her somewhere entirely different than her wrist. There was a heaviness between Ida's hips; all of her body was opening under his touch. A mosquito buzzed by his leg and he did not lift his hand away from hers to dissuade it. Its needle went into his ankle and still he sat, giving it his blood, watching her face. She looked back at him, forcing herself to hold his eye. There were little flecks of yellow in the green of his irises; his lashes were long. He had a small scab from a bug bite on his right temple.

"You got bitten," Ida said.

He smiled, and she saw his chipped tooth and wondered if it had happened when he was a child.

"This is brand new to me," Levi said.

It was not clear to Ida whether he meant the workday ahead of them, or the touching of her wrist, or their mission to establish an entirely new country. His words encircled all the possibilities. And something else too.

She looked back at Levi; he covered her hand with his own.

She reciprocated.

He placed his other hand on top of hers.

She reciprocated again.

Four hands, piled one on top of the other.

"I'm on night watch," he said.

"But it's morning."

He laughed. "This evening."

Ida said, "Okay."

Levi was quiet. Then he said, "Come with me."

"Where?"

"Keep me company tonight," he said.

After, as she walked back to her tent, she replayed the conversation, word by word. She was considering the implications of the phrase "keep me company" as she came around the corner of the dining tent and almost stumbled over one of the German twins. She touched her glasses and squinted. He was alone. Just standing there. She noticed again the strange spots of pigment on his lips.

"Where are you off to in such a hurry?" he asked her.

"None of your business," Ida said, impulsively, and immediately regretted being rude. It would only draw attention to her.

The German—which one?—puckered his lips. It was a look of both disgust and disdain, as if she was at once repugnant and not worth his time.

"Enjoy yourself," he said testily.

"Where are you off to?" Ida asked, because he was clearly going nowhere and they were meant to occupy all their waking hours being useful. But the German only waved his hand, as if dismissing a servant.

Sarah had told Ida that there was usually a way to distinguish identical twins—the voice, a birthmark or a scar—but if such a thing existed in this case they had not yet identified it. Why bother trying? Ida wondered. And later wished she had.

It seemed to take forever for evening to arrive. It felt to Ida as if she was hunched over the vat of boiling water for days, stirring the laundry like it was some kind of witch's cauldron. Sweat coated her buttocks and the back of her neck. When the bell rang, signalling the end of the workday, she took off her leather sandals and lay on her back, too tired to move the twenty metres to the thin strip of shade by the clothesline. An hour passed. Her eyes closed. She smelled eggplant.

When Ida finally made her way back to the tent, Sarah was there. She was wearing a silk skirt and a blouse with crimson sleeves.

"Where did you get that?" Ida asked.

"I brought it from home," Sarah said.

Ida had not seen anything like it pass through the laundry. There was a vee at the bust, offering just the barest hint of cleavage, the rose-coloured fabric falling in soft folds over the curves of Sarah's figure. A few delicate, clear beads decorated the cuffs.

"What?" Sarah asked, in answer to Ida's glance. "David said I could keep it." She held her bottom lip in her teeth.

Ida pictured her own beautiful candlesticks. Had she given them up for nothing?

"Did he really?" she asked.

Sarah drew herself up. "He didn't actually say it. But he didn't tell me to turn it in either."

Ida shrugged, drawing a breath and letting it out slowly. She scratched her cheek. "You look beautiful," she conceded.

Sarah smiled. She looked down at the red blouse tenderly.

It was too hot to stay for long inside the stifling canvas, so together Ida and Sarah made their way outside and down to the river. They crossed the mud flats, wading in water up to their knees, holding their skirts bunched up in their fists, Ida's bag-like, utilitarian, Sarah's like a prim lady's from the city. They stood for a long time watching the sky turn a deep shade of pink, and then purple, and then navy blue. Ida's feet were deep in the muck, and it occurred to her there might be leeches but she could not bring herself to move. The mud felt cool on her hot, blistered feet.

Finally Sarah spoke. "I sometimes get the feeling . . ." she said. But her voice trailed off.

"You get the feeling?" Ida prompted. She reached over and touched the sleeve of her friend's blouse absently, rubbing the red fabric between her fingers like a vendor in the Old City market sizing up its worth.

Sarah pressed her fingertips together, steepling her hands in front of her face. She's been acting oddly, Ida thought. They'd known each other only a short time, but Ida could tell that Sarah's long stretches of moody quiet were out of character. As was the muffled crying late at night. Once, when Ida had woken very early in the morning, Sarah had been gone.

"You were saying something?" Ida asked, more directly. Voices drifted through the dusk from the cooking tent: a peal of wild laughter. A single shout. Sarah looked up, surprised. As though she had forgotten the conversation entirely.

"I'm not sure," she answered at last. "Do you ever feel like there's an unwelcome presence here?"

"You mean the Arabs?"

Ida felt fondly about Fatima but could not think what else Sarah might be referring to.

But Sarah said, "No. I mean ghosts."

Ida smiled, and then removed the smile carefully from her face, unsure if this was meant to be a joke. She splashed at the surface of the water with her foot.

"Not really," she said. It was a nonsense notion, like Ayin Ha-Ra, the passage from Berakhot in the Talmud about how to ward off the evil eye by claiming yourself a descendant of Joseph.

"No?" Sarah asked.

Ida reconsidered.

"No," she said.

Sarah said, "I do."

"What kind of ghosts?"

"The kind with sheets over their heads and holes cut out for eyes."

Eva had worn this exact costume for Purim last year; Ida felt a pang of homesickness and closed her eyes against it. A night bird cried out.

"Not ghosts," Sarah qualified. "Not exactly. It's more like . . . I feel haunted."

"Haunted by?"

"A ghost."

They both giggled, and then laughed more intensely. It was a ridiculous conversation. Ida imagined someone overhearing it, and Sarah joined in. "The pioneers of tomorrow in deep discussion," Sarah narrated, as though she was reading aloud from a headline in a newspaper, perhaps the brand-new *Ha'aretz* from Tel Aviv.

A dragonfly floated above them, wings aloft, a bright emerald blue. Sarah pinched her earlobe between her thumb and her forefinger. "I'm not sure," she said. "It's hard to explain."

Above them I drifted. Had you forgotten I was here?

Sarah said, "It's like I'm haunting myself."

CHAPTER 3

*I*DA WALKED ACROSS THE FIELD with Levi holding her hand for everyone to see. They passed Dov, one foot balanced on a wagon axle, reading Bialik's Hebrew translation of *Don Quixote*. The thought came to Ida that her life was not dissimilar to a translated work: a story taken from Russian, lifted up and placed in a Hebrew context.

Dov waved his hand in front of his face absently, his eyes still on the book. The cloud of mosquitoes around him rose briefly into the air and then descended a moment later.

Levi led Ida not toward the newly installed water tap that the Agency had magically produced as though in apology for all the other supplies that were somehow stalled in Jaffa, but in the opposite direction, toward the Arab settlement. She followed without asking where they were going. From somewhere behind them came the sound of a motor turning over. A few high, clear notes as Zeruvabel played his violin.

When they passed the farthest edge of the field—a row of boulders had been placed there to mark a barrier—Ida asked, "Aren't you on night guard?"

Levi turned and smiled at her. "It's taken care of," he said. Ida hesitated. But he squeezed her hand and her trust returned, flooding through her body like golden liquid.

They kept walking further from the tents in search of some privacy, although neither of them said so. They followed the Arab donkey path as it wound around the base of the mountain. The slopes here had long been picked clean by Bedouin goats. The air was heavy and close, and hot as an oven. A hamsin was coming. They passed the dry well with the rusted bucket sticking out of the sand. Fatima's house loomed behind them, the flowers outside withered in their boxes. It would be nearly impossible to keep them alive in this kind of heat. Ida recalled the bundled candlesticks passed between their hands like a baby. A flutter rose in her chest, a mild nausea of guilt and uncertainty. For a moment she thought of telling Levi what she had done. How good it would feel to have someone to share her secret with, to have him know this part of her too. But Levi was a good halutz. He thought always of the group. She wanted to unburden herself, but the need was not equal to the risk of confessing.

They came, finally, to a bend in the creek that was sheltered by an outcrop of the mountain. There were bulrushes and mud flats and the river smelled like sweet mint and clover. A night bird sang the first four notes of the Marseillaise, and then sang them over again.

Levi squeezed her hand.

Ida had once held hands with a boy before. Shlomo's hand had been smooth, and the same size as hers, whereas Levi's was calloused from work, and engulfed hers entirely.

"I'm sorry I'm so sweaty," he said, and she felt the moisture between their palms. "Should I let go?"

"No," she said.

And then added, sweetly, "Please don't."

He did let go, though, and lifted his arms and took off his loose cotton shirt. He spread it out on a stretch of patchy grass, cracked earth showing between the tufts like a baby's first hair. Ida thought briefly how dirty it would be when it reached the laundry. Then Levi took off his trousers, as though it was the most natural thing to do, and laid them flat as well.

His underclothes had once been white but now were almost grey with wear. She could see the bulge of his testicles beneath them. And a hint of the cut that was evidence of God's covenant with Abraham, that marked him as a Jew.

Levi had taken a revolver out of his pocket and casually laid it in the grass.

Ida looked at it. An object entirely unrelated to the scene around it. It seemed innocent, irrelevant, like it was carved out of soap or wood.

"I thought the gun was David's," she said.

"It is."

"But I thought . . ." she paused, assembling her words. "I thought only David . . ."

"Samuel is on night guard," Levi said, meaning that one of the Germans had replaced him. But this only confused Ida more. She raised her eyebrows and squinted, asking for more clarification, but Levi waved his hand, like the topic was written on a chalkboard in front of them and he was erasing it.

"Are you sure?" she asked.

He patted the earth beside him.

She hesitated a moment, everything hanging in the balance, and then submitted. It was strange that he had the gun, but something more important was happening.

Ida followed Levi's lead and took off her dress.

"Help?" She knelt forward, and Levi undid the back button. He pulled the zipper down slowly.

She folded her glasses carefully and laid them in the grass.

If her mother could have seen her.

But Ida quickly dismissed the thought. She did not judge herself for her own willingness. If her father had been alive back home there would have been a matchmaker, and hushed negotiations between him and the father of some boy she might barely have met who was deemed suitable because his family attended synagogue. But her father was not alive, and the old world was dead. She would have no part of the chuppah, the superstitious circling of the bride by her groom. No part of the furtive fumbling beneath the sheets. If her father was alive he might have been shamed, but on some level she knew her mother would understand.

Ida slipped out of the dress and stood in her sandals and her brassiere, which she would have to abandon entirely soon— Shoshanna was on a tirade about how bras were demeaning to women, a physical manifestation of the impulse to keep them socially constrained. Easy for Shoshanna to say—she didn't have any breasts to speak of. Whereas Ida's were full.

When she released the clasp, though, she did feel relief in being free. Her breasts, she saw, and saw Levi seeing as well, were a shocking white in contrast to the deep tan on her face and arms.

Surely, nobody had ever felt before what she was feeling now.

Levi looked up at her face. He, too, wore an expression that was almost like pain. She saw the chip on his tooth and felt an impulse to bring her hand to his mouth and touch it.

He wiggled over so that his back was on the scratchy mud and the shirt was available for her more delicate skin. He again patted the fabric. "Come here."

Before she'd left Russia, Ida had said a prayer. She wanted to build Eretz Yisrael, yes. She wanted to do it in her beloved Abba's memory. And also, she had wanted things to happen to her. To become a new person suited to this new place and time. But she could hardly believe the ease with which this was happening, as though God had heard her and given her even more than she had thought to ask for. As though He had seen her crippling loss and was now trying to shower her with gain. If Ida needed proof that He existed, here it was. She was used to moving through her days with an unrequited longing in her belly—for a boy, for adulthood, for something more ephemeral she couldn't name. She had grown so accustomed to the longing that she had not conceived of the fact that it could be sated. That instead of the interminable waiting, action could be taken, events could occur.

A man who wanted to give himself to her had appeared. Her prayer had been answered before she had known what she was asking.

Ida lay down beside Levi, and he took her in his arms.

It was as if they were an old married couple in their bedroom on a Shabbos afternoon, endless years of tenderness and arguments and reconciliations already between them, laying down beside each other to let their bodies have the animal pleasure of speaking without the burden of thought.

"I've never done this before," she said, turning her face to him. She wanted him to know in case this changed his mind.

"Do you want to know the truth?" he asked.

"Yes."

"Neither have I."

This astonished her, and made her tender toward him, like a mother toward a child. She knew his inexperience was partly because of his religious observance, and this, too, engendered in her a feeling of recognition, like they were seeing each other at the most profound level. Some of the halutzim saw God and Zionism as incompatible, but within Levi the two were braided together inseparably. How could Hashem object? Unlike the strange and sin-laden world of the Christians, in Judaism it was a mitzvah to make love with the one you loved.

All her fear was suddenly gone. His arm was around her shoulders, and she curled onto her side and put her head on his chest. She felt the soft fuzz of hair against her cheek. It was like the act was already finished, like they were holding each other in the wide wake of a great thing already completed. His hair had grown shaggy in the short time they had been there.

"I could cut your hair," she said.

He laughed. "Like Delilah?"

"I would never betray you," she said, breathing him in. Sweat, and hay, and oil from the plow.

"We'd need scissors," he said.

She nodded. It would have to wait.

"Your hair is long too," he said. He rolled toward her and undid the ribbon at the bottom of first one braid and then the other. It took him some time to loosen the braids until her hair was free. He ran in his fingers through it, like he had never seen a woman's hair before. Their faces were nearly touching. He looked in her eyes. He did not look away.

Later, much later, they walked back together through the darkness. Their hands swung loosely at their sides, an invisible line between them, palpable and alive.

"How did your work go today?" he asked.

Ida smiled. It was like he was asking his wife what had

happened in the hours they had been apart. Like he wanted to know every part of her life.

"The clothesline fell down."

Levi laughed. "How?"

"It collapsed. Under the weight of wet clothes."

He laughed again at this. "What else?" he asked.

"The shirts are covered in stains that will never come out."

"Probably from Yashka!" Levi said. They all ate like wolves, but Yashka was notorious for how he slopped his food, pieces falling everywhere as with a toddler.

"Who can tell?" Ida said, thinking of how she laundered them, pinned them up to dry, and assigned them randomly the following morning. Yet again she admired the elegance of the system: no individual more important than anyone else. Nobody owning anything that could help someone else. But then, unbidden, came the memory of the candlesticks and she swallowed hard and held her breath. She turned toward Levi and blurted out, "I don't belong to you."

This was the exact opposite of how she felt.

Levi stopped and looked at her. His face was pained and solemn. He, too, appreciated the dictates of the shared life. He wanted her to see that he agreed, that he believed this fiercely and would give his whole being for the collective. But something else crossed his face, some words whose weight he was measuring, and finally he spoke. "But I wish you did."

"You wish what?" she asked, wanting to be sure.

"I wish you were my wife," Levi said.

In the tall grass the crickets were singing. The bullfrogs in the mud flats added their own symphony, and suddenly Ida saw that the entire world had a kind of existential harmony. That everything was animated with that sacred God-given spark, and all of it was trying to give birth to love. Her father might be gone, but he was here; she felt his presence as though he was in the next room. The feeling was so strong and consuming she imagined that nothing could change it.

If I could go back and warn her, I would. But I cannot.

As Ida approached her tent she heard crying. She hesitated outside. She wanted to give Sarah her privacy. On the other hand, she thought quickly, wasn't privacy bourgeois? And where else would she sleep? It was late.

She drew herself up and entered the tent.

Looking around, she saw the kerosene lamp had been lit, and had been left burning for some time. The wick was low, only a trace of oil remaining in the bottom. Still, it was enough to throw long shadows on the sloped walls, the dirt floor, the straw pallets. But Sarah wasn't there.

There was a pair of scissors lying on the floor, as if someone had trimmed the wick and then been startled into dropping them. Ida picked up the scissors and put them in her pocket.

Levi came to the laundry the following morning and said to her, "The light in the east is Zion in your hair."

She passed the tin cup she was holding, half filled with murky water, from her right hand to her left.

"Thank you," she guessed.

She saw his Adam's apple working, swallowing and swallowing again.

"The Tree of Life begets the Compost of Death," he said.

Ida squatted and put the cup down. She stood and held his face in her hands.

"Are your eyes okay?" she asked.

She peered more closely at him; his sockets were protruding slightly, and there were bruises beneath them as though he had been in a fight. The whites were tinged yellow.

"I'm fine," he said. And not quite meeting her gaze, "I'm happy. I had a wonderful time with you last night."

He tugged at his shirt as though to create some space between it and his chest. His face, she saw, was damp with sweat. What she had taken as ardour now seemed to be simple bodily heat.

"You have a fever," she said. "Your eyes are yellow."

"Like the lemons we will soon be growing!" He laughed.

Ida said, "Grapefruits."

Levi said, "Soon we will be like the wealthy pardessanim. But instead of keeping our profit we will turn it back into the earth like fertilizer."

"Bananas?" she asked.

"Why not?" Levi agreed.

They both knew that while citrus groves might one day be possible, the dark earth of the Emek was not suited to fruit from the jungle. Still, they laughed together, imagining it.

Ida turned and saw David bisecting the yard, a book in his hand, his face down, reading while he walked. It occurred to Ida that his wife, Hannah, had not returned; Ida pictured the wagon galloping from the yard. Where had it taken Hannah? Was she coming back?

As though David had felt Ida's eyes on him, he lifted his head. She motioned to him; he walked toward them, looking slightly disgruntled to be summoned.

"Shalom," Ida said when he reached them, but David didn't answer. Now he, too, was peering at Levi. He closed his book and put it in his back pocket.

"Kadachat," he said.

"Pardon?"

Levi blinked.

"Malaria," David said.

Levi said, "I'm fine!" but David was already taking him by the elbow and leading him like a child, looking for somewhere to help him lie down. Ida followed a few metres behind them, unsure of her role but unwilling to let Levi out of her sight. Some sound inside her had begun to ring, a low alarm, increasing in volume.

"This is why we need to plant more eucalyptus," David was saying, but more to himself than to Levi or Ida. He stopped, took the pencil from his ear, and extracted his book again. He made a note in the margin. "We'll need more quinine."

Levi swayed on his feet.

The settlement had not yet established a real infirmary, so David led them to Levi's tent and helped him lie down on his own pallet. Almost as soon as Levi was prone, his infirmity emerged fully formed, as if it had been waiting inside him for the correct context to assert itself. What had appeared to be a yellowish tinge to his skin now became a more pronounced jaundice, and the beads of sweat on his forehead erupted into rivulets of moisture. He moaned.

"Let it move through you," David said, but again it was as if he was speaking to himself, or to some former version of himself that had once been in Levi's position. "The more you resist the worse it will become. It is the land of Yisrael entering into you. Accept it."

Ida wondered briefly if David might be sick too.

"We must have some quinine somewhere," he said, and he looked at Ida as though she could somehow provide this.

On the straw pallet, Levi's body was clenching. They were small convulsions at first, and Ida crouched down beside him, holding his hand until the spasms increased in intensity and his whole body was thrashing as if he was possessed by a demon. Foam rose in his mouth as the panic rose in Ida.

"Where do we get the quinine?" she asked David desperately.

From the ground, they both heard Levi say, "We need to work!"

For a minute Ida thought David was going to agree with him. But then he said, "I'll go for it."

Levi was struggling to sit up, but before Ida could stop him he was overtaken by another fit of shaking. She groped around for a shmata to wipe his face with. It seemed absurd—not twenty minutes ago he had been talking about lemon groves.

"Where?" Ida asked.

"I'll saddle the donkeys and go to Tiberias," David said.

Ida didn't know how far the journey would be and didn't want to ask.

"Or I'll send someone," David said, reconsidering.

There was a sound at the tent flap: Levi's tentmate Dov returning from his work clearing the field. He ducked down to enter through the low opening. It was now late morning but it did not occur to Ida or David to ask what he was doing back so early.

"You'll have to move your things," David said. "From now on we'll be using this tent as an infirmary."

Ida waited for Dov to ask what Levi was sick with, but Dov only turned away and began cramming his belongings—a blanket, a pen knife, a small framed photograph of a woman in a bonnet—into an orange crate he had been using as a dresser.

"It's kadachat," Ida offered, not translating.

"I see that," Dov said, his face impassive.

He straightened his back, both his knees popping loudly. "Your turn next," he said to Ida.

She reached for her braid and inserted the tip of one finger under the ribbon. "That's a very strange thing to say."

"Look around you," Dov said. "Is there anything here that isn't strange?"

Dov left, and soon after David did too, reassuring Ida he would find quinine. Ida was alone with Levi. She perched on the edge of his mattress and held his hand through another round of the terrible shaking.

"I'm here," she reassured him, but if Levi could hear her he could certainly not respond.

When the worst had passed, she lay down beside him. His sweat smelled sour. He made a noise, and for a moment she thought he was talking. She drew him close and said, eagerly, "What?"

His eyelids opened for a moment, and she knew he had seen her. But almost immediately they closed again. His body softened; his breaths lengthened and deepened. She stayed with him then, like she was carrying him somewhere in her arms. She felt the little ticks, like an engine cooling, of his muscles twitching as he fell back to unconsciousness.

CHAPTER 4

*L*EVI'S CONDITION GAVE THE GROUP extra motivation to drain the swamps. The mosquitoes were dangerous and needed to be tamed. Another team of workers was formed.

"This will be tiring work," David explained the next morning after breakfast—as though any of the work here was not tiring, Ida thought—but a cheer rose up from the halutzim. Work! Tiring work! Work in the service of Eretz Yisrael!

"If not now, then when?" David asked the group. And Ida saw how David was using Levi's sickness to motivate them to do something that needed to be done regardless. But the halutzim were not deterred, and they answered back Hillel's famous words, "Im lo achshav, ayma-tay!"

The few pairs of rubber boots they owned were distributed; the rest would have to make do without. Groups were sent to different areas, some to the base of the spring, some to the main road from Jenin where the swamps extended for miles. They began by digging ditches to drain the muck. The ditches had to be deep—Zeruvabel the fiddler, who also happened to be very tall, was used as a gauge. When the team thought their ditch was deep enough they summoned him over, and he came gladly, like a child being called into a game.

He folded his long limbs and lowered himself down into the hollow.

"Not deep enough!" he declared, if he could still see over the edge of the hole in the earth. Or "You're done!" if he could not see over the top, at which point a collective cheer went up. The halutzim were sickly and hungry but they took any excuse to cheer.

A separate team, including the Germans, was working on the drains themselves, building a primitive system using gravel and clay pipes.

Ida was grateful for her position in the laundry. She knew the halutzim's clothes would now be even filthier with mud from the ditches, but her work gave her long hours in which to be alone, to sneak away and check on Levi. She was surprised by the strength of the protective instinct that rose up in her, as if from nowhere; she felt compelled to take care of Levi, and to do so in a way that succoured to his manhood. She went through the day as though her whole body was alight. She went over their night together, piece by piece, like a child who takes her treasures out of a box and lays them out on her bedspread to account for them. The contours of his biceps. The smooth, dark circles of his nipples. The trail of wiry hair that led down to the part of him that had split her open, revealing the genie of her new self.

In the afternoon Ida went to see him. She crouched down beside him and felt the heat of his breath. He was resting peacefully, his chest rising and falling, but no matter how much she stared at him he did not wake up.

She took the scissors from her pocket. "I can cut your hair now," she said.

Nothing.

Hesitating, she angled herself closer, sat down cross-legged beside him. She lifted the weight of his skull with one hand. It was surprisingly heavy. With her other hand, she angled the flat side of the blade against his forehead. She took a piece of the soft, dark hair and she cut.

The lock that fell onto her hand was fine like a child's.

It took her only a few minutes to make her way around his entire head. She held his skull, shifting its weight as she circled his nape, the hair over his ears, his shaggy bangs. When she was finished, his face was covered with a fine fuzz, and he sneezed in his sleep but still he did not wake up. She blew on him gently, and then brushed the few stray hairs to clear his olive skin.

"Just like I said I would," she whispered.

When she laid his head down he looked like a different boy. Like someone she had never seen in her life.

When Ida got back to the laundry, Sarah was there. Her wild curls stuck out from the edges of her kerchief, and there was a smear of crusted blood from a mosquito bite next to her collarbone. She saw Ida coming and hefted a log from the woodpile in her dress, holding the hem up to form a hammock. When she tossed the log on the fire a cloud of white smoke billowed up; Ida squeezed her eyes shut, tears on her cheeks. "Thank you," she said to Sarah.

The smoke changed direction and she squeezed her eyes shut against it for a second time.

"My pleasure," Sarah said. And then, "The tractor broke."

Ida understood she was bringing news from the far edge of

the kibbutz where a few dunams of land had been drained and cleared, and were ready for planting.

"How do you know?" Ida asked. She wiped at her eyes with her fists.

"There was an accident," Sarah said.

Ida blinked hard.

"Someone forgot to change the radiator water in the tractor. When Dov unscrewed the cap he got scalded."

"Is he okay?"

Sarah winced, like she was the one being burned. "I wouldn't say so." She tilted her head to her shoulder, as though listening. "I wouldn't say so," she repeated.

"Pass another log?" Ida said. But Sarah ignored this.

"His face is covered in blisters," she said. "He can't speak. He can't move."

"What—"

"He might die."

Ida thought that Sarah seemed both concerned about Dov and pleased to be the one to tell the news. She paused, letting the gravity of the situation sink in. It occurred to her that Sarah had left out a crucial part of the story. If there had been negligence, someone must be responsible.

"Who forgot to change the water?"

Sarah shrugged. "David," she said.

It was David who assembled them—for the second time that day—before the evening meal. He waited until the shovels had been cleaned and returned to the cage of barbed wire they would use until there was time to build a storage shed. It seemed silly to Ida to clean shovels that were just going to be dirtied again the following morning, but David insisted. He had learned this, he said, from a chaver named Meyer back at Kinneret.

David was solemn as he waited for them to gather. His black curls were growing, and they bobbed around his jaw like a girl's. He stood still, his hands hanging in fists, waiting for the halutzim to quiet. Ida could have sworn that even the songbirds in the meadow paused to hear what he would say.

"We are in a difficult situation," he began. "But we will be faced with many difficult situations this year."

There was a very long pause. David had a habit of clearing his throat when he spoke, as though to underline the important points with his voice. "And in all the years to follow," he finished.

Ida took the ribbon off her braid, undid it and rebraided it again.

David said, "The tractor is broken."

A murmur rippled through the crowd. Ida knew they all understood the implication of this, how a broken tractor would halt the wheel that made their whole collective turn.

"We need to repair it," David said.

He paused like a professor who has asked his students to solve an algebra equation, something abstract that had no consequence in the tangible world. It seemed to Ida that he was testing them, that they were all part of some great social experiment that David was conducting. "Who has an idea?" he asked.

There was a brief pause and then many voices started to shout at once.

"We could take the Arabs'!" someone called out.

There was general laughter. The Arabs did not have a tractor.

"Levi can repair it!" someone else suggested.

It was understood that Levi was exceptionally skilled; he had quietly emerged as the lead worker, and although this could not be made explicit, in the future he would be the one people turned to when something needed welding or a pipe had burst.

Ida felt a rush of pride, followed closely by an awful panic.

Shoshanna said what Ida could not. "Have you forgotten the kadachat?"

The man who had spoken up demurred, muttering his condolences.

"At the kutsva where I was before," he said sadly, "ten halut-zim died from the kadachat."

Ida sat up straighter, and looked around for someone to dis-prove this statement, but nobody did. Died? From malaria? Ten people?

She stood up. Her heart was pounding. She had to go to Levi in the infirmary. But David looked at her, one eyebrow raised, and she sat back down.

"I can try repairing the tractor," a chaver called Saul sug-gested; but Saul had been a literature student in his former life, and his fingers were smooth and sausage-like, and the silence that responded was answer enough.

"Unfortunately," David said, "we weren't able to repair it. We tried."

"Why not?" one of the Germans asked, disdainfully.

"There is a part missing," David said.

"We can make it from our bare hands!" That was one of the youngest men, barely sixteen. A boy, really, thought Ida. With a boy's enthusiasm.

David nodded benignly, indulging.

"We will have to find a way to purchase a new part," he said, gracing them with the answer he had been seeking.

"The Agency?" the youngster asked.

"Eventually," David said. "But they don't have the funds at the moment."

So far, Ida noticed, he had said nothing about the medical emergency unfolding alongside the mechanical one, the scalding of Dov that Sarah had referred to. Ida thought he would address this next, but David only repeated himself. "We will have to find a way to purchase the missing part." He cleared his throat for emphasis.

"I have twenty lira," the same boy called out. This was equivalent to the change in a child's piggy bank, and everyone laughed except David.

"It's a good point," he said.

He let his approval hang in the air for several long moments. "Does anyone have any money? Or anything we could sell?"

Ida saw immediately what David was doing. The halutzim had already been asked to turn in their personal belongings. But he was offering them another opportunity to come forward with anything outstanding. He was telling them implicitly that he would not fault them for not having done so already.

Ida pictured her heavy silver candlesticks. This was a desperate situation, David was saying. And also, a chance to make things new.

Levi was overcome by another round of convulsions and Ida stayed by his side, touching his forehead with a cool cloth, dipping it back in the pail of water and wringing it out. He still seemed not to know she was there. David had delivered on his promise and pumped Levi full of quinine, but if it was working the results were not yet visible. The words of the halutz rang in Ida's ears. *Died* from the kadachat.

Eventually she was forced to leave him; night was falling and she had neglected her work. There was a last load of laundry waiting to be dealt with before she slept. As she was hanging shirts on the line with wooden pins, one of the Germans approached her. "May I help you?" he asked.

Ida eyed him warily. She had given up trying to tell which twin was which.

"No thank you," she said.

"Hard work in the trenches today," he said, and he waggled his fingers to show her the mud caked under his fingernails. There was something effeminate in the gesture, something fey, despite the size of his knuckles and the cracks that snaked across his skin.

"Unfortunate about the tractor," he said idly.

"Yes," she agreed.

"A German machine would not have broken," he said.

He turned toward her basket of damp shirts, extracted one, and hung it on the line.

"I'm fine," Ida said.

"It's no problem," the German said.

The wooden pin clamped down on the fabric like teeth.

She looked at the German. There was something else he wanted to say. He had hooked his thumbs beneath his suspenders, taking the posture of a farmer, which was oddly incongruous with his perfectly polished shoes.

"You turned in your candlesticks?" he asked finally.

Ida swallowed.

The German raised his eyebrows, but his incredulousness was feigned.

She clenched her teeth, turned her back and selected a wooden pin from her wicker basket. The shirt she drew up was enormous; there was nobody on the kibbutz it would fit.

The air was still so hot that the shirt was almost dry before she got it to the line.

"Well," the German said. "Well, well."

From across the yard came the sound of one of the donkeys braying. They both turned their heads. Shoshanna was lifting the leather harness and rubbing a wound beneath it with salve. Beyond her was the infirmary, and Ida pictured Levi laying there, his own skin sore and hot, his eyelids fluttering in his sleep.

"You have forsaken the group for your own benefit," the German said.

"Hardly," Ida snapped, and then wished she hadn't spoken, for in her answer was a tacit acknowledgement.

"Levi is quite sick," the German said, taking another approach. His eyes drifted in the direction of the infirmary, then back to Ida's face to gauge her reaction.

She kept her gaze steady, but the German must have detected a trace of fear, because he asked, "What would Levi think if he knew what you'd done?"

She turned away and adjusted a wooden pin. She would not give him the satisfaction of an answer. But he had seen her weak spot. He held it to his chest like an ace.

"Samuel," Ida said, reprimand in her voice, like an adult trying to shame a child.

But the German only smirked. "I'm Selig," he said. His smirk broke into a full smile.

"You can't tell us apart," he marvelled, and she saw he had settled on a way to use this to his advantage.

"I suppose you could give the candlesticks to David now," he said. "But that would be a shame."

He bit his lip, considering.

"They're very beautiful," he added.

Ida tried not to picture the candlesticks, as though by banishing them from her mind she could banish them from his too. But the more she tried to ignore them the more they made themselves known to her, with Fatima's face beside them.

She saw them in her mother's hands.

She saw her father's torso bent at an odd angle, a pool of blood spreading out around him on the floor.

The German lifted his suspender and snapped it against his shirt.

He said, "You could give them to David, but I'd rather you give them to me."

Ida looked at him. "Pardon?"

"You heard what I said."

"My belongings are not your concern," she answered.

"Oh, but they are. Haven't you heard? We're all a family here."

She shut her eyes tightly, as if to make him disappear.

"There are two of them," he said.

"Two what?"

"What do you think? Candlesticks. One for each of us."

He snapped the suspender again.

"Otherwise?" she asked.

And he said, as though it had just occurred to him, "Otherwise I will tell everyone what you've done."

Later, of course, Ida would doubt herself. I go back and watch her reconsider. Could she have made a different choice? Was the German—Selig? Samuel?—calling her bluff? But the thought of being revealed as selfish was more than she could tolerate. To favour herself at the expense of the group. What would David think? and Hannah? Not to mention the first man she had ever loved, who was close to death in the sick house. The man who had told her he felt as strongly for her as he did for Eretz Yisrael, and the other way around. From where I am now I can see what held her back. She was worried about what Levi would say.

CHAPTER 5

*T*HE FOLLOWING MORNING DAVID was there when Ida came
out of her tent. His hands were clasped behind his back. It
seemed that he had been waiting, perhaps for a long time, a shy
suitor afraid to make his presence known. His little daughter was
hiding behind him, her hands poking out on either side of his
waist. David looked surprised to see Ida, as though he had been
expecting, or hoping, to see someone else, but he forged ahead.

"I need to ask you a favour," he said.

The last time they had spoken, Ida had petitioned David for a
day of observance—and thus no work—on Yom Kippur. For
Levi's sake. David had soundly rejected her. But his voice now was
different; from the repentant cast of his eyes, Ida understood that
the favour was a personal one.

He extracted the pencil tucked over his ear, then used its tip
to dig into his curls and scratch at the back of his scalp. "Would
you watch Ruth for a few hours?" he asked Ida, reaching behind
his back to tickle his daughter.

Any other request, Ida knew, would have been phrased in the

form of an instruction—an instruction phrased to make the listener think they had come up with it on their own, but an instruction nevertheless. This, however, was a genuine question.

"Of course," she said immediately. "I'd be happy to."

Beyond David, storm clouds were amassing on the horizon, dense, high castles of purple and blue. The air smelled wet. Ruth belonged to this land in the same way the clouds did, and the day birds and the night birds and the soft, lithe gazelles. She did not need "watching." But Ida remembered how David had gone to Tiberias to fetch the quinine for Levi. She owed him.

Besides, she missed Eva in a way that made her arms ache for want of hugging her. Ruth was younger than Eva, but only slightly.

Ida crouched down. She peered behind David to where the child was clinging to his back. "Shalom, Ruth," she said.

The child's wild black curls were identical to her father's, as though someone had snipped off a few of his locks and affixed them with glue to the top of his daughter's head.

"Have you seen my doll?" the girl asked.

"Oh no. Is she missing?"

Ruth nodded.

Ida remembered the doll from the first day, but still she asked, "What does she look like?"

Ruth's face lit up. "She's made of a puffy."

"A pillow," her father corrected.

"She has a headscarf that turns into a kippah," Ruth said, and added, "she's so pretty."

In the distance came the sound of someone shaking a tambourine.

A look of sadness came over Ruth's face. "My doll belonged to my friend, Sakina," she said.

David shifted and cleared his throat loudly, as if to distract Ruth.

Ida said, "What's your doll's name?"

"Salam," Ruth said, without meeting her eye.

Ida reached for Ruth's hand.

"Thank you," David said to Ida. He turned to leave but Ruth remained stuck to his backside, her face buried in his linen shirt. He tried to pry her fingers open one by one, but she was clinging too tightly.

"Look, bubi," David said. "Ida is your friend."

Ruth let out a small mewl of protest.

David pressed his lips together and raised his eyebrows at Ida. The gesture said, *You're the woman here. Do something.*

"I have an idea," Ida said, her mind going again to Eva, who could be convinced into most things if she was told it was a secret. "Would you like to go on a special adventure with me?"

Ruth poked her head around the corner of David's hip. She looked at Ida.

Ida said, "You can't tell anyone."

Ruth's eyes widened.

"You have to promise," Ida said.

Tears came suddenly to the little girl's eyes. "I don't want to go," she said.

But a sound of frustration came from her father's throat and Ruth reached out for Ida's extended hand. She knew she had no other option. She did not look back at David—Ida could see she was bracing herself for the separation, pretending she was not being abandoned.

The little palm was sweaty in Ida's and so small she could have crushed it with one squeeze. Ida waved goodbye to David over her shoulder, without turning to look back. She talked to

Ruth in a gentle voice, a steady stream of words like she was soothing a skittish pony.

"Here's the cook tent," she said, "where someone is frying eggplant. We only have a propane stove but one day we will have a real oven. And here is the garden with all the rakes and hoes— one day it will grow all our vegetables."

She was drawing a picture of the kibbutz of tomorrow in the girl's mind, but it occurred to her that Ruth was the one who could properly imagine a functioning commune, having been born at Kinneret. Perhaps Ida was painting this picture for herself.

"Here's Trotsky!" Ida said. The donkey hung its head over the newly built fence. The smell of sawdust still hung in the air, and wood chips coated the ground. A work sheet had been posted on it, hung by a single nail.

"Do you think he'd like some clover?" Ida asked.

Ruth nodded, and they stopped to feed Trotsky, his floppy black lips widening to reveal the pink gums and cracked yellow teeth. The sound of them grinding together made Ida wince. Ruth made her own sideways chewing motion, imitating the beast, and rubbed the smooth flank. Trotsky accepted the touch. Ida and Ruth continued walking, holding hands, through the maze of tents and past the edge of the field where some of the workers were stopping for their noonday meal. The break would be brief; there was a push now to plant before the heavy rains.

Beyond them, the plot of cleared land shimmered, the dark, neat square in stark contrast to the thistles and brambles that surrounded it. Yashka and Zeruvabel wrestled with a final boulder, attempting to pry it from the earth with a long bar of steel. Saul examined the plough, looking first at the handles, then at the blades, checking that all was in working order. The seeds waited in a burlap sack, glistening; their promise would soon be revealed.

Shoshanna, who had made it known that when there were children she would be the teacher, looked up from the water tap and waved.

Ida liked that the comrades were seeing her with Ruth. It was as if she had been charged with something special. She longed, suddenly and violently, for Levi to be well again so he could join them. Perhaps he could walk on the other side of Ruth, holding her other hand, like they were, the three of them, a little family.

As though she had heard Ida's inner thought, Ruth said sharply, "I want my Imma!"

"Where has she gone?" Ida asked, picturing the wagon galloping from the yard with Hannah's knot of hair bouncing wildly on the top of her head. She hoped she might get some information out of the girl, but Ruth only clenched her jaw, her bottom lip trembling.

"I want to see her," Ruth said.

"You will. Later," Ida said. "But first we have to have our adventure."

"Where are we going?"

"You'll see."

They passed the laundry, the big vat where Ida toiled all day, and she thought of a game that she played with Eva at home. She dumped a basket of fresh laundry over top of her sister's small body, pawed through the clothes pretending she was lost, and then feigned delight when she found her. But Ruth was restless, and on the verge of tears again, so Ida scooped her up and lifted her onto her shoulders. This cheered the girl up; Ruth took Ida's braids in her hands like they were reins. "Giddy-up," she said.

The child was surprisingly heavy, given that her limbs were spindly and she looked half starved.

Ida walked quickly and soon reached the donkey path. The

grass was dry as straw; she heard crickets and a sound like bellows being pumped. They passed the old well. Ida saw the place where she had begun to dig her burial site for the candlesticks, a dent of earth torn up and dark, as though there had been some kind of scuffle. She kept going toward the Arab houses. A group of children were playing marbles in the dirt. A baby toddled toward them, his bottom bare; he started to pee, and kept toddling, the fountain of urine spouting out in front of him. Ruth tightened her grip on Ida's head. Perhaps, Ida thought, the girl had not known there were other houses at all, and other people with dark brown eyes and skin like caramel. But Ruth leaned over her head and whispered in her ear, "Don't worry, I know Arabs. They're kind."

And the children! How long had it been since Ruth had someone to play with? Ida felt Ruth shift and wriggle on her shoulders; Ida bent her knees and braced herself and lifted her down. Ruth looked up at her through her long lashes, asking the silent question. Ida nodded her consent and Ruth ran toward the children. She hesitated at the edge of the circle, but when Ida nodded again, she joined in.

Ida took her moment. She walked purposefully toward Fatima's house, the one with the flaked wooden shutters and a thin white sheet in place of a door. Heat rose off the baked earth in waves. She pushed the fabric to the side—up close she could see it had once borne a pattern of stripes that had faded almost completely in the sun—and peered into the hut. There was a dull samovar on a rickety table, the cups around it arranged for tea. Fatima was crouched over a wicker basket, doing something Ida could not see. She raised her head, though, as if she had been expecting a visitor. Her eyes were even brighter than Ida remembered. The women exchanged a nod. Fatima rose slowly, her robe swaying with the movement, a hand on her lower back. Ida saw she was pregnant.

The sun slanted through the wooden slats and fell on the floor in hot white lines. In a dusty corner another child tried to pull a crumpled rag off a hook on the wall. Behind this, the mukhtar with the scar on his cheek observed from a chair. Ida remembered him from the day of their arrival, the stand-off between him and David. Then he had seemed threatening, but now he looked only tired and old.

Ida turned to leave but Fatima caught her eye, nodding to assure her it was okay.

One side of the mud hut stood in for the kitchen; there were some dry chickpeas in a chipped blue bowl, cheese in a mesh cloth, and a bundle of herbs tied with a string on the counter. Fatima moved toward it, and for a moment Ida thought she was going to give her a chunk of the cheese. Her stomach growled. But instead Fatima drew out an old woven box from under the counter. She rummaged in it and came out with Ida's bundle. It was still wrapped in the kerchief and tied neatly with a measure of rope. She held it close to her body, keeping Ida's gaze.

The sight of the pamotim hidden in the cloth brought sharp tears to Ida's eyes. She imagined her mother's horror if she knew what Ida had done. Ida reached out her hands in a gesture of supplication, asking for her belongings back, but Fatima stood her ground. And then, all at once, Ida understood. Fatima wanted acknowledgement. She wanted Ida to admit she was trustworthy.

"Thank you," Ida said, and whether or not Fatima knew the words themselves, the meaning in Ida's voice was clear. Fatima nodded, and spoke in Arabic. Then she passed the bundle to her solemnly, honouring her vow.

When Ida looked up she saw Ruth in the open doorway. The child was watching, her eyes wide.

"Let's go, metukah," Ida said, moving toward her, but Ruth's lower lip trembled and a large tear slid down her cheek.

"What's wrong?" Ida asked, moving the child back out into the bright sunlight. They both blinked, their eyes adjusting. Ruth pointed to her leg.

A long cut slashed down the front of her left shin. Blood ran from it, shocking red against her tender skin.

"Oh dear!" Ida exclaimed, and crouched down to get a closer look, but Ruth grabbed her and buried her face in Ida's hip the way she had done with her father just an hour ago.

For a moment, Ida pretended Ruth was hers.

"Let me see," she said, manoeuvring the girl back and peering at the cut. She used the edge of her sleeve to mop up the blood. It immediately soaked through, turning the material the darkest shade of crimson. Just like when Hannah had given her the blood-soaked rags, Ida thought of the laundry. These stains would never come out.

She felt a sudden panic. Where was the girl's father? But the face that came into her mind was not David's, but Levi's. Levi would know what to do.

"What happened?" she asked. But Ruth only began to cry in earnest, deep, wracking sobs that Ida could see were one part pain and another part shock.

"Oh metukah," Ida said. And then, lying through her teeth, because children were nothing if not suggestible. "It's only a scratch."

It took her a long time to clean up the cut. Fatima offered a tin pail of water and Ida wiped out the gravel as best she could. There were a few bits too deeply embedded, and Ruth screamed when Ida tried to get at them, the other little children watching slack jawed. One had had the eye sickness, Ida saw, and her left pupil was clouded with a milky film. The mukhtar emerged from the house, the scar on his cheek more visible in the bright light of the afternoon. He gave Ida an anxious half-smile and knelt before Ruth, probing at the wound and then wrapping it in a scrap of cloth. Ruth let him work, and eventually her crying lessened, but Ida could see that the blood was still flowing beneath the bandage. There was nothing else that could be done, though, and Ida lifted Ruth, and they waved goodbye to the gathering.

Fatima and the mukhtar both waved back, wishing Ida and Ruth well in words they couldn't understand.

As Ida walked, Ruth wrapped her legs around Ida's waist and laid her head on her shoulder. She played with the tip of Ida's braid, tickling her cheek with it like it was a paintbrush. She took off Ida's glasses and put them on her own face and squealed at how they distorted her view. This seemed strange to Ida, as the girl had been sobbing just moments ago. The cut must not be as bad as it looked.

"How does it feel now, yakira?" she asked, and felt Ruth shrug. The small body relaxed in her arms, and Ida smelled prepubescent sweat, so different from an adult's.

Ruth did not want to be put down. Ida continued walking, carrying both the child and the candlesticks in her arms; the metal dug into her ribs. Eventually the tents of the settlement came into view, that now familiar harbour full of sails. From this distance the halutzim looked like toy figurines in the fields. A silhouette with a shovel was bent over the vegetable garden plot. Ida saw it was David; Ruth saw this too.

Her mouth was next to Ida's ear; she whispered something.

"What's that, metukah?"

"My Abba has a gun," Ruth said.

Ida rubbed her back. "The night watch gun," she said.

She said it in the same voice she had used earlier, narrating what they saw around them: the garden, the donkey, the thresher waiting patiently for the corn to grow.

But Ruth shook her head against Ida's shoulder and wrapped her legs more tightly around her waist. "No," she whispered. "A different gun."

She must have felt a twinge in the poorly bandaged cut; she let out a whimper.

"He killed someone," Ruth said.

In the time they had been gone, evening had fallen. The nights were now starting to get cooler, and the sky was streaked with crimson. Cirrus clouds made ridges like the sand under shallow water. Ida heard birds, and the new tap squeaking in protest as someone turned it off.

"Shalom," Ida said to David.

Ruth didn't look at her father, her face now buried in Ida's shoulder.

"What are you holding?" David asked Ida, closing his notebook reluctantly and propping the pencil back on its perch behind his ear.

She thought to say, "Your daughter," and then realized he was gesturing to her right arm, where she held the bundled candlesticks.

"Nothing," she said, and then, before he noticed himself, "Ruth got a scratch."

She shifted the child in her arms, and then set her on her feet so they could inspect it properly. All three of them looked down together. The muslin cloth was soaked in blood. A rivulet had run out from under the bandage, crusting on Ruth's skin in the heat.

"It hurts, Abba," Ruth said, her voice small.

David's face was blank.

"I can take her to the infirmary," Ida said, worried by the length of the gash and the amount of blood leaking from such a small body. But David said, "Not to worry, I'll deal with it."

He seemed oddly distracted, his eyes rapidly scanning the horizon for some unidentified enemy or something else only he was aware of.

"Are you sure? I could just . . ."

"There is always blood," he said. And then, to himself, something in fast Hebrew Ida did not understand.

She took her cue and left, but not without giving Ruth a hug goodbye. For a moment, she clung to the girl tightly, burying her face in her hair, as though she was the one being comforted, and not the other way around.

Ida walked quickly to the German's tent, before she could change her mind. He was fiddling with the knob on his kerosene lamp, raising and lowering the wick inside the glass. An old leather saddle was heaped in the corner by one of the beds. He turned and saw her and a small sound of pleasure escaped his throat. Glee, or gloating. She saw he knew he should hide it, but he could not resist.

"You came," he said.

Ida set her package on a crate he was using as a bookshelf. She undid Fatima's neat knot and unfolded the kerchief, peeling back the layers of fabric, and selected one of the candlesticks. She did not make eye contact as she passed it over. The image flashing through her mind this time was of the Cossack's boots as they manoeuvred her mother backward into the shadows. Her mother's own shoes a sensible black, with a button. The German took the candlestick without comment and put it beneath his own mattress. They didn't speak.

His pale skin made her think of the belly of a fish floating upside down in the river.

There was nothing left to say so Ida turned and left. She went toward her own tent, cradling the remaining candlestick against her body. It was now the only thing she had left from her old life at home.

She stood at the flap and heard Sarah crying again. Even through the muffle of the canvas and whatever soft pillow Sarah was using to bury her face, Ida heard the full force of despair. She was about to go in and comfort her friend when she felt someone come up behind her. She stood still without turning. There was a tap on her shoulder. It was the German again, his face sickly and impassive.

"What do you want?" she asked bluntly.

"My candlestick," he said.

Up close she saw dirt at the edge of his hairline, and the skin peeling from his sunburned nose. He picked at it, and then brought his thumb down to examine the skin that had flaked off.

"I already gave you one," she said.

The German looked casually down at his hand, rubbing the dead skin between his thumb and forefinger like he was asking for money. He looked back up at her, shaking his head slowly.

"You gave one to my brother," he said.

Ida held on to the tip of her braid. She dug her forefinger under the ribbon and held it there; she could feel it turning red and filling with blood.

"Well?" he said.

"What do you mean?"

But the words of his brother came back to her. *One for each of us.*

How had she been so stupid? What stake did he have in her wellbeing? He knew she wouldn't tell. Ida was the one who had lied to the group, who had kept something back that could have helped the others.

The Germans would not let her keep a thing. One candlestick was for Samuel, and one was for Selig.

CHAPTER 6

*I*DA HANDED OVER the second candlestick and went straight to Levi. She found him prone, on his back, with his arms arranged neatly at his sides. His skin a clammy grey, his eyelids closed. He moaned in his sleep as though in greeting. Ida took the shmata from the pail beside his bed and wiped the sweat from his forehead and the back of his neck. Then she lay down beside him on his pallet and let her tears fall. She curled onto her side around him, her face and nose pressed into his neck, his bony hip joint digging into her pelvis. She tried not to think about what she had just given up. She lay there a long time in the shadows of the tent, the other patients like corpses all around them. Many more were falling ill with the kadachat. Necks and ankles and foreheads were covered in bites; the pioneers' eyes grew glassy and their collarbones protruded at their shoulders. Ida lifted her head and looked around: someone had been strapped to a backboard to be restrained during the convulsions. And there was Dov, his face was crusted over in black, like he was a monster in the Brothers Grimm or a golem living under a bridge in Prague. Suddenly Ida had a premonition that soon Ruth would be here too—the bandage had been so completely soaked in blood. She laid her head back down.

Was this Eretz Yisrael? She had been promised—had believed so fervently—that they were making something new, but instead everything was falling to pieces.

She moved her face against Levi's face. His stubble would soon be a beard.

"Wake up," she whispered. "I need you."

But he didn't respond, his body frozen against her like he was dead.

The following afternoon, though, Ida came around the corner to the dining hall and found Levi repairing a broken garden hose.

"What are you doing?" she asked, because she couldn't think what else to say, and he straightened. He made a sound like he was somewhere far away but trying to answer her back. The sound was, "Mere."

Ida ran the short distance to him and stood right in his face. His eyes were clear. The whites were white again; whereas before his view had been turned inward, a battle raging inside him, now he could see the person in front of him.

"I'm here," he said again, his speech clearing too, like fog off a pane of glass.

He put his arms around her waist. Yesterday she had been lying beside a dead man. Now she could feel his pulse where her face was pressed into the base of his throat. It was like the Christians' strange Yeshu'a, come back to life after three days.

"You're through it," she said.

"Eretz Yisrael is in me now," Levi said. "Branded on my soul."

He was repeating David's words, and Ida understood what he

meant, but she understood, too, that Eretz Yisrael had always been in Levi's soul. It was he, and he it. More than any of them. More even than David himself.

Levi squeezed her against him, his grip deliciously tight around her ribcage. She could feel him smiling against her head.

An image of the German came into her mind, and along with it what she had done, forsaking both her family in Russia and her new family here in a single betrayal. She squeezed Levi back. "Don't leave me again," she said.

"I won't."

But he trembled slightly and lowered himself beside the severed garden hose on the ground.

David must have known that the weaknesses would take time to recover from, because that night at dinner there was chicken. It had been purchased, and—pure extravagance—slaughtered. David himself set the meal before Levi at dinner with the pomp of a king.

Levi said, "Thank you."

He nudged the plate away. David waited to watch him eat. But Levi passed his plate to Ida—her mouth already filled with an embarrassing amount of saliva.

"You don't like chicken?" David asked, genuinely confused.

Levi pressed the pads of his fingers against the protruding bones under his eyes.

"Ida needs it more," he said.

David's gaze fell on her; she could see him evaluating, weighing Levi's words.

"You have to regain your strength," David said finally. "We need you in the fields."

Levi said, softly, "I don't eat meat."

"Oh?" David took a step back.

"I'm a vegetarian."

Ida could see the admiration in David's eyes, and she felt proud.

The next day, Hannah returned, along with the old man Yitzhak, the emaciated woman whose name was Rivka, and their son, a boy called Gabriel. He had black curly hair, and knobby knees, and wore short pants held up with a bib. He looked, Ida noticed, very much like Ruth. And now Ruth would have someone to play with.

Ida had heard a rumour that these people had been at Kinneret with David and Hannah in the old days—ten years ago!—when everything had started. Perhaps things had gone badly for them there and they were taking refuge here in the new place. People used the kibbutz for all kinds of reasons—many ideological, but some because they had nowhere else to go.

Ten days later, at Hanukkah, another large group of halutzim arrived. And like that, they were divided into two. The first group and the newcomers. Later, Ida would marvel at how they'd arrived mere months apart, but this distinction would remain in their minds, and in the minds of their children, for years.

The new group comprised maybe thirty people. Among them was an American doctor, short, with a bald patch on the back of his head the exact size and shape of a yarmulke. The lenses of his eyeglasses were also perfect circles, and the delicate wire hooks looped over his ears. He said his name was Dr. Lowen, and he was inspired by what he had heard about the young pioneers rebuilding the land of the forefathers. Other American Jews showed their support by sending money, but he wanted to see for himself. And what did Eretz Yisrael need but Jewish hands? He wanted to contribute.

He had brought with him a pretty young nurse, Elisabeth. She wore dark eye makeup, like the kohl the Arab women sometimes used.

"Do you think they're lovers?" Sarah asked Ida.

"I don't know," Ida said.

"I saw them kiss," Sarah said.

She stood on her tiptoes, then fell back on her heels. "America," she said, dreamily. "It's like a love story. Like Natasha and Pierre in *War and Peace*."

Obviously, Ida thought, she had forgotten how that story ended.

Ida took the ribbon from one of her braids and began rebraiding the hair. She tied the bow tightly. She was thinking of Levi.

"David saw it too," Sarah said.

"Saw what?"

"The kiss."

Sarah's tone implied that if David had seen it, the event had a different kind of weight.

The nurse Elisabeth was tall and willowy. She had almost no breasts but enormous brown eyes and creamy skin. When the newcomers arrived they were swarmed by the first group, who were eager to see what personal items would now become part of the communal pot. Elisabeth was disarmed of a beautiful hand-hooked lace shawl. It had been, she said, the blanket she was wrapped in as a newborn. Her mother had crocheted it. Ida watched Elisabeth's face as the blanket was taken from her, but she did not flinch. Either Elisabeth was a true believer in the collective or she was a very good actress.

Shoshanna held Elisabeth's shoulders, reassuring, and declared, "We will wrap the first baby born on the kibbutz in your shawl. I promise."

"What baby?" Ida asked.

But Shoshanna only said, "Soon there will be children," as though she could see something that the rest of them couldn't.

And of course there was Ruth. Sweet, quiet Ruth.

To Ida's dismay, the girl's cut had not healed. Her lower leg was now red and puffy, and the heat from the wound had spread up her body in a dark stain and caused a fever.

The following day, David came to the laundry to ask Ida about it. "What exactly happened to Ruthie's leg that day?" he said.

He was sweating, Ida noticed, and the small bump on the bridge of his nose was glazed with perspiration. His cheeks were pale and his forehead looked clammy. It occurred to Ida that he had been sent by someone else; by Hannah, perhaps.

Ida paused, choosing her words. Had Ruth mentioned their visit to Fatima?

"She scratched it," Ida said, tentative, like she was dipping a toe in very cold water. She pushed her glasses higher up her nose with the tip of her forefinger.

She expected this would elicit more questions, but David only gave her a puzzled look and said, "She has also lost her doll again."

It took Ida a moment to catch up to the change in topic. "Oh," she said.

"Her mother had it at Kinneret. If you can believe it."

Ida scratched her nose.

David said, "Hannah took the doll to Kinneret without telling Ruth. She brought it back. But now Ruth has lost it a second time."

"Where did she last have it?" Ida asked.

But David looked blank—she could see how hard it was for him to focus on the mundane—so she asked instead, "Can I help?"

David shrugged. "You could find it," he said.

Ida went to the infirmary to see Ruth. The child's straw pallet was the size of an infant's crib and had been covered in a canopy of white mosquito netting. The new little boy, Gabriel, sat cross-legged beside her, silent, like he was holding a vigil.

"I want Ruthie to play with me," he said to Ida right away.

"I think she's too weak," Ida said, and the boy nodded. He had seen this himself, but needed an adult to make it real. Ida lifted the mosquito net. She crouched down beside the children.

"Shalom, bubi," she said to Ruth.

Ruth opened one eye. She flared her nostrils; she closed the eye. Then she looked up at Ida fully, smiling weakly. "Gabriel's here," she said. "Our angel."

"I see," said Ida. "The Angel Gabriel?"

Ruth nodded.

"I missed Ruthie so I came to see her!" the boy said. But he wrinkled his nose at her leg. "I miss home," he said.

"We miss Liora," Ruth said to Ida.

Gabriel asked, "Where's Salam?" He, too, knew the doll.

"She's playing hide and seek," said Ruth, but her bottom lip began to tremble.

A look of alarm passed over the boy's face. "Don't cry," he said to Ruth. "I'll go look for her for you."

He got up and smiled. Ida saw he was missing his baby front teeth. One adult tooth was growing in at a funny angle.

"Salam was Sakina's doll," Gabriel said, as though it was his job to explain things to Ida.

"Who is Sakina?" Ida asked, but Gabriel didn't answer. He turned to go, pleased to have a mission to find the doll. "Goodbye Ruthie," he said, over his shoulder.

Ruth tried to answer but the effort was too much and she closed her eyes again. The blue veins spider-webbing across the backs of her eyelids stood out. She looked suddenly much younger, more nascent; an image came to Ida of Ruth as a fetus. A child of Eretz Yisrael trembling between this world and the next.

Ida stood up. All around her lay the suffering and the half-dead. Dov's blisters had ruptured and he looked like a creature that had been buried and clawed its way back out of the earth. A halutz named Reuven with a face like cooked ham had what must be dysentery, and spent his days crouched over a chamber pot from which the most foul smells rose. There were several cases of ringworm—red scaly rashes that broke and bled. A halutza named Rachel had even started to lose her hair because of it.

And of course there was now an ever-increasing number of malaria cases.

When the doctor approached, Ida saw that his delicate eye-glasses had already broken. The bridge between the lenses was held together with medical tape so they rested on his face at an odd angle.

Ida moved closer to speak to him so Ruth wouldn't hear.

"Can you help her?" she asked, urgently. Then, "Good morning," she added, smiling apologetically.

But the doctor understood, and nodded to show Ida shouldn't worry about niceties, not with what was facing them.

They looked down at Ruth's puffy leg together. The cut was crusted with puss and the circle of red surrounding it had grown to encompass most of her shin. Ida averted her eyes; she thought of the muddy yard with the Arab children playing marbles. Then she pushed the thought away. It made her feel guilty about too many different things.

The pretty nurse Elisabeth approached them, and the three

adults formed a ring around Ruth's prone body. Elisabeth was carrying a tray of silver tools.

"I can't keep them clean," she said to the doctor. She was speaking in English but Ida understood from her gestures.

Elisabeth said, "Did you tell her?"

"Tell her what?" the doctor asked, switching to Hebrew.

"About your mould cure."

The doctor shook his head no. A flush rose to his cheeks; Elisabeth was exposing something that made him ashamed, or proud, or some complicated mixture of both.

"Why not?" Elisabeth asked.

"I told the girl's mother," Dr. Lowen said.

Elisabeth looked at him.

"David's wife," he said. "With the brown curly hair."

The newcomers, Ida realized, were still trying to keep track of who everyone was.

"With the red sleeves?" Elisabeth pressed.

"I think." But the doctor lifted his broken glasses from the bridge of his nose to indicate their deficiency. And Ida knew the question was of no use anyway. There were several shirts with red sleeves.

"What did she say?" Elisabeth asked.

"She said nothing."

"But all your research . . ."

"We don't have any proof," Dr. Lowen said. "People think it's nonsense."

"That's not true. There was the British study. There was the—"
But the doctor shook his head.

"You need to have more confidence," Elisabeth said. "You're onto something important."

"Give me ten years," the doctor replied.

Ida's eyes went back and forth, back and forth between the doctor and the pretty nurse, like she was following a table tennis match. She could see that the nurse was bolstering the doctor, that this was the intimacy between them.

I look down from above. The plot turns.

It wasn't Hannah the doctor had told. It was me.

To be fair, he downplayed the issue of his research to such an extent that I thought it some half-mad side note. But I should have paid closer attention. Perhaps it truly was my fault; perhaps I deserved to die for what I'd done.

The next day, when Ida went to see Ruth, she found the doctor prone on a straw mattress. The bald spot on top of his head was glazed with sweat; Elisabeth was at his side, holding his hand. He was old enough to be her father. But who was Ida to judge? She backed out of the tent quietly so as not to interrupt.

Her first instinct was to find Levi and tell him the doctor was ill. She saw him at a distance, in the far field, ploughing. The sight of him upright, stretching his muscled arms in the air above his head, filled her with a kind of glee. He looked so strong it was as if the sickness had never happened.

He was working alongside Saul. The kibbutz owned one three-sided plough, and Saul had cleaned its blades, oiled the break and hooked it to the lone tractor. He rode upon it proudly, the black earth opening out like the wake of three boats behind him.

Levi, on the other side of the field, walked after his wooden plough, letting Trotsky and Lenin take the time they needed. For each furrow he opened, Saul opened three. But Ida loved Levi's great patience—with the mules, the primitive equipment, the rich earth beneath them. He saw the process of sowing seeds as one of coaxing out that which was already there. Give the land the things it needed and it would abundantly flourish. It was not an act of God alone, but of God working through the human hand.

Ida watched as Levi pulled on the reins, and Trotsky and Lenin came to a stop. Levi got down, and walked around to crouch in front of the plough. Ida couldn't see the object he picked up, but could tell what it was from the shape of his hands: there had been a nest in his way. This was the basis of his vegetarianism too: he did not want to hurt a single living thing.

"The doctor," Ida said when she got to Levi, taking his hands in her own. He had carefully placed the nest out of reach of the tractor.

"The doctor what?"

"He's ill," she said.

Levi looked as though Ida had told him his own father was sick. His brow furrowed. "Kadachat?"

She nodded.

"What can we do?" he asked.

"I'm not sure."

Ida thought that Levi would know the answer, having just been through the sickness himself. And she was not surprised when he said, in reply to his own question, "There's nothing we can do. Except wait and see."

The following week a road was paved. The men opened a quarry at the base of the mountain and schlepped rocks to the road on their backs. They used hammers to smash the boulders into gravel.

"A steamroller would help push the gravel down," Ida heard Yashka complain as she passed them in the field, and Zeruvabel said, "Steamrollers are bourgeois."

They laughed until tears leaked out from the corners of their eyes, and Ida, hearing them, laughed too.

Zeruvabel said, "Work will provide our people with the bread of tomorrow, and moreover, with the honour of tomorrow and the freedom of tomorrow."

"Easy for Herzl to say," Yashka answered. But he turned back to his shovel, inspired once again.

A dance was planned to welcome the newcomers, who were arriving every day now. The stacking chairs were pushed to the sides of the dining hall, which had been built, in a hurry, to accommodate their increasing numbers. Zeruvabel was outside the back doorway—there was no actual door yet, only the frame—running rosin up and down his bow.

Ida stopped to listen. "You should play in Paris!" she said.

She had no musical talent, no expertise on which to base her judgment, but there was something in the high, clear notes, the ease with which the music floated out from the instrument as though it had been caught there and Zeruvabel was simply releasing it.

A pained look crossed Zeruvabel's face. His red freckles seemed to stand out more sharply.

"What?" Ida asked.

"I once wanted to do that," he confessed.

"To go to Paris?"

"New York."

"Why didn't you?"

"Good question." And then, as though remembering an answer he had trained himself to believe, "I decided my music was for our cause."

Ida looked at him quizzically.

"It's not just all wealth that belongs to the worker," he said. "Knowledge too. And beauty. They belong to us all."

Ida could see that, despite himself, these ideas pained him. He knew he had talent. He could have travelled the world.

Zeruvabel lifted his palms to his head, pressing his red hair against his scalp. He raised his rosin to his nose and sniffed it delicately, like a bouquet. He said, "My name is from the biblical hero who led the Jews out of Babylon and built the Second Temple."

Ida tried to think what the right response to this might be. She said, "So your music can lead us out of our drudgery and into the world of beauty?"

Zeruvabel nodded, appeased.

Out by the quarry the halutzim had heard the sound of Zeruvabel's instrument being tuned. A seed of a song was planted, and as in all things terrible or beautiful, a seed was all it took for a consequence to grow.

Ida heard a far-off voice from the field, and knew it was Levi's.

Bo ha-baytah, ben chaviv;
Bo ha-baytah, ben chaviv . . .
Come back home now, dearest son.

He was singing to himself, plaintively, but across the furrows Raya and Aaron had heard him, and their two voices rose, joining in:

Come back home now, dearest son,
your father's dead, your mother's sick,
come back to Russia . . .

And the answer returned from a row even further off where Shoshanna, who had insisted on being in the fields, was digging her spade into the rough earth to the rhythm of the song:

Never budge! Never go away from here!

The shovels rose and fell. The melody changed quickly to "Kadimah," their most beloved and familiar song:

Come home now, come home now,
come home now, labourer!
Go forward, go forward,
go forward working man!
Kad-i-mah, kad-i-mah,
kad-i-mah ha-poel! . . .

The sun was beginning to set. It was the end of the work day. The halutzim kept singing as they loaded the wagons and harnessed the mules for the short ride back. In place of "working man," Yashka shouted out "young at heart!" and the chorus changed to, "Go forward, go forward, go forward young at heart!" Then "strong of will." Then "joyful youth."

By the time the wagons reached the tents, there were ten of them singing at the top of their lungs, improvising behind Levi, who himself improvised the words to a nonsense song based on their beloved Hillel:

Im eineni ani, mi ani?
V'ahni l'atsmi mi li?
V'ihm lo achshav aymatay?
Ay-ma-tay?

Ida caught Levi's eye as he drove the wagon into the yard, and joined in, the two of them singing together as if theirs were the only voices:

If not myself then who am I?
And to myself what am I?
And if not now, then when, then why?
When, when, why?

CHAPTER 7

*T*HE DANCE WAS NOT supposed to start until later, but who could resist the singing? The men from the quarry, with the fine dust of ground rock streaked across their faces, jumped down from the wagons happily. Hannah and Rivka, who had been preparing the evening meal, put down their knives and came into the field, wiping their hands on their aprons. They hesitated briefly, torn between their duty in the kitchen and their love of celebration, but the latter won out and they tipped their faces to the sky and started to clap. Ida saw that Rivka was pregnant. Behind them were Elisabeth and Shoshanna, their skirts hiked up, carrying aprons full of wheat sheaves. The women shared a conspiratorial glance and ran to join in too, crossing the field with their arms linked together: now there was critical mass. A ring formed. They would all dance the hora.

Zeruvabel, who had a foot propped up on a pile of lumber, began to play in earnest. He picked up the pace and bent over his instrument, his cheeks flushed with pleasure and responsibility. His foot tapped, keeping time. He drew his bow back and forth over the strings with such speed Ida could barely see his arm. She suddenly understood how, for the story of the kibbutz to turn, Zeruvabel's music was required. He may have given up a career in the concert halls of New York, but it was not for nothing. This was what it was for.

Ida couldn't stop herself; she ran to get in on the dance and was swept up immediately into the sway. She linked arms with Shoshanna on one side and Levi on the other. His muscled elbow hooked her in. Once things had started on a good path they wouldn't change. She was being guided by something bigger than herself. They could renounce God all they wanted, but how could anyone deny that He was here with them in their enterprise, in the sowing of the fields and the growing of vegetables and the sharing and most of all the dance? The circle had formed almost of its own accord, young people joining from every corner of the kibbutz: someone who had been currying the new mules in the new stable now crossed the field; someone else who was practising balancing an earthen jug on her head—like Rebecca from the Bible—carefully took the vessel down, set it beside some oilcloth and a jar of kerosene, and joined the dance as well. Saul's whistle bounced wildly on the lanyard around his neck. Zeruvabel leaned forward into his fiddle to draw from it everything possible. Levi's body was warm and alive beside her. The wheel tilted one way, then tilted the other, the circle of life unsure which way to spin; then all at once it began to whirl and there was no stopping it. Several latecomers stood at the sidelines unable to break in. They stomped and whistled along. Then, a miracle, there was a slowing of the circle and they, too, were linked in.

When the circle got too big, the women made a smaller one in the centre, Sarah and Shoshanna taking Ida by the arm and pulling her in. The three of them spun in the opposite direction to the men, and now there were two concentric circles moving against each other, interlocking gears that made a wheel turn. Ida flew past Levi, and both of them grinned. Nothing would stop them. They would dance forever.

I look down at Ida. I wish I could warn her. What she was living then was the happiest moment. The moment before things went wrong.

Many hours later the hora wound down. It was well after midnight. Ida bent to take off her sandals—her feet were pulsing. When she straightened, she noticed David and Sarah standing by the tractor. Their heads were bent together, discussing the Arab effendi, she suspected, or the eucalyptus saplings due any day from the nursery outside Damascus.

Around Ida, other comrades were catching their breath. They stood in the dark night, stars sharp like knife points above them. Heat beat from their faces. Spent as they were, they were unable to fully stop moving, as if their bodies had been cranked tight by some invisible hand and could only rest once the spring had fully unwound. Shoshanna bounced back and forth from one leg to another like a boxer at the start of a match. The pretty nurse Elisabeth must have thought the same thing; she made a jab at Shoshanna and got her head under her arm and held it there and made a chomping noise like she was going to eat her ear. The two of them laughed uproariously. Only the German twins, a few paces from the others, seemed less than engaged. They were in some kind of argument.

"Du idiot," one said.

"Na, du musst was reden!" the other replied.

"Wenn du wilst dass ich dein Geheimnis halten, du mal lieber etwas netter zu mir!" said the first. They fell into a strained and huffy silence.

Yashka leaned back to look again at the stars. He said, "Work is early! I guess we'd better . . ."

He paused before he could finish his sentence. Head cocked to one side, eyes alert.

"What?" Shoshanna asked.

But they were quiet, their hearts still banging in their ears from the dance. And then they heard what Yashka had heard: the gallop of hooves passing.

"The Arabs," Zeruvabel said.

"At least it's not the Cossacks," said Yashka.

"They're probably razing our crops," said one of the twins, who had removed himself from his brother and inserted himself back into the group conversation.

"What crops?" Saul asked, his fingers pulling idly at the lanyard around his neck.

"The wheat is growing! Give it time," Levi said.

"Never trust an Arab," the twin answered.

Ida pictured Fatima standing with a hand on her low back to support the child in her belly, her skin brown with the sun and the wind. She recalled the pantomime when they had first met, Fatima showing Ida that she would protect her candlesticks, and her secret—whatever it was—as well. And the way she had held her lip between her teeth as she tried to help bandage Ruth's wound.

"I don't think they're so different from us," Ida said.

"Who?" the twin asked.

"The Arabs," Ida said.

The circle fell silent. A look of surprise crossed many faces, like wind spreading across an open sea. Ida supposed it was not so much what she had said as the fact that she rarely spoke out in the group at all.

The twin waggled his fingers at her like he had done the other day by the clothesline. "And why do you say that?" he asked.

Ida held onto the tip of her braid.

"It's just a feeling," she answered. She saw Levi nodding across the circle from her.

"She's right," he said, leaning down to pick a stone from his sandal. He straightened again, holding it as if it was an oracle in which he could see the future. "We can live peacefully with them, if we make the effort."

"Have you read what they published in the *Falastin* in Jaffa?" Saul asked. "Hatred. Jew hatred, pure and simple."

Leah said, "That paper is owned by Christians. Not Muslims."

From the tents came the sound of other halutzim still singing as they changed into their night clothes:

Am Yisrael chai,
Am Yisrael chai!
The nation Israel lives,
The nation Israel lives!

The twin ignored this, remaining focused on Ida.

"How do you know there are good people among the Arabs?" he asked. He took a half-step toward her.

Her stomach tightened.

"What does it mean to be good?"

"I wouldn't expect you to know," she said.

He raised his eyebrows. "Aren't *you* a little Hündin."

Ida steeled herself. "Speaking like that has already marked you," she said.

He looked confused for a moment, and then laughed. "You think God has stained my lips for blasphemy?"

He laughed harder, and puckered his lips as if he was going to kiss her.

Ida closed her eyes. The happiness that had been filling her body moments before was suddenly gone, as though she had been punctured. She imagined the hiss of a tractor tire deflating. But in the face of his challenge her own indignation rose. She had hidden something from the group, yes, but so had this German. And he had blackmailed her in order to do it.

He said, "Aren't you going to tell me what it means to be a good person?"

"You know what it means," she said pointedly. "And does not mean."

But the German would not back down. "I'd prefer you to enlighten me," he said.

Ida noted that, despite the vigour of the dance, Samuel—or Selig?—had kept his clothes perfectly neat, his suspender straps dividing his torso into three equal rectangles.

"Your preference doesn't interest me," she said.

He raised an eyebrow. "Doesn't it?"

Ida remembered an infamous ghoum between two Arab groups she had been told about, a clan from near the River Jordan and their enemies who lived nearby; decades passed, nobody forgave, the dead piled up like timber. She stared hard at the twin for a long moment, then turned on her heel.

She felt the group's eyes following her, and then felt Levi separating himself from them and coming after her. She stopped walking only when she had reached the river. She stood

with her back to the tents and waited for him draw up beside
her. He put a hand on her shoulder. His fingers crept into the
tangled hair at the base of her neck, tugging gently.

She smiled at him over her shoulder, but brushed his hand
away.

"Do you want to tell me what's wrong?" he asked.

The moon had come up, three-quarters full, a last little
slice needed for completion. Its reflection on the surface of the
water was a trail of silver. From the shadow of the mountain
behind them a jackal screamed in the final moment before
landing its prey.

"What's wrong?" he asked again. "Why do you dislike him?"

Ida felt the urge to unburden herself to Levi, but what would
he say? She saw the twin's leering face in front of her. She heard
again Levi telling her that Zionism was the logical fulfillment of
the history of the Jewish people; that taking care of the group
was the highest calling of their cause.

Levi's hand felt good, kneading her neck.

"Did he do something to you?" he asked, his voice gentle,
like he was coaxing a pony to accept a saddle.

Ida drew in her breath. "He blackmailed me," she said.

Levi took his hand away.

He walked forward to face her and tipped his head to the
side as though he had just heard a gunshot far away. Ida saw this
was not the answer he had been expecting; she saw that he wondered if the twin had violated her sexually. And although he
hadn't, her body contained what she imagined must be a similar
mixture of shame and rage.

"What do you mean?" Levi asked.

He folded his hands neatly in front of him, and desire to
unburden herself again warred against her desire to be loved

by him. She couldn't risk him judging her; she had started her story, and he would not let her draw back. The combination of love and protectiveness on his face emboldened her. He would defend her. He would be on her side regardless of what she had done.

"Tell me," he said softly.

She examined his tanned face, the dark hair she herself had cut growing shaggy again in the heat. She wanted to know everything about him—what he was afraid of, what he dreamed of, what he had been like as a boy. Because surely to love meant to know someone completely. And the other side of the equation—she wanted him to know her too.

"I did something," she said.

She ran the pad of her thumb against the tip of her braid.

"What?" he asked. "Something . . . bad?"

There was a hint of laughter in his voice, like he could not believe she was capable of any such thing. But he did not laugh outright.

"Questionable," she said.

He was silent, waiting for it.

"I had candlesticks from home," she said. "They belonged to my great-great-great grandmother."

Levi looked at her, and raised one eyebrow, the way he had on their very first day together. "There's nothing wrong with . . ."

And then his face showed he understood.

"Where are they now?" he asked, his voice careful.

"I gave them to Fatima," she said.

A beat.

"Who?"

"A woman from the Arab village."

He was looking in her eyes; she saw his face begin to close down, from the forehead to the chin, like a row of slatted blinds. It panicked her, and she forged ahead, as though she could talk her way out of it.

"I tried to hide them. But Fatima saw. She offered to keep them. She was really very kind. But the twin knew I had kept them—I don't know which—"

"Which candlestick?"

"Which twin."

Levi gave a half-smile.

"He took one candlestick and gave the other to his brother. He said that otherwise he would tell David what I'd done."

And you, she wanted to add. He said he would tell you.

But Levi had gone back one step.

"We were supposed to turn in our valuables."

"I know," she said quickly.

His forehead was wrinkled.

"You kept your candlesticks?" he asked. "We could have sold them. The group needs money."

This was the crux of it.

"And he blackmailed me!" Ida said.

But Levi was less interested in what the twin had done. It was Ida he was worried about. The look on his face was not one of anger but one of profound disappointment. He didn't reprimand her or judge her verbally. He was too kind. But she saw, once again, that his ideals were real. He wanted a partner who shared them. She pictured him, still shivering from kadachat, refusing to eat the meat that would make him stronger. She had seen him with the eucalyptus saplings, planting the weaker shoot and setting the stronger one aside. He loved her, yes. But she felt the door to his heart sliding closed.

Ida lifted her eyes. One of the German twins was crossing the field. He was holding something in his hand. A pillow, the size of a small loaf of bread. It had a flap of black fabric attached to one end and a patterned ribbon around its middle, like a sash.

Was it?

Yes. It was Ruth's doll.

Ida turned back and opened her mouth to tell Levi, but the expression on his face stopped her. He was looking down at the dirt, his cheek puckered where he was biting it inside his mouth. It was as though she could see the thoughts passing across his face: the rainy season was coming. They were behind in their planting. They could have used the money from Ida's candles to repair the tractor.

She didn't know what to say, and so she asked, bluntly, "Can you forgive me?"

He reached for her face. She thought he was going to pull her to him and kiss her, but instead he lifted her glasses off and placed them on the bridge of his own nose. She laughed—he looked so ridiculous—but he said, seriously, "We see this differently."

The smile left Ida's face. "Please?" she asked.

Levi hesitated. "I have something to tell you too," he said.

She held her braid, waiting.

"I saw David . . ." he started.

But he stopped, as though the full impact of Ida's secret was sinking in and he could no longer trust her with his own.

"What is it?" she asked.

She wanted, desperately, to know. Everything depended on it. She could see it was something important, and she could also see Levi was changing his mind about trusting her.

"It's nothing," he said. "Never mind."

All the while he had been talking he'd been weaving a long string of fragrant grass, and now he tied the circle together and set the crown atop her head.

As though to spite her, Ida thought, the rains that came that winter were torrential. They washed away the taboon and drenched the straw pallets and everything smelled like mould and fermented grain. At night she shivered violently in her tent, unable to keep warm. The roof of the dining hall was made with reed mats, and fat drops smacked into her soup. The other pioneers picked up their bowls and began to dance and sing:

> Rain, rain, good rain,
> God of heaven, grant bane!
> Look for each son and daughter,
> Pure water, clear water.

Only Ida was unhappy. Levi had ceased seeking her out entirely. The cold nights seemed to last for an eternity. Then, when the rainy season was over, as though to spite her again, the land erupted into a kind of beauty she had never seen before. The grass shot up, the wildflowers tangled themselves on the hillside, purple sticker weeds and bright red anemones and blue irises. From out in the fields you could hear the drone of the bees as they pollinated the hillside, and the collared doves singing. The kibbutz had been given four horses from the Agency, and all of their bellies hung low with foals. One died, but the other three survived and stood on spindly legs in the pasture. The wheat, too, grew heavy and high. It was time for threshing.

None of the settlers had ever threshed a field.

Levi, though, seemed to know what to do intuitively, and

this, too, pained Ida, to watch his quiet competence revealed in front of the group. To see them all witness to what once had been hers. He demonstrated how to win the trust of the new foals and then, ever so gently, how to attach them to the sledge and nudge them forward. He showed the rest of the group the correct way to turn up the crops with the pitchfork. He showed them the wide arc they must make to scatter chaff in the wind.

Partway through the first morning, though, the thresher broke. From over at the laundry Ida heard the bang of something caught in the gears followed by the sound of crumpling metal. She crossed the perimeter and joined the others peering into the back of the machine. Grains of wheat were leaking out with the straw.

Yashka cursed in Russian. "That's what we get for buying it second-hand."

"What else could we have done?" Zeruvabel asked.

Levi climbed in at the open end to see if he could figure out what was wrong.

"Careful," Ida cautioned, but he didn't look up at her. She could see the soles of his sandals sticking out, the leather treads worn away entirely.

Around him, the halutzim stood poised and waiting. "Pass me a wrench?" Levi called.

Yashka obliged.

"A different wrench."

"How many wrenches do you think we have?"

But Yashka dug around in the rusted red toolbox.

"This might take some time," said Levi.

Yashka gestured to the thresher that was now making a gagging noise as though trying to spit something out. "Maybe there's a rock in it?"

"Of course there's a rock in it," spat Zeruvabel. "There are a hundred rocks in it. Because we didn't clear the field properly, because we didn't have the right machine!"

"We had the machine," someone corrected, "but it was broken."

Saul slid down from the mountain of wheat. There was nothing to do but wait.

From across the field David was approaching. His black curls bounced with his step; he was holding his daughter, Ruth, in his arms. She was pale, collapsed against her father's chest. The nurse had placed a new bandage loosely around her leg; Ida kept her eyes away from it, but could not ignore the feeling of guilt and regret that landed in her gut whenever she thought of Ruth.

David stood in front of them and waited until everyone was listening. "There are brambles to be cut at the bottom of the yard," he said.

As he spoke, Ida noticed how hollow his cheeks were as well. He wiped at sweat on his forehead with his billowing sleeve. From the back of the group came a voice. "We're going to cut brambles? In planting season?"

They all turned to look. It was not every day someone challenged David.

The voice belonged to Yitzhak, the new halutz who had arrived back from Kinneret with Hannah. Ida could see from the way David looked at him that the two men had some kind of history.

"You can clean the toilets if you prefer," David said.

Insult beyond insult.

"In planting season?" Yitzhak repeated again. He cracked his knuckles.

"There's a whole work crew waiting. What would you suggest?"

David shifted Ruth higher on his hip and wiped at his forehand again. He scrunched his eyes like he was trying to focus and steady himself.

"I'll tell you what I would suggest," Yitzhak said. "I would suggest we send men to work at the factory to make money. Then we purchase proper machines. Poof! The field is down. Then threshers, then wagons to carry the sheaves to the machine, then done. Easy! That's what I would suggest."

Ida had heard rumours of a contingent of workers who wanted to abandon the fields—only briefly!—to work at the factory in Tiberias, but up until now nobody had voiced this idea aloud to the group.

The look on David's face was difficult for Ida to read. It was as though he was weighing his words very carefully lest he say something he regretted.

"I don't know what kind of utopia you're trying to build," he said finally, "but my utopia doesn't include—"

But Yashka interrupted. "Forget the factory. Let's just steal the Arab's wheat!"

"There's no need to be disparaging," someone said.

"He's not being disparaging," chimed in another voice. "They really don't have any!"

"Exactly. So they steal ours! Every time the one with the scar on his face passes he leaves with his thawb puffed up twice as large as before."

"I don't know why you persist like this about the Arabs!" Leah said. "This is their home too."

But her comment was ignored.

"We have watchmen," Yashka said.

"A watchman, not watchmen. One! And with a whistle instead of a gun." The old argument hung in the air.

Yitzhak said, "When I got here it was taking three hours to get around the field. Today we went three times before lunch. The threshing should be started."

"I am aware," David said hotly, his face pinched.

"Well, I'm just noting. Now *three* of our machines are broken."

"The machine from Prague just needs cleaning," David said.

"But it needs seven men to do it!" Yashka jumped in.

"We sent Zeruvabel to clean it," Yitzhak said. "Let me tell you something. Zeruvabel is not a mechanic! Yesterday I watched him tightening a bolt with all his strength. He leaned in and gripped and sweated and pushed. And then? He'd forgotten to put the washer on first. Would you like to know how long it took him to unscrew the bolt?"

But nobody wanted to know.

"We must be patient while he learns," David said, as though Zeruvabel himself was not right there in front of them, flushed with shame.

"Do you think we should be patient?" Yitzhak asked. "Because Zeruvabel is really a musician. A talented violinist! Aaron over there, on the other hand, is a trained mechanic."

"But Aaron is in the gardening crew."

"My point exactly."

Ida had been thinking the same thing, but she would never in a million years have given voice to the thought. She wondered who this Yitzhak had been to David at the old place. How did he have such confidence to stand up to him?

"What about talent?" Yitzhak went on. "Can we not admit that each of us is not identical to the other?"

Raya jumped in, unable to restrain herself. "What about the American machine?"

"Broken as well," Saul said.

"Once we fix it, though! It cuts its own straw, blows away its own dust."

"It only takes two men," someone else agreed.

"So what's the problem?"

Saul rolled his eyes. "The carrying device. The elevator."

A cork had been popped and the entire kibbutz's frustrations sprayed out. A side argument erupted about whether buying the plough had been the correct use of resources. What about a chicken incubator? Come to think of it, what about some chickens? A water pump to irrigate the fields? Leah railed against the women's assignment to kitchen duty—was it or was it not a world where equality reigned? Shoshanna launched into a tirade about the treatment of the Arab girls who could be married off to a man four times their age and forced to labour alongside his other wives while he drank bitter coffee in the souk. Did the pioneers not have some responsibility to try to prevent this? Then from the back of the crowd there was a ripple as someone tried to come forward. Ida saw that it was one of the German twins.

As Ida watched, the twin took David aside and whispered something in his ear. He must have spoken loudly enough to rouse little Ruth, for she lifted her head from her father's shoulder and leaned in so she, too, could hear.

David's eyebrows lifted and a smile pushed at the edges of his cheeks. He turned from the twin and faced the group. Their voices died down as they waited to hear what he would say.

"Selig has received some valuable candlesticks from home. We can sell them to repair the machines."

In her father's arms, Ruth straightened her torso, squaring her little shoulders. Into the bowl of silence, her voice rang out high and clear. "Those candlesticks are Ida's!" she said.

Instinctively, Ida took a step backward, trying to conceal herself among the halutzim. She had clearly underestimated Ruth's capacities on several different fronts. The twin—Selig—looked at Ruth in alarm too, as though his own fate hung in the balance. But David only put his hand on Ruth's head and guided it back to his shoulder. She struggled for a moment, her determination evident, but a moment later she was quiet, her breathing heavy and her papery eyelids closed.

David boosted Ruth higher up on his hip and Ida remembered how heavy the child was. David turned again to Selig. "We are grateful to you," he said, so everyone could hear. "This will help."

He hoisted the candlesticks like a prize. "I'll take them to Tiberias and see what we can get."

Selig nodded curtly. He turned away from David and scanned the group. Ida knew he was looking for her. When he caught her eye, he held it. His face like smoke.

Later, Ida saw David walking toward the tents with Ruth in his arms. The child was happily holding her doll. A look on her face of dreamy contentment. Ida smiled. This, at least, had worked itself out. The doll had been found.

From here, of course, I know better.

CHAPTER 8

*T*IME PASSED QUICKLY; soon Passover was coming. There would be more visitors, Jews from abroad who wanted to see the miracle being worked in Eretz Yisrael. David had been negotiating with the railway company to build a proper station for the kibbutz. The company required a commitment to a certain number of passengers. David had promised to deliver. He was confident; the railway company was skeptical. But as soon as the station was built the quota was surpassed, almost doubled. It was good news for them all.

The coming of Passover also gave the group the motivation to finally move to a permanent spot beyond the stream. The Arab tenant-farmers had left their homes after some negotiations with David that the other halutzim were not privy to. Ida realized she would no longer see Fatima. She found herself disproportionally sad, as if she was losing a sister, the only person who really understood her. Nobody knew about her relationship with Fatima—she recalled how she had tried to tell Levi that day she'd confessed, with disastrous results—and so she had no one to share her sadness with.

She might have tried to tell her tentmate Sarah, but Sarah's own mood had been volatile. The crying had increased. Ida had tried to talk to her about it, but Sarah repeated that she was homesick, and how could Ida argue with that? She, too, thought about home constantly, wondering if her mother and Eva were okay.

The Arabs had left behind their mud houses and a handful of stone buildings that the halutzim argued over how to best make use of. Saul suggested a communal hall, but the building would be too small to house the wild dancing that would take place on rainy January evenings. Shoshanna wanted the largest one to be designated for the school.

"We have no children here," Zeruvabel said.

"Other than you," one of the twins answered.

"Just wait," Shoshanna said.

The image came to Ida of the baby she and Levi could have had together. A boy with his father's pure heart. He would have grown up in Eretz Yisrael, speaking Hebrew. A child who had nothing left to long for. But Levi had now withdrawn from her entirely.

New spots for the tents were chalked into the dust, like a ghost town. Nobody could imagine the settlement being there, until, all at once, it existed. One day, a handful of halutzim stayed back from the field to move the camp, and at sunset, when the others returned, the new world was ready: rows of dazzling white peaks had been raised. The halutzim were ecstatic. Finally their move was permanent. Only Ida did not want to go. Everything that had happened between her and Levi had happened in the old place. To let it go was to acknowledge their failure, to release the dream they had shared.

The mud house that had been Fatima's stood vacant, deemed even less sturdy than the canvas tents. Ida could not look at it without nausea rising in her belly. In the end, the stone houses, too, were left empty, for the children who would surely soon be conceived. The grain was stacked, and now couples went to the gorens. They nestled into the mountains of hay as evening fell, like lovebirds into their nests. But Levi would not go, and so Ida would not go either.

The coming of Passover also meant that everything was cleaned. The air smelled of bleach and kerosene. Straw was taken out of the mattresses and changed. Ida saw the twins polishing their shoes.

Elisabeth came to Ida at the laundry and asked her to cut her hair.

"I heard you're the barber," she said.

"From who?" Ida asked.

"Everyone knows," Elisabeth said, and she held up a pair of gleaming scissors.

"Where did you get those?"

"From the medical kit."

"Of course."

"Will you do the honours?"

Ida sat the girl down on one of the few folding chairs. Her hair fell almost to her behind, a dark chestnut colour, and the weight of it in Ida's hand was heavy like rope. It smelled uncannily like she had just emerged from a bubble bath.

Ida twisted the hair around her wrist, gathered the ends together to be trimmed. It was satisfying to cut through the resistance. When she had finished removing the dead ends, she patted Elisabeth's shoulder. The girl twisted around in her chair.

"What?"

"I'm done."

Elisabeth laughed. She said, "You haven't begun."

"What do you mean?"

"I want it all off."

Ida tilted her head. "Your hair is so beautiful," she said. Surely Elisabeth must know this, but the girl just looked at her, staring her down.

Ida asked, "Are you sure?"

"I've never been more sure of anything."

Who was Ida to disagree? She lifted the scissors.

The tractor was fixed using the money from Ida's family candlesticks. David himself went to Tiberias and sold them. Four, five, maybe more generations of memories lost to a godforsaken stranger. Ida was alone with her grief; the others only knew that everything would now be easier because the machine was repaired. The whole enterprise was a giant interwoven mosaic. Back home this had been only theory, but here the truth of it was plain for anyone to see. If someone made a mistake in the morning and added too much salt to the gruel, then the workers went into the fields with resentment rather than joy. The fields felt their dejection. The weeding was slower. The threshing was incomplete. And this, in turn, affected the gruel they would be eating—or not eating—the following winter.

There had been a fevered debate as to whether or not to hold a Seder, but Zeruvabel, whose father was a famed Torah scholar in Minsk, assured them Passover had originally been a celebration for the cutting of the winter barley. Observing it could be seen as the renewal of a long lost agricultural festival. It didn't have to be religious.

Unspoken relief rippled through the halutzim. Godless as most of them professed to be, they had been raised with Pesach their whole lives, and although nobody would have admitted it aloud, they would have felt bereft without it. They took care to make it an event of great celebration. In the dining hall that still smelled of sawdust, cloths were placed over the roughly hewn tables. Wheat sheaves, barley sheaves and olive branches were used for decoration. To Ida's mind this made the celebration look more like Sukkot than Passover; the scythe made out of wheat—similar to the sickle and hammer of the Communist Revolution—would have been entirely out of place at any traditional Seder. Wheat—and anything leavened—was forbidden on the holiday. But perhaps that was the point?

A Seder plate had been placed in the middle of each table; that much, at least, was traditional. They had no lambs to slaughter but each plate was adorned with a chicken bone. These had come from Tiberias—Shoshanna had tried to raise chicks, but without an incubator most of them had died. The smell of soup from the vats on the propane stove made Ida's mouth water, but lately her stomach was refusing food. She had no appetite—only panic when she woke in the early mornings, and a crippling kind of heart-sickness that she could hardly stand. Sarah was gone from the tent as often as not and Ida was alone with her heart hammering as the great weight of consciousness flowed back into her body.

Although Levi had not explicitly judged her, her sin stained their every interaction. It was as though the love that had been so abundant one moment had the next been baked dry in the stifling sun.

Levi was distributing Haggadot when she came into the dining hall for the Passover Seder. He, too, had polished his shoes. His hair was partly neatly at the side, and combed. He was wearing a kippah. The sight of all this made Ida almost physically ill with longing.

He reached over to pass her a Haggadah, and they both looked at it in his hand, as though once it was exchanged something more would be officially concluded.

Ida remembered that first day they'd met, when he had passed her his canteen.

"The Haggadah," he said, as if to reassure her that was all he was giving her.

"I saw you by the river earlier," she said.

She did not say "at our place in the river," but Levi flushed and pressed his lips together. In her mind's eye she replayed the sight: the contours of his bare muscled back, him pausing on the bank, his eyes closed. He had been purifying himself for Pesach, using the river as his mikveh. Later, he had wrapped a prayer shawl around his shoulders, rocking back and forth as he davened.

"Will you sit with me?" she asked. The tables were filling up.

"Okay," he said. But then he hesitated. "I'd better keep passing these out."

They both looked down at the Haggadah on the top of the pile he was holding. The glue at the binding was coming apart. It, like Ida's candlesticks, was somebody's family heirloom. The story of Passover brought back to the place where it had originally happened.

"Haroset," she said, looking over his shoulder at the Seder plate.

"Yes."

"Strange that something symbolizing mortar and bricks, the slavery of—" She broke off.

"Ida," Levi said.

"And maror!" she said, trying desperately to keep her voice light. She gripped her braid.

"Ida," he said again.

If she refused to listen, she would not have to hear what he was saying. "I hate horseradish," she said.

"Ida?"

"What?"

"I'm sorry," Levi said.

"For what?"

"For everything."

Ida understood. He was sorry for the death of what they had dreamed. He was sorry they would never have a child. He was sorry for his idealism that made him unable to forgive her.

His heart had closed, but he, too, wished it had not. He saw its closing as his own shortcoming. But that didn't mean he could change it.

They both turned at the sound of someone's hobnailed boots clomping across the new floor. Ida seized the moment to take the Haggadah from Levi's hand and push past him. She saw Hannah sitting at the front with her daughter, Ruth, in her lap; the girl looked pale as a ghost, as though she weighed almost nothing. Ida kept her eyes averted from the child's leg. Ruth made a small noise in her throat when Ida passed them, but Ida kept going. She found a place beside Elisabeth, who had announced at breakfast that she would now be called by her Hebrew name, Esther.

The candlesticks on the table in front of them were the same cheap tin ones they had used at Rosh Hashanah. David reclined at the head of the table as was customary and led them through the Seder.

"This is the bread of affliction that our forefathers ate in Egypt," he read from the Haggadah, and Ida felt the affliction as if her flesh was burning.

I go back and listen from above as they say the prayers, but I can hear that these are prayers to themselves, praises of their own ingenuity. They forget that there are forces bigger than their own, forces that have been leading them all along.

CHAPTER 9

*A*S THOUGH TO MAKE UP for the ambivalence about Passover, the halutzim celebrated May Day with wild abandon. The Day of the Worker was something they could all get behind, and they danced and danced, stamping their wild hora into the night. In darkness the work was forgotten, the terrible back-breaking, never-ending work. There was only the realization of an ideal, like something conjured through sorcery, or through pure desire alone. Ida heard the song of Zeruvabel's fiddle while the stars spread out above like a bridal veil. But she would be nobody's wife.

She was young enough that she could not project herself into the future. She could not imagine that something else would happen, and then something else, and another thing. That life would keep on changing.

Ida felt keenly that there was only the present moment. A blessed state of affairs. And a cursed one.

She could not stand to see Levi dancing; could not tolerate his elbows linked with Yitzhak on one side and Leah—a woman!—on the other. She extracted herself and slipped away into the darkness, the full moon above like a lamp. The new settlement had the semblance of a street running through the middle, with the stone Arab houses on either side and the tents in the far distance. Beside the stable Ida saw two silhouettes, their heads bent together; it was Sarah and David. Sarah was in her red-sleeved blouse. Ida thought how the landscape around them took everything, but the blouse was something Sarah had been allowed to keep.

Ida did not want to talk to these two. She wanted to be alone. She carved a wide circle around them, but the moon was so bright she could see the stitching on Sarah's sleeves, and her friend's gaunt cheeks, as if she'd survived some ancient famine. The night was still, and despite the music from the dance in the distance, Ida could hear their conversation as if they were beside her.

"I'll bring it to the group," David said.

"But you know it isn't like that."

There was an edge to Sarah's voice, a shrillness.

"It *is* like that," David said. "Everything here is like that."

Ida slipped past them. She went beyond the old encampment, the ghosts of everything that had happened there invisible and more alive because of it. It astonished her to see the physical place where their tents had first been erected, where they had arrived that first day, the bend in the river where they had taken refuge from the heat they could never get used to. It was as though, if she looked hard enough, she could see the outline of her former self, sitting on the bank with her feet in the water and Levi's arm around her shoulder. That self was only a little behind her in time. She wished for a door to step back through.

She walked until she could no longer see any part of the kibbutz at all. She followed the donkey path by the base of the mountain, its shadows falling on her like water. She felt entirely alone, now, under the canopy of stars. She thought, with a terrible pang, of poor, sweet Ruth, so sick in her mother's arms, and of the day they had gone together to give her candlesticks to Fatima. She thought of little Eva back home, and of her own mother. How good it would be to have her mother stroke her forehead, push her hair back from her face. Her mother would have been able to fix this, to ask the matchmaker about a boy for Ida. A nice Orthodox boy whose Zionism was an idea, not an everyday reality, and who would have given her lots of babies. But it was too late for that.

Later, much later, Ida returned to the tents. From half a mile away she could see that the door to the infirmary was open, a bright rectangle of light standing out against the darkness. Somebody screamed, and someone screamed back. Someone else shouted, "Esther!" Then, "Hurry!"

Now Ida heard crying. Voices overlapped, excited, agitated. They made everything bigger than it was, thought Ida. Bigger than it needed to be. The debates, the fights. The wild dancing late into the night. Things were so exaggerated here, as though there was some great silence at the heart of their enterprise and they were frantically trying to cover it over with sound.

Ida didn't stop to investigate. She walked straight to her tent. When she lifted the flap, Levi was there.

The light from the kerosene lamp fell on his face, bisecting it perfectly. Half of him illuminated, the other half in darkness.

"What are you . . ." she started to ask, and then she saw Sarah crouched on the straw mattress with tears running down her cheeks.

"Oh!" Ida said. "I'm sorry to interrupt."

Her mind flashed to the scene of Sarah being lectured by David, so intently, at the edge of the field. But that must have been hours ago.

"Are you okay?" she asked, even as she knew it was a ridiculous question. She pushed her glasses up on her nose. She felt Levi's presence as if he were a giant light beaming down on her. Every part of her vulnerable, exposed.

She remembered the heat of him inside her. His smell of salt and sweat and something else that belonged only to him. But he had given it to her. After that, it had belonged to them both.

"I've never done this before either," he'd said back then.

It was all she could do now not to reach out and touch his face. But he was no longer hers. And here he was with Sarah.

Ida looked around the tent. There was half a shell, upturned, holding a spool of thread, a needle and a button. She looked at her own bed, then looked again. The revolver lay on her wool blanket.

Sarah's red-rimmed eyes followed Ida's.

Behind Ida, Levi's body was dark and dense, a magnet she felt pulled toward helplessly.

"Why do you have the gun?" Ida asked. It was as though she was not speaking the words, but the words were speaking her.

In fact, it was me making her ask.

As Ida spoke, Sarah lunged forward, grabbed the gun and pulled it to her body. She looked up and saw the question on Ida's face.

"I'm on night guard," Sarah said, defensive.

"Sarah," Ida said. "What's going on?"

Tears began to leak again from the corners of Sarah's eyes. She didn't brush them away; it was as if she didn't notice them at all.

"Something happened," she said.

"Something?"

Sarah began to cry in earnest, leaning forward and holding her head in her hands. Her curls shook as she sobbed.

"Oh achoti," Ida said. "Can I help?"

Sarah lifted her head and caught Levi's eye. The two of them exchanged some silent signal that Ida couldn't read. Was Sarah trying to tell Levi something? Or was it the other way around?

"Can I help?" Ida repeated.

"No," Sarah said. And then her expression changed. "Actually," she said, "yes. Would you give me an hour to myself?"

She glanced around the circumference of the tent with her eyes, indicating the privacy she wanted within it.

Ida hesitated. "Where will I go?" she asked. But she knew right away it was not a good question.

"Go with Levi," Sarah said.

Ida froze. Sarah knew that she would not want to go with Levi, that her shame at her abandonment was so great as to make it impossible. But Levi nodded. Ida saw his beautiful olive skin, his long eyelashes. He would take her away. And yes, she would allow it. Even though he was not doing it for Ida. He was doing it for Sarah.

It was the middle of the night when Ida returned to her tent to sleep. Across the field, the halutzim were still gathered around David and Hannah's tent. Ida again heard the sound of a woman crying.

She vowed that what had passed between her and Levi was something she would never reveal to anyone. It was something that had changed her forever.

As soon as she entered the tent she knew something had changed here too. The full moon shone through the open flap, revealing a frozen tableau. Silence filled the space; even sound had stopped. There was a tear in the fabric of time; for a moment there was pure existence.

Sarah lay on her bed. Her curls were spread out around her and her cheeks were flushed, as though moments ago she had been running. The revolver lay beside her hand, as if it had fallen from her grip. But even before Ida saw the gun, she knew Sarah was dead.

I was dead.

But I wasn't yet released.

My spirit was still contained in my body; it would take several hours for it to leak out, to drift up over the tents, the infirmary and the stable. The house for the babies not yet born. From above, the encampment looked shockingly small and inconsequential, a set laid out by a child for her dolls. I was pulled up and almost got away, but the jagged face of the mountain caught me, delicate lace snagged on a nail.

PART TWO

David

CHAPTER 10

*A*GAIN, I GO BACK. I hover behind David at the top of the thresher's floor and look out over the kibbutz with him. The fields are spread across the land in squares of colour like a woman's quilt. The garden bristles with vegetables; the stable is at maximum capacity, and there are plans to build an extension as soon as threshing season is over. The Baby House is full of children. There were meetings—many meetings—to discuss the ideal number for the first cohort. The final decision was six, and then Thin Rivka became pregnant by mistake—oh, the broiges it caused. But late was better than early, as had happened with Hannah. And now there were seven in the first kindergarten class.

From where David stood he could see Rivka bending over the tap by the shower house, tinkering with the nozzle. Always looking for something that needed fixing. But to David, for the moment at least, the commune was a perfectly oiled machine, functioning exactly as it was meant to. The halutzim stood in a perfect line, stepping together and swinging their scythes. And there were sickles for those not strong enough for a scythe. For the women.

The ground man pitched the sheaves up for the wagon man to pack. The wagons drew up to the thresher, sailing smoothly across the field and docking like ships in a port. They unloaded the wheat sheaves, long and heavy. David watched as Yitzhak manoeuvred his wagon according to the direction of the wind, letting nature help in the lifting of the sheaves to the rick-top. Yitzhak's sheaves were perfectly ordered. It always gave David a queer kind of pleasure to be the one on the receiving end of such fastidious work, and to add his own flourish by cutting each cord—like slicing the mother from the child—relinquishing each bundle into the thresher-mouth. The cylinder took the grain and sucked it down.

What happened inside the machine was like what happened inside a woman. The body volunteered, the body offered itself, there was the banging of steel rods, the giant vibration. Inside, the shibboleth came away, and then the grain, and then the chaff from the seed. What remained was only the golden kernel itself, like the essence of a man that could make another human.

The wheat poured out through four different funnels into four different sacks, each one better quality than the last.

It was the pure kernel, the perfect kernel, that David aspired to.

Afterwards, the sacks were tied, one by one, and carried away to feed Eretz Yisrael.

"Switch!" someone shouted from beneath the thresher floor, where dark orifices discharged the straw and the chaff. David could picture the halutz, goggled to face the stream of straw. It could bury a man alive—it was a race to shove it away before you disappeared under it entirely. Someone had to stand midstream, flinging the straw into high piles. The piles became the gorens where the halutzim would later go for love.

Which—perhaps the idealists were right about some things?—was the greatest result a man could hope for.

David looked over to the east where the baler, too, was functioning perfectly. Daniel fed straw into it; Yonatan set the wires and stacked the completed bales. The belts slapped in time, like the slapping of bodies in sex.

Yes, the whole enterprise was like the wrangling of eros into form. The heavy work, the climax, followed by the birth of the world anew.

Hannah would have called this romantic pontificating. But how could she deny its truth?

What chutzpah they had had at the beginning, to believe the revival of a homeland was something they could accomplish. David thought back with a strange nostalgia to the early battle with the Bedouin, whose scrawny billy goats gobbled up every growing thing. The crops had suffered a blight, and the grains of wheat were hard and dark like pebbles. Then when the wheat was good the locusts had come, in a black cloud that covered the sky, their mouths clicking; they had devoured every inch of the fields. But somehow, after years of broken fan belts and kadachat and babies dead from dysentery, of scorpion bites and starvation and fields turned fallow from the drought, the whole show was up and running. The wagons sailed in from the valley, one after another, the machine's maw opened to the bundles of wheat, and the gold currents of grain poured forth, as though taps had been turned on.

He turned away from the sight of all this.

There would be no gold where he was about to go.

In the new place, they would have to grow it all from the earth up. As Hannah kept reminding him.

Why, after all, had they been working all these years? she had asked. Just to pick up and leave?

But David couldn't stand the accusing look in Yitzhak's eyes. The shadow of the accident hung over everything he did here. In the new place, nobody would know.

He climbed down from the thresher. He would take a last walk around the kibbutz. In the store room, the jars of nails were perfectly ordered according to size, and each tool hung in its place against its own outline that had been chalked on the wall. This was Meyer's work—his mark was still on everything.

For Hannahleh this had only led to grief.

Down at the schoolhouse, Ruth was in a circle of children crouched in the garden; her beloved Liora was showing them how to gently remove the weeds by pinching them from the base of the root. The children looked to Liora as if she were their mother; their curly heads—every one of them curly, noted David—bent in her direction.

Liora felt David's gaze, and lifted her face. The light that she was named for was woven like ribbons through her hair. They held eyes briefly; David looked away.

He thought he should tell Ruth she only had a few minutes left, that she needed to say goodbye to her playmates, who she thought of as brothers and sisters. But he knew the fuss that would ensue, how she would protest that she didn't want to leave, she did not understand why they had to go, and David did not want to endure it, especially not with Liora right there. He would leave it to Hannah. It would be a better use of his energy to go to the stable and help with the loading of the wagons.

On his way he passed the eucalyptus grove, there on the shore of Kinneret. He touched the trees he himself had planted in the muddy banks almost a decade ago. How he had worried about them, crouching over the saplings with his watering can in the days before they had a proper irrigation system. Now they were broad and tall; the long, narrow fingers of their leaves pointed downward, as though to stroke one's head in comfort.

He whispered goodbye to them and then turned up the trail that had been worn into the slope of the bank. Beside the dining hall he saw Rivka. It was different with her than it was with Liora. He and Rivka barely acknowledged each other. It had always been this way, any connection between them covered by an act of mutual denial. And if both people denied it, could anyone prove the act itself had happened?

Rivka was Yitzhak's wife. She had a son, Gabriel, with a mop of black curls just like David's.

Sometimes David wanted to go to the boy, to tell him. But of course, he and Rivka had their agreement.

Rivka's new pregnancy was starting to show.

She lifted her head up to him. Her smile was kind. And although they almost never spoke, she now said a single word, "Matok."

My sweet one.

A feeling rose in him then, a feeling of such sadness and remorse that he almost cried out, like a man does in the final moments of love. He tucked his chin against his chest, steadying himself.

"Shalom," he said, offering her the generic word for peace, hello, goodbye, but by the time he managed to lift his head she had already looked away.

While David had been walking, Yitzhak must have parked the wagon and cleaned himself off from the day's work before coming to the stables. David found him singing to one of the horses, rubbing salve on her wound. The harness had chafed and there was an angry red slash on her hind leg.

"All set?" he asked David, looking up.

David nodded.

"Malka packed you a lunch," Yitzhak said, motioning to a basket covered in a white checked cloth that had been wedged beneath the seat.

"The oilcloth is rolled inside the canvas," Yitzhak said. He straightened, cracking his knuckles. "There isn't enough but you can get more in Jaffa."

David nodded like Yitzhak was the one in charge—although it was he himself who had organized the details of his and Hannah's departure. Their banishment. They would stop along the way and gather the two parties of the Work Brigade, and then in Jaffa at Mother Lobinsky's to collect several other stragglers. Seventy-five of them in total. He would join in the excitement of the young halutzim as though he was one of them. As though Kinneret, and the accident, had never happened.

He had not meant to do it, of course. But there was no telling that to an Arab.

And of course the Arabs did not think of it as an accident.

The piece of white cloth had been spotted by Yitzhak, pinned beneath a rock like a trapped bird, its loose fabric flapping like a wing. It was a good thing Yitzhak had been the one to see it: another chaver might have missed it entirely. But Yitzhak knew, as he had made it his mission to learn everything he could about the Arab dialects and customs. The white cloth was their sign. They had enacted a blood feud. For what David had done, a Jew would be killed.

The kibbutz had sent Yitzhak to the Arabs as an ambassador of peace. Somehow he was able to talk them out of the feud. He had given them all of their demands: a portion of wheat and a portion of barley. Access to the water along the better donkey path. The right to turn their wagons on the Hebrew fields.

Medicine from Tiberias for the eyes of the Arab children. But this had not been enough. Yitzhak had been forced to tell the Arabs that David would leave. They would not see his face again. Not in these parts.

That should settle it, Yitzhak had said. They are good for their word.

But David was not convinced. He thought that still, on a stony pathside, on a remote hillside . . . He would have to keep his guard up. Always.

He was sad to go. He was repentant. But he also couldn't deny his excitement at what lay ahead. It was like being able to rewind and begin his youth again. The whole adventure of arriving in Eretz Yisrael with a sense of purpose, a sense of being chosen. That same chosenness he spent so much time trying to deny. But it was there, always, behind every action, the sense that he was carrying out God's will.

He thought back to when he had come to this place, full of hope, full of promise. And now the new place lay ahead in much the same way. Empty. Waiting for him to make his mark. He thought of Ezekiel's vision of the valley of dry bones, and of the valley they would reclaim today. God promised that Israel would be returned to her homeland under the rule of David . . .

He thought—he was certain—that the worst was now behind him. When of course the opposite was true.

David could hear shrill crying from over by the Baby House. Hannah would be trying to extract Ruth from the other children. Eventually she appeared, carrying Ruth in her arms. She must have bribed her with something, for the terrible noise had stopped. Hannah installed Ruth in the wagon carriage with her doll, where the child sat with tears rolling down her cheeks but no sound emerging from her mouth.

"You'll have a wonderful time, bubala," Yitzhak said, ruffling Ruth's hair. She looked at him with an expression of such betrayal that David turned his head away.

Hannah, he knew, did not want to go either. She was afraid of what would happen if she left her father. She had promised, at her mother's deathbed, that she would stay and take care of him. It had become an obsession for her. But even Hannah saw—must see—that now they could not stay. Not after what had happened.

David would not let little Sakina ruin him.

Still, he was shocked by how easy it was to leave. He'd expected a gathering to come and wave them off, but in the end, the threshing was a huge machine that could not be stopped. To pause one cog was to halt the entire process. So it was only Gaby and Lenka who came out of the kitchen, rubbing their chapped red hands on their aprons, and Yitzhak with the accusing look in his eye.

Hannah climbed up beside David and sat on the bench, her jaw set and her hands folded tightly in her lap.

"The tractor is making a sound." David lifted his chin in the direction of the field, and Yitzhak nodded but did not turn to look. He would take care of it later.

"Shalom," Yitzhak said. He was standing with his hand on Thin Rivka's back; Rivka held eyes with Hannah but did not look at David himself.

Nobody else saw them off; it was as if they were making a secret getaway. The halutzim were in the fields, making the big wheel turn. David took the reins. He lifted a hand; Yitzhak lifted a hand in return. So much unspoken in that one gesture.

David turned the horses and they galloped out of the field.

CHAPTER 11

*I*T TOOK DAVID AND HANNAH longer than expected to collect the halutzim. Someone from the second Work Brigade was late meeting them in Petah Tikva, and a young woman in glasses had seemed to be lost within the walls of Mother Lobinsky's boarding house in Jaffa; only at the last minute did she emerge, hair coming loose from her braids and sticking out in all directions. But finally they were off, and it seemed like a minor miracle to David that their straggling line of pioneers reached the Emek while the sun was still high. And then, a minor catastrophe: the Arabs appeared almost immediately after. He had hoped for a day or two to establish his authority with the new group. It was a tricky job, leadership in a movement that was about equality, and he would have to be subtle, earning the young halutzim's trust. He needed some time. But as their motley group wound its way through the valley, the Arabs from the nearby village came out of their mud houses to watch. David spotted the leader immediately, an old man whose face had been disfigured in some ancient battle. The black and white keffiyeh always made David think of a chessboard. Did the old man know what David had done? Of course. Word spread between the Arab villages, through market stalls and Bedouin tents, like wildfire. He felt the mukhtar looking at him knowingly, as if they were sharing some kind of terrible secret.

"The Hebrew tribe is here to settle this valley," David said, motioning to the long line of halutzim like a snake's tail stretched out behind him. And then he switched to Arabic; he wanted this understood.

"I am the mukhtar," David said, and touched his nose.

His Arabic was passable; what he had learned came from watching Yitzhak deal with the Arabs. Yitzhak had been the lead negotiator of land purchases in the Emek; once the land had been bought, it was Yitzhak who determined exactly where new settlements would be put up. He was a universal farmer; he bought cows and horses in Damascus, mules from Cyprus, sheep in Turkey. This old Arab would surely know Yitzhak, and for a moment David considered invoking his friend's name to work as a salve on the slow-building tension. But more than peace he wanted respect; he wanted to assert his authority.

"David. Mukhtar," he repeated, to make sure he had been understood.

"Ya seyyed David," the Arab said. *Oh! Sir David.*

But there was something insincere in the greeting. He could not quite call the Arab out, accuse him of disrespect, but it was clear this old man was not glad to see him there.

"We'll be off," David said. "The sun is already high."

The Arab followed David's gaze skyward. He made a noise in the back of his throat and David looked at him, squinting. The Arab had a smile on his face, but it was frozen tightly in place. He said, "This valley is already settled."

He spoke in bastardized Hebrew. He, too, wanted to be understood.

David could feel Hannah stiffen behind him in the wagon. He didn't turn to look, but he knew she was drawing Ruth closer, under the shelter of her arm. Where they had been, at Kinneret, was perhaps not exactly safer, but it was known. Whereas this situation was unfamiliar.

David shifted his weight. Somewhere behind him in line, a halutza started to cough. He resisted the urge to turn and look, instead staying upright and holding the mukhtar's eye. But the coughing increased to a violent pitch, as though she might choke, and he finally was forced to cast a glance over his shoulder. It was the plain girl with the braids who had been late to the meeting point at Mother Lobinsky's. She was bent double, making the terrible noise. He wished she would stop; how was he supposed to negotiate? The hacking increased and he worried briefly she might pass out. Well, at least she would be silent. But she expelled whatever had been stuck in her maw and straightened, and David turned away. What had he been saying to the mukhtar?

"It doesn't appear settled," he said in Arabic. He swept his eyes across the swampy, uncultivated land. This was the crux of the matter: there were people here, true. But the land itself had gone to waste. The Eretz Yisrael he envisioned was another country entirely.

Besides, two thousand years ago his people had lived here. The Romans had brought them down, the last stand at Masada. Since then the Jews had been exiled from almost every other place on earth. They had wandered in the wilderness, longing for their home, the yearning lodged in their bones and hearts like so many painful splinters. They had been cast off, divided, scattered like seeds in the wind. Some had taken root in other lands; most were promise unfulfilled, persecuted and baited wherever they went. Now, finally, they were coming home to blossom and bloom.

David looked up. The old Arab was watching him.

"The land is already settled," the man said again, as though David had not heard the first time.

"Your flowers are beautiful," David said, magnanimous, gesturing behind the Arab to the dusty village, to a few straggling begonias that had been planted in window boxes.

The mukhtar continued staring, his keffiyeh like a red scarf in a bullring.

"I see you," he said, finally.

It was perhaps a bad translation, coming out in broken Hebrew, but David had a feeling the old man was saying exactly what he meant: My eyes have apprehended you. With my vision, I have taken you in.

The unspoken corollary: I won't forget this.

He had moved to stand in front of David's horse. His toenails were long and yellowed, curled over his toes.

"Please excuse us," David said. He gestured to the halutzim whose impatience was a wild thing bristling behind him.

"You're excused," the Arab said.

But he said it in a way that implied he was accepting an apology, that he was the one who had forgiven David. It came to David again that this Arab knew what he had done. He could see in the man's face that he thought David had got off too easily; the old code was an eye for an eye.

He suddenly recalled, too, like a wind passing through the valley, that Yitzhak had told him about this old Arab, warned him even. The one with the scar. A fierce, volatile soul. He would have to be shown who was boss.

"I ask you to move," David said.

"And yet you do not use my name."

"What is it?"

"It is Mukhtar."

Yitzhak's advice was to submit to the Arabs whenever it did not cost you, thus saving yourself for the moments when submission was impossible.

"Mukhtar," David repeated, deferring, although it pained him.

As he said the word, an Arab woman approached the mukhtar, and said, "Yallah, Habib."

David smiled. He couldn't help himself.

The Arab with the scar was Habib. David had won the first round.

The Arabs left, their keffiyehs swaying, their bony shoulder blades visible through the fabric. Behind him, the line of halutzim had given up and taken off their shoes; they were lolling on the muddy earth. David would pretend it had been his idea to stop. He would use the opportunity to address them.

There was a heap of canvas on the back of the wagon and he mounted it like it was a podium. He imagined Theodor Herzl ascending the stage at the first Zionist Congress in Switzerland in 1897. David had been only a boy but news of the distant event had reached even him, back home in Bessarabia. He remembered his parents discussing it in a feverish hush around the dinner table.

He stood now, unmoving, his hands loose at his sides. The sun was thick and heavy. It pinned you down, made it hard to move. David waited until the group was silent. When they were all facing him, he lifted his palms to the heavens. "Today is yom ha aliya ha karka. The day of the ascent to the land."

The halutzim leaned forward to absorb his words. A portion of them, he knew, had been assigned to this brigade without understanding the true magnitude of what they were doing. It was his job to explain it to them, to instill in them a sense of awe at their monumental collective task.

"I don't believe we are God's chosen people," he began. He waited for a moment to let the blasphemy sink in. He touched one of his back molars with his tongue.

"But I do believe we have been called here. It is up to us to make the dream of Zionist Socialism a reality."

Behind him, Ruth was muttering to her doll. How he hated that doll for what it made him remember. David made a small flapping gesture with one hand, without looking at Hannah, and she silenced the child.

He let his eyes roam over the assembly. So many boys, their faces barely shaven for the first time. His eyes roved like search-lights, skipping over the plain girl with glasses and landing finally on a woman toward the back of the group. His breath caught in his throat. The long curls. The strong shoulders. She was both so beautiful and so Jewish. If David had an image in his mind of the women who would bring forth the children unto the new land of Israel, this was it.

As he read to the group the passage from Judges, he imag-ined he was reading a love poem into her ear.

So he brought down the people unto the water: and the Lord said unto Gideon, Every one that lappeth of the water with his tongue, as a dog lappeth, him shalt thou set by himself; likewise every one that boweth down upon his knees to drink.

That word. *Lap.* With all its connotations. He looked at the girl with the long dark curls. He felt himself growing hard.

And the number of them that lapped, putting their hand to their
mouth, were three hundred men. . . . And the Lord said unto Gideon,
By the three hundred men that lapped will I save you . . .

The halutzim were looking at him.

David lifted his eyes higher, to the edge of the clearing, and saw the silhouette of an Arab on his horse. The shape was backlit, but David did not need to see the scar to know who it was.

His hand went to his pocket, where he touched the weight of the gun.

It took them several days to organize the digging of the security trenches. David worked alongside the new pioneers. He measured his body, ten years older, against theirs. When they had taken a break and were leaning on their shovels, he asked the boys what they thought about a night guard system. A young halutz named Dov volunteered to take the first shift.

David said, "Wonderful."

Dov said, "May I have the revolver?"

David straightened and gripped the handle of the shovel. He tried to think of an acceptable reason to deny the boy his request. But he could think only of the blood feud, and how cautious he needed to be. He could not be caught off guard without a weapon around the Arabs.

As though reading his thoughts, a girl said, "The Arabs mean us no harm."

"Are you joking?" someone answered, so David didn't have to.

"You can't really blame them," someone else said. "I'd hate us too."

David angled his body toward Dov. "You'll have your whistle to blow," he said.

Dov said something David could not discern.

"I couldn't hear you," he challenged.

Dov spoke clearly, enunciating. "I said, I'll kill them with my whistle."

David said nothing, letting his silence speak on his behalf, but it irked him to have to deal with juvenile egos. He had almost forgotten this early jockeying for power: they had gone through it at Kinneret as well, when the pioneers were first establishing themselves as a group. Except back then, he himself had been one of those jockeying.

David gritted his teeth. He took another approach.

"Does anyone have thoughts about how to enclose the encampment? To protect ourselves?"

He immediately had to brace himself against the clamour of ridiculous suggestions.

"We could roll ourselves up in the barbed wire!" someone shouted.

"But we don't have enough for everyone."

"Three people per roll!"

"Blintzes!" someone else said.

David's eyes fell on a dark-haired boy who was silent, considering. He had noticed this halutz several times in the days that had passed—he had a steady determination about him, a dedication to their cause.

"What do you think?" David asked.

The boy smiled up at him, and David saw his front tooth was chipped.

He said, "Digging trenches is the obvious answer. But, in a way, it makes us look afraid."

"In what way?"

The boy shrugged. "In the obvious one."

STRANGERS WITH THE SAME DREAM

David nodded. "What's your name?"

"Levi."

"Okay, Levi. So we should forsake the trenches?"

"I didn't come here to take the Arabs' land, or to displace them," the boy said. "We will eventually be able to live peaceably together."

David smirked internally but kept his face impassive.

The boy paused and then continued, "But for now we need a divider of some kind. Theory versus practice. It would send a strong message—not of threat, but of confidence—if we camped freely, out in the open air. But in reality we cannot take that risk."

David made a mental note of this boy. He moved his gaze along; his eyes fell on a pair of twins, with bowl cuts and suspenders. They looked about five years old, he thought. He half expected them to be wearing buckle shoes. Their lips were stained with scars from some childhood disease they must have suffered. A pox of some kind, or measles. He pitied them a moment, but he didn't acknowledge this aloud.

"Could you please coordinate the digging of the trenches?" he asked the first instead, the one with the higher forehead and bigger ears. The obvious choice was to select Levi, but he wanted to show his equanimity.

"Certainly," the boy said, although he looked barely old enough to coordinate building a castle out of wooden blocks. His brother echoed him. "Certainly."

So: what one said was reinforced by the other. David was not fooled into a false sense of security. Two empty promises were no better than none.

"Please dig east of the river," David said.

The truth was that he did not care where they dug. The trenches would only be temporary; the Arabs would move off within the month. David had counted no more than ten buildings, a few made of stone, most made of straw and mud. The yards were overrun with brambles. The mortgage holder had assured them that the Arabs would be easily dispatched to their brothers in Nablus, their sons in Beirut. Wherever.

But the next morning, Dov reported that the Arabs had come, and had stood watch on horseback late into the night. His voice was sullen as he said this, as though, in this loss, he had won.

CHAPTER 12

*I*T WAS THE TWINS who volunteered to build tables in time for Rosh Hashanah. The halutzim had been taking their meals on the bare earth, and while this had a rugged charm, the Germans saw a job that David wanted done, and stepped in to oblige.

"With tables, we'll need chairs," Selig said.

"There are orange crates in the tent with the motor parts," Samuel said.

David had little trouble telling them apart. Samuel was the one whose forearms were more defined. He had the bigger ears. He spoke excellent Hebrew; Selig's was merely passable.

"We'll need some *proper* chairs," David said.

He had in fact been campaigning for some from the Agency, saying the halutzim were more likely to fall ill with kadachat if they sat directly on the muddy earth, although he had a second, ulterior motive. In his mind a game was forming, a game they could play with the chairs. He and his cousins had played it as children, his beloved Bubbe looking on and clucking and laughing. She turned the crank to the music box; when the music stopped you had to find a seat. Each round, a chair was removed, until there was only one remaining and a winner was declared. The game was called Going to Jerusalem.

Well, they had gone. Here they were.

Sometimes the hair rose on David's arms when he thought of the task they were accomplishing, of everything his people had had to overcome to make it to this land of milk and honey.

Yes, in the game, the players were knocked down one by one until there was just one man left standing.

David would be that man.

The boys were looking at him. Samuel and Selig. Levi had wandered over too.

"We can bring back the boulders for chairs," Levi said. They had just finished the work of clearing the field, hours and hours of back-breaking labour.

"You're kidding?" David said.

But he saw that Levi had pressed his lips together, bracing himself for the labour.

"I can help," Selig said, in halting Hebrew.

His brother jumped in. "I'll help Levi. You rest."

"I'm fine," Selig said, his voice sharp. His eyes were sunk deep within their sockets, and his gaze was otherworldly, as though perpetually seeing something from the well of the past.

"Are you sure?"

There was something between the twins that David could not identify; some desire of Samuel's, perhaps, to protect his brother. Selig sank to his knees, as though exhausted. This seemed to confirm Samuel's resolve; he squeezed his brother's arm, and then glanced toward the pile of rocks at the perimeter and then at Levi, who smiled, his broken tooth flashing like a charm.

David left them to it. On his way across the field he came upon a girl, sitting on a tarp. White material surrounded her like the train of some elaborate wedding dress. She held a needle aloft in a plump hand, and a spool of red thread.

"Shalom," David greeted her. He noticed how her curly armpit hair sprouted from under her blouse.

"Shoshanna," she said. She lowered her needle, and made to hide it among the billowy folds.

"I'm sewing," she said hastily, as though she needed to justify her work to David; as though he had asked. But drawing David's attention toward her task had its desired effect, and he came closer.

"Are you embroidering?" he asked.

Her cheeks were already rosy in the heat, but she flushed more deeply. "Just something small."

She held up a sleeve for him to see; it was covered in an elaborate pattern of red roses. The petals blossomed down the shoulder; the vines wove their way around the cuff. Shoshanna looked both pleased, as though she had done something she would be praised for, and ashamed, as though she knew she had done something wrong.

David was of the second opinion.

"Is that necessary?" he asked, leaving her space to conclude, herself, that it was not.

"Beauty is necessary," she said.

He drew himself up, surprised she had answered back.

"It is a secondary necessity," he said.

"Children need beauty to grow into adults."

Her round cheeks shone pinkly, filmed with perspiration. There was something slightly porcine about her. The upturned nose.

"There are no children here," David said.

She raised her eyebrows.

"Other than my daughter," he said.

From somewhere across the field came the sound of a motor starting up, then failing, then starting up again.

"We have to work," he said, frustrated.

"Work is beauty made manifest," Shoshanna said.

"Beauty is for later," he said, annoyed that he had to set his foot down. "When work is done and we need inspiration."

"Necessity is the mother of invention," Shoshanna said, and he almost laughed out loud. This was not an especially bright girl, only a girl capable of memorizing quotes. He had simply to learn how to bring her alongside.

He asked her to stop her embroidery, and left assuming she would obey. He went to the place where a greenhouse could one day be, and bent over his tray of seedlings. Each sprout neatly arranged by species. He carried the seedlings, tenderly, over to the new water tap. Beside it, in the open-air kitchen, Hannah was preparing the meal, elbow-deep in a bowl of mush, her hair pulled back from her face with a kerchief.

"Eggplant?" he asked her.

"Chicken," she said.

It was a silly joke, he thought, but Hannah always found it funny.

She laughed and said, "Something from nothing," but he could hear the edge creeping back into her voice. She did not like to cook, and David knew it. At Kinneret, she had worked with the livestock.

"Good thing we are somewhere where we have the freedom to celebrate our holiday," David said.

But Hannah snapped back, "Don't lecture me. I'm not a child."

At her feet, by the water tap, Ruth was pulling out small sprouts that the chaverim had painstakingly planted for herbs. Her dark curls were bent over her work.

"Ahuva," David said. "Stop that."

"What else would you like her to do?"

"She could plant rather than uproot," David said.

He glanced at his precious seedlings. He lifted the pencil tucked behind his ear and gestured with it as though it was a conductor's baton.

Ruth held up the dirty brown pillow she called her doll. To David's eye, it was a glorified pincushion. Sakina had also had a little clay pot you could pretend to balance on the top of the doll's head, but Ruth had broken this almost immediately. She held the doll up now to the uprooted shoots, ramming them against the face where a mouth would have been and making chomping noises.

"I'm full!" the doll said in a high, squeaky voice.

Ruth made noises like gas emissions from her pursed lips.

Back at Kinneret she would have been occupied with Liora, memorizing a Bialik poem or practising a traditional folk dance for performance at the Sabbath meal.

"We need to ensure there is culture on this new kibbutz," David said. He lifted his eyes skyward, picturing lectures, art exhibitions. Maybe one day an orchestra.

"She just needs a playmate," Hannah said.

David lowered his eyes to his wife's small, apple-shaped breasts.

How he longed to clasp his palms around two full handfuls of milky, lusty abundance. A girl took shape in his mind's eye, dressed in a dirndl and blonde braids. She was a hybrid between someone who milked cows and someone who produced the milk herself.

"There will be other children," he said.

"She needs a sibling," Hannah said. And then, "I want to have another baby."

David squeezed his eyes shut. He should have known this was where the conversation was heading. He was making so much effort to not relegate women to biological determinism; to treat them like workers, equal and competent. He wished Hannah would reward him for this effort. Instead, she let her womanly urges eclipse the communal good. Surely she could see they were in no position to have another baby.

"Look around you, Hannahleh," he said. "We're starving. What would we do with another child?"

"Starving is a little strong," she said.

Her stomach growled audibly; they both laughed.

It was me trying to reach down and add a drop of levity, hoping it might spread between them like a drop of blood through water. This was how it used to be all the time. At Kinneret. Before Kinneret. When they had fallen in love, as children.

I was trying to repent, to create the conditions in which something better would happen. Something redemptive, with its root in love. But no matter how I tried I could never change what would come. The horror would happen, regardless.

"The halutzim will have children," David said to Hannah.

"They *are* children."

"That won't stop them."

"What about populating Eretz Yisrael with little Jews?" she asked, but David was tired now, and frustrated. He rubbed his fists into his eyes. The desire to end the talk and leave came over him like a fever; he leaned his head in toward Hannah and whispered, "I'll be back."

He tried to imply that they would resume the conversation later, or that in place of the conversation would be another kind of more physical intimacy. Perhaps the kind of intimacy that would lead to more children. But his resentment showed through and his words came out sounding like a threat.

His wife heard this: she took a step back and placed a hand protectively on her daughter's dark curls.

"Come here, Ruthie," she said.

Ruth had abandoned her performance and was putting her doll to bed under a blanket of grass she had ripped up from the newly planted pasture. Now she came to her mother and clung to her tightly, desperately, as though to a life raft. The child never came to him in this way.

David turned his back on both of them and walked away toward the tents, a purpose in his step that implied he had something urgent to attend to.

If there was a woman standing beside her tent, alone and beautiful in the late afternoon light, it was not his fault. It was not his fault if her breasts were full, and if, in her dark curls, in the shadow of her cleavage barely visible beneath her shift, the vision of the milkmaid he had just conceived sprung to life. It was not his fault that his body responded, every part of him rising to attention.

It was the halutza he had noticed on the first day; the Jewess who could single-handedly make enough babies for all of Eretz Yisrael. The one named Sarah. Had he imagined he'd escape her?

She said, "I need help unzipping my dress."

He blinked, then blinked again. He ran a finger over a hangnail on his thumb.

She turned her back to him and lifted her dark curls to reveal a zipper that had snagged on the fabric.

What was she doing wearing a dress with a zipper? A dress with crimson sleeves and a skirt that looked to be made out of silk?

"It was my mother's," she said, looking back at him over her shoulder apologetically.

And then: "It's two pieces, actually. A skirt and a blouse."

He waved this away like a fly.

She did not acknowledge that she was supposed to have relinquished it. She said, "All I need are red slippers to match," and gestured to her heavy workboots and laughed. But David did not dwell on her dress because beneath her dress was her back.

Was she asking him to touch it?

"So I should just . . ."

"It's stuck," the girl said.

"I'm David."

She laughed. "I know."

She had a dimple. It was almost too much.

"I'm Sarah," she said.

He nodded. There was so much at stake here, in every moment; he knew from Kinneret how quickly things could go wrong and how, once tipped, the boat of social convention was difficult to right.

He lowered his eyes from the beautiful face to her shoes, caked in mud like everyone else's.

"Working makes us individually stronger," he said. "And in this way, we will grow infinitely strong as a group."

But Sarah's eyes laughed, telling him that she knew exactly what she was doing, trying to diffuse the sexual tension. It was not by coincidence that she had chosen him to unclothe her.

"My body is yours," she said, and he flinched at the directness.

"Every body belongs to the collective?" he stammered, wanting to be sure, to clarify what she meant.

She nodded, her eyes amused.

"Eventually the Arabs will see it too," he said. "If we set our example, they, too, will eventually free themselves from the medieval clutches of the effendi and . . ."

Sarah was laughing outright now. She saw through his inability to surrender to the situation, the way he was using theory as a shield against unruly human desire, the sort of desire the collective was trying to normalize.

"Monogamy isn't natural," he said, in a high voice that he recognized, although surely it did not belong to him. "It's a kind of bourgeois property owning."

He was like a record, the needle skipping back and forth between tracks, trying frantically to land on something that would diffuse what was happening. The zipper, too, would not come unstuck. Its little teeth dug into the fabric just as he wished to dig his own teeth into Sarah's flesh. He could smell her sweat, the heat from the fields, mixed with a tang he imagined coming from the triangle of her groin. He wanted to bury his face there.

When the zipper came unstuck, there was a hiccup of sorrow within him, and then a sharp pain of longing as it opened to reveal her back, pale as milk.

She turned toward him; for a moment he thought she was going to kiss him. But she only smiled and said, "I couldn't have done that on my own."

As though he was just some man who had helped with a stuck zipper. As though she had not wanted him especially at all.

CHAPTER 13

*O*N THE AFTERNOON of Erev Rosh Hashanah two horses galloped into the yard. They pulled a wagon; in it sat Yitzhak with his hands clutching the reigns, Thin Rivka at his side, and the Angel Gabriel wedged between them. They had come to fetch Hannah. Her father, old Avraham, had died.

Hannah, David thought, was strangely calm in the face of this news. But when he looked more closely he saw that her reaction was really a kind of frozen terror. She stood by Yitzhak's horse, who recognized Hannah and whinnied happily, with her hand buried in the rough mane and her eyes wide.

"I should have gone earlier," she whispered, her lips barely moving. "I should have taken Ruthie."

But when David asked if she would be taking Ruth now she told him in a furious whisper that she was unable to deal with a single additional thing. She wanted to see her father's body alone. And so she packed a small bag and mounted the wagon. Thin Rivka hugged Hannah and helped her get settled in her seat; she did not even look at David. David nodded at Yitzhak like they were concluding a business deal, and Yitzhak nodded in return.

"How long will you be?" David asked his wife, who had started to sob violently when she reached the safety of Yitzhak and Rivka. She ignored him, and then the wagon was gone from the yard.

Ruth began to sob, too, when he told her. Her Saba had died from loneliness without her, she cried. She had known he would die and nobody had listened to her. Ruth's sobs deepened when she learned her mother had left and she would have to stay here with the adults. With her father. Why could she not return and visit her beloved Liora, and kiss her grandfather goodbye one last time? Silently, David agreed—it would have made the most sense. But Hannah was already gone.

The girl was stuck beside him throughout the Rosh Hashanah meal. She wasn't eating and then he saw she needed him to cut her food, which, David had to admit, did not taste as good because Hannah had left her post in the kitchen. He stood at the front and addressed the group and Ruth refused to let go of his hand. He recited prayers he knew by heart but did not believe or even really hear. After, he and Ruth stayed to help clean up. He was not on the kitchen crew but he wanted to set a good example. He scraped the tin plates, which had already been licked clean by the hungry halutzim, and submerged the cutlery in the vat of soapy bleach. One of the stray cats had drunk from it recently and died, its body stiff and maggoty the following morning. He thought about rolling the boulders they had used as chairs back out to the field but it would be a waste of his energy, and the stones could still be used as seats until the Agency came through with more chairs. Ruth said, "I'm tired. Where is Imma?"

"She'll be back soon."

"When?"

"I don't know."

She hung on him and dug her little fingers into his arm.

"Ouch!" David said.

"Happy New Year," Samuel nodded to them as they were leaving.

"Happy New Year," David said. And then, "I have to put my daughter to bed."

He felt the need to explain his departure. And he told himself to remember that Samuel had seen him leaving.

At the communal bathroom he helped Ruth brush her teeth with baking soda and spit in the trench that had been dug for this purpose. It gave him satisfaction to see this; the utility of it.

In their tent, his notebook was open on the bed to a page with a sketch of an open-air oven called a taboon they had built at Kinneret in the early days. The Arabs had come down and spent an afternoon showing them how—Youssef, who David still admired, and several of his sons. They had helped the halutzim adapt to the new land in other ways as well, showing them which herbs were edible and which worked as a salve for mosquito bites. Teaching them how to predict the volatile weather. David closed the book. The gun was wedged beneath their straw mattress. He took it out and turned it over in his hand, admiring its heft and shine.

"Abba?" Ruth said.

He looked up. Then he put the gun back in its place carefully and tucked her in.

"I'm still in my clothes," she giggled.

He said, "It's okay."

"Where's Salam?" she asked.

"Who?"

"Salam. From Sakina."

His heart started to pound at the sound of the girl's name but after a moment he remembered. "Your doll," he said.

She nodded. "I need her to fall asleep."

David looked around the tent; Hannah had made a mess of things in her haste to leave. He lifted shirts and the wool cover and something that looked like a half-sewn receiving blanket for an infant.

"I can't find the doll, ahuva," David said.

He looked over, expecting a fuss, but Ruth had grasped on to her mother's only pair of stockings instead—David knew Hannah would not like it but he let the girl wind them around her hand and then stick her thumb in her mouth and start to suck. The little eyelids fluttered. She fell asleep quickly, and he watched her chest rise and the darkness descend on her body.

He began to recite the Sh'ma, but it was not to God that he spoke. It was to silence. It was to existence, or eternity; to the big open nothing out of which each moment was born.

He remembered the sense of possibility from childhood, when he would lie in his bed on a dusky summer evening and hear his Bubbe moving around in the kitchen below him, feeling safe and loved and exquisitely cared for. In those sunset hours, the sound of the milk horses and clinking glass in the street below, a girl calling out to her mother, he had felt that the world outside was entirely up for the taking. That the safe containment he felt was the launching ground for something bigger. Adulthood was ahead of him like some unimaginable play. How would he act? Who would he be? Ruth's breathing deepened and he watched her turn over beneath the mosquito netting. He reached beneath his own bed and found the gun again. He pulled it out, shifted it in his hand, and gently touched the trigger. Like a boy in a game of Cowboys and Indians. "Bang bang," he whispered to himself.

He knew what he was doing without letting himself know. Ruth was asleep; if she woke she would find the tent empty and dark, but that didn't stop him. His feet moved across the perimeter like they were in charge. When he passed Levi he followed his impulse to speak.

"I'm on night guard," he said. "I need you to take my shift."

The air around them was cooling almost imperceptibly. The sound of laughter floated out over the dusk.

Levi said, "Of course." He rubbed at his left eyebrow with his right hand. He inserted a forefinger under a string looped around his wrist.

David turned the revolver over. He held it out like an omen.

"But isn't . . ." Levi started.

"Take it," David said. And the boy didn't question him, didn't make explicit the thought so obviously in his mind: the rule was that only David would have the gun.

Truthfully David was not entirely sure why he was passing it along, but a long-buried instinct had chosen this moment to assert itself, and he knew enough to obey.

Levi said, "Shall I go?"

David looked up and blinked.

"Go where?"

"To stand guard."

"Oh," he said. "Yes."

At Sarah's tent he scratched lightly on the canvas. The stars were coming out and the shadow of the mountain was black and cool like the inside of someone's mouth. There was a cleanness in it, David thought, like a soul scrubbed pure of imperfections. David did not let himself think about what he was doing. He did not think about his wedding vows, about the chuppah on the banks of the Sea of Galilee when Hannah was pregnant with Ruth, about the veil over her face or the ribbons braided into her hair. About Liora before this, or Rivka.

Sarah's head poked out from the slit in the tent, her curls wild around her face. She said, "I was waiting for you."

"You were . . . ?"

"My zipper is stuck again!" And she laughed uproariously, like she had told him the best joke ever.

David said, "I can just . . ." He lifted his hands and mimed the gentle pulling of fabric from the teeth of the zipper.

"No," she said. "I was kidding."

He flushed the deep scarlet of his Bubbe's borscht; his hand rose automatically to his cheek, its evening stubble.

"Okay," he said. "I'll just . . ."

He swallowed several times; he touched his Adam's apple with his pointer finger.

"It isn't like you to seem nervous," Sarah said.

"Do I seem nervous?"

He took a step backward.

Sarah's eyes were on him. The beautiful Jewishness of her face. He knew there were halutzim—Yitzhak for one—who would object to this characterization, but to David she was gorgeous, and she was an Israelite, and the two were braided together like dough in the Sabbath challah. She said, "What I need help with is actually untangling some wire."

Untangling wire was a job for one person. And woman's strength must be respected. But what if she truly couldn't accomplish this on her own? Was it a test?

He tilted his head.

"It's over behind Gilboa," she said. She turned her gaze

toward the mountain, the pool of shade it cast in the twilight. The sky now almost as dark as the mountain itself, but not quite.

His eyes followed hers and they both saw the place where the field levelled out under the plane of stars, beside the river, the place where nobody would see them.

He looked at her again, to be sure. She raised her eyebrows.

"Yes," he said. "I can help you with that."

They walked across the field in silence. He heard the loose threads of Zeruvabel's fiddle, and the halutzim singing, "Who will build Galilee? We! We!"

Night was falling fully, and the hora had begun.

When they had passed out of earshot of the rest of the encampment, Sarah said, "I'm so glad you can help me with my wire!"

She laughed gaily, for the second time, at the ridiculousness of her pretense. There was not a trace of guilt, nor any awareness of consequences. It was like she, too, was bowing to something preordained. Like it had been written in the stars the whole time.

The week passed like pages in a book and Yom Kippur was upon them. Who would be written in the Book of Life for another year? Some of them would die. That much was certain. Scorpion bites, malaria. There would be dysentery. Untreated heat stroke. Then there would be the less predictable deaths—an infected wound. There might even be death by revolver.

David methodically set this thought aside.

Hannah was still away, back at Kinneret. Her father one of the ones who had not made it.

Young Ida came to him in the vegetable plot where he was showing the halutzim the choking weed called yablit.

"It's the Day of Atonement," she said, and there was mild

reproach in her voice. She paused, working up her nerve. "And Levi is very sick with the kadachat."

David saw that it cost her to say this, that she was by nature obedient and mild. But she was worried that they were provoking God; she thought Hashem would be angered by their refusal to cease working and observe the Day of Atonement, and would take out his mighty wrath on Levi.

Their work was subversive, David agreed—but it was, in his mind, more like a child's kind of mischief. Yom Kippur was the day to ask forgiveness of sins, the day to petition that the vows they would not keep in the coming year be annulled so they were not accountable. It was a prayer that anti-Semites used to justify their belief that Jews were not trustworthy. But, he reassured Ida, there was no part of him that thought Levi would actually die from their transgression.

"So—do you think we can risk ignoring the greatest of all Holy Days?" he asked Ida.

She whispered, "No."

Her eyes were downcast but large behind the lenses of her glasses. He knew she shared a tent with his Sarah. One so beautiful and the other so unremarkable. David almost felt sorry for her: her plainness meant life would be hard. But the halutzim needed to be disarmed of their religious superstition. Here was a chance that would not come again for another whole year.

"We need you in the laundry," he said.

She lifted her eyes.

"Salvation is to be found in wholesome work in a beloved land," he said, quoting Herzl.

Ida opened her mouth but closed it again.

"Your work is necessary," he said. "Today, as every day."

And that was the end of that.

Ida, however, was correct that Levi was sick with the kadachat. It was not a bad case; the boy's convulsions were nothing compared to the ones David himself had experienced many times before. Still, the appearance of the affliction meant that the mosquitoes had found them and others would be sick soon; they would have to find quinine, and quickly.

David was happy to have an excuse to saddle the donkeys and go to Tiberias. There was, he knew, a clinic run by Christian nuns that would provide quinine, gratis, more quickly than the Agency. The Christians believed that the return of the Jews to the Holy Land was a sign that the return of their Messiah was imminent.

The nuns spoke English. It was a queer language, to be sure. But David had been to the clinic before, when Igor from Kinneret was ill, and the young nun with the blonde hair and the big wooden cross around her neck liked him. Through the gesture of the prick of a mosquito he would be able to communicate what he wanted.

There were other things he could do in Tiberias at the same time. They were already low on kerosene. He would purchase some oil lamps and one large glass chimney, and hire a carpenter who could build an extra trailer for the wagon. They needed bolts, and a wrench, and as much mosquito netting as he could find. And while he was there he would look for red harem slippers for his love. Not the one who was away. The one who was here.

CHAPTER 14

*L*EVI'S CONDITION GAVE THE group extra motivation to drain the swamps. David organized them into teams, one girl in each to keep the boys in line. He had heard there was a doctor back in Vienna who was writing about every boy's desire to kill his father and sleep with his own mother—it made David laugh when he thought of it. All a boy wanted from his mother was comfort, and to be the centre of her universe. It was this they were trying to get back to their whole lives, and this would help them behave when a girl was around.

"If not now, then when?" David asked the group.

And they called back, "Im lo achshav, ay ma-tay!"

As he spoke, Ruth was hanging on his arm; he shook her off.

"That hurt," she said, indignant.

"I'm talking, ahuva," he told her. The eyes of the halutzim were on him, watching closely how he responded to his daughter. Hannah was still away, and some of them knew he had gone to Tiberias for supplies and forgotten Ruth. It was not clear exactly what had happened in his absence, but when he'd returned she had clung to him and cried like an infant. And since then, she would not let him out of her sight.

David was not used to dealing with Ruth without Hannah, and although he loved her he was irked by her neediness. He sent her off, and she went, her little shoulders sagging. He turned back to the job at hand. His energy was needed now to motivate the workers. In addition to draining the swamps, it was also critical that they get going on the one field from which they had removed enough rocks to plough. If they wanted any crops at all, now was the moment. There was even a tractor ready to pull the plough—a luxury he hadn't dreamed of in the early days.

When David went to bring it around to the field, he found old Habib peering into its motor.

"Salam," David said, keeping his voice as neutral as possible. He was thinking of Yitzhak's advice: Be kind to the Arabs whenever you could, give them the benefit of the doubt. And of course it made sense that the old man would want to see this machine.

"Habib," the Arab said, jabbing at his chest with his bony finger.

"I remember," David said.

Habib looked into the gears, then looked at David with a plaintive expression.

"Ya seyyed David," he said. "Oh, Mr. David. It is hard without a plough. And our children are hungry. Some are dying."

David straightened, his mind leaping straight to the blood feud he feared. Could old Habib be talking about Sakina? Was he threatening him?

David responded in Arabic. "Chabibi, my friend. I trust in Allah, as do you. The hard days we are all enduring will one day pass."

But this did not satisfy Habib; it only encouraged him. He launched into a story about how the Arabs had not cultivated their own land last year because the Lebanese money-lender would take almost all the final crops away. He glanced again, furtively, at the tractor. David remained impassive; the Arab's problem was not his problem. Everyone knew you had to work the land to claim it. And did Habib not even understand that the Lebanese money-lender had sold the land to the Agency—to the Jews?

Finally, Habib turned on his heel and left. His threadbare thawb reminded David of the yellow robes of the Sephardim. David knew the man was telling the truth about the hungry children, but the uncultivated swampland surrounding the Arab village spoke volumes. What did Habib expect?

He knew, too, that the unworked earth would be in the Jews' favour when they made the Arabs move.

David turned back to the tractor. There were clods of mud in the big back wheels and he brushed them off. He touched the axle and ran a gloved hand over a spoke. But when he climbed up to the seat and turned the key to start the motor, an awful grinding sound came out.

He winced and took his hand off the throttle but the noise continued until he removed the keys entirely and jumped off the machine.

It sounded as if a rock had been caught in the gears. But he had just cleaned them—what could have happened in the intervening time?

An image came to his mind, unbidden, of Habib's plaintive face.

Anger rose up in David's belly all at once, like a wave. He thought, I could kill someone.

From across the field, Dov had heard the grinding, and now he approached, his arms swinging at his sides. His bony elbows bulged, like a famine victim's, but his voice was cheerful. "What's wrong with the machine?"

David gritted his teeth. "There's a rock in the gears," he said.

Dov knelt down. "It sounds like you forgot to put water in the tank," he said.

David would normally have taken offence at such an accusation, but he was busy reviewing, line by line, the conversation he had had with Habib. It sounded different now, replayed in his head: the sad story had been a threat.

"Take a look," he said to Dov.

"I don't see a rock," Dov said.

If David had learned anything over his years toiling in Eretz Yisrael, it was to never trust an Arab. Let Yitzhak say what he wanted; David didn't need to justify himself. He knew what he knew: old Habib had placed a stone in the machinery of their progress.

David climbed back up on the tractor and turned and turned the key. The grinding continued. Eventually the engine coughed, but just as quickly it sputtered again, and died.

"May I look?" Dov asked.

David nodded, indulgent.

Dov walked over to the tank and stood on tiptoe. David could see that the boy did not want to override the more experienced man's judgment, but that Dov's expertise—what was his expertise?—would not allow him to let it go entirely.

Was there water in the tank?

The question crossed his mind and disappeared.

Dov crouched down and unscrewed the nozzle.

David was seated on top of the tractor so he did not see the eruption itself, but he had a clear view of the astonishment on Dov's face, as though he had seen a ghost or something even more terrifying and unnamable. It was like a wave was rushing toward him, and when it hit, his mouth and nose contorted and spasmed, the entire face pulling back from itself, his teeth bared, his eyes wide. And then a sound came from Dov's mouth that David had not heard the likes of before. It was a sound that would haunt him for a long time to come.

Later, he gathered the halutzim together. Ruth was pulling at him, saying something about her doll, and he told her roughly to go sit by the eucalyptus tree and he would come and talk to her later. She started to cry but obeyed him, and he felt remorse at the sight of her little figure crossing the big horizon, her shoulders shaking.

He knew he had to address the halutzim first, though, to nip any panic or loss of authority in the bud. There was a way to leverage every situation, but he wouldn't be sure what it was until he began speaking. He was a thinker who discovered his own thoughts by talking. The words came from his mouth in many interwoven trails and he saw which one was best and followed it.

He found, this way, that he was often startled by his own intellect and insight, as he might be when reading a new book for the first time.

"We are in a difficult situation," he began. "But we will be faced with many difficult situations this year."

He cleared his throat, and looked out at the young faces. Their cheeks were sunburned, their necks covered in scabs. Some had tape on the palms of their hands to cover blisters from the shovels. But they were quiet, attentive. He let the silence hang. He let them imagine the worst, and in this way the real news would seem comparatively benign.

He caught a glimpse of Sarah at the back of the group, and slid his eyes past her. He could not let himself be distracted.

He said, "The tractor is broken."

Unspoken dismay travelled through the crowd like a wave. Was God was punishing them for working on the Day of Atonement? David knew they were thinking this, but none of the group voiced it, and he felt their silence as the pulse of blood through his veins. Workers were expendable. Where one fell, another would rise. It was the machinery, the hardware, that kept the whole enterprise running. They needed the tractor to plough. David thought again of Habib. Especially if they wanted to be different from the Arabs at all.

"We must repair the tractor," David said.

He touched the pencil tucked over his ear.

"Who has an idea?"

His voice was the hand that wound the instrument, and the sound came right away, the chorus of voices, all young, all male: "We could take the Arabs'!" someone called out.

"I refuse to take Eretz Yisrael by stealing," the idealist Zeruvabel scoffed. "I don't know about the rest of you, but I didn't come here to displace Arabs."

"It was a joke," the first boy said. "The Arabs don't have a tractor."

"Levi can repair it!" someone else suggested.

"Do you forget the kadachat?" Shoshanna said. David noted that she was the first girl to speak.

"There is a part missing," he said, giving them another piece of the puzzle. In fact, there were several parts missing—a bolt had been blown off in the explosion, and the plastic gasket had melted in the heat.

"We can make it from our bare hands!" This from one of the youngest, barely sixteen.

David smiled, indulging. He felt something touch him from behind and flinched, but it was only Ruth.

"Abba . . ." she started, but he said, sharply, "I'm busy!" The girl sat down, silent, but he felt her there, a heavy planet in his orbit. He turned his focus back out to the group.

"We will have to find a way to pay for the repair," he said, gracing them with the answer he had been seeking.

"Can't the Agency do it?" the youngster asked.

"Eventually," David said. "But it would take longer than we can afford to wait."

He cleared his throat for emphasis. "We will have to find a way to purchase the missing part."

"I have twenty lira," the same boy called out.

There was a smattering of laughter. This amount of currency would not even buy a handful of halvah at the market in Jaffa. It irked David that the group of them seemed to not understand the gravity of the situation: without the tractor, they could not plough; without ploughing there could be no planting; without planting there could be no new settlement in the Jezreel valley. No new big kibbutz.

He steadied his face. "It's a good point," he said. "Does anyone have any money? Or anything we could sell?"

But nobody did, and eventually he had to dismiss everyone with the request that anyone who had an idea about how they might find money to come to him any time, day or night.

When he spoke the word "night," he felt a rush of blood to his loins. As the others dispersed, he looked out to see Sarah whispering something into Ida's ear. Where he had avoided her before, now he stared directly at her. The large group breaking up afforded him disguise.

He felt an urge to give her the new slippers. After all, Hannah was gone. And even if she had been here, it would not have mattered. She would never suspect him.

But at the thought of his own guilt, his own culpability, the image of Dov convulsing in pain flashed in front of him and he winced. He found himself wishing the boy would not recover so that his own mistake would not be revealed.

CHAPTER 15

*T*HE THINGS DAVID NEEDED to forget were mounting inside him and he threw himself into work in order to avoid them. He was only a decade older than most of the others here, and yet it seemed a lifetime ago when he'd had no wife, no child, and was free to live as big and as wild as life would permit him. He remembered when Eretz Yisrael had seemed to have no edges at all, stretching and opening wider and wider, like the rim of the birth canal when something new was being born. Now, in this new place, he could see the adventure the land afforded, could see how the young halutzim were experiencing it as a rebirth, but he felt only an intense responsibility—to his Bubbe, to Bessarabia, to all Jews worldwide, as though the building of Eretz Yisrael was resting on his shoulders entirely.

He had almost killed a man with his negligence.

And there was the girl from before. Sakina.

It had been an accident. But she didn't know that as she died.

The tryst with Sarah was of a different order. He did not let it puncture his conscience.

And in any case, where was Hannah and why had she not returned by now? She was the one who had abandoned him.

He let himself feel the indignity of this, the shame and embarrassment, and in this way absolved himself of what he had done. In some distant part of himself he could see his own child- ishness, his hypocrisy. Hannah's father was *dead*. Her beloved father Avraham. She had gone to sit shiva, or as close to shiva as the secular Zionists would allow. But David clung to the feeling inside him, lodged like a piece of gristle in his maw that he could never quite chew through and swallow down; the feeling that he had been wrongly abandoned, and the wild rage that came over him in return.

On top of it all, Hannah had left him with Ruth. The girl hung around his neck like a stone. How did anyone accomplish anything at all with a child? He cast about in his mind, trying to think what he could do with her.

"Where's your doll?" he asked in the morning when he woke up to find her limbs wrapped around him.

"Salam," Ruth said, supplying the name.

"Salam," David repeated.

"I don't know," Ruth said. "Remember?"

Her bottom lip protruded and David silently cursed himself for bringing it up.

"Where could she be?" Ruth said, and began to mimic the pulling open of drawers, the opening of closets to peer inside.

"Let's go find her," David said.

She nodded, her anxiety temporarily allayed.

He held her hand as they walked across the field. Several of the halutzim noticed, and smiled, and with this small dose of external approval his annoyance was relieved and replaced with pride.

Ruth was his life's greatest accomplishment. He saw the image of his own face in hers and felt an odd mixture of pleasure and repulsion, that nature was capable of something so profound and so entirely outside the realm of human control. The act of fucking produced and reproduced the means of labour, but not through a generic worker—no, in someone so specific, so particular, that the rest of the world saw who she belonged to, and therefore who was responsible for her. He held Ruth's hand tighter and tickled the inside of her wrist. The little giggle sent pleasure through him entirely unmediated by the mind. It was almost sexual, he thought, for a moment—and wondered if Hannah was right about him. She said that his own body was so unfamiliar to him he needed sex as a way to get inside it. He thought about the intelligent design that made children resemble their fathers, the deep understanding of the male psyche that it implied, the knowledge that otherwise a man might wander away. Because, after all, why wouldn't he?

"I have to pee," Ruth said, and he looked down at her, startled from his reverie. There was a smear of dirt across her cheek; she was still wearing her night dress.

"Okay," he said.

"I need help."

"Okay."

But he did not know what she meant by help. He remembered the first glimpse of her vagina, the tiny slit when she had slid out of her mother. The months when his relationship to her involved wiping shit out of it when he changed her cloth diaper. The repulsion and attraction he felt at what he knew it would grow into.

When they had finished with the bathroom—she did not need help, it turned out, only supervision and approval—he took her under the armpits and lifted her onto his shoulders. She leaned down and repeatedly kissed the crown of his head, so grateful for his attention. It came to him suddenly that he had been ignoring her these past days—and worse, when her mother was gone and she needed him most. Shame overwhelmed him. "I'm sorry, ahuva," he said, but she didn't answer.

He took her to see Trotsky and Lenin. He took her to see the little shoots of the carrot tops poking out in the new garden. He took her to dangle her feet in the stream. It was 10:30 in the morning. He wanted to repent. But what was he supposed to do with a child for the next eight hours? The day was meant for working. Or better yet, thinking.

He let his feet lead him. They found themselves outside Sarah's tent. When he cleared his throat loudly, though, it was Ida who came out. Her glasses were sliding down her nose in the heat.

"Shalom," she said.

He could see that she didn't know what he could want from her. She was worried, perhaps, that it was something about their previous conversation about Yom Kippur.

"I need to ask you a favour," he said, without greeting her first, and with an urgency in his voice that surprised him when he heard it. "Would you watch Ruth for a few hours?"

He had lifted the girl down off his shoulders; he felt her clamp onto his thigh. She dug her little fingers in and he grimaced. Did she not know that he was a person too, with a body that felt things?

"Of course," Ida said immediately. "I'd be happy to."

Her cheeks were pink as though she had been working, and when she raised her hands to her face he saw her knuckles were chapped and scabbed. She smiled, genuinely pleased.

"I have a little sister," she said, but this only made Ruth whimper. She had heard from her mother that she, too, might—one day—have a sister, and she wanted one desperately. David cursed Hannah silently; and he cursed Ida for bringing it up.

Ida crouched down.

"Shalom, Ruth."

The girl looked up. "Have you seen my doll?"

"Oh no. Is she missing?" Ida asked.

David winced but Ruth seemed happy to launch into an in-depth description of the doll's headscarf, which you could tie around her head, and how her mother had added a button so it could also be transformed into a kippah. David sought to extract himself from the situation and took a step backward. He could smell the heat, like something burning far away. A hamsin was coming.

"I have an idea," Ida was saying to Ruth. "Would you like to go on a special adventure with me?" Ida slid a finger under her ribbon. With her other hand she pushed her glasses up on the bridge of her nose.

Ruth lifted her lashes.

"It will be a secret," Ida said. "You can't tell anyone."

Ruth's eyes widened.

David heard the sound of a halutz shouting something—not the actual words, but the command in his voice. A mosquito lazily circled David's head.

"You have to promise," Ida said.

Ruth nodded, agreeing. She was a malleable child, David thought, and happy to go wherever there was adult attention. And he was grateful to be relieved of the duty he had taken on twice, first at conception and again now with Hannah gone. Ida had freed him. He didn't wonder what their adventure would be.

It was only later, when Ruth was returned to David with a red line sliced cleanly through her calf, that he paused. Blood trickled down from a poorly wrapped bandage; a clot had crusted in the hollow between her toes. How had this happened in such a short time? He was momentarily alarmed, but then the thought of cleaning her up made him feel tired. This was women's work. He was not meant to say it, but it was true; if he had been unsure before, the glob of blood in the child's sandal rendered him certain.

It was Yitzhak who drove the wagon that brought Hannah home. Thin Rivka was beside David's wife, holding her hand. The Angel Gabriel was beside them on the bench. A beautiful but silent child—the opposite of Ruth in disposition, David reflected, even though he was the father of both—looking around, bewildered.

"Shalom," David said, addressing Rivka directly, but she refused to look him in the eye or to acknowledge he had spoken.

He patted Gabriel on the head roughly.

Hannah stepped gingerly down from the wagon, as though returning from a long convalescence. She was thin; even her heavy bottom that he liked so much was now less substantial. When Ruth ran at her mother shouting "Imma! Imma! Imma!" she almost knocked her down.

Hannah reached out a hand to steady herself, using Thin Rivka's shoulder instead of David's.

If she noticed the cut on Ruth's leg, she didn't say.

When David kissed her cheek he could smell death on her.

"Hannahleh," he said into her ear. But her look was filled with a sorrow that made him flinch and step away.

Yitzhak and Thin Rivka unloaded the wagon. There were carpet bags and a satchel and three of the blue cargo trunks they had first brought from Russia.

"Provisions?" David asked. And Yitzhak shook his head no.

"We're staying," he said.

"Where?"

"Here."

"For how long?"

David took a deep breath and held it.

"Indefinitely," Yitzhak said. He cracked his big knuckles.

Gabriel had climbed down from the wagon and found Ruth, who was still clinging to Hannah, and he clung on as well, all three of them attached to each other like souls on a ship going down.

David wondered, briefly, if something else had happened when Hannah was away, some calamity even larger than Avraham's demise that would merit Yitzhak staying. But then, from the irrigation ditches, he heard the ring of Sarah's laughter, high and girlish, and his thoughts turned to which halutz was drawing this sound from her, like a string of pearls. The question of what had happened to his wife at the old place vanished from his mind.

Yitzhak had heard the laughter too. He watched David. And David could see that he had recognized the look in his friend's eyes. Already Yitzhak knew the whole story, without having been told a thing.

Was this why Yitzhak had been sent? To keep an eye on David and the women? But when Yitzhak asked if he could see the infirmary, David suddenly knew otherwise. It was because of what had happened with Dov.

Chaim the messenger must have carried the news throughout the land on his camel. Along with mail and telegrams and bolts of fabric from the market, he delivered gossip from kutsva to kutsva, farm to kibbutz. And soon David saw that the Agency had heard too; they had sent Yitzhak with bandages and creams, with his doctor's patience and eye for detail.

Yitzhak was here to heal Dov. They could not let David become a murderer a second time.

CHAPTER 16

*I*T WAS NOT DAVID's fault that the girl fell in love with him. He took her to the mountain and laid her on her back and hitched up her dress; he talked to her about the mechanics of building a water wheel by the river. Trotsky or Lenin could make the wheel turn; they didn't even need an engine. And how much simpler than having some poor schmuck schlep the pails to the barrels and then the barrels to the kitchen, the laundry, the farthest fields.

He talked to her about the mysterious ways of history: Chaim Weizmann had moved to Manchester not to further the Zionist agenda but because chemical dyes, his specialty as a research chemist, were critical to the weaving industry there. But while in Manchester he had spoken publicly about Eretz Yisrael and the Jews, and several prominent Englishmen had caught his enthusiasm. Who exactly? The Secretary of State, one Lord Balfour. And Winston Churchill himself.

David told Sarah the thoughts in his head, his theories and predictions, his hopes. But he might as well have been saying, My beshert, my destiny, it is you and only you. For you I will leave my family; my wife, my child. For you I will do anything.

He had given Sarah the new red slippers, to match her red sleeves.

It had been so long since Hannah had clung to him like she needed him; so long since he'd felt a woman's desire for him to fill her with his heart and his mind. Hannah wanted his semen for reproductive purposes. The more she wanted it, the more he withheld, pulling out at the last minute and ejaculating like a teenager on the clammy white skin of her belly. Her stretch marks from the earlier pregnancies were still visible, like scars. Hannah's need was perfunctory. But Sarah wanted the essence of him, as much as she could get, the essence that was spread throughout him like a thousand stars in a brilliant night sky.

David did not think, in the deepest part of him, that what he was doing was wrong. The Hebrew patriarch Jacob, after all, had taken two sisters for wives, Rachel and Leah, and their descendants had become the Jews of Eretz Yisrael today. And this was nothing compared to how some of the Arabs lived. But Hannah would see it differently. Now that Hannah was back, he had to be more careful.

Just before Hanukkah a group of new halutzim arrived. Their ranks had been changing, as those who couldn't handle the harsh conditions slipped away in the night. These new young Zionists arrived to take their place. Some were focused on populating Palestine with young revolutionaries so the sickness of imperialism and capitalism would not take hold here as well. Through the simple act of working with one's hands, the whole world could be shown how to live a life of justice. So it was written in Prophets; and so the idealists in Hapoel Hatzair—The Young Worker—who followed A.D. Gordon would do.

David was wary of this idealism. It embodied a naïveté that he had learned could only hurt their cause. He thought of the boy, Levi, who had gone so far as to refuse to eat the only thing— meat—that would heal him from his sickness.

A chicken had been bought at the market and the boy had turned his face from it, as though it insulted him.

"You don't like roast chicken?" David had asked, feigning ignorance.

"Ida needs it more," the boy had said, but David refused to let him get away with this.

"You're a vegetarian!" he said, the word in his mouth like sour milk.

Still the boy had pushed the plate away, and with that gesture David felt a disdain that bordered on rage. He might have been dealing with a belligerent son. It made him feel that he himself had failed to accomplish some critical task, failed to impart the crucial knowledge of how precarious their situation here really was.

He felt the same frustration when the new group of pioneers arrived on foot, lugging their belongings through December's thick mud. Every fifteen metres or so the carts got stuck and Trotsky and Lenin had to pull them out. David, despite months of trying, still had not been able to convince the railway company to build a new station for the kibbutz. He took his failure as a judgment against himself. He promised himself the next group— the third group—would arrive by train.

As he stood in front of the new and old faces that evening, David let the image he had seen earlier in the day inform his words.

"You have come here as wandering Jews, carrying your belongings through the mud," he said. "For centuries you have wandered, homeless in the wilderness. But now you are here. In your own place. In your homeland."

He looked out at the group. It was as if they were gathered on some old railway platform in Europe with their heavy cargo trunks and their valises, wearing clothes all wrong for the season. He had an image of the boats some of them must have arrived on, the long journeys from whatever Cossacks or pogroms they were fleeing. He felt the burden of their untried ideas about what the Jews could become. He saw the kibbutz as a kind of net, wide enough to draw them all in, strong enough to hold them, flexible enough that what they would grow here would push its way through the empty spaces.

"What if nationhood is a thing of the past?" he heard a halutz say, thinking surely of Leon Trotsky, and someone else answered simply—and correctly—"It isn't."

The old group was spread among the newcomers— Shoshanna with her armpit hair poking from her sleeves, Ida fiddling with her braids, Yashka and Zeruvabel and Selig running their eyes through the gathering to see if there were new women they wished to talk to. And there was Levi, who had recovered despite his refusal of meat.

Yitzhak stood alone, slightly off from the others. At Kinneret he would have addressed the newcomers. But here, he hung back, his arms folded across his chest, watching David, evaluating him, as though he was some old Rabbi on a Beit Din.

David had read about an ancient sage, Gamzu, who was known to reply to every event, even a calamity, with the words "Gam zu l'tovah"—*this, too, is for the good*. David tried to remember this, tried even to believe it, but with the arrival of Yitzhak his own authority was compromised. He and Yitzhak had fought, years ago, over the issue of a German plough. Yitzhak had said it would cut twice as deep into the earth and produce twice the yield. The Arab plough, David had said, was suited to the rocky earth, but Yitzhak, friend of every Arab in the land, had insisted on the German one. And hadn't he been right?

The harvest the following year had proven his point.

This was the kind of thing David was now determined to avoid. He heard a boy he didn't recognize—a newcomer—say something about dialectics and historical imperative. The workers had only to correctly turn the wheel of time to bring about the objective of true justice.

At the word "justice" David thought of Sakina; then he pushed her small brown face from his mind.

Among the newcomers was an American doctor. He was chubby and short, with a calm born of entitlement, and carried a field kit with a cross on its side. David was immediately suspicious of him. No doubt he would get a taste of the harsh conditions and return straight home to New York or Boston or wherever he had come from. Still, the kadachat was ravaging their ranks and they desperately needed medical help.

After David had addressed the group he went out to shake the doctor's hand. The man's fingers were smooth, like a desk worker's.

"Shalom," David said.

The doctor spoke a long sentence in English that David could not understand.

David raised his eyebrows. The doctor spoke again in a butchered Hebrew, saying something about how grateful he was for everything the Jews in Eretz Yisrael were doing for Jews in the diaspora.

There was a woman beside him; David tried not to look at her, but the more he tried the more his eyes moved toward her.

"This is Elisabeth," the doctor finally said.

David rubbed his nose.

"My nurse," Dr. Lowen said. He touched the girl's shoulder. Her dark hair hung all the way down her back, landing just above her behind.

"Shalom," David said.

He reminded himself to shake Elisabeth's hand the same way he would a man's. But she was so feminine, with ridiculously long eyelashes and a tortoise shell comb above her ear.

Perhaps they could sell it.

Elisabeth said, "Where do we start?

David blinked at her. Maybe she knew what she was getting into after all. But he didn't feel right giving her directions—she was at once too assertive and too delicate. Without acknowledging she had spoken, he turned back to Dr. Lowen. "We have many cases of kadachat," David said.

The doctor nodded. He tugged at his beard. "Of course," he said in his slow and laboured Hebrew. "The quinine from the tree in Palestine is different from . . ."

But his gaze was unfocused and drifted away from David.

"My spectacles were broken on the trip," he said, mostly to himself.

The doctor was looking in the direction of the infirmary, and it came to David that there was someone who needed medical attention more urgently than the malaria victims.

"My daughter was also . . ."

Dr. Lowen cocked his head to the side.

"Your daughter?"

"She's six."

"Is she ill?"

The doctor placed his palm over his bald spot as he listened.

"She got scratched," David said.

The doctor's forehead furrowed. "What do you mean?"

"More like . . . cut."

He waited for the doctor to ask him how, and was grateful when he did not. David continued, emboldened. "It seems . . ."

"Yes?"

"It's red, and hot. It's getting worse."

From the direction of the tents came laughter. Someone began to sing a rousing rendition of "Eliyahu Ha Navi," the Sabbath song calling for Elijah to appear, to make himself known.

"I'm sure it will heal," David said, his voice revealing the opposite of his words.

The doctor took a deep breath and let it out through his nose. "Why don't you show me?" he said.

He rolled up his sleeves. His work had begun.

David led Dr. Lowen and Elisabeth across the marshy flats to the hastily erected sick house. He lifted the flap of the tent as though it was the entrance to a circus, a freakish collection of ailments housed within, and with more than one of the patients gravely ill from his own negligence.

He forced himself to enter. The doctor and the nurse followed behind him.

Inside it was stifling hot, and it stank of iodine and feces. The number of kadachat patients had increased. David himself was surprised to see perhaps ten of them—some on backboards, some covered loosely in mosquito netting—in various stages of the illness. He watched the doctor's face to gauge how they were doing, but Dr. Lowen remained impassive. He went from body to body, looking in his patients' pupils and feeling their foreheads. Elisabeth circulated on her own; she was the first to see Dov.

"What happened here?" she asked, and the men looked over to where she was crouched beside the boy, lifting his bandages gently and peering beneath them.

"Accident," David said.

Elisabeth bobbed her head. "What kind of accident?" she asked.

David didn't answer, hoping she was too engaged in her exam to press the issue.

But she looked at him from under her long lashes, and touched the hair gathered by her tortoise shell comb.

"What kind of accident?" she repeated.

"He got scalded."

Elisabeth exhaled and mercifully turned back to the patient, calling the doctor over. He, too, crouched by Dov, his face steady in response to the charred flesh, the oozing black wounds.

The two of them conferred in quiet whispers. David saw their familiarity and envied it, the way they spoke without using words, the way they functioned as a team, two different arms on the same body. They had obviously been working together for a long time back in America. Shee-ka-go, they had told David. It took him a minute to understand: Chicago. How fortunate to not have to work at communicating; to have your inner thoughts known by someone as though they were her own. Was this not the desired thing? To not have to work for love.

As though David had summoned Sarah, there was a rustle at the tent flap and her head poked in. She had piled her hair on top of her head like a model in a fashion magazine from Paris. She was so young she would surely live forever.

When she saw he was there—that, he fantasized, she had finally found him after searching the whole kibbutz—a smile broke across her face. David thought that perhaps he had never been as happy to see someone in his entire life.

"I came to—" she started, but she saw the doctor and nurse and closed her mouth.

The others were occupied; they barely noticed someone new had arrived. David took advantage of this, and ushered Sarah in with his eyes. He was practising the familiarity he had seen between the doctor and the nurse, and Sarah took him up on it. She came in, and stood beside him, silent at his side. Their arms pressed against each other. Without exchanging a word, they were playing at being seen together in public, right here where Hannah could walk in at any moment. There was something subversive in this, something reckless. For a moment, David thought that Sarah's own hunger was as big as his, maybe bigger. And this was why he wanted her.

It was not love, it was appetite.

He would have to be sure that she, too, did not confuse the two.

Dr. Lowen chose that moment to look up from Dov. He saw Sarah and David standing together, and David knew he must think this woman was his wife.

The doctor's eyes flitted back to Elisabeth, who stood up from Dov's bedside. The doctor now raised himself too, and lifted a hand and put it on the small of her back. He kept it there.

David summoned his courage. He lifted his own hand, and put it on the small of Sarah's back. As if they were a mirror, or a younger couple imitating what it was to be an older one.

As though there was nobody else in the world, the doctor leaned over and kissed the nurse's shoulder. But this was too much. David flushed at this intimacy. He removed his hand from Sarah's back as though burned.

A cry came from the corner of the room and David started. Ruth. Her body was so tiny compared to the other patients she might not have been there at all.

"It hurts, it hurts, it hurts . . ." she cried.

"This is your child?" the doctor asked.

David nodded. "Yes."

Ruth was twisting under her mosquito net as though trying to rid herself of some kind of demon.

"Metukah," the doctor said, pleased, David could see, to know the Hebrew term of endearment and be able to use it.

He crouched down beside Ruth, steadying himself with one hand. He lifted the mosquito netting carefully and touched her leg as gently as possible; still, Ruth's crying grew louder.

"What did she cut it on?" the doctor asked David.

David weighed his options. "I'm not sure," he admitted.

He waited for the doctor to say that Ruth must be ill with something else, that a cut alone could not lead to this kind of fever, but he did not.

Ruth moaned. "Salam!" she cried out. Her black curls were stuck to her face with sweat.

"Peace?" the doctor asked.

"It's also the name of her doll," David said. And then to Ruth directly, "I'll go find her."

"I gave her to Selig," Ruth said, with a crazed and feverish look in her eye, and tried to say something else but her voice trailed off and she began to cry.

David hushed her. His failures nested inside him like Russian dolls.

Elisabeth turned to David. There was a look on her face that said the child's rotting leg was too much even for her, a nurse, to bear; she needed a break, a brief distraction.

"How long have you been in Eretz Yisrael?" she asked, like she was making small talk at a cocktail party back in Shee-ka-go.

"A long time," David said; he watched Elisabeth's pretty face.

But the doctor had summoned Sarah over and was speaking to her; David tried with to listen to the other conversation with one ear.

"The leg is . . ." He heard the doctor say. Then something undecipherable. Then something that sounded like the word "mould."

"I have wanted to make Aliyah since I was a child," Elisabeth was saying. "I grew up with stories of . . ."

David nodded, but he continued straining to listen to the doctor.

"You could always try . . . unproven . . . unclear results . . ." he heard.

But Ruth cried out again, begging relief, and David, too, felt the irresistible urge to unhook himself from what was taking place. He could not stand to see Ruth in pain, to hear the pleading for help in her cry. The mould vanished from his awareness. His mind fled to Sarah like a swallow glides across the back of the wind. All he could think was how he wanted to take her somewhere away from here and fuck her senseless.

Later, when he did just that, Sarah began to cry, asking bothersome questions about Hannah. He tried to reassure her as best he could—the marriage was sexless, and it was a bourgeois institution anyway—but Sarah only cried harder and eventually David had to leave her. He said he had duties to attend to.

I go back over those moments. I watch them replay. Yes, I could have acted differently. But I had not understood the magnitude of what I'd been told.

Why not?

Now I know: Because the doctor himself did not understand.

CHAPTER 17

*T*HAT NIGHT THERE WAS a dance. Someone had thought to light torches around the perimeter of the field, creating the shape of the room where no room existed. David felt, as he crossed the tall grass, that he was approaching a country wedding, with dazzling little lights suspended in the blackness.

So many grooms, and only a handful of brides. He was surprised to see Hannah, his real bride of all these years, among the younger women. Why was she not back by Ruth's side? Instead, she was talking to one of the young pioneers. David squinted; it was Samuel. She was chatting as though she had known him for a long time; as though they were sharing in some great ambition together—which, of course, they were. But it irked David to see the way Hannah's face was tipped up in pleasure, with a look he himself never drew from her anymore. It shamed him—so subtly that he was almost unaware of it—to see her displaying her fellow-feeling for another man in public.

He took the image of her laughing with Samuel into his heart and stored it for when he might need it.

Hannah felt his gaze and looked up. For a moment he held her eye. She looked so gaunt, and so old. But Hannah was not suspicious. There was not a suspicious bone in Hannah's body. She was goodness embodied.

This had once been enough to hold him.

The pioneers were dancing, the wheel of the entire company spinning, and at the centre of the wheel was a smaller wheel where three women had giddily inserted themselves. They were the shimmering jewel on the ring. There was Ida and Shoshanna. There was Sarah. Her hair fell over her face as she danced, and her cheeks were pink with exertion, and her eyes were bright. It was as if light sparked off her in every direction.

David had not planned on dancing. He had danced, all those years ago, when he and Hannah had arrived at Kinneret and were filled with the same wild optimism of these new halutzim. But the music was surprisingly compelling. The young halutz Zeruvabel was talented. And David could not forsake a chance to be close to his Sarah.

He approached, unexpected shyness asserting itself in his body. He had authority, but he did not know if he was liked on his own merit or for his position. But when he wedged himself into the wider circle, nobody seemed to notice. The boys, too, were watching Sarah—Ida and Shoshanna might as well not even have been there—and something clenched in his gut, a longing that was almost intolerable, a rage at his impotence to make her his own. She *was* his, he reminded himself. She belonged to all of them. And he was hers. But there was a hollowness to this idea that infuriated him, reminding him of all the ways his beloved theory had failed when put into practice. He gave himself over to the dance, to the wild frantic energy of the circle itself. His feet spun beneath him, back and forth and back and forth, moving him rapidly nowhere. His right knee ached as he landed on it. He was thirty! But the circle kept spinning, the same thing over and over, like the closed circuit of Nietzsche's Eternal Return.

When she came to him it was like a miracle. He had thought he would have to wait all evening, until the dance, like a spinning Hanukkah dreidel, had wound itself down and toppled over. But as the inner circle rotated Sarah passed in front of him and held his eye briefly, a light of happy surprise registering on her face. She had not expected to see him there. She unlinked her left arm from Ida, her right arm from Shoshanna. The two lesser women looked disoriented, abandoned by the brightest light on their string. They were not confident enough to hold the centre themselves, David thought. But they had no choice, and they let Sarah go like a bubble floating out over the darkness. She walked until her shadow fell outside the square of light from the lanterns. David looked across the circle; Hannah had not noticed. She was occupied with the dance. Her mind would not wander elsewhere.

David waited as long as he could manage—maybe two minutes—and then detached himself from the circle as well. He had to make several attempts at it, as the bodies on either side of him interpreted his movement as enthusiasm, and clutched him even harder with their own sweaty elbows and quickened the pace. Yitzhak was across the circle, watching David's efforts, his face impassive. Finally David succeeded in unhooking himself and leapt out backward so as not to get trampled. There was a slight waver in the circle, the dancers unbalanced, and for a moment it seemed that the whole thing might come undone. But the hole mended itself, the two boys who had been on either side of him found each other's arms, and the spinning continued.

David stood on the perimeter, panting heavily, his hands on his knees. When he caught his breath, he righted himself. He took a large step backward. He took a second large step backward. Then he turned and ran.

Sarah was standing by the edge of the river where the mountain loomed high like a dream. She was waiting for him. She did not try to hide it, or to pretend she wanted to speak with him for some reason to do with livestock or threshing.

"Ya seyyed David," she whispered, her voice husky and almost inaudible. "Oh Sir David."

He stood close to her, glimpsed her face in shadows. She smelled like lavender and hay.

He leaned in and took her bottom lip between his teeth and held it there. Their bodies were still not touching, but the tips of their tongues brushed, like feathers. They closed their lips together as gently as possible. He ran a hand along her lower back, along her right hip, but he still did not pull her against him. The warmth between them built like black clouds, dense and loaded with rain; he drew back from the kiss even more, so their lips were barely touching, just their breath, the low heat. The tip of his cock was pressing against his trousers. He felt like he might ejaculate without even touching her.

He thought of the first time he had lifted her skirt and entered her against the side of the wagon, with the sun falling in tassels all around her. The look on her face, part pleasure, part rapture, and something else he could not quite name, but recognized, a kind of escape or absolution of the self. And then he saw, over Sarah's shoulder, a blur. An outline. Someone had come around the corner and seen them. David's eyes met Levi's.

The following afternoon, he took the boy aside.

"May I speak with you?" he asked.

Levi nodded and followed him obediently. But there was a confidence to Levi's step that unnerved David. He was so young, so genuinely humble, and yet so sure of himself.

David led Levi to a private clearing near the base of the mountain. He ushered the boy in as though welcoming him into his study, as though he were a great Rabbi. "I'm sorry I don't have any babka to offer you," he joked.

Levi smiled, but it was a smile that indicated he wanted to move on to the real matter at hand.

David had decided the best recourse was honesty.

"I want to acknowledge what you saw yesterday," he said.

He thought for a moment that Levi was going to make him spell it out, but after a pause the boy nodded, and didn't say a word.

Later, David wished he had left it at that. But as he often did, he felt compelled to fill in the silence. It was like the words were prepackaged inside him, prepared by his brain for a time when they might be relevant, and the correct context called them forth. Sometimes he felt that the content of his speeches was less important than his ability to deliver them convincingly.

"You know that here on the kibbutz we believe in equality. Women are equal to men. In all ways."

Levi nodded.

David said, "There are institutions that preclude this equality. Marriage is one of them." He clasped his hands in front of him and shifted from his right foot to his left. There came the protesting squeal from the new Agency tap as someone tried to turn it on.

"Monogamy hinders a woman's freedom," he said. "It relegates her to the sphere of the domestic. Marriage is not about love between two people, as has been spoon-fed to us as children, but about distracting women from their deepest longing for creative, meaningful work."

An unspoken question hung in the air: If David was so against marriage, why had he gotten married himself? The answer was, of course, that he had been too young and unschooled to know any better. If he had known then what he knew now . . . but to acknowledge this aloud would shine a light on his own ineptitude. He reached to his back molar with his tongue and tried to dislodge a piece of leftover eggplant. He looked at Levi's face; the boy was alert, attentive. David was encouraged.

"Here on the kibbutz we not only support a woman, but demand that she partake of the full breadth of her inheritance, her right to be a worker. And with that right comes the fulfillment of her potential not just as a woman, but as a person."

There was a small splash in the river, some frog or fish. He looked at the bulrushes, tall and turgid, their cock-like heads gone to seed.

"Women have sexual urges too," he said. "For too long we men have seen women as our property. As something to fill our own needs with little acknowledgement of their own. I'll tell you, Levi"—he was on a roll now—"I'll tell you. One of the things I am most excited to see here on the kibbutz is the fruits of a new, modern paradigm."

He scratched his nose.

"Do you see?" he asked, but the question was rhetorical. He talked until he almost forgot what it was he was trying to say. He was trying to get out of the conversation without naming *what* the boy had actually seen—David kissing a woman who wasn't his wife. He said, keeping his voice neutral, like a professor presenting a summary of his lesson, "I hope you understand."

"I do," the boy said.

But hearing the boy's voice brought David back out of his head, out of the pleasure of speaking and into his fear.

"Please don't tell Hannah," David said, and regretted the words immediately.

By explicitly stating what he did not want, he had put the idea into Levi's mind. He saw that the boy had not considered doing so, but now that he had been warned against it, the idea was planted.

"I won't," Levi said. The chip in his front tooth made him look so young. He rubbed the back of his hand down a rash of mosquito bites on his neck.

But what David heard was something else. In the words "I won't" lay the opposite: I will. If I choose to.

And worse: You can't stop me.

David went to look in on Ruth, both to see how she was and to steady himself after the conversation with Levi. When he saw his child's crumpled figure, he scooped her up into his arms. He crossed the kibbutz holding her against his chest, taking slow breaths to steady himself. At the water tap, a number of halutzim had gathered; they were turning on the tap and splashing each other with the spray. It was high noon, working time, and it irked him to see them there frolicking like a bunch of children.

"There are brambles to be cut at the bottom of the yard," he said when he reached them.

The halutzim looked up, surprised, as though they had been caught smoking the hasheesh that sometimes came to the Arabs from the Syrian fields. Several of the girls stood, brushing the grass off their skirts. The boys began to gather their things.

He knew the fact that he was carrying Ruth lent him additional authority. He was a father, a serious adult in more ways than one. But Yitzhak was a serious adult too, and he approached now, his shirtsleeves pushed up. Like David, he had heard the childish play at the water tap, the squandering of scarce resources. There was a look on his face that David recognized from years of group discussions and debates; Yitzhak had smelled blood. David shifted Ruth in his arms; he felt something clench in his chest, like a nut on a machine being tightened.

"I don't need you here," he said briskly, so only Yitzhak could hear.

He meant that he had the situation under control, but his tone conveyed his deeper resentment—what was Yitzhak doing here at the new place at all? Did nobody—at the Agency, at Kinneret— trust David's judgment?

Yitzhak caught the whiff of aggression in David's voice and bristled. The frustration that had a moment ago been directed at the young halutzim changed direction like a sail in the wind.

"We're going to cut brambles? in planting season?" he asked David, but loudly, so everyone could hear.

Ruth made a noise but kept sleeping.

David knew he could still step away. But instead he snapped back, "You could clean the toilets if you preferred."

Yitzhak's eyes widened. But he was quick on the draw.

"In planting season?"

He had always liked a fight.

David remembered how Yitzhak had fought on Hannah's side about her first pregnancy, and how they had lost. Perhaps that decision still accounted for the rage simmering in each of them.

"The tractor is broken," David said. He resented being forced to say it, as though it was his own personal failure.

Yitzhak was silent, but in his silence was a sullen refusal to be dominated by David. The other halutzim had paused in the gathering of their belongings and were watching to see what would happen.

David squinted. He felt dizzy and wanted to sit down. "There's a whole work crew waiting," he said. "What would you suggest?"

"I'll tell you what I would suggest," Yitzhak said. He cracked his knuckles. "I would suggest we send men to work at the factory to make money. We purchase proper machines. Poof! The field is down. Then threshers, then wagons to carry the sheaves, then done. That's what I would suggest."

The two of them had been through this a thousand times before, but the halutzim didn't know it. It gave David a perverse kind of pleasure to perform it for them, to ignite one of the old classic debates in this new group. To take the land using Jewish labour alone? Or to allow Arab labour? And what counted as labour exactly? These were questions with so many angles. All the actual working made less room for conversation about working which was, if he was honest, the part he really enjoyed.

He asked, "Is that why you think we are here? To recreate the capitalist machine with the few precious resources we have?"

Yitzhak said, "I think we are here to make a homeland for our people. However we are able."

David had an argument for what Yitzhak had said, and he knew what Yitzhak's argument would be in return. The truth was that he could argue either side of this debate—Eretz Yisrael at any cost, versus Eretz Yisrael by Jewish labour alone. But before he could trot out either side, a boy jumped in: "Forget the factory. Let's just steal the Arab's wheat!"

The boys began arguing, some of them yelling, about the thresher, their Arab neighbours, the timing of the planting and the harvest, the pros and cons of sending the men to work at the factory in exchange for money. David took a step back, clutching Ruth, who was somehow sleeping through the uproar, against his chest. He found himself strangely satisfied that the halutzim who had, moments ago, been like children running through a garden hose, now seemed to care so deeply about their cause. He saw the German twins coming toward him. Selig leaned in to whisper in his ear, and David instinctively drew back slightly, not wanting another man to touch him in this way. But he listened. "I have a solution," Selig said, bashful.

"A solution to what?"

"The broken tractor."

He spoke in his bad Hebrew, looking to his brother to translate, but Samuel shifted away, like he wanted no part in this. David nodded to show he understood Selig, that the boy should continue. He expected the solution would involve hiring Arab labour, something that had been tried before and led to chaos and disaster, and he was happily surprised when Selig said, "I have something we can sell."

David felt Ruth adjusting her position in her sleep, and thought again of when she was a baby. It occurred to him that maybe Hannah was right, that maybe it would do them all good to feel the bright new life of an infant again.

Selig held open a satchel, produced from behind his back. David peered into it and saw a frayed brown pillow with stuffing escaping from the seam. He looked up, questioning.

"Sorry," Selig said, and jostled the bag to shift the contents. David looked again; there were two beautiful candlesticks, tall and silver, engraved with the Sabbath blessing.

His mouth opened. "Where did you get those?"

Selig averted his eyes and cleared his throat. "My mother sent them to me from home."

David was surprised; he'd thought the twins had no mother. And there had been no delivery recently from Chaim. Still, here the objects were, and they looked valuable.

"They're candlesticks," Selig said in German, and then translated, to show David he did have some Hebrew. "Pamotim."

Without delay, David turned to address the group. He must not forfeit the opportunity to be the bearer of good news. He cleared his throat, noticing only then that Samuel was standing very close by, as though he wanted to tell him something. David stepped away from him. He stared into the group of halutzim, willing them to quieten; he felt impatient.

"Shalom everyone!" he cried out. "I have news!"

They looked up from the fight, interested, but also unhappy to stop their own shouting.

David said, "We have some valuable candlesticks we can sell!"

There was a long pause. Then, all at once, a cheer went up. The haltuzim were still so enthusiastic, thought David; they still took any chance to cheer.

At the roar, Ruth wriggled in his arms, a worm on a hook. She tried to lift her head. He could feel her struggling to speak, forming a sentence against the heat of her fever. When she managed to finally raise her head, her cheeks had two almost perfect circles of pink on them. Her eyes glassy, like marbles.

"Those candlesticks are Ida's!" she said.

Her voice was high and clear, and the halutzim turned to stare.

Under their scrutiny, a strange feeling came over David. His girl was speaking nonsense, obviously, as she could not help herself from doing because of her age. But there was some kind of truth in her words. David had been formulating a theory about exactly this, the way in which things could be both true and untrue, if not factually then essentially. There was a seed of truth in some things even if their content was false.

It was a theory that served him well in his relations with his wife.

Ruth wriggled more, clamping her legs around his waist, and seemed to be trying to say something else. But David placed a hand on the back of her head, lowering it down to his shoulder again. She submitted, and rested against him, and was fast asleep in two seconds flat.

Yitzhak, he saw, was watching Ruth closely. He believed, David knew, in the uniquely perceptive capacity of children.

David felt suddenly exhausted. He needed to lie down.

"We will sell the candlesticks and see what they bring in," he said, to end the debate. He turned to go, to take Ruth back to bed. He was almost at the infirmary when I put the image in his mind, the gentlest of reminders, which is all I am capable of anyway: the brown pillow in the bottom of Selig's satchel.

David turned abruptly, Ruth still in his arms, and walked back to where the halutzim had mostly dispersed. The tap was running, precious clean water spilling onto the earth. David turned it off. Selig was still standing there, his hair sticking out at odd directions, the knees of his pants worn through until you could see the hairy kneecaps beneath.

"You have my daughter's doll!" David said.

Selig made a noise that David couldn't read, then opened his bag. He looked in.

"It seems that I do," he said. His voice was calm, almost bland, like he was commenting on something that had nothing to do with him.

"May I have it?" asked David, for some reason tentative, like he was asking for a favour.

Selig looked at the doll. "What if I want to keep it?" he asked.

There was no threat in his voice, only a mild curiosity as to how David would answer.

Selig said, "I gave you the candlesticks. What if I need the doll in return?"

"I can assure you my daughter wants it more than you do," David said.

"What if your daughter gave it to me?"

"I highly doubt that," David said.

Ruth made a sound in her sleep, a little cry that sounded like the word "truth," or maybe "thief."

"What if I need it more than she does?" Selig tried. He inserted a finger under his blue suspender and gave the strap a little snap.

This was the rationale behind the distribution of goods on the kibbutz; those who needed most were those who received. Medicine, clothing. A whistle. A revolver. Selig was trying something, pushing a limit, but David could not quite discern the shape of his request or the little experiment he was conducting.

"I don't think that's possible," David said.

He expected Selig would raise some further objection, but the boy all at once capitulated, whatever game he had been playing come to its final conclusion.

"Very well," Selig said. "If you think it's better."

He fished in the bag and handed Salam over. He seemed satisfied, a bright new smile on his face. David looked down at the doll. There was a new stain on the markings that stood in for eyes, and a rip in the miniature headscarf. But David was able to lower a curtain in his mind. He did not ask what he couldn't see. And I didn't push him.

Soon enough that curtain would open.

David took the doll and boosted Ruth higher on his hip. She was getting heavy; his arms were suddenly sore from holding her for so long. He knew that he should take Ruth back to the sick tent, but a wave of exhaustion was cresting over him. He did not want to walk the extra fifty metres. He barely made it back to his own tent before collapsing with Ruth beside him. His eyelids were heavy as though weighted down with coins. An intense gratitude came over him, that he had a mattress, a bed, a place to rest his body. It took just a few seconds for the rope of consciousness to slip its knot, for his body to start to drift out onto the black and heavy ocean, but a scratch on the tent canvas flipped his eyes open. He was immediately awake and alert; he knew who it was.

He had told her not to come here.

Ruth was snoring at the foot of the bed, her leg puffed out and held apart from the rest of her body, but the doll Salam was still in David's arms. He had been drifting off to sleep with it clutched to his chest.

He shoved it under his mattress so Sarah would not see.

She was carrying a kerosene lamp even though it was only late afternoon.

"What are you doing here?" he asked in a whisper. She opened her mouth to answer and he put a finger up to his lips. Ruth was tossing in her sleep. It was true that Hannah wasn't there, but she might have been.

It did not occur to him to wonder where she had gone.

He stood up slowly on wobbly legs and let Sarah lead the way. He was powerless to her pull. He could have no more resisted than he could resist the force of gravity. The weight of his whole life piled onto him—his sick girl, who seemed to be getting sicker, his own endless sweating, Hannah's sad face, Yitzhak's accusing face, the broken machinery, the field lying thick with wheat they could not bring down. He watched Sarah's behind as she walked in front of him. The swing of her hips, her small and smooth bottom, so young and taut compared with his wife's.

Behind the shed he bent her over the hollow of an over-turned wheelbarrow. He jerked her dress up roughly. He unzipped his pants and took himself out and thrust into the fabric of her white undergarments, unable to stop and take the two seconds to pull the cotton to the side. When he finally slid into her he thought he was going to finish right away. She was there all around him, hot and tight. He slipped in and out and covered his cock in her wetness. When he exploded it was like he was giving her all of his problems and she was saying, Yes, yes, I will take them.

CHAPTER 18

*T*HE FOLLOWING NIGHT there was a light at the edge of the field. It was shifting and changing against the shadow of the mountain. David realized it had to be a person carrying a flame. He saddled Lenin, for distances were deceiving here. What appeared close, within easy reach, was often far away.

The donkey had been used to pull the water-barrel wagon back at Kinneret; once they got a pump, the animal was free for more adventurous pursuits. It pulled at its halter now and thrashed its tail, but David looped the reins tightly in his fist. He was not trying to sneak up on the torch-bearer, but neither did he want to announce himself too loudly. Still, the old Arab saw him approach. He was holding his flame high in the air and it threw shadows on his face, making the shiny taut line of his scar stand out more brightly.

"What have you come for?" David asked.

"Salam," said Habib in greeting. He was showing he was the civilized one, the one to say hello before accusing another man. The horse beside Habib was lean and muscular, with a wide chest and flared nostrils. It had saddle tassels and baubles, matching the tasselled headscarf Habib himself wore.

"Shalom," David conceded.

He was trying to be more like Yitzhak, not just because it was the right thing to do but because it yielded better results. But Habib took a deep breath, and released it audibly. When he spoke it was in slow, clear Arabic. "Your wagons are turning on our fields."

David snorted loudly. "What fields?"

He shouldn't have said this, but he couldn't help himself. What could their Hebrew wagons possibly want on the swampy muck the Arabs called fields? This was obviously an excuse for Habib to come spying. He did not say what was rising next from his throat: that soon it would not be an issue anyway as the Arabs would have to relinquish their land.

Around them was scattered the detritus from the halutzim's day's work. David watched Habib's eyes fall on the thresher—it was broken, but Habib did not know this. The sacks of grain were plump like Russian babushkas and David saw Habib observe this too, and the loaded wagons, and he saw a look creep into Habib's eyes. It was envy, which David understood, and a kind of disgust, which he did not.

"I would ask you to stop doing it," Habib said.

"Stop—?"

"Turning your wagons on our field."

David stayed silent. He would not give him the satisfaction.

The quiet lengthened. David heard the cracking of the fire on the end of Habib's torch. The Arab stuck it into the earth now, like an explorer's flag claiming new ground. Except the ground was already his. David could see the thought on Habib's face and for a moment felt an intense rush of remorse; he wished it did not have to be this way. Were they not both the beloved sons of

Abraham? But the Jews had lived here two thousand years ago. They were reclaiming what was rightfully theirs.

And no one else in the world wanted them. In his mind, David listed the long history of Jewish expulsions, the countries that wanted nothing to do with the Jews. Where else were they to go?

The men looked at each other, neither wanting to be the first to turn away.

"I'm thirsty," Habib said finally.

David almost laughed out loud. In Habib's comment was everything he tried not to believe about the Arabs: they were simple. Unteachable. They thought only of their immediate needs. They had lived on this land for so long, and what they had done with it? Almost nothing. The fields Habib referred to yielded hardly enough for the villagers to feed their own families. Their houses were made of mud. In the rainy season they brought the goats inside to sleep beside their children. David had seen this with his own eyes.

His gaze settled on a fence post nearby. Balanced on it was a jar of drinking water that the halutzim had left behind after their day's labour. In Habib's declaration of thirst David understood that he was being tested; and yes, he wanted to demonstrate the goodwill that he knew was crucial to things going well. To allow the Arab to drink from this water would show his humanity, his compassion. But the counter-argument rose up inside him: it would also show submission. The two impulses tumbled around inside him, his yaetzer tov and his yaetzer harah, an angel and a devil wrestling for dominance.

"There's water in the barrel," he said, finally.

Habib's head flicked up, like someone had jerked his neck on a leash. The water in the barrel was for the livestock. Habib knew it, and David knew he knew it. It was murky and green. Little specks made visible by moonlight floated on the surface.

David saw Habib recalibrating; he knew the Jews' presence was bad for his people, but now he understood the full extent of things.

After, David would think back to this moment. What if he had let the man drink from the clean water? What then?

Another moment passed. Habib was weighing his options. He, too, had worked a full day. He had travelled by horseback to deliver his message to David and the night had provided no respite from the heat. Finally, he knelt down and put his face to the barrel and drank.

This confirmed something for David, something he tried not to express aloud but that he nonetheless believed about the primitive essence of the Arabs and the way they lived. But their land itself had potential. It had sunlight, a good view; once the kibbutz took it, the halutzim would be able to look over the fruits of their labour as the fields filled out and were brought down. There would be room for babies. Not his and Hannah's, but future pioneers'.

David had been biding his time, and he took the chance now. The old mukhtar had come to him. It was always better to negotiate on your own territory. Even Yitzhak would agree.

"You will need to move your encampment," David said to Habib.

Habib looked at David. His tongue clicked once, the word for "no."

And encampment, of course, was the wrong word. David knew it implied something makeshift, temporary—something more in keeping with the pioneers' situation. Whereas Habib's family had been here for generations.

Habib did not ask what David meant. He lifted his head, and reached over to touch the shaft of his torch. Then he made a flicking motion with his hand; all it would take, the gesture implied, was one misplaced flame for the entire Zionist enterprise to burn to the ground.

At the thought of a fire David began to sweat. He dug his fingers into his heavy dark curls and pulled them back off his face. He turned for the jar of good water, the one the halutzim used while they worked. It had a silver dipper attached to it with a string. He did not meet Habib's eye, but dipped the cup in the water and drank deeply. He did it a second time, and a third.

When he looked up he saw that the resentment in Habib's eye had transformed into pure hatred.

At Kinneret there had been an Arab named Youssef who lived in the village nearby. He was related to Anisa and Amir, and to Sakina—before she died. An uncle. Youssef was a true mensch, David thought. He had invited the halutzim into his home and gave them sweetmeats and rose wine, and let his women wait on them hand and foot. The women served dark red pomegranate seeds in a blue porcelain bowl; they too knew the Jewish fable that there were 613 seeds in every pomegranate to correspond to the 613 mitzvoth. There were almond and fig trees in the yard. David remembered how Ruth and Gabriel and the other children had looked upon a trip to this house as a special occasion. Youssef and his mishpocha let David and the other founding fathers feel that what they had done was okay; not just in regard to the Zionist goal but in regard to the Arabs themselves. He let them feel that their presence was a welcome one, and thus justified the entire enterprise.

But all Arabs were not Youssef. On the contrary.

David had believed the banker in Beirut's promise that the Arabs would leave this land. But Habib and his people seemed to prefer their dilapidated mud houses and barren fields to their relatives' villages in Syria or Lebanon. It was dawning on David that he would have to take a trip to Tel Aviv, back to the headquarters of the Central Labour Organization, to discuss how to remove the Arabs forcibly. He resented Habib for this, even though he knew it wasn't reasonable, as if it wasn't the man's right to defend his own home in the same way that it was the Jews' right to claim theirs.

"You're a bad man," Habib said, and David knew he was referring to what had happened to little Sakina.

"You can't stay here," David said bluntly, clenching his jaw. Habib touched his scar. "Where should we go?"

For a moment it seemed to David that this was a genuine question, that Habib was a friend who was asking advice, and his heart softened. But the torch flame lengthened and he remembered the fire and he hardened it again. No vigilance would be too great. He saw that a heavier night watch was needed. Not one man, but two. And to protect the kibbutz he would have to give up his gun.

The tractor was fixed in a few short days. David had sent Samuel to the market to sell the candlesticks and then to town to buy a replacement for the nozzle and the tank, which was in pieces after the explosion. The younger man seemed keen to help, and it felt good to give orders and have them carried out. He remembered being a small boy in cheder, the older boys with their long sidelocks who taunted him about his high voice. How invisible he'd felt at the back of the classroom, like he would never amount to anything. Like he would never have an idea that was worthy.

Now though, he could *see*, unfolding in front of him, in real time, the success of this big kibbutz. It had been his brainchild. His and Yitzhak's, and Samuel Scholessinger's and Meyer's too, in a way—but David had been the one who'd believed it most deeply and look, here it was! Kibbush Avoda Ivrit: the conquest or triumph of Jewish labour. There were hands in the fields and hands in the vegetable garden and the kitchen and the laundry. Labour took everything they had. But soon, if he got it right, there would be time for study groups and for language groups and the life of the mind. His vision was of a working class that was culturally and spiritually developed: one that would lead all of Israel to become "am oved," in the broad sense that encompassed not just physical work, but intellectual and artistic work as well.

The Zionist Executive had been divided on the idea of the big kibbutz, as had been the Battalion of Labour. David had fought the battles, and David had won them.

He told the halutzim all of this as he stood before them after their dinner of pita, olives and yellow pudding. They had taken to gathering in the cooling evenings in the quarry, each pioneer choosing a rock to sit on, forming a ring with David at the centre. The sweating had recently left him; he had willed the kadachat away. He was capable of anything.

Still, the air held the memory of the day's heat, and the thick smell of manure from the fields, a choking, cloying scent. It was almost too oppressive for talking. But many of the young pioneers were desperate to cut their teeth on ideals. They had been part of Zionist Youth back in Russia or Poland; they had argued and debated for years, and now they wanted the chance to live what they had studied.

David was speaking tonight about "creating facts" with action—with Jewish hands and Jewish labour. If you waited for diplomacy to grant you permission you could be waiting forever.

He touched the pencil behind his ear.

He said, "For example, we fixed the tractor. We used the money from the candlesticks. If we had waited for the Agency . . ."

"I have a question," one of the boys called out.

David was mildly irked to be interrupted, but he said, "Of course."

He flexed his hands. "You do not need my permission to speak."

The boy nodded. "What about 'Hagshama Ishit'? Personal realization. Aren't we required to help attain the goals of Zionism by our own labour and sacrifice? Not by giving money for someone else to do it?"

David ran his fingers through his beard. It was getting long; it made him feel wise, avuncular.

"Yes," he said. "But Hagshama Ishit doesn't apply to us selling the candlesticks. It is primarily in response to the Jews of the diaspora who want to be invested from afar, financially, while keeping their bodies clean and unsullied."

There was a canker sore on the inside of his cheek and he ran his tongue over it.

"There is no future for us in the lands of dispersion," David said. "If we stay back, we will either be destroyed by pogroms, or will cease to be Jews as a consequence of assimilation."

"That sounds extreme," Zeruvabel said.

"It's a fact."

"How do you know?"

A bird called out, three high notes followed by three low ones.

Normally, David believed in explaining one's logic, in taking a listener step by step through a thought process, but now he said only, "I just do."

And as he said it, he was overtaken by a sense of certainty, and beneath this by the urgency that sometimes visited him in the middle of the night, a fierce awareness that now was their moment. Eretz Yisrael was the only place of safety for his people.

Hannah thought the Armenian genocide was so horrific, and had been felt so intensely throughout the world, that nothing like it could ever be repeated. But David knew—how? but he did— that she was wrong.

Greater slaughter was coming.

The halutzim were watching him, waiting. So he said, "We, here, have committed to Hagshama Ishit. We *are* the principle. Even if the tractor part was not made by Jews, a Jew walked to town to buy it. A Jew will use it to make the soil bear fruit, to bring about the triumph of Jewish labour. We will expand into areas that were previously monopolized by Arabs."

Here he paused, thinking of Habib, the tassels on his scarf that matched his mules' tassels. What could make a man dress to match an animal?

"There is another discussion we need to have," he said.

The assembly grew quiet.

"I have had an interaction with the Arab mukhtar."

He waited for this to sink in.

"The shcik," he said, using the term more of them knew. "We will be making a change in our night watch policy. From now we will need two night guards at once."

He paused for impact.

"And I will be giving whoever is on duty my gun."

This news was greeted with solemn acceptance from the halutzim. They looked like children being granted a long-desired privilege: the chance to stand on the bimah, perhaps, and be blessed.

"What happened with the sheik?" Zeruvabel asked.

David shook his head. "It doesn't matter," he said.

What he really meant was, I am the guardian of that secret.

And: I am too ashamed to tell you.

He looked out again at the group, and saw the accusing look in Levi's eye. But he was finished speaking. He took the pencil from behind his ear and put it back with the notebook in his satchel.

CHAPTER 19

*I*N THE END IT WAS Yitzhak who made the Arabs move. David had wanted to deal with the mukhtar himself. Wasn't it his responsibility? But he'd had to concede that he had already sullied his relationship with Habib beyond repair. So Yitzhak was, again, forced to intercede on his behalf.

"How did you convince him?" he asked Yitzhak afterwards.

The argument about cutting brambles had been forgotten, or if not forgotten, dismissed. If there was one thing both he and Yitzhak had learned from a decade of living in a collective, it was that holding a grudge did not work. David understood this intellectually, but he knew it was Yitzhak, the man whose own child wore David's face, who understood the brutal reality of it.

Yitzhak was on his knees clearing a new vegetable patch next to a tangle of castor plants from which they would extract oil. His knuckles were cracked, and the cracks were filled with dirt. His broad face was sunburned despite the wide brim of his hat. He looked up at David and smiled, like he was talking to a simple child. He said, lightly, "A little bit of kindness goes a long way."

And the old rage flared inside David. Just as quickly as the fight had been forgotten it was reignited, like a flame touched by wind.

David stalked off and his mind followed his feet to the infirmary. If Ruth didn't get better soon, he told himself furiously, something would have to be done. Before he reached Ruth's pallet, though, he was shocked to find the doctor himself on a make-shift bed, unconscious, his cheeks pale above his beard and the beard itself mottled with saliva.

"What happened?" David asked, frantically looking for any-one who might know. They could not lose the doctor; they needed him.

"It's hot in here," he said to nobody, blousing out the sleeves of his white shirt, and a voice behind him answered, "Do you find?"

He turned to see a boy he didn't recognize, a boy with deli-cate features, high cheekbones and long eyelashes, his voice not yet broken.

"I do find," David said, his voice rough and sarcastic. "What's happened to Dr. Lowen?"

"Kadachat," the boy said, shaking his head.

"Clearly," David said, dryly. And then, "Why did you not come and find me?"

The boy said, "Do you have a solution? Something the doctor himself doesn't know about the kadachat?"

"I have experienced it myself many times," David said, remembering back to when Eretz Yisrael had first entered him, the fits of shivering and convulsing that Yitzhak had assured him were the usual rite of passage. It had come so close to killing him.

The boy repeated his question, his voice now sounding dis-concertingly effeminate. "Do you have a solution?"

Colour rose to David's cheeks. "I would like to stay informed," he said.

"Should I equally inform Shoshanna? Or Leah?"

"Go ahead. See where that gets you."

"Easy enough to talk about equality," the boy said. "But where is the action?"

David snapped. "That's enough," he said. Who was this rude child? He squinted to try and place the face.

"You don't recognize me," the boy said.

"No."

"It's Esther."

David's mind was blank. Was this supposed to help?

He squinted again, and like a drop of dye added to a glass of liquid the face in front of him transformed; where before there had been a boy, now he saw a girl.

Esther, he thought. A Hebrew replacement for Elisabeth.

He looked at her, eyes wide, his amazement momentarily eclipsing his rage. "You've remade yourself," he said.

"The land has remade me," she said. "In its own image."

David knew she was referring to the harshness of Eretz Yisrael, the heat and the dust and the mosquitoes. But beneath all that, there was a softness to this earth. It would, with the right touch, cleave open under the blade of the thresher like a woman under a man.

A trickle of sweat slowly rolled down between his shoulder blades. "You're not hot?" he asked Elisabeth.

She shook her head no. "You're sick," she said flatly.

It was as though she had transformed completely, thought David. Not just in looks but in personality, the kind, capable nurse replaced by some strident bitch.

"It's your doctor who is sick," David snapped.

"He's not my doctor," she snapped back.

David said, "Okay."

He saw that tears had risen to her eyes; who could say why? He softened, feeling suddenly fatherly.

"It's all right, Elisabeth," he said, moving toward her. But she retorted, "It's Esther."

David felt a sudden, desperate need to escape. The emotions of women were like wounds you could open, accidentally, meaning no harm, and the blood would gush over you forever. He did not understand this changeability. And because he did not understand it, he detested it.

He turned away, crossed the room and knelt down before his Ruth. He wanted to take her away from here. She would grow into one of these women, raging, unpredictable, like Elisabeth—Esther—like her mother. Was it contagious, this glaring femininity? Could little Ruth catch it, like kadachat?

Was kadachat contagious?

His head spun. He had not considered this angle. Once a person had it, could they give it to someone else?

But reason returned, and he shook his head, a dog shaking off water. He crouched down again and looked at his daughter, as thin and fragile as if she might break. He lifted her up as he had when she was a baby. The miracle of that little loose bundle of a barely formed person in his arms. How glad he'd been she was a girl. With a boy he would have felt threatened.

What would it have been like to claim his place as Gabriel's father? He didn't let himself wonder.

Sometimes Sakina came to him in his dreams. She had been Ruth's age, had been playing with Ruth when the accident happened, but in the dream she seemed younger. She wore a thick braid over her shoulder and already her eyebrows had grown together into one long row of dark hair. Her lips were plump and moistened, the woman she would become showing through. She was probably not too young to be sold into marriage—he would not put it past the Arabs. She might have already been promised to some old grandfather without a tooth in his head. For the Arabs, he knew, a daughter was an excellent investment, fetching four camels, or five, or even ten.

What had they been thinking, the old men in their threadbare jalabiyas, so occupied with their games of dominoes, with smoking their harghileh, and not noticing that a little girl had wandered out in the evening to where she did not belong. And what was David supposed to think, hearing an unfamiliar sound coming from the stables, the shadow of someone he did not recognize rooting through the hidden food stores? The locusts had ravaged every field that year, without distinction between Arab and Jew, the Arab men smoking in the cafés while their women desperately fanned the fields with their robes, and so of course the little girl had been hungry. The Arabs themselves had put her in a vulnerable position.

It might as well have been they who had killed her.

Still, David saw Sakina in his nightmares, forehead beaded with sweat, the tatty night dress that came down past her knees. She clutched the pillow doll Salam to her chest. Her eyes were impossibly wide, but it was the whimper he could not forget, the little sound that had escaped her in the moment before he pulled the trigger.

Passover came as it always did, along with the accompanying predictable debate about how to celebrate, if at all. The truth was that David had been waiting for his Passover for a very long time. Back at home, his own father would lead the reading of the Haggadah, the story of the Jews' emancipation in the desert in

Egypt, and how they followed Moses to the Holy Land. At Kinneret, Yitzhak had been given the honour. But here, now, David was the Patriarch. He pictured himself as Abraham or Isaac, ensconced on a plush red cushion at the head of a very long table, doling out speaking parts, reciting the holy text deep into the night. He looked over at Ruth's pale face, her little body crumpled into nothing in Hannah's lap, and remembered how he, as a child, had looked to the front door that had been left open a crack to welcome in Elijah, the Messiah, half expecting the prophet to appear any moment and take his place at their family table.

Hannah smiled at him, her chin resting on their daughter's head. She knew this was a triumph for David. She was encouraging him. He was pierced for a moment by love.

Once, in the green hills of Samaria, a land of sheep and lush olive groves, he had found himself lost and stopped at an estate to ask his way home. David loathed these early settlers, the ones who had come at the start of the century and now lived no differently than Lebanese landowners, with the fellaheen slaving in their vineyards and new Arab villages erupting from the soil around them as they came from near and far looking for work. What about Jewish labour? Was this any way to build Zion?

But the day had been so hot, and the man, who wore a blue silk kippah, had brought David into the house where a maid offered him a cool, milky drink she called lebeniya. A girl who must have been the man's daughter, in a perfectly starched dress, played scales up and down the piano. Somehow, despite the stifling heat, there had been a cool breeze at the loose billowing curtains. The drink was sweet on David's tongue. But it was that girl he often thought about, the girl with the plump pale hands on the piano keys, and the clean, shining hair.

And it was she he imagined he was speaking to, convincing even, when he intoned the famous words, "This is the bread of affliction that our forefathers ate in Egypt. All who are hungry, come and eat—"

The only problem was that the meal was so meagre. What would that girl, who was used to a full plate, have thought? There was the usual pita, fried eggplant, gruel. David tried not to judge. The women were managing with very few supplies.

The young halutzim seemed to relish most the chanting of the plagues—locusts, blood, darkness. In their voices David heard an eagerness to show they could relate, that they thought their own suffering was equal to that of their forefathers.

Well, maybe it was. It was hard not to be moved—David felt a shiver as he spoke, his ears straining for the sound of Arab hoofbeats just as the Hebrews had listened for the sounds of the pursuing Egyptians in the ancient times.

After the Seder, Samuel came to him and said quietly, "There's something I need to tell you."

The men had gone out into the evening; the women were back doing the dishes.

David waited.

"It's not on my own behalf," the boy said.

"Okay," David answered.

"I'm uncertain whether it's something you need to hear," Samuel said.

David fidgeted. He could see Sarah across the yard, filling a watering can. Was she as beautiful as his phantom practising her scales? No. But almost.

"What's the meaning of confession?" Samuel said. His eyes were focused on something distant, as though he was addressing no one in particular. "And to whom does one confess? God? One's self?"

David sighed and gritted his teeth. "This is Pesach, not the Day of Atonement," he reminded him.

Sarah, he noted, was bending over, and he pictured coming up behind her, surprising her, so she would not have even a moment to protest. He stretched a calf muscle, an old injury that seemed to be returning. Samuel was usually a sweet boy. Why was he droning on like this? "Your allegiance is to the kibbutz," David said. "To the group."

He could see that this was not the answer Samuel needed in order to cough up his secret. There was some magic password he was waiting for David to stumble on, which would then absolve him of whatever sin he feared he was committing. David did not want to participate.

When Hannah approached he was relieved.

The relief lasted briefly, however. The warm look they had shared at the Seder was gone. He could see she was angry with him again; he could tell, even before she spoke, that her words would have the glassy calm that was designed to camouflage fury. He tried to think what she might be mad about, but the options were both too vague and too numerous.

She came and stood in front of him. She said nothing. He waited.

"Do you know where Salam is?" she asked finally. Her right eyelid twitched almost imperceptibly, but it was a sign David knew well.

Out of the corner of his eye David could see Samuel watching. The boy's mouth was halfway open; there was still something he wanted to say. But David ignored him and shifted to angle his back to him. Finally Samuel slunk away.

"Pardon me?" he asked his wife.

Now she was glaring at him. She was close enough that he could smell her sweat.

"Salam," she said. "Your daughter's doll."

A volley of feelings rose inside him: guilt, anger, guilt, annoyance, fever, guilt, heat. He *did* know where the doll was. Or he had once known. But he couldn't remember.

"Ruth says you have it," Hannah said. Her voice rose at the end like she was asking a question.

"She's right," David said. This was not Ruth's fault. He did not want her doubted. "But I can't think of where it is now."

"What do you mean?" Hannah snapped. "How many places could it be?"

But David was telling the truth. All day he put on an act for the halutzim, a bravado that betrayed his true essence, but with Hannah he was far beyond that. With her, he could at least be himself.

He tried to remember. He summoned an image of the dirty doll, stained and losing stuffing, but a shiver came over him, a tremor. He disciplined his body, refusing the weakness.

Hannah's hand slipped beneath her kerchief, massaging the back of her own neck.

"I'm sorry," he said instead. Sometimes an apology helped. But Hannah was not mollified.

He said, "I have something to do," although it was as clear as day that he had nothing to do, that this was just a shell of an excuse. David turned to leave. His wife did not respond.

As he crossed the field he saw the pretty nurse Elisabeth. She was standing beside Shoshanna, their shoulders touching. Not Elisabeth, he corrected himself, but Esther. Her new boyish haircut was really a shame.

CHAPTER 20

On MAY DAY THERE was gruel and eggplant again. Summer was coming, but Ruth was getting no better.

She was getting much, much worse.

David had gone to the infirmary and was shocked by her leg, swollen almost comically, and now with a blackness around the original wound. The flesh was dead, and it was rotting. It smelled putrid, like raw meat left out too long in the sun. He saw a fly crawling over it lazily, hungrily, and he bent down to fan it frantically away.

A little moan came from Ruth's pale face.

"Abba," she said.

There was no hook that could pierce him more sharply than her high clear voice. Eretz Yisrael was his one true dream, and he wanted to populate it with workers, but the act of raising them in this land was so difficult. He had seen, back at Kinneret, a fetus lost halfway through the pregnancy due to malnutrition; Lenka had laboured and then delivered a clot of slippery blood that, on closer inspection, had eyelids and tiny little hands that might have worked the fields. He had seen the way Meyer's woman had wanted nothing to do with him after their daughter was stillborn. And of course he had seen what had happened with Hannah, with his first child. Or, if not his first, then their first together. He did not believe in regret, yet regret was eating him from the inside out. He shuddered to think of how he had behaved, and he could feel how that emotional shudder led to the physical convulsions he was fighting off now with every breath. He refused to be hooked—by the kadachat, by his daughter, by the things that tied him down to the world of his body, where he could control nothing, where deep inside him there was a desperate need and he could not retreat and be safe inside his head.

"Abba," Ruth said again.

In contrast to the swollen leg, the rest of her had wasted away, her skin white as cream, the blue veins on her eyelids standing out, nearly translucent. An image of that fetus flashed through his mind. He pushed it away.

"Ahuva," he said, and he bent forward to lift her up. But as he bent forward his head began to spin; the world tilted and he laid a palm flat on the dirt floor to steady himself. There was a long moment when he thought he would have to lie down. The thought of being tended to, cared for, had an infinite appeal. He remembered his mother's featherbed when he was a boy; he remembered being sick with the stomach flu and staying home from cheder, the pretty maid bringing him berries and cream with a silver spoon. But once he lay down here, beside his daughter, in the infirmary, he knew he would not get up again.

He raised himself unsteadily and stood.

"Abba," Ruth pleaded. "Stay with me. Don't leave."

There were fat tears on her cheeks now. David pretended not to hear her crying as he left the tent.

Later, though, he went to find Hannah. She was sitting cross-legged beside the quinine tree with a play by David Pinsky open in her lap. He was glad to see she had not forgotten how to read. He lowered himself down beside her; when his knee touched hers he did not move it away.

"What do you think?" he asked, and he did not have to say what he meant. They were both wondering, day and night, if the time had come.

"I don't think I can do it," she said.

David said, "It wouldn't be us. We'd ask someone else. Yitzhak?"

They were silent for a moment.

"Yitzhak couldn't do it either," Hannah said.

"You're right," he agreed. "Someone who doesn't know her."

"Remember, with Igor . . ."

They were both remembering how Igor had fought when the time came, even though he was an adult and had agreed beforehand to the amputation. They had given him a horse's bit and as much whiskey as they had, until he was almost unconscious, but when the saw pierced the skin and then the muscle and then the bone, the look in Igor's eyes was something David would never forget. And the sound from far inside him. Human beings were not built to withstand that kind of pain.

"It saved him," David said.

"He was never the same."

"He was alive, though."

David touched his nose and squeezed his eyes closed. He was trying to imagine the circumference of Ruth's femur inside her skin. There was a feeling rising inside him that he hoped was vomit but knew was really tears. He looked over at Hannah, her elbows on her crossed knees, her head in her hands. When she looked up there were tears on her face too. He reached over, tentative, and took her hand. She let him. They sat in the half-light that would be there for the rest of their lives if they went ahead with what they were considering.

It was Hannah, finally, who said, "I can't do it."

Relief crashed through David, hard as any wave. It was the decision he wanted but he could not be the one to say it. He couldn't bear the responsibility.

Hannah was stronger. She always had been.

"Okay," David said. "You're right, Hannahleh."

"We'll give her more time."

"Can we take her to Tiberias?"

"The nuns could probably help," said Hannah.

"Let's try that first."

Hannah nodded; it was agreed.

"I'll take her tomorrow," David said.

From the field they heard a motor dying, sputtering to life, dying again. David held Hannah's hand a moment longer, then squeezed it and got to his feet. His knees popped. He arched his back. When he left the sun was starting to set and she was still sitting there, the Pinsky open in her lap.

CHAPTER 21

*S*ARAH WAS WEARING a tailored blouse with a low neck and loose red sleeves. David had seen it before, he thought, but only now did he register it. What was striking was not that she looked beautiful wearing it—although she did—but that she looked unique. In the crowd of interchangeable halutzim she looked to be herself.

A line from "Eshet Chayil," the Sabbath poem that a man recites to his wife, came to David: "A woman of valour who can find? She is far more precious than jewels . . . All her household are clothed in scarlet."

There was an odd look on Sarah's face, though, a pinched sort of anticipation, as though she had something to tell him but was trying to prevent it from leaving her own mouth.

"Where are you coming from?" she asked.

He did not want to tell her about his conversation with Hannah, so he said, simply, "The infirmary."

Sarah asked, "Was the doctor there?"

David raised his eyebrows. "Why?"

Sarah tugged at her sleeve. "I want to ask him some questions," she said. "How sick is he?"

David didn't answer.

"You like the doctor," he said.

"Yes," she said, distracted, and then saw what he meant. "What? No!" She wrinkled her nose. "What do you mean?"

"That day," David said, although he knew he was being ridiculous. "When we were in the infirmary together."

He did not want to say he had seen the doctor's hand on her shoulder, just lightly, but nor could he deny how he felt about it. "What were the two of you talking about?"

Sarah widened her eyes in frustration. Clearly, she had something else she wanted to tell him, and she had finally worked up the nerve.

"He was talking nonsense," she said. She shut her eyes and pressed her forefingers against her temples.

David knew he should let it go but he couldn't help himself. "What kind of nonsense?"

He imagined the doctor whispering English sweet nothings into Sarah's ear, little American rhymes, love songs his father had long ago sung to his mother before conceiving him.

"He told me you should feed Ruth mould."

This bald statement was so far from what David had been anticipating that he thought he had misheard. "Mould? What mould?"

He remembered, now, overhearing something like this, but only very vaguely.

"How should I know?"

"Like from a rotten cheese?"

"Exactly." She hesitated. "I think."

There were tears were in her eyes.

"What's wrong?" David asked. All at once, peering more closely at her, he could see a kind of darkness closing in around Sarah, something she would not be able to resist for much longer.

"I'm pregnant," she said.

He touched the edge of the fence to steady himself. One of the posts was coming loose; he would ask Samuel to repair it.

He looked up and saw the straight line of the Arabs' stone houses they were now using to store gardening hoes, harnesses, sacks of grain. Behind the houses, there was the outline of the triangular tents, like so many beautiful women's skirts. All this he saw by moonlight, while the night pressed in so there was no space between it and his body. The night did not distinguish the Arab air or the Jewish air or the last thin breaths his Bubbe had swallowed back home in Bessarabia.

Sarah was looking at him.

"You have to get rid of it," he said.

Sarah's hand was flat against her stomach. David suddenly saw how gaunt she was, her cheeks caved in. He had the thought that the pregnancy would not last, that they were all so hungry it would not be viable.

"I'm sorry," he said.

"For what?" she asked roughly, as though there were too many options to choose from.

"For everything."

But Sarah's voice had turned belligerent. She reminded him of Hannah.

"What's the point of being here? If we aren't to have children?"

"The point is for us to survive," David said.

Now there was an edge to his voice too. It was cresting over him, what he had not let himself know: he had seen this coming.

All of Sarah's crying had been leading somewhere. This, of course, was its final destination. There were the rubber sheaths at the Agency headquarters and David knew full well what they were for. He understood cause and effect. He was not like the Arabs who did not understand, for example, that the kadachat came not from the swamp itself, but from the pointed prick of a mosquito. He cursed himself for falling into the gulf between things as they were and things as he wanted them to be, a gulf he was powerless against. Again.

"You have to get rid of it," he repeated. He ran his tongue over his sore tooth. "Look around you. We're sick. We're starving. What are we going to do with another child?"

"We'll raise it."

"Wait a year, maybe two."

"But you have a child."

"That's different."

"It isn't."

"I'll bring it to the group," he said.

Sarah's face contorted, like Dov's had when the scalding water hit it, and the look of shock and rage reminded him again of his wife. "What business of the group's is my pregnancy?" Sarah asked.

"What business? It's everyone's business."

"You're kidding me."

He said, "The group will vote."

A strangled cry came from the back of Sarah's throat.

His hands clenched. Rubber sheaths or no rubber sheaths, she could have been more careful. Perhaps she had done this on purpose.

"I'll bring it to the group," he said again. He didn't say, It wouldn't be the first time.

"You know it isn't like that," Sarah said, her voice now like a small child pleading.

"There's nothing else to do," David said, and in his confidence he almost convinced himself. There was another cry from the woman, like a pain of labour. The world spun. David lowered his hand to the fence post again to steady himself but it wobbled under his grasp.

When he finally looked up into the blue-black sky he saw Ida. She was maybe a hundred metres away, walking with her eyes fixed on the silhouette of the godforsaken hills. In the way she was so studiously not looking at them, David understood she had heard.

Tears poured down Sarah's cheeks.

"How would I even get rid of it?" she spat. This was something he had not considered. How had Hannah done it? Salt? Quinine? No, she had gone to the Arabs. To Anisa. His mind moved to logistics, the reassuring question of what steps to take, but Sarah interrupted. "I want to keep it," she said. "You have a child."

David steadied himself. "My daughter is dying," he said.

Only as he said this did he know it was true. The realization came over him, a warm tingling that began in his groin and rose through his belly and his chest until his whole torso was vibrating with heat.

His daughter was dying, and it was the result of his negligence. He had left her alone with that Ida.

It was *her* fault. Ida's.

She might as well have cut Ruth herself.

But it had only been a scratch, his inner voice protested. Surely nobody could die from a scratch.

He thought of Igor, how the halutz had fought when David held him down. He thought of the nuns in Tiberias who also would not be able to help. Rage came over him then, at the whole situation, at the heat and the scorpions and the land that had not yielded half of what he'd expected it to. The rage extended to Sarah, this woman in front of him made out of flesh and blood, with bodily needs, with a human heart, and who wanted something from him he could not give. Ruth was dying. What would he do with another baby?

He had always taken refuge in his competence; it had protected him from himself. He could use it to get out of almost anything. But here, now, in this new place that was meant to absolve him, the unsolvable problems were piling up. He felt this in his body as the desire to fuck, but fucking only promised so much. This rage would have to be released through his hands. Sarah was waiting. Her face was so vulnerable. In its pure submission it was like she was asking for punishment.

CHAPTER 22

*D*AVID WALKED BACK to his tent. Sweat poured off him. Convulsions were coming on now like something trapped inside him clawing to get out. He saw the tip of Mount Gilboa seemed to be covered with snow, as if it was a mountain from his childhood home. Beams of light lengthened around it, then retracted, then lengthened, the sky itself a living, pulsing thing. It had turned a deep purple, the clouds outlined in black like a woman's eyes painted with kohl. There was a young philosopher, an Austrian, who had just published a text called the *Tractatus Logico-Philosophicus*. Chaim had brought David a copy when he'd delivered the mail. David had enough German to understand the bare bones. *That which we can't speak of we must pass over in silence.* But had God not conjured the world out of language? Tohu va'vohu. God had said, Let there be light.

At the edge of the stream David saw two young halutzim. Their faces had become interchangeable, different features on one generic background, from Shoshanna the childless teacher to the motherless German twins to the insolent fiddler Zeruvabel.

They were, he thought, simply different iterations of the idealism he had lost. Dov, whose enthusiasm had cost him his face. Leah, who genuinely thought the Jews and Arabs could coexist in peace.

The dark sky had a pinkish crimp to it, and light leapt up like flames at the edge of the horizon. Finally his shivering eased and the faces settled. He saw Levi, the good son, and Ida, the negligent one who had let his daughter cut her leg. The good and the evil standing shoulder to shoulder—which was, he saw through his fever, the way the world was. The good did not exist on the back of the evil, at its expense, but was part of it. One and the same. They were inseparable.

Ida had heard him speaking with Sarah.

The full realization crashed over him; he bit down and his body shook.

Sarah was pregnant, and Ida knew.

She was, right now, telling Levi.

He had to go and find Hannah. He had to tell her himself, before someone else did.

The convulsions had become like visions. They came over him, wracking him with shudders, and he saw himself as a boy on the bimah, unable to make it through the Torah portion he had been called up to read, the one that would make him a man. His body heaved. He stopped beside the steel wash basins and braced himself and the wave crashed over him: "If you will it, then it need not remain but a dream." Herzl. Why had he waited so long to take quinine? Had he not already been branded with the fire of Ha'aretz? Yes. But he would be branded again.

When the convulsion ended he staggered upright. He forced himself forward, toward Hannah. In the distance, their tent flap was pulled back; light streamed from the slit. He could see his wife cradling his child in her arms, Ruth's body limp like an infant's. It struck him that there was something vaguely Christian about the pose, the Madonna and child, the easy way the mother was supporting the child's soft head. There were other halutzim, whose names he could not say, gathered at the entrance of his tent as though at the door of the manger where a great miracle had taken place. A wolf howled in the night, and David felt the sound racing through his veins. The pounding in his temples increased. This was the blood that kept him alive, that had brought him here to his homeland, that was now tainted with a sickness he could not name. It was the sickness of capitalism. The sickness of desire. The sickness of personal failure. Kadachat did not come close to naming what gripped him.

As he approached the tent, sounds trickled into the silence between his heartbeats. He heard a soft hush that might have been the wind, but turned out to be crying. It grew louder: sobbing. And then wailing.

It was Hannah. There were others around her, bent over her, but she was the one making the noise.

"Hannahleh," he said to his wife's feet. "I have to tell you something."

He could not look at what was in her arms, or even at her face, which was bright red with bodily fluid, contorted with an emotion that did not fit into the shape of any word. The wailing eclipsed all other sounds. It was like he was speaking only to himself when he said, "I'm having another child."

He saw no recognition in Hannah's face that he had spoken; she had not heard, or if she had heard she had not understood, or if she had understood she did not care. Her body was crumpled over little Ruth. She rocked back and forth, back and forth, like she was trying to shake something vital back into her child. The sounds that came out of her were like nothing David could describe, and so he lifted his hands and covered his ears.

The following day, he thought, they would put Ruth in the ground. They would wind her in Tachrichim, white linen sheets, and bury her in Eretz Yisrael itself, as though she was the sacrifice it had exacted. The great hollow of the earth would swallow her whole.

Hannah wailed.

Must she cry so? Ruth had come from Eretz Yisrael, and to Eretz Yisrael she would return. And now there was another child on the way. But when David's mouth opened to tell Hannah this—had he not already told her?—it was another sound that came from deep within his body, and his legs buckled beneath him. He shook, and his eyes lost focus, the yellow appearing in the whites. Saliva foamed around his mouth. And from the depth of the seizure, he felt the gun in his pocket. He could not move to touch it, but his mind rested on the fact of it. It gave him a clear place of respite, somewhere to aim.

Later, when he woke up, he remembered nothing.

CHAPTER 23

*F*ROM MY PLACE OUTSIDE TIME I can tell you something true: God exists, but not as people conceive of Him, a vengeful Adonai who dispenses merciless judgment. He is here, the God of the Jews, the One God, in everything—the thickets, the dense acacia bushes, the vast swampy marshlands. In the land of barley and vines and fig trees, of olive oil and honey. And He wants to stay animated in each of us. We are His effort. No more than the flowers and the river stones, the Arab taboons, but no less either.

I look back at David stumbling out into the field alone. The moon was torn in ragged shreds on the tips of the barbed wire fence. But he saw at last what I can now see: there is no keeping anything in, and there is no keeping anything out. The attempt to do so is an attempt to order a universe that is, at its heart, pure chaos. It is an attempt to control something the halutzim refused to call God, but that could equally be called nothingness. It could be called time, or eternity; it has the same wide emptiness at its core.

By early morning there was a second body. Mine.

David was the first to kneel over my bed, to touch the curls spread out around my head, to touch with his fingers the place where the bullet entered. He did it mechanically, like a child in a science class, examining the skin of a frog held open by pins in front of him, each organ neatly labelled. This was the kind of teaching Yitzhak would do later, with the children, when there were new children. But Ruth would not be among them.

David saw my blood and stood up and walked quickly out of my tent. He was bracing himself against an onslaught of feeling he didn't know if he would survive. He got as far as the fence before the wave overtook him, forcing him to his knees, forcing his mouth open, drawing from him a substance neither animal nor emotional nor spiritual but all of these in every combination. The wordless thing that had made him human was pulled from his mouth like a string of knotted scarves. He retched, retched again. It was only when this terrible tangle had been pulled clear of the trap of his body that the crying started.

Only then did he understand, in some far-off place deep inside himself, that his daughter was gone. He had planted the seed of life in this earth, and what had grown up had belonged to the land, and also to him. As sure as the almond trees belonged to the desert and the wind to the empty mountainside, the girl with the black curls had come from his thought and his longing. He had held her to his chest the moment she was born, when she smelled of blood and yeast and her only instinct was for the nipple. She had turned her head toward his chest and he had nothing to give her.

He had passed the baby to her mother, where she belonged, but the sadness and frustration of that moment had never entirely left him. Nothing he could provide had filled his hunger to be needed. Later, he found other ways to love Ruth. He had taken her to the barn when the cow was in labour, one half of the calf emerged from the protrusion and the cow, seemingly unaware, chewing grass. He had helped Ruth gently pull the young animal into the light. He had waded with her into the high wheat that came almost over her head, and showed her how to strip a stalk, rubbing it between her small palms so the chaff came free. He had walked with her on the hillside in Zichron, waving to the Arab girls, only slightly older than she was, who bent in their colourful dresses to cut the vines. He had picked, from a lone tree, a sweet pod of carob for her to suck on. And high in the hills, he had shown her a tumbled-down stone door, the crumbled rock still holding a handle. It was old almost beyond comprehension. Before the time of Isaac and Rachel and even Abraham. From earlier even than the Canaanites.

Ruth had been unmoved. Perhaps she was too young to appreciate it. Perhaps if she had been a boy. But David had a boy, a son, and was helpless to exert his influence on him either.

Ruth took in everything he showed her with wide open eyes. She loved him. But at the end of the day she returned to her mother.

In death I understand what I did not in life: David's refusal of my pregnancy did not reflect on me. He had always had a resistance against anything feminine, a fear of being eclipsed and surrounded. And under that, a hatred of the female in himself. Everything he had ever done had been an attempt to clear a space between him and his mother. The motherland, Russia, and the land that was his, Eretz Yisrael. His flesh and blood mother, and the mothers of his children. All of us.

Hovering over my own body, I look back at David. The sweat had congealed on his body as a kind of carapace, coating all of him. The breeze rose against his bare skin and he shivered. Another convulsion was coming on. The tremor started at the nape of his neck, the place where a wolf held her cub in its teeth, and travelled down his back, his arms, so that all of him was shaking uncontrollably. He was freezing cold; he wanted to stand next to a fire. An image came to him of a hand raising a match, of Habib's torch. The Arabs, too, were looking for light in the darkness. He had done wrong by them. The burning of the world was needed in the same way death was needed before life. As the flame in the back of his mind rose, a wind rose up as well. It was a ghostly wind, of things gone by. And of everything still left to come.

PART THREE

Hannah

CHAPTER 24

I GO BACK AND SEE BLOOD. The group's, and my own. Hannah's, getting heavier each month. She squatted over the hole in the ground and contracted her uterus and the clots eased out, slick black cutlets that reminded her of afterbirth, and before that, of the abortion. They smelled of iron and winter and stained the ground scarlet.

She knew that periods like this meant her time of child-bearing was coming to an end. She was still young. But it had been like this for her mother too. A little window in which to birth her world and then the doors sliding shut.

She also knew what it meant to be without her mother. It was as if a part of her own self no longer existed in the world: a map of contact points, of context. Her mother's hazel eyes; Hannah's hazel eyes. Her mother's rugelach; Hannah's love of the smell of dough rising that seemed to both surround her mother and *be* her. As though Hannah could swallow her mother and hold her inside the way she herself had risen inside her mother. A reversal.

Hannah remembered her mother's watery eyes on the day before her heart gave out and she slumped over by the stream where they'd built the tannery.

"Promise me something, Hannahleh," she had said, in Russian.

There was something in her mother's voice that made Hannah pay attention.

"Don't leave your father here without me."

Hannah laughed. "Are you going somewhere?"

Her mother's face was stern, and Hannah saw what she meant. "Mamochka," she said, "don't be ridiculous."

Her mother's eyes smiled in return, but her mouth did not.

"Anyway, why would I ever do that?" Hannah asked. "There's nowhere else to go." She gestured around Kinneret, to the Baby House, the fulsome fields, the water. "This is my home."

But her mother had seen something that Hannah had not, and she insisted.

"Okay, okay!" Hannah said, laughing. "I promise."

Her mother nodded, but Hannah could see she was still not entirely sure.

"Your father will need you," she said.

Hannah took the bloody rags to the girl, Ida, who had been assigned to the laundry. It was high noon, the sun directly above them, not a spot of shade or reprieve anywhere. Ida held one of her braids in her own hand, like she was anchoring herself to the land with a rope. She held her other hand out for the bundle of rags, but Hannah did not yet pass it over. She saw the horror and disgust on the girl's face; she felt a desire to protect her and a competing desire not to hide. Defiance in the face of Ida's revulsion.

"I need you to wash these," she said.

"Of course," Ida said. Her nose bunched up.

Hannah stood there biting her tongue, the apology for her own blood trying hard to escape her, fighting its trap like an animal.

"Thank you," she said.

But it took her another moment to relinquish the bundle, tied together in a knot of clean fabric, it, too, now soaked in blood. This halutza, Ida, with her long braids and her glasses, still had the innocence of a child about her. And in the passing of the bloody rags Hannah absolved her of it. Somehow, her innocence would be taken.

When Hannah returned from the laundry, Ruth looked up at her from the corner of the tent.

"Why did Sakina die?" she asked her mother.

"People die," Hannah said. How many times had she answered this? A hundred? A thousand? "They get old or they get sick."

"Sakina wasn't old or sick," Ruth pointed out.

"Sometimes there's an accident."

"But?"

"Savta was old."

"Come here, Ruthie."

"Did Sakina have an accident?"

"I wasn't there when she died," Hannah said.

It was Ruth who had been there, but perhaps she had instinctively looked away, or perhaps she had truly forgotten—or been unable to hold the memory in her young mind.

"Did Abba make the accident?" Ruth asked, like she could tell what Hannah was thinking. "David?" she translated, just to be certain.

David should have been the one to deal with this. If there was anything he should have taken on, it was this. "What's Salam doing?" Hannah asked, trying to distract her daughter.

Ruth reached for her doll, and bounced her up and down on the tent's dirt floor for a moment, as though she was dancing. She undid the round button on the top of the doll's head that Hannah had sewn on for a kippah. Poor Ruth had no toys and here in the new place she had no playmates either; the least Hannah could do was give her a way to change the doll's appearance. Ruth loved to transform the doll from Arab to Jew and back to Arab again; she smoothed the headscarf down the doll's back.

"Salam is planting eucalyptus," Ruth said. The girl's fingers were thin, bony, her baby fat almost all gone now, although it was hard to know whether it was because she was growing or because she was starving. Her eyes were huge and behind them unfolded the scene on the riverbank back at Kinneret, the children helping Yitzhak and Liora dig the small holes and deposit the saplings into the muddy banks.

"Come and put your shoes on," Hannah said.

"Where is Noam?" Ruth asked.

"He's back at the old place."

"I know that," Ruth said.

"Shoes," Hannah said.

"Noam's sister is me, and his other sister is Susan."

Hannah smiled, thinking how the children in the Baby House had assumed they were siblings. Ruth had been competitive with Susan in the way real sisters often were, although she did love saying her name, so unusual in their group. Leah had a relative in America who'd died, and when Leah gave birth she had given her daughter the English name.

Ruth was repeating the names of her cohort from the Baby House so as to enshrine them in her memory.

"Plus Gabriel," Ruth said. "Our angel."

The only one, Hannah thought, who was actually related to Ruth.

"Left foot first," Hannah said.

"The light of Zion is in the wild animals' eyes."

Hannah said, "Put your heel in here."

She held Ruth's foot in her hand, and it took up almost her entire palm. The shape and distribution of the toes were the same as when she'd been born six years ago, the second toe slightly longer than the big one. Hannah was sure she could pick those feet out of a lineup. Yes, if she was shown the bare feet of all the children in Eretz Yisrael, she would be able to choose the ones that belonged to her daughter.

"I want to stay here," Ruth said.

Hannah lifted her head, smiling. "At the new place?"

"In our tent."

The tents had just gone up; the young halutzim had spent all night erecting them. Their hope and their energy exhausted Hannah.

"It's time to go out and look for your Abba," she said.

Ruth jumped up and down on the spot vigorously, one sandal dangling from her ankle.

"Where does Gabriel live? And Susan and Mikhol?"

"At the old place. At Kinneret."

Ruth's face fell. Each time they discussed this, it was like a recurring bad dream for the girl, the same scene replaying over and over. It still confused Ruth that the boundaries of Kinneret— the Sea of Galilee to the east, the Arab village where Anisa now lived, without her daughter Sakina, to the south—were not the boundaries of the entire world. Hannah watched Ruth struggle to arrange the places in her mind, locate where she was in relation to the children she thought of as her brothers and sisters.

"Can we go back?"

Hannah sighed heavily, and Ruth jumped in. "To visit."

"Not now, Ruthie."

They would visit, of course. Hannah thought of her father, sick with no one knew what. Old age, it seemed—only he was not so old. She would not forget the promise she had made to her mother. It was Hannah, after all, who had brought her parents from Russia to Eretz Yisrael. She had convinced them, and they had come.

"Put your foot in," Hannah said.

Ruth flicked the sandal that was dangling from her ankle and it flew across the tent, hitting the canvas and landing on the floor. Ruth giggled. Hannah closed her eyes as tightly as she could.

"What are you doing, Imma?"

"I'm taking a moment."

"For planting you need just the right amount of mud."

Hannah was quiet.

"Imma?"

"Yes, bubala."

"Growing a baby is like growing a seed."

Hannah nodded. This was the line Ruth's beloved Liora had taught them.

"First you put the seed in the earth," Hannah said, starting the story, but Ruth stomped her little foot and crossed her arms over her chest and puffed out her cheeks. "I want to see Liora!" she shouted.

At Kinneret, babies had been raised collectively. Mothers, it was decided by the group, could not maintain the objectivity required, so other women were assigned to the Baby House. Women with the interest of the group at heart. Without the personal bias that biology seemed to engender.

Hannah remembered—would never forget—the panic of handing Ruth over to Liora at the Baby House on the other side of the Kibbutz when she was three days old. A vote had been taken; only non-mothers would be accepted for the position of caretaker. Only childless women had the objectivity to see what was needed. The babies would be breastfed—that was only natural—but one lactating mother was as good as any other. The mothers were not meant to feed their own child. And yet, when baby Susan had fallen sick, Leah had wormed her way in through Liora. Hannah was sure she had fed Susan more than the others. Susan's little legs were plump and dimpled, while Ruth was just a spindly pile of sticks. She could still remember hearing a baby cry across the kibbutz at night, knowing it was Ruth, not being able to go to her.

And then, slowly, the impulse had faded out of her. Not the intense love, so sharp it could cripple her, could cut her in half with pleasure and pain. But the instinctive part of her that knew what to do with her child, without thinking. When to come close and when to give her daughter space; what to do to make her listen and especially what to do to make her stop crying.

Ruth took the second sandal off her foot and threw it across the tent with the first. A puff of dust rose off the canvas into the air.

"David made that accident," Ruth said. She was not asking a question, but making a statement. "Sakina is dead now," she concluded.

"Go get your shoes," Hannah said. She felt a scream rising up in her throat.

Ruth shook her head no and looked to see what her mother would do. She saw Hannah's exasperation and came over and hugged her hard. She pushed on Hannah's breasts.

"No milk," she said. And then, "Imma, I love you so much I could die."

"What?"

"Like Sakina."

"Sakina was far too young to die," Hannah said. And then, "I love you too, Ruthie." Tears had come into her eyes, of exhaustion and exasperation and frustration and loneliness. She wasn't prepared for any of this.

"Will I die?" Ruth asked her.

Hannah pulled her daughter against her. "Not for a long, long time."

At first they thought it was kadachat, except without convulsions. Hannah's father was jaundiced, and losing weight.

"I'm old," he had said to her, as she was packing to leave Kinneret, and she had said, refusing, "You're young!"

His face stayed serious. He was a big man, tall with wide shoulders that filled his tallit, and only by knowing this could you see how he had deteriorated. In contrast to what he had been before.

"I'm sorry I'm going," she told him.

She wanted to be absolved, but she wanted his honesty more. And when he said, "I'll be fine, but you disrespect your mother's wishes," Hannah had closed her eyes against the pain.

"They're making me go," she said, like she was a small child. "Because of what David did."

Her father softened, and motioned her over to his rusted metal bedframe. She passed him the water glass beside his bed, and he sat up awkwardly, braced against one elbow. He drank deeply and lowered himself back on the bed, wiping his mouth with his arm. "Thank you," he said.

He kept his hand resting on her hand; he would never have done this back in Russia, but Eretz Yisrael had softened him in this way as well.

"Ah, bissela," he said. "If only life were simple."

"Isn't it?"

He laughed. "You're still your mother's daughter."

With that, he seemed to have said what he wanted to say. Hannah didn't understand the message, only that one had been delivered, and that delivering it to her had somehow made him feel better.

"Go on," he said, flicking his hands like he was getting rid of a fly. His eyes were smiling, though. "You have my blessing."

He did not mention David, which was better for them both.

"I'll come back to visit. With Ruthie," Hannah said.

"And your other new babies," Avraham said.

"Soon," Hannah said.

Her father's eyes were closed as she exited his tent. The ghost of her mother whispered in Hannah's ear. "Don't leave him. You promised."

If only I could have warned her then, too.

CHAPTER 25

"*I* WANT TO HAVE ANOTHER BABY," Hannah said to her husband.

"I'm aware," he said.

"Now," Hannah said.

David was bent over a tray of vegetable seeds, each type in its own cup; he looked up at her. There was a smear of something on his cheek, which she thought at first was dirt from the fields but on closer inspection was pencil lead. "We have nothing to eat," he said.

"I'm making dinner," she said, although she knew this was not what he was referring to. Still, she had found some potato peels and thickened them with the last bit of flour and was up to her elbows in the dough for latkes. There was almost no oil so they would be dry. But at least it was food.

She had a ridge of flesh on the inside of her cheek where she had been trying to eat her own flesh in her sleep. She ran her tongue over the angry line.

"It's Rosh Hashanah," David said.

Hannah paused. For a moment, she had forgotten the time of year. At Kinneret you could tell by the crops, but there were no crops here yet by which to measure.

"Today?" she asked.

"On Tuesday."

"We will eat for a different holiday," she said, referring to the latkes.

"Eggplant?" he asked.

"Chicken," she said, playing her part. It was a silly joke, she thought, but David always found it funny. But his brief smile was weak, and his expression grew angry, and he gestured to a gathering place at the base of the mountain. The halutzim had formed a circle around a tall redhead who was serenading them with his fiddle. Every once in a while, a loud whoop rose up.

"Don't they see there's work to do?"

"Let them celebrate," Hannah said. "They've made it to the homeland!"

There was truth in this—and sarcasm. She remembered her own wild optimism from the early days, and longed for it back. Eretz Yisrael was still her dream—but dreams took so much work and she was so tired.

"I suppose we'll mark the New Year," David said, his fingers buried in his black curls.

Hannah nodded, too tired to form words. Whether, and how, to celebrate the Jewish holidays was a debate they had been through a thousand times. They agreed, without needing to discuss further, to mark them, but lightly, focusing on their agricultural significance.

"I'll choose some girls to help you cook," David said.

Hannah imagined, wearily, how he would look over the young women.

"I want to have another baby," she said again. She was think-ing of her father's words to her before she'd left him. She didn't let herself think about the first baby she'd had taken from her, or about the other children who had been playmates for Ruth at Kinneret and had absolved her of the need to produce a sibling. Here, the air was filled with a ghostly silence, despite the halut-zim who never stopped laughing and singing. It was a silence that ran under sound. A hungry silence.

"Not yet," David said.

"We don't have much time," said Hannah.

She and the other women had come to Palestine thinking they could make a new world. But now she saw that sexual equal-ity made it easy for men, not women, to settle their urges. What women wanted—what she wanted—was deeper than a climax. It was something more elusive, something she found hard to name for herself, and if you could not name something, how could you claim it?

A child was easier.

It hadn't occurred to her that David might say no a second time.

"Look around you," he said. "We're starving. What would we do with another child?"

"Starving is a little strong," she said.

"The moment isn't right."

She could hardly believe he dared to say this to her again, but she forged ahead.

"What about populating Eretz Yisrael with little Jews?"

In the distance the halutzim had linked arms. The red-headed fiddler raised his bow and the dancers hummed with anticipation. Night was falling and the wheel began to spin and the fiddler poured himself into his instrument. The pioneers in their loose white shirts and khaki shorts bounced up and down and sang at the top of their lungs. They were surviving on instinct alone, as Hannah had once done too. In the first years at Kinneret they had eaten salty Arab goat cheese and drunk water and lost half their body weight and things had been fine.

More than fine. Wonderful.

"Ruth needs someone to play with," Hannah said.

David looked far into the distance, squinting. And then Hannah heard the sound, over the music, of someone calling his name, emphasizing both syllables: "Daaa-vid!"

David got to his feet; dusk had fallen and no doubt he could no longer see the seeds he had been sorting.

"I should go," he said, gesturing with his chin toward where his name had been called.

"I'm not done talking," Hannah said.

"Later," he said, already leaving.

"Fershtinkiner," she said, loud enough for him to hear, but he didn't turn around. He had the privilege of being only where he wanted to be in his mind. Whereas she was forced back into her body again and again.

Ruth grabbed Hannah and held on to her waist; she tried to use her mother to hold herself up, lifting her own feet off the ground and hanging there.

"Ouch," Hannah said.

It was early morning, and already sweltering. Sun fingered its way under the fabric of the tent. The first tent erected had been for Ruth and Hannah; it was ostensibly David's tent too, although he had not come to sleep with them last night, but had stayed awake until all hours of the night, dancing with the teenagers. Hannah had heard the sound of them singing "Hatikvah" as the sun finally rose.

She could not help but feel that the halutzim giving the first tent to Ruth had been a way to both provide shelter for the child, and also to remove her from view.

"Imma?" Ruth asked.

"Yes, Ruthie."

"Shalom!"

"Shalom bubala."

"Can I swim?" Ruth asked, and then flopped down on the mattress and began to pull at the white thread that had come loose from the edge of her bed sheet.

"Don't do that love."

"Don't do that love," Ruth said back.

Hannah cocked her head to the side.

"Ruthie," she said, cautioning.

"Ruthie," the little girl repeated.

"Not now, Ruth," Hannah said.

"Not now, Ruth."

Hannah turned her back and began to straighten their things. There was a corrugated washboard and she put it outside the tent, and she took the thread Ruth had pulled and bit it off with her teeth. "It's too early to swim," she said. "Let's go find someone for you to play with."

There was nobody for Ruth to play with. And when her daughter repeated, "Let's go find someone for you to play with," a kind of quiet desperation came over Hannah that she had not felt before. Was this really the plan? To have a child here, alone, in the company of adults? A lone girl in the wilderness of Palestine, stubborn and powerful enough to drive her mother insane?

She had not wanted to leave the old place and the resentment drew up again inside her body, filling her like smoke. She was so worried about her father. She was disappointed in herself for breaking her promise to her mother, and afraid, and she did not know what to do. The Agency had said they needed her and David to establish the new place, the new idea: the first big kibbutz after the small ones. It was an honour to set the stage for the new Zionism that would eventually cover the whole land. But everyone knew the real reason David had been asked was because of the blood feud. His face could not be seen around the old parts.

Ruth had found another thread and was pulling at it like she'd done with the first.

"I said stop, bubala." And before Ruth could echo her she said, "What would Liora think?"

But it was an empty threat. Hannah knew Ruth would have been delighted to be back in Liora's sphere, the woman who had shepherded her from infancy into toddlerhood and then childhood, the one who had been her mother in everything but name. Ruth would have been grateful to receive even Liora's reprimand. And she seemed to sense Hannah's impotence and rage, because when Hannah exited the tent, shoving the canvas aside and nearly toppling the whole structure, Ruth followed on her heels, grabbing at her waist again.

"Ani ohevet otach, Imma," she said. She hung onto Hannah, as though for dear life.

Hannah softened as she looked down. Ruth had picked up her doll Salam and was carrying it tucked under her arm, where it fit perfectly.

They walked together into the sweltering morning. A group of halutzim was trying to work the old wooden plough. It swerved, refusing guidance, the line behind it bending wildly back and forth. Laughter rose from the halutzim.

Someone called out, in Arabic, "Inshallah." *If God wills it.*

Someone else had been assigned the task of ordering the storeroom, and there was a stretch of muddy earth where supplies had been laid out like at a rummage sale—halters for the horses and frayed leather reins. Big iron wash basins, a fiddle bow, a large metal box containing glass lanterns with spare wicks. Trowels, hobnail boots, a pair of valuable binoculars that should have been in a case. In the middle of the chaos stood a pair of identical twins with bowl cuts and suspenders. Ruth looked from one to the other and back to the first, and then up to her mother for explanation. But Hannah felt too tired. She was surprised when Ruth marched up to the men and said, emboldening herself, "You look the same. Are you twins?"

Ruth had learned about twins from Yitzhak when the old workhorse Shira had given birth to two foals. She must have extrapolated from this to human twins, and Hannah could not help but feel a rush of pride.

She quickly reminded herself, as she had been reminded so many times over the years, that she was no more responsible for Ruth's achievements than anyone—and certainly less responsible than Liora.

"Obviously," one of the twins said.

He inserted an index finger under his red suspender and smirked at her.

Ruth looked to Hannah, questioning—she could not interpret the man's unkindness. It was not in her realm of reference.

Hannah took a deep breath. The smell of clover in the sun.

The second twin gave his brother a slantwise look, and said to Ruth, gently, "You're a smart girl. Have you seen twins before?"

"Horses only," she said. She stood on her tiptoes and peered at his face. "What happened to your lips?" she asked.

Hannah winced, but the German laughed. "Nothing happened. They're freckles!"

"On your lips?"

"Funny," he said, "isn't it."

He ruffled Ruth's hair, which she submitted to happily. He extended his hand. "I'm Samuel. And my brother is Selig."

His brother looked at the interaction without bothering to conceal his disdain, his forehead wrinkled and his marked lips puckered. Then he turned to leave.

"I'm Ruth," Ruth said, oblivious to Selig's retreating back. She shook Samuel's hand, happy to have been taken as a person of consequence.

Samuel was larger than his brother, slightly, and had a higher forehead and larger ears.

"He doesn't speak very much Hebrew," Samuel said of Selig, now that he was gone, and as though this could somehow account for his rudeness.

"I speak *only* Hebrew," Ruth said proudly, and Samuel raised his eyebrows to show he was impressed.

"You've been in Eretz Yisrael for a long time," he said.

"For my *whole life*," Ruth said. She held up Salam so Samuel could see. "My doll speaks Hebrew *and* Arabic," she said.

She arranged the headscarf so it covered the doll's forehead.

"But mostly Arabic," she said. "Because she was Sakina's." She passed gas loudly, and giggled. "You can button her headscarf into a kippah," she said, and started to demonstrate.

"Sorry," Hannah said, trying to manoeuvre her daughter out of the way so Samuel could leave, but he said, "For what?" and moved to take Ruth's hand.

"Ma shlomech?" he said.

"Tov toda," Ruth answered.

The two of them sat down among the spread-out jumble of objects. Lye soap and red plastic jerry cans of gasoline. Hannah hesitated and then sat down too. It felt good not to move.

"My brother experienced something very difficult," Samuel said to Hannah right away, like he had been waiting to unburden himself; like he had spent so long—all his life—being attached to Selig, viewed in the same light, and he wanted to snip the cord that bound them in other people's eyes. He had been waiting for someone to tell, and Hannah was there. Or so she thought. Later, she would wonder if it had been more calculated.

Samuel was not looking at Hannah—in fact he was looking away—but she could sense from the rigidity of his body that he was waiting for an answer.

"I understand," she said.

He nodded without lifting his eyes.

"He was in a prison camp," he said. "In Siberia."

Hannah made a noise of sympathy but she didn't ask why; the reason was that he was a Jew. This was the truth that Eretz Yisrael was built to counter. A place where Jews could be safe, and not fear being carted away to a random jail cell at any moment.

"Terrible things happened to him," Samuel said.

Ruth was arranging the items around them according to size, from largest to smallest—washtub followed by washboard followed by the horse-hair brushes and then thinner paint brushes—but now she looked up. Her cheeks were bright pink from the heat. "What terrible things?" she asked.

Samuel looked to Hannah, apologetic.

"It was cold," Hannah said.

"Was there snow?" Ruth asked.

Samuel said, "And ice."

"I've never seen snow," said Ruth.

Hannah said, "It snowed once when you were a baby."

"In the winter the rain is freezing cold like ice," Ruth conceded, as though preparing Samuel for something he could not now imagine in the heat. Then a look came over her face; she realized her mother had succeeded in distracting her. She turned to Samuel directly. "What happened to your brother in prison?"

She ran a tin fork over the corrugated washboard, making Hannah grimace.

Hannah could see that Samuel was a kind man, but a man who had no experience with children. "Sometimes people are unkind to Jews," she said to Ruth. She stretched her legs out in front of her and pointed her toes.

Ruth nodded, impatient. She knew this; she had known it always. "And also to Arabs," she said, which had been another important part of the teachings in the Baby House.

"Maybe they did things to his body that hurt him," Hannah said.

"Like Abba did to Sakina?"

Samuel looked up sharply, his dark hair shining in the heat. None of the halutzim knew what had happened at the old place. Hannah and David had agreed to this covertly; there was no need to state it explicitly. It would make him look bad—it would make them all look bad—if the young pioneers knew they had been exiled.

"Maybe they hit him," Hannah said to Ruth. "Maybe he didn't have enough food." She wiped her face with the back of her arm.

Ruth was interested now. "Hit him where?" she asked.

"I don't know, bubala."

"On his face?"

"No," Hannah lied.

"On his tuchus?"

Hannah imagined a matronly Bubbe in a Siberian prison putting grown men over her knee and whacking them with a wooden spoon. "Maybe," she said.

Samuel was examining his fingernail, a pink tinge on his pale cheeks.

"Liora went to Yerushaly'im once, to learn about Maria Montessori," Ruth said. "No spanking," she added. "Children are human beings to whom respect is due."

She bit her lower lip with her teeth, but could not recall the rest of the quote. "I had brothers and sisters at the old place," Ruth said to Samuel.

"Which old place?"

"Kinneret," Hannah explained. "Where we came from."

But she knew that these new halutzim barely registered that anything had come before. They thought themselves to be the first Jews ever to settle in Eretz Yisrael.

"They were other people's children," Hannah added. "The kids were raised together in the Baby House."

"How many children?" Samuel asked.

"Six."

Hannah plucked a blade of grass and twirled it between her thumb and forefinger. "I did have another pregnancy," she said, although as soon as the words escaped her, she could not believe she had said it.

Ruth's head snapped up.

"Imma?" she asked.

Hannah ignored her, but Ruth said, "You did?"

How, Hannah thought, had she arrived at this dangerous subject? Talking with another interested adult; Samuel had a calmness to him. It was like they were a family on a Sunday picnic. Her guard was down.

"Girls can wear a kippah too!" Ruth said now, forceful, repeating what Liora had taught her. She held up her rag doll and gazed at it with a look of such adoration that both of the adults laughed. Ruth lifted the small headscarf and buttoned it, completing the transformation.

"That's true," Hannah said. "Why is that?"

She was hoping to distract the girl, but Ruth said, "What other baby did you have?"

"No other baby," Hannah said. "Only you, bubala."

But Samuel, she knew, had understood. A pregnancy was not the same as a baby. There were many things that could happen to a pregnancy in this wild land, just as there were many things that could happen to a Jew in prison.

Ruth pushed her face into her doll and inhaled deeply. Hannah hated to think what the doll must smell like, but it seemed to give Ruth some comfort. She set Salam down in Samuel's lap. "My sister," she said, reverently, batting her eyelashes.

Samuel smiled. "She's lovely."

Ruth nodded, solemn. She stood up and grabbed a long poker meant for a fire and began scraping it around the inside of the washtub. She threw the poker into the tub, where it made a terrible clang like metals doors closing. She tried to climb inside the tub, and the toe of her sandal caught on the rim and Samuel leapt forward to stop her from falling chin-first onto the metal surface.

"Thank you," Hannah said. Her hand on her heart.

"You're welcome," Samuel said. And as he looked at her, Hannah saw that he knew; not everything, but he knew enough.

Later, when she was bleeding again, she went to see Ida. She carried the rags with less shame than when the girl had been a complete stranger, but it still embarrassed her to have to hand them over. She tried to think of a decoy, another reason she might have come. David had forgotten what he had promised, to find some girls to help her prepare Rosh Hashanah, and so Hannah asked Ida.

"We need tablecloths," she said. "For the meal. Or something to use as tablecloths. Just a bolt of fabric maybe?"

Ida nodded.

Hannah said, "We need a kiddish cup. Could you try to drum those things up?"

Ida nodded again.

"And pamotim," Hannah said.

Ida's hands went to the sides of her face like she was being held up in a robbery at a bank.

"I don't have any candlesticks!" she almost shouted, her eyes wide as if Hannah had pointed a gun at her.

Hannah took a half-step back.

"I know, achoti," Hannah tried to soothe her. "But could you look in the unpacked crates and see if you can find some?" She thought of the mess of things Samuel had been standing in earlier. Surely there must be some there.

"Check with Samuel," Hannah said.

"The twin?"

Hannah nodded.

And Ida ran off before Hannah could say thank you.

CHAPTER 26

HE HALUTZIM HAD RAISED the tents and established the laundry, and now they began to work the fields. Hannah was grateful for it and resentful that she did not get to participate. All day and night Ruth was stuck to her like tea leaves, asking a thousand questions and refusing to put on her shoes. Wasn't the promise of Eretz Yisrael that Hannah would not have to do this alone? That the halutzim would raise the children together, like a big bunch of grapes on the vine, ripe in the natural sunlight and growing into sweetness? The traditional family was a path to isolation, one they would leave to the capitalist cities of Europe and America. But Hannah found herself doing things she had never had to do: wiping her daughter's behind and coaxing her to eat the last bit of porridge, which she left on her plate even though she complained constantly about being hungry.

What I would have given to do those things. All of them. But of course, I never got my chance.

Hannah fell asleep with the girl pressed to her side, and Ruth kicked her in the ribs and in the legs and she woke up with bruises

in places she'd never had them before. A kink in her neck from
contorting herself to make room for Ruth's doll. All those years of
longing for her child beside her, of imagining her cries from across
the kibbutz, and now that she had an excuse—a reason—to sleep
beside her daughter, she longed for freedom and space to move.

And yet, contact with her girl worked its magic. She breathed
in the smell of Ruth's sweet warm skin in the morning when the
hot sun pushed in at the sides of the canvas tent; she marvelled at
the dust motes in her hair and the downy fuzz still on her upper
arms and her earlobes. Hannah nibbled on her girl's cheeks as if
Ruth was made out of brisket and Ruth giggled wildly and tried to
squirm away. Hannah had never had this intimacy before—the
intimacy of waking in the same place as her child—and the loss
of what she had missed crashed over her. A milky morning with
her baby, bare skin on bare skin, both of them drifting back to
sleep with the little mouth still fastened on the nipple. The short,
pudgy legs carrying her daughter toward her when she'd fallen in
the stable and skinned her knee on a nail; Ruth pulling up her
mother's shirt to get the milk. To get the love and comfort that
was rightfully hers.

Hannah rose to go to the outhouse. When she came back,
Ruth had taken all the mosquito netting for herself.

"Saba is sick," the girl said. She stuffed the edge of the filthy
doll into her mouth and sucked.

"Don't do that, Ruthie," Hannah said.

"Did you hear me?" the girl asked.

"Yes," Hannah said.

"Sicker," Ruth said. "More sicker than before."

She got off the pallet and untangled herself from the mosquito net. There was a small hole she had poked into the mud
floor the previous day, so she could bury her blue marble and

uncover it again. She resumed this game now as though she had never stopped it, as though no time had passed while she slept.

"Are you sure?" Hannah asked.

Ruth nodded. She picked up the dirty marble and inspected it; she put it in her mouth.

"Ruthie! Spit it out!" Hannah said.

Hannah put out her hand and Ruth spat the marble into her palm obediently.

"I'm sure," Ruth said.

Next Ruth put out her palm and Hannah returned the marble. "Don't eat it," she said.

"Touch but don't eat?" Ruth asked.

Hannah recognized this as a mantra Liora had used with the children when they were toddlers; when everything around them went straight into their mouths. Although, truth be told, the thinking on the kibbutz was that children could follow their instincts and no harm would come of it.

Hannah thought of Sakina.

Harm had come of that.

"Can I come with you home?" Ruth asked.

"Home where?" Hannah asked, although she knew what Ruth meant.

"To Liora."

"To the old place?"

Ruth nodded. "When Saba dies."

"What do you mean, bubala? Saba is alive."

Ruth shrugged. "I want to go home."

Her shoulder blades were so thin, thought Hannah. So fine and chiselled as to be wings.

"We have to build Eretz Yisrael," Hannah coaxed. "Remember what Liora said? It's the most important job."

"I hate you," Ruth said. She lifted up her blue marble and threw it, hard, at Hannah's face.

"Ouch! Why did you do that?"

Sharp tears came to Hannah's eyes. She rubbed at the spot the marble had made impact, her cheekbone below her right eye. "You could have blinded me!" she reprimanded, wiping her cheeks. "You could have killed me!"

Only when she heard her own words did Hannah realize the effect they might have. Ruth's eyes widened—and Hannah could see what was replaying in her daughter's head as clearly as if it was a play the halutzim were putting on in the quarry in front of them. The lifting of the gun. The small girl's body falling. The silence in the air after Sakina's head hit the ground, and later, the adults—Arab and Jew—looking down together. The doll—the one that was now beside Ruth—thrown into the corner, her scarf pushed back off her face.

"I'm sorry, Imma," Ruth said, and started crying.

Hannah wrapped her arms around her daughter. She rubbed her back but did not try to talk her out of her tears; they would come, they would exhaust themselves. To prevent them would just lead to more later.

And comforting Ruth was comforting to Hannah too. The pleasure went in both directions. Maybe it was wrong to meet her own needs through the child's more pressing ones, but it had been such a difficult journey here and she wanted the warmth of another human body. She wanted to be needed by someone, and Ruth needed her.

"It's okay, bubala," she said, and held the girl against her chest while she cried.

"Are you going to die?" Ruth looked up, mucous smeared on her cheek.

Hannah wiped it away with her thumb.

"Why? Because of the marble?"

Ruth nodded, her eyes wide.

"Of course not!"

Ruth sucked her lip. Her black curls hung over her face.

"But Saba is."

Hannah was silent.

"Saba!" she said more forcefully, as though Hannah was hard of hearing.

"Everyone is going to die one day," Hannah said, resigned.

The great tiredness was creeping over her again; she wanted to lie down. She wanted to be left alone, even for a moment. To pull a pillow over her head and rest.

"Not one day," Ruth said.

Hannah didn't answer.

"One day," Ruth said. "Not eight days."

She had picked up Salam again; Hannah saw the upside-down semi-circles inked on the doll's face that made it look like she was asleep. Lucky doll. Ruthie was now rubbing the doll's fabric against her cheek, hard enough to chafe the skin.

"What means the Hebrew? Who went around there?"

What was Ruth talking about now? Hannah had no idea.

"Salam went around there and so did all the children," Ruth said, now narrating some private story to herself. "If you can't see what's coming, don't say anything mean at all."

"Bubala," Hannah said, absently. She rubbed at her elbow.

"The berry is poison," Ruth said, holding her blue marble to the doll's mouth and making her eat it.

David was gone all day, and came to their tent in the evening. He crouched down and kissed his daughter on the top of her head.

Hannah thought of the Angel Gabriel with his own mop of dark curls, his own ears that made the perfect ledge for a pencil to perch on.

"I'll see you in the morning," David said to his daughter.

"Inshallah," Ruth said. And, "Why do you have a gun?"

"I'm on night guard," David said.

"I thought you were going to study?" Hannah asked.

"I am. On night guard."

This had made sense in the old place, where they were so established that guard duty was merely a formality. But here, it seemed to Hannah, he could do better than reading Marx while the Arabs galloped past with their flaming torches.

The fierce old Arab Habib knew what had happened to Sakina! David seemed the only one who had forgotten.

He stood, his knees popping, and stretched his back. He tucked the gun into his satchel, along with his book.

Ruth said, "Abba?"

He looked at her; she passed him a stone.

He went to put that into his satchel too, but she said, "No, here," pointing to a little pile she had started of stones that held her interest.

"Then why did you give it to me?" David asked.

"Put it on the pile," Ruth said.

"You could have put it there yourself."

"I wanted you to have it."

"You want it on the pile."

"I want both," Ruth said.

"That's ridiculous," David said, much too harshly.

Ruth shrugged, as though to say this was just the way it was. Don't blame the messenger.

Hannah looked at the pile of stones. It resembled a grave.

"Saba is going to die," Ruth said.

David did not disagree. "Everyone dies," he said, echoing Hannah's earlier words. "Every one, and every thing."

But this was tiresome to Ruth.

"Come on, Salam," she said. "Let's go home."

CHAPTER 27

*T*HE FOLLOWING AFTERNOON a wagon galloped into the yard. Hannah thought it would be a tourist come to witness Rosh Hashanah in Eretz Yisrael, but it was Yitzhak at the reins. The horses heeded him perfectly, stopping and looking around with their huge rolling eyes, like they were silently judging the new place and how much—or little—had been accomplished here.

Yitzhak's hairline had receded further in the time since she had been away. He looked heavier than she remembered, sturdier, and somewhere in the back of her mind she thought that perhaps David was right. Perhaps they really were starving here at the new place.

When her old friend climbed down from the wagon and said, "Avraham has died," it took Hannah several moments to understand what he meant. Later, she briefly wondered why he had used her father's first name—but death belonged to the group along with everything else, and to identify the old man as Hannah's father might privilege her grief. Still, she saw the intense compassion in Yitzhak's eyes, and how he hated to be the one to tell her this news.

"But I was planning to come soon," Hannah said, thinking of her promise to her mother. "I *am* coming soon."

Yitzhak rubbed the corner of his eye with his knuckle.

"I'm sorry, achoti," he said.

It was not the news itself but his expression of endearment that broke her. Hannah sunk to her knees, like she was a marionette and her handler was slowly putting down the strings. One by one her joints collapsed; onto her knees, onto her face, her hands stretch out in front of her head in the dirt. She tasted Eretz Yisrael. She whispered the blessing with her face pressed into the earth: "Barukh atah Adonai Eloheinu melekh ha'olam, dayan ha-emet."

Blessed are You, Lord, our God, King of the Universe, the Judge of Truth.

Hannah had been nine when she first bled, older than Ruth was now, but still several years too young. The blood was her shame, and she did not tell her mother, but found some bleached rags in the cupboard under the sink. At the table, her mother drew the light from the Sabbath candles over her own face, her cheeks pink and warm, and Hannah saw the monster of flesh and need that she herself was growing into. But after the meal her father came to her. He was carrying a bouquet of wildflowers he had picked from the riverbank and the ditch by the dirt road. The purples and yellows and blues like splatters of paint. His white beard touched the flowers he held against his heavy black coat.

"Mazel tov," he said, and his smile was so warm and kind, her eyes filled with tears.

"What for?" she asked, but she knew. And she knew, too, that he would not embarrass her by saying it. It was not proper. It was not of the world of men.

"Like the flowers you grow," he said instead, quoting from the Torah, and he handed them to her.

He did not touch her cheek. But she could smell tobacco and the leather of his teffilim and she knew that if the rules permitted he would pull her close and hold her in pride and love. Her father. The man who had made her. To Hannah, there was no other God.

She looked up, remembering where she was.

Why was Yitzhak crying too?

Seeing his tears sobered her; if they both cried it would allow this thing to have actually happened. A moment ago she hadn't known; the horses, all morning, had been galloping toward her from Kinneret, carrying the news of her father's death, but she had been innocent until it reached her.

"The chevra is preparing the body," Yitzhak said now.

What chevra? What body? But even as Hannah wondered, she knew that they would wrap her father in winding sheets and place him in a hole on the hillside with the others. The young halutz Gesher who had taken his own life. Several who had died from the kadachat. And the clot of blood that had been her first child was in that same earth, under a boulder.

In his early adulthood, Hannah's father had resigned himself to a life—noble but loveless—of Torah. And when the niece of his teacher came to town and he fell in love at the ripe age of thirty-one, he had never stopped being grateful for God's intervention. He was grateful even when all the children were daughters—Shulamit, then Anna, then Hannahleh, the baby, whose eyes were an unlikely blue that reminded him of his own mother. He had let her play with the tassels on his prayer shawl; on Friday nights when he blessed her she felt him linger a little longer with his favourite.

Would he have followed Shulamit or Anna here? For him, Eretz Yisrael was a concept, a symbol of Jews' spiritual freedom more than an actual place. She still remembered the look on his face when she had told him what she was planning to do. Make Aliyah? His baby Hannahleh? And she wanted her Abba to come with?

Now she forced herself to stand; her bones felt hollow, made of straw. Someone might blow her over at any moment.

"I'll take you when you're ready," Yitzhak said.

"Are they digging the grave?" she heard herself ask.

Yitzhak nodded, the smallest gesture he could afford that would answer her question.

She saw that his shirt was torn. The halutzim did not believe in God, but there were still superstitions that nobody wanted to forsake.

"I'll tear my shirt too?"

He shrugged, to say it was up to her, and then nodded his agreement.

She looked down and saw she was wearing the shirt with the red embroidered sleeve. It had landed on her in its rotation through the laundry, as though she had been singled out, or marked. But not to be passed over. It was as if the vanity had marked her for pain.

The cotton tore easily. In tearing it, Hannah was tearing her father out of this world. She felt that she had been the one to kill him.

"I'll go and pack my things," she said. "It will just take me a moment."

And then: "How long will I be gone?"

She felt like a young child who needed to be told what was happening.

"Shiva lasts a week," Yitzhak said. He rubbed at his elbow where the skin was chapped hard as a callous.

It came back to Hannah that Kinneret had adopted an abbreviated shiva, a version that lasted two or three days, giving comfort to the bereaved but allowing everyone else to continue their work.

"Who is digging the grave?" she asked.

He said, "We'll talk on the way."

Hannah returned to her tent. She took a shirt and the bonnet she had been sewing—for a baby—and she saw Ruth's doll Salam that had once belonged to Sakina. Why was it here? Why had they not given it back to Anisa? She saw how any belonging of her father's now held a weight she could never have imagined; how every shirt and tallit and teacup he had touched would be now immediately precious. Surely Anisa must feel the same about her child's belongings? She added Salam to her meagre pile of things and went back out into the yard.

The tears had started down her cheeks again, and there was something in the depths of her stomach crawling up, up, trying to escape. Soon she would not be able to keep it down any longer.

One of the young women, Sarah, was standing by the water pipe in a gorgeous red dress. Even in her grief, Hannah felt the shock of it—she had no right to be wearing such a dress. Hannah asked her to go and tell David she was leaving.

The girl nodded dumbly.

"I'm ready," Hannah said, turning to Yitzhak.

"Don't you want to bring Ruth?" he asked, tentative.

Hannah thought for a moment. She wanted to be alone with her father, to say a proper goodbye. She shook her head no.

Hannah could almost not believe how established the old kibbutz was in comparison to the new one. It felt similar to when she'd first arrived in Jaffa, with the boats going in and out of the harbour, merchants with their spices, the souk smelling of fish and goat meat and salty cheese and bargains. Menachem was in the distance in the special protective netting they had ordered from America; the bees were producing enough honey to sell in Rosh Pina. The dining hall shone with a fresh coat of paint in preparation for Rosh Hashanah. Several new buildings had been built in her absence, and the sawdust was still fragrant in the air.

It was threshing time and long rows of men—they seemed much older than the boys at the new place—were stepping and swinging in time. And in the garden, Liora, with the golden complexion she was named for, was doing what she had always done. The children were gathered around her; they were dipping apples in honey. How Ruth had loved that. Liora's laugh rang out. The vegetable plot around her was in heavy bloom, the cucumbers long like phalluses, the tomatoes fat and pungent; you could almost taste the salad that she would be able to make. She would sprinkle it with the salty feta Anisa gave her.

How could Sakina's mother stand to share her food with the Jews after what had happened?

Well, she had other children, Hannah thought. But no, that was ridiculous. That must only make her grief more difficult.

Liora had seen Hannah. She smiled brightly, happily surprised, and waved. She and Hannah were friends; there was no reason for them not to be. David had taken it upon himself to ignore Liora after his indiscretion, which left Hannah in the role of friendly compatriot. And Liora loved Ruth as her own. Hannah knew that Liora wanted to run over and hug her, ask how she was, ask how Ruth was, say how much she missed her, but she would not leave little Susan and Noam and Gabriel in the middle of a lesson. Education was of utmost importance.

"Shalom!" Liora called out, and the little ones waved too, momentarily curious to see if Ruth was with Hannah. Then they were pulled back, as children so easily could be, into what was happening directly in front of them.

It was Rivka who came over while Yitzhak tied up the horses and Hannah stepped down from the wagon. Despite the constant press of shock and sorrow inside her, Hannah almost laughed— they didn't call her Thin Rivka for nothing! And her new pregnancy somehow made the rest of her seem skinnier than ever, as though every ounce of fat had been given to the baby. Her arms were like sticks, her legs long and coltish, her cheekbones sharp. Nothing showed she was expecting a child, other than the protrusion itself, which looked like she had taken an enormous melon from the garden and stuffed it up her shirt.

Another boy, Hannah thought, from the way she was carrying. She had looked the same when she was pregnant with Gabriel.

"Shalom, chabibti," Thin Rivka said, which was what they had all called each other in the early days, when they were as determined as possible to respect the Arab character of the land. "I'm so sorry." She took Hannah's palm and pressed it in her own. "May his memory be for a blessing."

Hannah knew she could ask Rivka about her father's last days, but she didn't want to, not yet. That would be for later.

She felt with Rivka, as with Liora, that they were part of a sisterhood—and although neither other woman had ever given voice to this, it was understood between them. She imagined it was the fondness that wives of the same man—like the Arab wives?—might have. She and Rivka loved each other. And both were grateful to not be in the other's position.

They each had borne David's child. When Rivka had become pregnant, Yitzhak had stepped in as the child's father. And for some reason there had never been resentment between the two women. Perhaps, reflected Hannah, it was because she had been so occupied with baby Ruth at the time. The arrangement was odd, but it worked. There were so few women; they refused to let the men come between them.

I can now say that this hurt me. Why was it was so different later, for me? And I admired Hannah so. If I could, I would have told her.

I would have said just how sorry I was for what would happen.

Hannah hugged Rivka, and stepped back to admire her protrusion.

"B'sha'ah Tovah," she said. *All at a good time.*

Rivka said, "Come Shevat, inshallah, there will be a new child in the village."

Hannah had heard, via Chaim who delivered the mail on his camel, that Gaby from the kitchen was pregnant as well. And Malka had her cherub. The kibbutz had voted; there would be a whole new cohort.

"Where's Ruth?" Rivka asked, as though she was asking about her own child.

"I left her with David," Hannah said.

Rivka's silence contained a mild kind of reproach—David still had a soft spot for Thin Rivka, but it wasn't reciprocated. "I hope he takes care of her," Rivka said. "I hope he pays attention."

"I do too."

"I miss her," Rivka said. And Hannah was thankful for those words. A child, after all, belonged to them all.

Hannah had become pregnant too early. The Agency had sent the new rubber sheaths but the halutzim were young and sex oozed from their pores and the supply was gone barely one week later. After all, they had made their way to Eretz Yisrael. There was a whole field heavy with wheat; they had planted it themselves. They had cleared the rocks and ploughed the earth and sewed it with the seed of their new hope. Now they would reap. Nothing could stop them.

David's idealism had been pure in those days, and his belief in complete equality had been unfettered by any real experience. Hannah knew that his desire to take her pregnancy to the collective was not, to his credit, because of unkindness. It was based on a kind of clear logic that Hannah had begun to feel was somehow above her. There was no space between his theory and his practice.

"We need to tell the group," he'd said, when she came to him shyly with the news that for two moons she hadn't bled. But it was not the lack of menstruation that had made her realize what was happening. She had felt the conception. There had been a little hook, like a needle making a stitch. A tiny, surprisingly painful tug. The men said that kadachat was Eretz Yisrael branding itself on them. But for Hannah, this sharp pinch was what tied her to the land.

She was here. Her child would be born here.

"I'd like to keep it between us for a while," she'd answered, bashful—when she thought back to it now, her naïveté made her cringe. How little she had understood about so many things.

David had taken in a long breath through his nose and held it. Then he exhaled.

"We agreed in the meeting that we wouldn't start having children until after Yom Kippur," he said.

The Day of Atonement was still eleven months away, and Hannah was already three months gone. Their child would have almost a year of experience the other children did not.

"Does that matter?" she'd asked. She was being rhetorical.

But David took her literally. "We don't have the resources yet. Remember what the group discussed? And we can't give up the labour. We need every hand in the fields."

A chill had come over Hannah as she'd remembered—how could she have forgotten?—the seriousness of that particular debate. Those were the days of ridiculously long meetings; the issue of pregnancies had been discussed as though they were discussing the breeding of poultry or the cross-pollination of the olive and almond trees. Finally, after a week of discussing pros and cons, of some people remaining rational and others losing their cool, of one person even storming out and eventually leaving the kibbutz, they had decided there would be no babies for another year.

The couples—she and David, Liora and Yonatan, Lenka and her chaver Reuven who later left her, and Eretz Yisrael, entirely—had been left to their own devices to prevent it from happening.

Part of the reason for stalling was the hope of finding a chavera for Yitzhak, so he, too, could be among the first generation of parents. Everyone was equal, but it went without saying that Yitzhak's fine genes and political experience were especially desirable. For there to be, among the first children, a son or daughter of Yitzhak Cohen would be a boon for the kibbutz, and for history.

There was the sense, in everything they did, that history was something they were writing, that their version of history remained to be told.

"We will need to take it to the group," David said.

"And ask them what?" Hannah had said.

"Whether we should have the child."

She looked at him; his dark eyes were on her, and there was tenderness in them, a look of concern that told her he loved her and that the baby, after all, was his too. But there was something else underneath that. Something that had been there all along, but that Hannah was recognizing for the first time.·

Her heart began to pound. David continued to talk, but she was counting. She was adding up, in her head, the way the voting would go. They would try for a consensus, but if they could not reach one they would take it to a vote. Reuven would vote no. Yonatan would vote no. The women, surely, would vote with her. But perhaps not Rachel, who had fought in the Russian Revolution alongside the men and who had arrived with a pistol in her knitting bag.

And her parents? They were like mascots—old people, granted a place of honour for having crossed eternity to get here, but their wisdom and experience was discounted when it came to anything meaningful. They would not be given a vote.

There had been, in the early days, a chaver named Meyer. If he had come later, they might have understood he had some kind of illness. An obsessive need to control things, to line up the calves and their corresponding pails of milk, and to go back and check that he had done it correctly. He remembered entire pages of Herzl and could recite them verbatim. There was no nuance to his thinking. He had grown up in an ultra-Orthodox home, and although he had abandoned his observance he brought with him a rigid adherence to rules, rules that did not necessarily make sense but were God-given and therefore irrefutable. A person's job, a man's job, was to follow them to the letter. And Meyer's God was now Zionism.

It was Meyer who suggested the voting be blind. That for the halutzim to have Hannah watching as they cast their ballots would influence them too heavily.

"And should they not be influenced?" Yitzhak had asked, his big hands loose in his lap. "By the feelings of their comrade? The one who is actually carrying the baby?"

A silence fell at the word "baby." The halutzim had somehow managed to forget it was a human, and not livestock, they were discussing.

"Are we not here to make a better world?" Yitzhak had asked.

Even Meyer was quiet in the face of that. But eventually he said, with the slightest hesitation in his voice, "Indeed. We are. And the issue is whether this better world includes children now, or in another year."

Hannah could have left. She could have gone to Mother Lobinsky's, or to the Jaffa Port and sold her body, or to the big city of Yerushaly'im that she had not yet seen despite having crossed the ocean for Zion. But what would she have done alone with a child in the walls of the old city? And she had her parents to think about. She had brought them here, despite their aging bodies, despite the fact that their dream of Eretz Yisrael was so divorced from the thing itself as to be something else entirely. She couldn't just leave them with the young and impulsive halutzim. Nor could she drag them away from the little comfort they had finally established.

Unless David had insisted. Unless he had agreed to go with her. But he did not agree.

He did not agree.

In the time it took them to debate Hannah's pregnancy, the cow had given birth to two calves. Both had survived, and were now producing more milk than the kibbutz was capable of using.

Liora had had to make preserves out of the abundance of field berries. And what did a baby need besides milk and fruit and love? Hannah had wanted to say that, but the panic making its way through her body would have meant her words coming out shrill and tinny—womanly—and the kibbutz was about calm logic and rationality.

The discussion lasted longer than any had before. Longer than the debate about buying the American thresher instead of the chicken incubator, which had ended in Reuven throwing a glass storm lantern that had shattered against the wall. They were not able to come to a consensus. They talked all night, and worked all day, and talked the entire following night. Then they slept. But there was barley in the fields that needed to be cut. They could not—not even these pioneers who liked nothing more than to debate—continue any longer. They had agreed, as Meyer reminded them. In the absence of a consensus, they would vote.

Meyer had set up a macabre kind of polling station, and had them enter one at a time. Thin Rivka sat with him to ensure fair play. Hannah could surmise, from the way the debate had gone— which she had observed, silently, like a person waiting for the gallows—who had been on her side. Thin Rivka, of course. Yitzhak, of course. Reuven had gone back and forth, but in the end he had come down on waiting another year until the dairy herd was more robust. He must have voted no. Rachel had voted no. Yonatan had voted no. Meyer, obviously, had voted no.

They had, at the last minute, allowed her parents a say—after a long side-debate about the importance of each voice being equally valued. It was clear how they would lean, but it was agreed eventually that their life experience could not be discounted.

Hannah's parents had entered Meyer's booth, a corner of the

chicken barn, with such sorrow and resignation Hannah could not bear to think of it. Her father wearing his tallit, like he was entering synagogue; her mother's hands gnarled and wrinkled, as if she had become an old woman overnight. Their daughter was pregnant, and they would vote on whether to abort the baby. For this they had left their homes? For this?

Still, the tally did not add up. Hannah went over it after, tears rolling down her face, blubbering incoherently. She made columns and put check marks in them and sobbed with her head in her hands. She was three moons gone. A boy, she knew. Would that convince them? It would not.

David sat watching her, not trying to soothe her because there was no soothing her.

"How does this add up?" she asked. "Did Lenka lie to me? Did Gaby?"

She had her hand pressed against her belly. It was too early to feel the baby move but she imagined a half-formed heart beating its protest.

"Who?" she asked desperately. "Who?"

When she looked up at her husband, she saw the answer. It made her catch her breath.

"No," she said. "You didn't."

David was silent. He knew better than to answer.

Hannah blinked in the light as though seeing a new world.

Somewhere out over the vast land of Palestine a high note of mourning had started its sound.

She ate the Rosh Hashanah meal with Yitzhak and Rivka in the old dining hall. It felt so good to be surrounded by people she knew, people who knew her, like family. The special holiday challah was fat and round and gleaming like the wheel of life. There was a pilaf with raisins and almonds, and Gaby's famous cucumber salad. Several chickens had been killed and roasted. Hannah knew the pain this caused the children, for whom the chickens were playmates—after school every day they went straight to the barn, the boys lunging at them to make them shoot upward into the air in a display of squawking feathers, the girls clutching them tight on their laps and stroking their heads like they were kittens. But Susan and Noam and Gabriel sat quietly with the meat on their plates; they understood that Ruth's Saba had died. He was the old man in their village. He had been, in a way, a Saba to them all, with their own grandparents back in Minsk and Berlin and, in Susan's case, Philadelphia.

Thin Rivka held Hannah's hand through the meal. Hannah barely ate. After, she passed mechanically through the orderly line with her plate: a bucket of soap, one of water, one of bleach. Rivka brought her to an empty tent that was used, on occasion, to sleep visitors to the kibbutz, but Hannah hesitated at the sight of the bare pallet, the lamp with no oil and nothing to light it besides.

"Would you rather sleep with us?" Rivka asked, meaning with her and Yitzhak. Gabriel slept in the Baby House with the other children.

Hannah shook her head. "I'm fine," she said. "But I'll go for a walk first."

"Would you like company?"

"No thank you."

But she was glad that Rivka knew where she was going without her having to say it: down to the Sea of Galilee, past the tall reeds and Lenka's long-suffering flock of geese, along the path by the water to the Arab village.

There, she found Anisa in her yard, as though she had been waiting for Hannah.

"Salam," Hannah said.

Anisa had aged, observed Hannah. It was as though, in a single year, ten years of life had ripped through her body. Her black hair was now streaked with grey and the circles around her eyes had a purplish hue. Behind her, at a distance, four men sat around a card table smoking their pipes.

"Would you like to come in?" she said, in Arabic, although Hannah knew she could have asked the same thing in Hebrew.

"Just for a minute," Hannah said. "I have something to give you."

Anisa looked surprised, but she turned and led Hannah into the mud house. To say that Anisa had been Hannah's friend would have been overstating things, but they had been amicable with each other, balancing their menfolk's virulent distrust. In the early days Anisa had sent her brother Youssef down to show the halutzim how to build a taboon. The Arab's mud oven was more suited to the land than the open fires the pioneers had been using. Later, she had shown Rivka and Hannah how to make strong mint tea—it was still called Anisa Tea in the kibbutz, and, Hannah supposed, it always would be.

And when Hannah had needed help ending her pregnancy, Anisa had shown her how.

"How are you?" Hannah asked now.

Anisa nodded, but didn't answer. It was not a snub, it was her way. Hannah could read so much in her silence. Anisa turned to get some kindling so she could boil some water, and Hannah saw she was pregnant again. She was not surprised; to her eyes, the Arab women seemed always to be pregnant, and in this Hannah envied them. There was no haggling over who would plough the field and who would fix the threshing machine (although of course, they did not have a threshing machine) and who would raise the babies. They did not have long meetings into the night to discuss the politics of childcare or the division of labour. The mothers would raise their babies. How complicated did it need to be?

"You're with child," Hannah said.

Anisa nodded. "Come March, inshallah, there will be a new child in the village."

Had not Thin Rivka just said the same thing? Surely, this was what everyone wanted—for new life to take the place of the old.

Anisa did not say to Hannah that she hoped for a girl, that the new child would replace her Sakina, but she didn't have to.

Hannah felt a sudden terrible longing to put a hand on Ruth's forehead, to lean in and smell the back of her daughter's neck— warm and damp like yeast.

She fished in her satchel and came out with Salam. She held the doll out to Anisa.

"Ruthie still had this," Hannah said. "I thought you might want it back."

Anisa leaned over to see what Hannah held; she was only a few feet from Hannah when she saw her dead daughter's doll. She inhaled sharply, as though she had been slapped.

"Oh!" Hannah said. "I'm so sorry! I just thought . . ."

She looked down at the doll, the upside down crescent eyes that made its face look like it was perpetually crying. "I know Sakina must have loved her," Hannah said.

Anisa was busy rearranging her features, burying the grief as quickly as it had ambushed her.

"No," she said, "I don't want it."

She was carefully, studiously keeping her eyes away from the doll.

"I'm sorry," Hannah repeated.

"Ruth can keep it," Anisa said. But she couldn't help herself, and when she did glance at the doll she flinched again. Then she paused. "What's that?"

She pointed at Salam's head. The headscarf was pinned up with the button, so the doll was wearing her kippah.

"That's nothing," Hannah said. "It's just a button I added for Ruth to play with."

But Anisa had seen that Salam had been made into a Jew.

Once, at the beginning, the halutzim had sent their children to the Arab village during the rainy season while they tried out a new drainage system. The Arab children's eyes were often clouded with trachoma, but the kadachat did not affect them in the same numbers. Anisa's mother had said the Arab women would take care of the Jewish children. And they had. It was not so long ago, really, that this had happened. But now a line had been crossed. Hannah had come, hoping to reconcile, to absolve herself of her husband David's sins, but now she saw it was not to be. She had known Anisa a long time—ten years, even more. Youssef had always treated the settlers kindly. There had been a measure of good will between these particular groups of Arabs and Jews. They had traded recipes and medicines for their children and tips on where to pick the wild herbs.

"My father just died," Hannah said, thinking of this long history. But Anisa looked up in disbelief a second time. Was it grief for old Avraham that Hannah could see on Anisa's face? No. Anisa thought Hannah was looking for pity. She thought Hannah was trying to liken the death of a grandfather from old age to the death of a six-year-old by revolver.

The bonds between them were now broken. A grown man had murdered a child.

Hannah had hoped her and David's exile would be enough. That by leaving Kinneret—by David leaving—there might still be room for something to grow back up through the cracks. But in Anisa's expression lay something larger, dark and without contours, without shape. A kind of stain that was spreading now and wouldn't be stopped. Could Hannah blame Anisa? She could not.

She, too, knew what it was like to lose a child.

"I think of Sakina," she said. The words were like sandpaper in her throat. But it was worse, to pretend nothing had happened.

How she longed to hear her own lost baby named out loud. She would have called him Avraham, after her father. Avramchick. Little Avraham.

Anisa nodded. "Thank you," she said. And then, "Please go."

Tears sprang into Hannah's eyes; she blinked them back. "Of course," she said.

As she turned to leave a little boy ran to Anisa and tried to climb on her lap; her pregnancy prevented him from making it all the way up.

"Yallah, Mahmoud," Anisa said.

She stood up wincingly, one hand on her lower back. But she waited for Hannah to leave first.

"Happy New Year," she said.

And Hannah said, "Thank you."

They washed her father's body, carefully removing anything extra from his skin, but his beard they left as it had been. They immersed his corpse in the swirling pool at the edge of the river used for a mikveh. Then her father's body was wrapped in tachrichim. The sash was tied around him in the shape of the letter Shin. The hole was deeper than it needed to be, but nobody wanted to risk jackals, and they all remembered what had happened at the beginning, before they had learned this lesson.

Like the others, Hannah believed death was an extension of life. The land of Israel needed Jews to nourish it, with their work and their sweat and then with their flesh. Avraham would grow again in the barley harvest and the reaping. It was a kind of pagan confidence that would have horrified the religious Jews back home, but she belonged to the young halutzim who saw how the land worked. They had succeeded in removing themselves from the money lending and the textile mills and the diamond trade. They were connected with the life cycle in a way that gave them confidence to say what was plainly true: God was not only in the synagogues. He was here in the wild purple wind and the dark clouds and the cold sky in the winter as the sun went down. And this, all around her, was the heaven where her father would now reside.

This much, Hannah was right about. I wish I could have told her.

Hannah watched the burial, unblinking, refusing to look away. She remembered how her father had let her play with his tallit when she was a child, using it as a tent under which all the little Israelites gathered. Bubala, he had called her. And sometimes bissela. His little bit. And now he was dead. It seemed absurd.

She stayed at Kinneret until the following Sabbath. On the last night, she dreamed her father came to her and stood in the open tent flap and told her another child was coming. The birth would be hard and she must give herself to it fully. When she woke with her heart in her mouth she knew she had been dreaming in Hebrew. After ten years, it had eclipsed Russian as the language of her deepest self.

She slowly opened her eyes. Yitzhak was at the tent's door. Dust motes danced in the shaft of sunlight behind him. He came in, like a brother, and sat on the edge of her pallet.

"It's morning," he said.

She was still half asleep; she nodded. She ran her tongue over her fuzzy teeth.

"We'd like to come back with you," he said.

She rolled over to face him.

"Where?"

"To the new place."

"Okay," she said, and closed her eyes for a long moment. Then opened them again.

"Why?"

Yitzhak hesitated. "You seem very lonely."

She looked at his face and saw there was another reason. "Yitzhak," she said.

"There was an accident," he said.

Hannah sat up. "Ruth?" she asked, as the quicksand seeped into her limbs.

But Yitzhak shook his head, reassuring her. "Someone else," he said. "Some young halutz."

"Samuel?" she asked. "A twin?"

Yitzhak thought. "No. Dov?"

Hannah strained to bring a face into focus, but there were so many pioneers.

"There are always accidents," she said.

Yitzhak nodded. "Apparently it had something to do with David."

Hannah lay back down. She shielded her eyes with the back of her arm like she was a sunbather on a beach.

"How do you know?" she asked.

"Chaim," Yitzhak said.

News travelled faster by the postman's donkey than by any telegram back in Russia. Hannah had heard that in Jerusalem, on the desk of the head of the Agency, sat a telephone. She supposed this would be faster still, but it was as hard to imagine the telephone as it was to imagine Moses actually parting the Red Sea.

Hannah put the pieces of Yitzhak's words together in her head. David had done something wrong. It would be some act of bad judgment, some harsh acting out. Yitzhak and Rivka had heard, and they wanted to come and supervise him. The Jews could not afford David making another mistake.

She knew how David would feel, that he would want her to object. But she didn't have it in her. How good it would be to have Yitzhak and Rivka at the new place, people she knew and loved.

"Okay," she said.

Yitzhak nodded.

"And Gabriel," he said.

"Of course. Ruth will be happy to see him."

Hannah wondered for the thousandth time if the children understood their relationship. Was it possible for children to know things without ever being told?

I could have answered then: It was not just merely possible, it was the very way they learned. They saw what was around them and they took it in. It grew. It changed. There was a kind of mutation. And then it came back out of them—in unimaginable time and form.

CHAPTER 28

*H*ANNAH SAW RIGHT AWAY that Ruth had been injured.
"What happened to your leg, bubala?" she asked
when the girl jumped into her arms.

"I hurt it."

"It looks sore!"

The cut itself was very thin, as though a finely sharpened
knife had split the skin open. On either side was a ridge of
flaming red, puffed up and corrugated. At the top and bottom
of the cut, yellow pus wormed its way out; it made Hannah
think of the grubs that sometimes made their way into the
almond trees. She pictured her father, who had taken to horti-
culture at Kinneret after all, carefully cutting a gash into the
bark and extracting the culprit, the location of which he could
somehow divine.

"Capnodis," he had said, while the cream-coloured worm
withered on the end of his knife in the light. "This bug is the
enemy of every fruit tree in Eretz Yisrael."

"How did it happen?" Hannah asked Ruth now.

She touched the cut, tentative, and Ruth winced.

"I missed you, Imma. Where did you go?"

Ruth looked so much taller than she had when Hannah had left, as if in ten days she had grown into a different girl entirely.

"I had to go back and say goodbye to Saba."

"Why goodbye?"

"He died," Hannah said, simply.

Her directness was not because she wanted to take the moral high ground and be honest, but because the thought of lying exhausted her.

She braced herself for crying, but Ruth had an empty look in her eye, as though she could not properly remember who it was they were talking about, who her grandfather had been.

"I cut it with the candlesticks," she said.

"Pardon, bubala?"

"In the yard with the marbles and the boy's bare tuchus."

Hannah took her daughter's chin, and gently moved her face so she could look her in the eyes.

"Your Saba died," she said. "He is buried in the earth now, back at Kinneret."

"Abba told me," Ruth said. And then, "Did they hurt him?"

"Who?"

"Like Selig."

How had Hannah forgotten this endless parade of non-sequiturs? Returning to motherhood was like returning to a different world altogether.

She sat down; she put her head in her hands. How she missed her father. There were suddenly a million things she wished she had asked him, about his ancestors, about his childhood, about his faith. Now he was gone. There was nobody left to ask. And there never again would be.

Ruth rammed her head gently into Hannah's ribs. She made some mooing noises. She said, "If I had a twin, there would be two me's."

"Yes," Hannah said.

"Gabriel is here!" Ruth said, remembering.

"You can play with him tomorrow. It's time to get ready for bed," Hannah said.

"I'm not tired."

"You have to sleep so your leg will heal."

Ruth looked down at her leg like she had forgotten it was there. "It stinks," she said, and then, "I lost Salam!" Tears appeared in her eyes. "I can't find her anywhere."

A wave of guilt hit Hannah. "I have Salam," she said. "I'm sorry, bubala."

She fished again in her satchel and came out with the doll, arranging its headscarf neatly around its face. She tried not to think of Anisa's stricken look. She expected rage from Ruth too, but there was pure joy in her voice when she sang out, "You have her? I thought she was gone!"

Ruth grabbed the doll and pushed her face into it and inhaled deeply, like she was smelling a spring bouquet, and then held it at arm's length and gazed at it with a look of such adoration that Hannah had to laugh. "You sure do love Salam," she said.

"Sakina loved her too," Ruth said. "And now I'm her Imma instead."

Hannah shut her eyes.

"Let's go brush our teeth," she said.

"When Selig was in jail, did he get a cut on his leg?"

"Teeth," Hannah said.

"Moo! Moo! Moo!" Ruth declared, meaning, I asked you a question. I want an answer.

"I don't know if he cut his leg," Hannah said. She cleared her throat. "Maybe."

"His brother said they hurt him." Ruth paused. "Imma?"

"Yes, Ruthie."

"I want to give him Salam," Ruth said.

"Samuel?"

"Selig."

"It was Samuel who was playing with you." By this, Hannah meant, Samuel is the nice one.

"I know," Ruth said. "But Selig is sad."

"He is?"

"Because they hurt him in jail."

Hannah looked down at her daughter. Ruth's face was thinner, more angular, than it had been just last week. Her curls were knotty; it had been some time since anyone had combed them. Hannah put her hand on the top of Ruth's head; she curved her fingers like she was about to play a scale on the piano and dug the tips of her fingers into the scalp, massaging.

"Ah," Ruth said in pleasure.

"You're a nice girl, bubala."

Ruth said, "My leg hurts." A tear appeared at the corner of her eye. "It hurts so much!" she said, and suddenly she was wailing.

Hannah hoisted her up onto her lap. Clearly, Ruth had been waiting for her mother to come home. The tent smelled vaguely of urine and Hannah wondered if Ruth had had an accident in her absence. Or maybe they just needed new hay in the mattresses. At Kinneret they had stuffed them with dried seaweed from the Sea of Galilee.

Ruth cried, long, satisfied sobs, sobs she had been saving up for the safest person she knew who was not Liora. Hannah held her patiently. Ruth was full of pain and she was discharging it, the way the body would cough up a chicken bone lodged in the throat.

"Tell me again what happened?" Hannah asked.

"I cut it!" Ruth choked through her tears, angry that her mother was focused on the cause of her injury instead of the effect.

Hannah sighed, and ran her hand along the neat row of vertebrae down her daughter's back. Ruth felt warm. Hannah looked again at the wound on Ruth's leg; the circle of red around it seemed to have grown wider in the few minutes they had been talking. It now encompassed most of her leg below the knee. "Let's get you to bed, bubala."

But Ruth grabbed Salam, and hugged the doll fiercely to her chest, and kissed its filthy face, and breathed in its smell. She shouted, "I want to give Salam to Selig."

"In the morning."

"*Now*," Ruth said.

"Hush," Hannah said.

"You're stupid!" Ruth screamed.

Hannah raised her eyebrows. Ruth liked to whine, to wheedle and get her way, but she had not spoken to her mother like this before. She would not, in a million years, have spoken to Liora in this voice. But Hannah knew that she was paying the price for having left her daughter and for whatever casual negligence might have happened in her absence, and she braced herself, willing her voice to come out calmly.

"In the morning," she tried again, but Ruth caught a whiff of her lack of certainty, her surprise, and stamped her foot and started to scream more loudly, an undifferentiated stream of sound like an alarm.

Young halutzim were walking past the open tent flap;

Hannah saw them crane their necks toward the terrible sound. Ruth thrashed about looking for something to kick. She bared her teeth. She slammed her clenched fists into the straw mattress, and lunged for her mother's face; Hannah pulled away just in time.

Soon Hannah would wish for this rage, for this lashing out, for this embodiment of the life within her daughter. But now she was embarrassed, ashamed.

The halutza Shoshanna stuck her head in. "Can I help?" she asked.

Hannah was so grateful she could almost have wept—but a child took up all the space for feeling. The mother was left with the task of making a container for the child's emotion. Where was the mother to put her own emotion? Nowhere.

"I'm okay," Hannah said to Shoshanna. And then, "I'm sorry."

Later, Hannah would remember this, and reflect that if Shoshanna had been a mother herself she might have known to tell Hannah there was nothing to apologize for, that she wasn't responsible for her child's bad behaviour. But Shoshanna must have believed that Hannah could control what Ruth did. Turn it off or on, like the new water tap. And Ruth, feeling Shoshanna's presence, increased her performance, relishing the larger audience. She held on to her leg and shouted, "It hurts, Imma. Make it stop!"

Shoshanna's bushy eyebrows went up. "Is she okay?"

Hannah was about to say yes, she was okay, but there was an edge to her daughter's crying that made her panic. There was a performance happening, true, but the pain at the core of it also seemed real. She shrugged, admitting that she didn't know.

The screaming increased, seemed to peak—and Shoshanna covered her ears. Then it dissolved back into crying.

"Does it really hurt that much?" Hannah asked, and Ruth looked at her with complete disdain.

She said, "I want to give Salam to Selig."

Hannah had forgotten entirely that this had been the trigger for the outburst.

"Oh," she said. "Okay."

Ruth blinked. She rubbed her eyes and looked up to make sure she had understood correctly. "Can I?"

"Yes."

Like that, the storm was over. Shoshanna quietly stepped away.

"Let's put your shoes on first," Ruth said to her doll. "And brush your teeth." She looked up through her drying tears, to make sure her mother got the joke.

Hannah watched anxiously as Ruth stood. The child winced when she put weight on her leg and sat back down on her bottom. "Uppie me," she said to Hannah, her expression for please pick me up.

Hannah hefted the girl with effort and thought how she would not be able to do this for much longer. Her baby was now a child. She needed a new baby to replace the old. To replace what she had lost, and lost before.

Selig was cleaning the rifle. The parts were spread out in front of him on the ground, and several dirty rags, and a jerry can of oil. The bullets lay scattered, like the gun had just been repeatedly fired.

"I brought you my doll," Ruth said.

Hannah braced herself, but Selig only smiled.

"Salam," he said.

How did he know the doll's name?

STRANGERS WITH THE SAME DREAM

Ruth nodded, solemn. "To make you not sad anymore."

Hannah set her daughter down on the ground.

"Thank you," Selig said, with no trace of surprise. It was as if this was the formal completion of something that had been envisioned earlier, by the two of them, the result of a long negotiation. Hannah felt like she was coming in halfway through a story. Something must have happened when she was away.

Selig took the doll. He put it up on his shoulder like she was an infant he was about to burp. His palm entirely covering the doll's back.

"I'll take good care of her," he said.

"And give her back," Ruth said.

Now Selig was the one to nod solemnly.

"You have my word."

He was speaking only to Ruth; he had barely looked at Hannah to acknowledge her presence. He clearly had no feelings about her one way or another. But Ruth he treated as his equal.

"I hurt my leg," she said. As always with Ruth, saying it made it true, and she suddenly winced and lifted the weight off it and then sat down on the ground.

Selig nodded. "I'm sorry to see that," he said.

There was a dark shadow across his jaw where a beard was growing in. In the distance they heard someone singing, in butchered French, "Allons, enfants de la patrie, le jour de gloire est arrivé!" There was the tantalizing smell of frying onions in the air.

"Did they hurt your leg in prison?" Ruth asked.

Hannah was about to shush her, but neither Ruth nor Selig looked at her.

"Yes," he said. "But mostly they hurt my back." He pursed his lips, and scrunched up his nose. "Would you like to see?"

Ruth nodded.

Selig put the doll down tenderly on an upended orange crate. He adjusted its headscarf, then turned around. He wriggled his suspenders to the side and lifted his loose linen shirt. Beneath it was a stretch of skin almost completely covered in scars.

Gnarled, knotty ridges twisted like the branches of a tree. Hannah drew her breath in sharply.

"They did hurt you," Ruth said, pensive. She reached for her mother's hand, to reassure herself of her presence, but she did not take her eyes off Selig.

Selig pulled his shirt back down, tucked it in and rearranged his suspenders. He turned back to face Ruth.

"They did," he said. "But I got better."

They looked, together, at Ruth's leg. The hot red oval with the black line through it, the crusted pus, the swollen ankle.

"Will I get better too?" she asked.

Selig didn't answer.

"I suppose I didn't heal entirely," he said instead.

Ruthie stuck a finger up her nose and dug around with it.

"I'm not as kind as I used to be," Selig said, like he was speaking of somebody else.

"What do you mean?" Ruth asked.

Selig tilted his head. "People bother me," he said. Then added, "Only adults," so Ruth would know she was excepted.

"Are you mean to them?" she asked.

A slow smile crept over Selig's face. "I do like to play tricks," he said.

Ruth bent her wounded leg and jumped up and down on her good one. "I like tricks!" she said, and hooted like an owl.

"It's easy to play tricks when you're a twin," he said. He looked at Ruth, weighing her trustworthiness. "Would you like to hear a trick I played on Ida?"

Now Hannah felt that she was genuinely intruding, that she was overhearing something private. She took several steps away and turned her back. But not before seeing first the look of wariness on Ruth's face. "I love Ida," the girl said.

Selig said, "Do you?" In his tone, Hannah could hear that he was truly interested.

Ruth must have nodded, because Selig said, "You're right. I don't know what gets into me sometimes."

"What did you do?"

"I made her think I was my brother. She gave me two gifts, one for each of us. But I didn't tell Samuel. I kept them both for myself," Selig said.

There was silence from Ruth, but when she spoke her voice was conciliatory. "Everyone makes mistakes," she said—a direct quote from Liora. "You should just say you're sorry."

"I suppose," Selig said, but Hannah could hear his doubt. "No," he said. "It's too late for that."

CHAPTER 29

*R*UTH AND GABRIEL PLAYED together all the next morning. Ruth sat with her leg propped up and Gabriel pretended to be the doctor and then he pretended to be her mother and then he pretended to be Liora. Ruth endured this with a happiness that bordered on ecstasy. Hannah was certain that if her leg had not been so sore she would have stood up and danced.

After a while, Hannah left them and walked down to the fields. The harvest was going so slowly. The project of the new Work Brigade Camp, which had sprung up with such vigour, had now slowed almost to a standstill. Arriving back, she could see the enterprise through Yitzhak's eyes, and also the questions: Was David capable of spearheading this new kibbutz? How had they trusted him with it in the first place?

Something had happened to one of the machines when she was gone—she did not care to ask for the details—and now there were halutzim making flower crowns while the ripe wheat and barley went to seed all around them. Her desire for a new baby rose up in her again, a vine climbing a trellis, and then, when she tried to ignore it, a vine wrapping around her throat and strangling her. Being home had revived it in her—seeing the young girls pregnant, the sense of purpose Liora had as she presided over the next generation. And the halutza Malka walking around with the little cherub on her hip. His pink cheeks and fat hands; his eyes following everything with alert intensity.

At the same time, Hannah's father was in a hole in the ground. He would never again fill the bowl of his pipe with tobacco, or don his prayer shawl and walk down to the river to bathe before the Sabbath. He would not call her bubala as she now called Ruth. He would never again press his long beard against Ruth's cheek and make her howl with laughter.

Saba, Ruth had called him. Using the new Hebrew word. But Hannah knew her father wanted to be called Zaidy.

Were there any of her father's wishes she had not sacrificed for the new land?

David was by the machines, fiddling with the back of the gas tank on the tractor, his face creased as though he was trying to solve a puzzle. He straightened when he saw her.

"I'm sorry about your father, Hannahleh," he said.

David had known her father for almost twenty years; and her father had loved him, if not exactly like a beloved son, then like an estranged one. But now when David tried to draw her into his arms, she bristled involuntarily.

He looked up, over her shoulder, and she knew without turning that someone was walking behind her; she knew it would be the halutza with the long curls and the bright red embroidered shirt, the one with the flowers on it.

Hannah remembered what it was like to be the object of David's affection. He was what the grandmothers called chedevnik; something in him shone in a way it did not in other men. It was understood he was not a safe choice. It was understood he was a heartbreaker. But a woman would have to have an incredible amount of resolve to say no to him. He was the kind of man that, if you were so lucky as to be chosen by him, you went to. Willingly. With the feeling that the world was showering you with flowers and they would rain down around your head forever.

How sorry Hannah felt for the halutza with the red sleeves. Sarah. Whatever was coming for her would cause so much pain.

"How was it at home?" David asked, turning back to Hannah. He ran a finger over the bridge of his nose.

"It was fine."

"Did you sit shiva?"

"No," she said.

In truth they had done what they had always done, since the first halutz had died from kadachat: the abridged version of shiva. But Hannah knew that David's question was not really about her father's passing. It was about his own legacy: Were they still doing things the way he had arranged them?

"Liora says hello."

David nodded curtly. He adjusted the pencil behind his ear.

"Why are the halutzim not in the field?" she asked.

He looked over to where the others were lounging by the new water pipe. One of the boys was doing handstands. He would take a few steps on his palms, wobble, and then fall over to applause from the others. Someone else was juggling oranges.

"It's a circus," Hannah said.

David lined the heel of one foot up with the toe of his other foot, like he was walking a balance beam.

"And what about the boy who got burned?" Hannah asked.

David looked up.

"You heard?"

"Chaim."

A look of defiance crossed David's face: this meant she was right in thinking the accident had something to do with him.

"I don't know," David said.

"What do you mean? Weren't you here?"

"Accidents happen," he said.

"And your daughter's leg? What happened to her?"

He shrugged.

"Well?"

"I don't know," he said. He was like an insolent child with one non-answer to every question posed by an adult.

Hannah laughed, a sharp, loud laugh. She thought how different this David was to the one he showed everyone else. How he had given up with her: he no longer tried to hide the selfishness at his core.

Why was it, wondered Hannah, that to love someone was to show them your worst side? Love was like an anaesthetic that slowly wore off, leaving the throbbing pain and the bloody open wound. There was no preventing it. All love progressed on a downward trajectory from euphoria to resignation to disdain.

She supposed this was how David saw her too. As something to be tolerated, even endured.

"She has a huge cut that is oozing pus. She has a fever," Hannah said. As she said the words, fury rose inside her. She had left for one week, because her father had died. And this is what had happened. "She won't stop crying," Hannah said. "She's in so much pain."

"Who?" David asked.

Hannah reached out and slapped him.

He flinched, but only lightly, as though she had been helping him by removing a mosquito from his cheek.

"It was Ida's fault," David said. He rubbed at the red mark on his face, but said nothing else about what she had done.

"The girl from the laundry?"

David nodded.

"What was she doing with Ruth? What happened?" Hannah asked.

David didn't answer.

Hannah tried again. "Did you even bother to clean the cut?"

David's black curls were dirty and there was mud on his right calf. She knew he thought having Eretz Yisrael on his body made him part of Eretz Yisrael himself.

"Of course I did," he said.

"With soap?"

He shrugged.

"It's infected! You need to use soap," Hannah said. They were silent, both thinking of Igor.

David shrugged again. "This is different," he said. "It's only a scratch."

Thin Rivka and the Angel Gabriel wanted to light the Hanukkah candles with Ruth and Hannah. It was something the children had all done with Liora, who had an uncanny knack for reinstating old Hebrew festivals that nobody knew had existed in the first place. She had plucked from the air the Israeli folk dances that had been lost to time, and taught them anew to the children. She had shown them how to celebrate Tu B'Shevat, a holiday nobody had even heard of. And she had found an old menorah that Rivka pulled out of her bag now, along with the tapered candles to fill it.

The rains had come and the day was cold. Ruth had been moved to the infirmary, which Hannah saw afresh through Rivka's eyes: a dirty tent with almost no medical supplies and a barrage of near-corpses struck down with malaria. And not nearly enough blankets to keep anyone warm. There was a man in the corner covered in terrible burns. Hannah realized with horror that this must be Dov.

Ruth had taken a turn in the night; her breathing was shallow and rapid. But when Rivka began to arrange the candles, she perked up and said, "Refill from the right, light from the left," the mnemonic Liora had taught them.

The Angel Gabriel said, "She's right," confirming Ruth's words. He, too, remembered what Liora had taught them.

"Pass it to me," Ruth said, holding out her hand for the menorah.

"I want to do it," Gabriel said, sulking.

"Gabriel," Ruth said, imitating Liora's voice when she wanted to be obeyed, and the boy did as told.

Hannah smiled at the sight of the two children beside each other again, their heads bent over the menorah. From the back you could hardly tell them apart.

Thin Rivka said, "New halutzim arrived in the night."

"Oh?"

"Thirty of them!"

"The big kibbutz," Hannah said. "It's what he wants." And then, "It's what the committee decided on."

"I heard there's a doctor," Rivka said.

She gestured discreetly to Ruth's leg. The child had fallen back on her mattress, her eyelids closed.

"Really?"

The Angel Gabriel was intoning the blessing, solemn, with reverence: Blessed are you, O Lord, who kindles the light of the Hanukkah candles.

Why had David not told her there was a doctor?

"Are you sure?"

Rivka nodded.

Hannah said, "I'll go look as soon as we're done lighting the candles."

After, Rivka confirmed that Hannah had fallen asleep beside Ruthie. She and Gabriel had tiptoed out to let them rest. It had been such a long day—a long week, a long year. Hannah could have slept forever. But a red shadow on the back of her eyelids woke her, and a crackling sound. She was dreaming of a bonfire. The fiddle played, and the hora wheeled wildly while the sparks flew up into the night. When she opened her eyes, the straw mattress was on fire. The menorah had fallen over, both of the lit candles—the shamash and the candle for the first night of the festival—flaring out into a blaze. She leapt to her feet and stepped on a tinder and screamed. Ruth's eyes flew open. The girl looked around her and saw the flames; she tried to stand but her leg wouldn't take her weight and she, too, shouted, and then started to cry.

There was a bucket of dirty water by the door. It had been placed there not in case of a fire, but so wet rags could be submerged and placed on the burned man's body and on the fevered necks of the kadachat victims. Hannah lifted the bucket and threw it on the mattress. It didn't put out the whole blaze—she used a stray sandal to stamp down the rest—but the fire was easily quelled after that. She stood, breathing hard, a hand on her chest. How had she fallen asleep? How quickly everything could go up in smoke. What if she hadn't woken up in time?

The following afternoon, Ruth wormed her way over to her mother and clung onto her calf. She said, "I want Salam."

Hannah ran her tongue over her eye tooth.

"You gave her to Selig. Remember?"

"I want her back."

"Okay, bubala. I'll go get her."

She took Ruth back to her own tent, and laid her on the mattress. The child closed her eyes and lifted her little fists over her head, the way she had done as a baby. She was asleep immediately. Hannah went to find Selig. He was exactly where he had been the day before, only now the pieces of the gun had been reassembled and he was holding it in his hand.

"I'm sorry to bother you," she said. "But could Ruth have her doll back?"

But Selig's mood had changed. If he had ignored her before, he now spoke with utter disdain.

He said, "I gave it back."

"You did?" she asked.

"To David."

On her way to find her husband she kept an eye out for the doctor, asking the halutzim if anyone had seen him, but nobody had. She eventually located David by the partly built cow shed—a frame with no walls, so you could see right through it—watching Sarah. Hannah could almost see the fantasy that would be playing in his mind: a chalet in the Alps, stumbling across a young milkmaid. For a moment she was caught off guard, and the soft part of her emerged unexpectedly, like a child popping her head around the corner.

Was she not good enough? How had this happened?

"Ruth wants her doll," she said to David.

She didn't say anything about the fire the previous day, that Ruth could have died, that the thing that pretended to be an infirmary was now filled with wet coals and soot.

"I almost fixed the tractor," he said. And when she was silent, "I have the part."

"He said *you* have it."

"I do!"

"The doll?"

David scratched his forehead. "Who said so?"

"Selig."

"Who?"

"The twin."

David touched his nose, and then the pencil over his ear.

"Did Selig give it to you?" Hannah asked.

She could see that it was hard for David even to pretend to pay attention. He began to page through his notebook, looking for some unnamed item. "I don't know." Then his eyes focused, remembering. "Yes."

Hannah cleared her throat.

He looked at her blankly.

"Can I have it?" she asked.

He looked around, as though it might materialize in front of him. Then he said, "I don't know where it is."

The flames of rage rose in her again; she held her breath to try and keep them down.

"Thin Rivka says there is a doctor who can help us," she said.

"With the kadachat?"

"With our daughter."

"The doctor is sick," David said.

It was like he was telling some twisted joke. Was this possible? A doctor had arrived and already fallen ill?

But I knew David was right, of course. And the doctor would not recover. He would join the ranks of the lost, rising past me, and away.

"There's a nurse," David said. And from his voice Hannah could tell she was beautiful.

"The doctor is too sick? How bad are the convulsions?"

David said, "He's from America," like this explained everything.

Hannah thought of Ruth back in the tent, alone without her mother, as she had been in the Baby House. Hannah carried around a longing for her own child, even when the girl was right there in front of her. There was nothing she could do in the face of this kind of love. The only recourse was to try to make her child happy.

"Please find the doll," she said.

David ran his eyes over her, evaluating her mood, the seriousness of her request and the consequences if he ignored it. He bobbed his head. He saw that she meant it.

CHAPTER 30

*T*HIN RIVKA CAME AND TOOK Hannah's arm and tried to lead her out to the field where the pioneers were dancing.

"But . . . Ruth," Hannah said. "I need to find the doctor." She remembered what David had told her, that the doctor had fallen ill. "The nurse," she corrected herself.

Rivka looked at her, all cheekbones and pointy chin. "We'll find the nurse," she said. "Come and dance first. You need this. Ruth will be fine for an hour."

Hannah let Rivka take her hand. They passed Samuel by the water tap, and said a brief hello.

"Will you dance?" Hannah asked.

"It is all one big dance," the boy said.

Hannah laughed. They kept walking and soon drew up to the spinning wheel. The redheaded boy was bent over his bow, sweat pouring off his face. The moon dripped down like nectar. The wild ring was like something at a carnival, with lights strung up and flasks of whiskey that had appeared out of nowhere circulating freely.

She saw the girl that David loved—Sarah—in the beautiful red blouse he had allowed her to keep. She was in the centre of the circle, like the cherry on the top of a cake.

"They're all so young," she said to Rivka, gesturing with her chin.

Rivka laughed. "We were that young once. Not so long ago!"

Hannah was only ten years older than these pioneers, but she felt like she had a hundred years on them. The wheel spun madly. These were the people who would make Eretz Yisrael? These children?

She joined the dance and let it take her over. It was like falling into the arms of an old familiar lover, one who knew—had always known—exactly how to please her. The night was so hot, the Milky Way smeared across the sky. When she linked elbows she felt the heat and sweat of her neighbours, their pulses beating there, just under their skin. Her feet had always known these steps, the hora of her childhood, the hora that would be her old age. She was taking her rightful place in the circle of things. She danced and she danced.

When the circle finally wound down, Hannah walked back toward her tent; two halutzim, a boy and a girl, were standing by the river. The girl was Ida, who had washed Hannah's bloody menstrual rags so discreetly. A sweet girl, all innocence. Had David tried to blame her for Ruth's leg? Hannah scoffed to herself. She tried to remember the name of Ida's chaver. He was a boy David had told her about, an exceptional worker, a true heir to the Zionist project. This boy led Ida by the arm out to the fence at the edge of the field. Even at a distance, Hannah could see their cheeks were flushed from the dancing. The girl's skirt was still swaying around her knees. As Hannah watched, the boy took

Ida's glasses off her face and put them on his own. The intimacy of it was almost more than Hannah could bear. It was, she thought, as though Ida's body was an extension of his own; as though he needed to see something clearly and she would be the one to help him do it.

Levi. The boy's name was Levi.

Had Hannah ever loved a man like this? She had. But her memory of it was in her mind; she could not remember that particular bodily joy. Was she capable of a love that pure now? Romance was done for her. But a baby might tell her about other forms of love.

When Hannah reached her tent she saw a girl walking unsteadily toward her.

"Elisabeth," the girl said, and extended her hand. She looked at Hannah expectantly, as though her name should mean something, but Hannah looked back blankly. There were so many new people arriving every day now.

"Elisabeth," the woman said again. She giggled. "The nurse."

Everything in Hannah stood at attention. "Oh" she said, "a nurse!"

Elisabeth just laughed again. "I hear you have a sick daughter," she said, more seriously.

Tears sprang into Hannah's eyes.

"Would you like me to come and look?" the young woman asked.

She had long, smooth hair almost down to her bottom and Hannah had the impulse to reach out and stroke it. "But it's night," she said.

Elisabeth's eyes softened. She swayed on her feet and let out a quiet belch that she covered with the back of her hand. Hannah suddenly saw the girl was drunk.

"Why don't you come in the morning?" she said.

Elisabeth nodded. She hiccupped and swayed again. By the time Hannah left, the girl was on her knees in the ditch, vomiting.

CHAPTER 31

*T*HE NEXT MORNING THE HALUTZIM were up at dawn, and back to work. It amazed Hannah, their ability to exist on no sleep—to thrive even. She felt there was not enough sleep in the world to sate her.

Of course, it was a mother's tiredness. But there was also a deeper exhaustion, one that was existential. Did everyone feel so tired from just being alive?

She went to the infirmary and found Elisabeth waiting as promised, repentant from her night of drunkenness, her cheeks a greyish hue. They crouched beside Ruth together. The girl was on her back with her fists in a tight ball on her belly and her cheeks flushed. Her dark curls were plastered to the sides of her face with sweat. Sometimes she still made nursing faces in her sleep, trying to extract milk from the long-lost nipple. There was a doctor in Vienna who was writing about this, a doctor David had spoken of, but Hannah could not remember his name.

Elisabeth looked in the girl's throat and in her eyes and her ears, perhaps steeling herself before getting to the leg.

"It should have been cleaned right away," she said, matter-of-factly, when she pulled back the linen—a bandage would no longer contain the swelling. She got a warm salt solution and dabbed it gently on the wound; Hannah averted her eyes.

"The salt is just beading off the skin," Elisabeth said, catching Hannah's gaze. Her eyes held an odd mixture of sorrow and acceptance. How she wished she could help.

Elisabeth left, saying she was going to look for a new bandage, her long hair swinging behind her like the pendulum on a grandfather clock. Hannah had a violent urge to remove Ruth from this place. It was too dirty, too filled with decay. She didn't want to wait for the nurse to return. She managed to get an arm under Ruth's shoulders and another under her knees, and to stagger to her feet. She tried to heft Ruth up onto her shoulder, expecting her daughter to conform to her shape, rest her head maybe, but the child's body was limp.

"Bubala," she whispered into Ruth's ear.

She wanted her daughter to rest and heal, and she also wanted her to wake up, to look at her mother with love and recognition. But Ruth didn't stir.

Back at the tent Hannah almost tripped trying to lower Ruth to the mattress. She got her down finally and took off her own shoes and lay beside her. She curled her body around her girl's. They woke up several hours later in exactly the same position.

"Two Hanukkah candles in a box," Ruth said sleepily.

"I'm a Mama Bear," Hannah said.

She ran her fingers through Ruth's soft curls. The girl's breath smelled like garbage.

"No. Two things," Ruth said.

"Pardon?"

"You're a Mama Bear and I'm a goose." She changed her mind. "You're a lynx and I'm a goat."

"What would the baby say to the Mama?"

"I. Want. My. Pudding." Ruth giggled. "I. Want. To. Pee."

"Really?"

Too late, Hannah felt the spread of the warm liquid over the mattress.

"Oh, bubala," she said.

It was like Ruth was regressing in every way. Like the balloon that was her life was slowly deflating. Bit by bit her abilities were leaving: she couldn't walk. She couldn't eat. And now this.

"I'm sorry, Imma," Ruth said in a tiny voice, ashamed. Hannah's heart ached, an actual, physical pain beneath her breastbone.

"It's okay," she whispered into the small ear. "It's only an accident."

Ruth rolled over on her side and held her head, as though she was trying to protect it from something too hot, or too loud. "I want to play with Gabriel," she said. And then, "I want Salam."

Hannah said, "Let's just get this wet sheet off," but the child had fallen asleep. Her lips were parted, and her breaths were ragged and uneven.

Hannah managed to remove the sheet by manoeuvring it around the limp body. When she had finished, she forced herself to look down at her daughter's wound. Each time she had done this, she had thought that somehow, magically, Ruth would be healed, and each time she was shocked that the opposite was true. The site of the cut itself was now pale in comparison to the skin surrounding it, which was crimped and black and rotting. A section of the skin had turned hard, like the shell of a turtle. The smell of it was like the kibbutz latrine, but worse. A smell with death in it.

"Imma," Ruth said, stirring.

"Yes, baby."

"Help me."

The child's eyes opened momentarily, their clear gaze focused on Hannah's. But Hannah couldn't help. It was as though, without Hannah answering, Ruth could see this. A look passed over her face. It wasn't disappointment in her mother, only sadness and perhaps surrender. Her eyes fell shut again. The rapid breathing resumed.

Yitzhak came to find Hannah in the middle of the morning. "I need to go talk to Habib," he said.

They both knew David had been making no progress on getting the Arabs to vacate their houses. Habib's father had been born here, and his father's father, all the way back, he claimed, to Ishmael in the Bible.

Hannah was scouring Ruth's bedpan with boiling water and a ball of steel wool.

"I don't want what happened to Igor to happen to her," she said to Yitzhak, nodding at Ruth. They were both quiet, remembering the limb that had to be removed altogether at Kinneret.

"No," Yitzhak said, pensive, and then, "I think it would help if you come with me." He cracked his knuckles loudly, one hand cupping the other fist like a ball in a mitt.

"Come with you where?"

"To speak with Habib."

Where David would have scowled at Hannah's lack of focus, Yitzhak's eyes were full of compassion.

Hannah knew that Yitzhak had been acquainted with Habib from the early days, when he had ridden his horse up and down Eretz Yisrael, visiting every tent and souk, drinking zouhourat, or mint tea, and smoking harghileh with the Arab men.

"You want a woman along," Hannah said.

Yitzhak nodded. "It would help."

"Where's Rivka?"

"She's taken Gabriel to Tiberias to try and find quinine."

Hannah inhaled. "Do you need to go now?" she asked.

"I think . . ." Yitzhak said. "I just have a feeling."

Hannah understood that Yitzhak felt the land like a current through his body. He could sense unrest like a cold coming on: if his instinct told him it was time to take action, then it was time to take action.

I knew, of course, that because of this he would go down in history as one of the great founders of Eretz Yisrael.

But Hannah hesitated. She did not want to leave, even for an hour. "Can we bring Ruth?"

"Of course, achoti," Yitzhak said gently. He paused. "But isn't she too sick?"

Hannah nodded sadly. Of course she was.

Yitzhak went to put in an hour in the fields—Hannah knew he was trying to set a good example for the halutzim, even if the machines were broken—and then ate a bowl of kashi and polished the horses' saddles. The sun was high when he and Hannah arrived at the Arab village. Yitzhak nodded to her, a gesture that told her he was going around back to look for Habib—he would know the sheik's hut because it would be taller than the others.

There was only one other woman about, and a gaggle of children. The woman approached Hannah and motioned her into a mud house. A wrought iron chair sat in the centre of the room, entirely covered in red-brown rust. Hannah smiled in grateful acknowledgement and sat. A serious little boy approached and jumped right up on her lap. He batted his long eyelashes at her and held her earlobes, looking intently into her eyes.

"Salam," Hannah said.

The Arab mother smiled. Her eyes were a shocking green in her hijab. The women exchanged knowing glances. They both knew which man in the village this little one would grow up to be.

"Fatima," the woman said, and she held up a teapot she seemed to have magically produced from beneath her long robes. Hannah nodded; Fatima poured. It smelled like Anisa Tea.

Another boy approached, six or maybe seven years of age, with skinny legs that showed the contours of his kneecaps and his ankles. Hannah could see that his right eye had once been infected with trachoma, and a skim of clouds was still visible across it.

"I have a girl, Ruth, who is just about your age," Hannah said, speaking in halting Arabic.

The boy seemed to understand. "I know Ruth," he said.

Hannah drew herself up. She lifted the toddler off her lap and he scampered away.

"Really?" she asked the older boy. And then, to check, "Who is Ruth?"

Fatima was refilling the teapot at the counter, and she turned toward her son. "Abdul," she said. Reproach in her voice, a slight warning.

"She's a girl who came here," Abdul said, shrugging as if he was indifferent. But Hannah knew children, and she could see that Ruth had made an impression on him.

Abdul leaned down and made a flicking motion beside his leg, like he was cutting the flesh open with a knife.

Fatima looked up.

"Ruth is my daughter," Hannah said quickly; she wanted to prevent anyone from saying something they would regret in her presence.

A look of pity crossed Fatima's face; Hannah flinched away from it.

"Ruth got cut when the children were playing," she said quickly to Hannah.

A pit of dread opened inside Hannah's stomach. She had been repeating to herself, despite how sick Ruth was, that the wound had simply been a scratch. David's words. But Fatima had seen the outcome in the genesis of the injury itself. Here was someone whose family had been living in these hills and marshes for centuries. She knew about jackal bites and hamsin and the eye sickness; she knew about kadachat and malnutrition and ringworm.

Fatima had seen people die. Children.

And of course, she would know what had happened to Sakina.

"You didn't see the cut happen?" Hannah asked.

Fatima shook her head.

"I was inside talking to Ida," she said.

For a moment, Hannah thought she must have misunderstood the other woman's Arabic, but Fatima mimicked long braids at the sides of her head and little circles around her eyes for glasses. Had David been telling the truth about Ida being somehow involved? And then a look crossed Fatima's face, as if she understood she had said something she should not have. She glanced across the dirt floor to the counter, as though looking for something specific. Her eyes darted to a large cupboard box, overflowing with a spice grater, a manual coffee grinder, a mortar and pestle. It was like she was trying to not look at something she did not want Hannah to see.

If Hannah had not been so worried about Ruth she might have paused to wonder about this. Instead, she said, "It's not just a scratch," more to herself than to Fatima.

Fatima asked, "Is the child okay?"

Her question was tentative, like she did not really want to know the answer.

Hannah shook her head slowly. She ran her tongue over her front teeth. "No," she said. "She isn't."

"You could try a clay poultice," Fatima said, but Hannah knew this was an old witches' remedy, as useless as the smelly dried herbs they used to try and cure the kadachat.

"Thank you," Hannah said. "I will." But both of them knew a poultice would not help.

Abdul had taken his chance and fled, followed by his little brother, into the yard. Hannah saw, in the corner of the room, a charm hanging on a string; a blue bead with concentric circles to indicate an iris. It was meant to prevent the evil eye. Perhaps Fatima would lend it to her. Here, she considered, the Arabs were right. The halutzim were so against anything that suggested the universe was bigger than themselves. Bigger than what they could control. And yet, Hannah understood, it was.

Yitzhak was successful in his negotiation with Habib. Hannah did not need to hear the details to know how it had been done: graciously. With diplomacy. Not by making empty promises that could not be kept, but by drawing on the Arab sense of honour, their commitment to their word. This was, ironically, the same system out of which came the blood feud. A righteous sense of justice. An eye for an eye.

Hannah watched Yitzhak and Habib come out of the mud hut where they had been talking and she knew it was done. Habib looked not so much defeated as old. He had grown up here. His father had grown up here, and his grandfather. He had known which nettle was poisonous, how to remove the venom from a snake bite, the ratio of mud to straw to build the sturdiest walls. He knew the caves where the old prophets had lived, the mountain where Ishmael had spoken to his people. But now the Hebrews had come and his people were forced to accept the money they so desperately needed. Hannah saw the scar on Habib's cheek and knew it was from another time, an era to which he must want desperately to return. A time when he had had power, and was to be feared. Habib, Hannah also saw, was a kind man. He touched Fatima's shoulder, gently, giving some signal only the two of them understood. Perhaps he was telling her what he had done. For at his touch, Fatima stood, and gave Hannah a half-bow, like she, too, was surrendering.

Habib saw Hannah and Yitzhak out to the yard. In raising his hand he was saying goodbye to more than his visitors; he was saying goodbye to the land itself. Hannah thought that Habib deserved to be furious, that fury would not even begin to describe what was happening in his heart, and she marvelled at his grace. Was he bluffing? Hannah herself could not have pretended. For her, surrender came with rage.

CHAPTER 32

*P*ASSOVER WAS CELEBRATED IN the new place, which Hannah could not help but think of, still, as Fatima's. Where had the Arabs gone? Hannah both wanted and did not want to know.

Passover, Hannah reminded Ruth—although of course the child already knew—was the celebration of the emancipation of the Jews from slavery. God sent ten plagues on their enemies, the Egyptians, then formed a nation of the Jews.

"We were slaves in Egypt," Hannah said, and pointed south, and Ruth lifted her head weakly, following her mother's gesture as though she might see Pharaoh himself emerging from the hills.

Hannah was determined to bring her child to participate in the Seder; she would at least witness what her parents had accomplished in the revival of a dream that had come so close to being lost. On their way into the new dining hall they passed Ida, and Hannah heard her say to Levi, "I saw you at the river earlier."

A look passed between the two so laden with import it could only mean one thing.

"Will you sit with me?" Hannah heard Ida ask then, and she also heard the gladness in Levi's single-word answer, "Okay." What she would have given for a conversation so sweet and simple.

She held Ruth in her lap at the table, the child's body hot and limp. She rested her chin on Ruth's head, and watched David, who stood at the front like a small boy preparing to recite a lesson. She saw he was nervous, and her heart softened, and she felt proud. She gave him an encouraging smile. The holiday was, as David told them all, an agricultural marking of the first harvesting of the barley. There was no faith involved whatsoever. But to Hannah it seemed like an act of faith to have laid out the Haggadot, and to have sent red-haired Zeruvabel to Tiberias for the wine and the horseradish. The young halutza Shoshanna had decided to make the matzah herself, over an open fire, the way the Jews would have done so many years ago. Perhaps, reflected Hannah, matzah was supposed to be the bread of affliction, but it was as delicious as anything they had eaten since arriving. The halutzim devoured every last bit.

Ruth was the only one who had no appetite. How long had it been since the child had eaten anything at all? Her body felt like a pile of sticks, the same as when she had been a newborn. Partway through the meal she lifted her head to look around. She saw the tin candlesticks and said, "Ida's were more beautiful."

Hannah drew the girl into her chest and shushed her.

The halutzim chanted the names of the plagues with relish, dipping their baby fingers in the wine and spilling a drop for each on their plates: frogs, lice, locusts, blood, darkness. The killing of the firstborn sons was the tenth and final plague; the Jews had marked their doorposts with blood so God would know to pass them over.

Yes, God had saved the firstborn Jewish boys. But Ruth was a girl. Did she count?

Hannah thought, too, of the binding of Isaac. God had asked Abraham to sacrifice his firstborn son. Abraham had taken his boy to the mountain, the son sweetly asking who would be sacrificed? It will become clear, Abraham told Isaac. When they arrived, he bound his own son to the altar, and raised his knife. Only then was the ram in the bushes revealed.

In the Arab's Quran, Hannah knew, it was Ishmael who was to be sacrificed.

Hannah had sacrificed her first child. She had waited for God to intercede, but He did not. Her version of the altar had been a tent in Anisa's village with an old woman who knew which herbs to use. The bleeding had lasted forty days and forty nights, like Noah's flood when the world was being cleansed.

She thought of little Sakina, the Arab girl who also had not been saved.

Was this what Eretz Yisrael was for? The casualties piled up as though part of some predestined plan; as though the land itself was not able to abide peace.

Hannah carried Ruth out after the Seder. Gabriel had wandered over and was kicking a stone around the driest part of the yard. "Come play Ruthie-Ruth," he said, but the girl was too tired to even raise her head.

Shoshanna was in the garden, beside someone Hannah didn't recognize. An androgynous-looking girl, her features fine and chiseled.

"Shalom," said the girl, and smiled sweetly.

Hannah looked again. It was the pretty nurse, Elisabeth.

"You cut your hair!"

"I did."

"You look so . . . different."

Hannah tried to put her finger on what was changed about the girl. It was cosmetic, but there was also something deeper, something more essential. Hannah shifted Ruth in her arms and peered at Elisabeth, unashamed, trying to make it make sense.

"Elisabeth," she said, the answer coming to her suddenly. "You're in love."

Elisabeth smiled. "Call me Esther," she said.

Romantic love was all around her, but Hannah could not, for the life of her, remember how it felt. She thought again of the boy Levi, putting Ida's glasses on his own nose to see her point of view. And of Rivka, who had loved Yitzhak for so many years now, and who was beloved in return.

"You're happy," she said, to Elisabeth. Esther.

The girl laughed. "I am."

"A man can make you happy?"

Esther laughed again. "I didn't say a man."

They were both silent at the wonder of it. The nurse had transformed herself entirely. Hannah was awestruck. How incredible—how truly empowering—to take up a new life when you were called to.

Ruth moved and moaned in Hannah's arms. She was trying to say something but her words came out in a string of gibberish. Hannah walked with her daughter, out into the silky purple night. Ruth pressed her mouth to Hannah's ear, and one word came, and the word was "Salam."

Hannah went to the new tent and laid her love down. She arranged the mosquito netting perfectly around her, like she was arranging a bouquet of wildflowers. Then she went to find David. He was standing beside a red jerry can, his brow covered in beads of sweat, his black curls plastered to his forehead.

"Did you remember to find Salam?"

"Yes," he said.

But his glassy eyes were focused over her shoulder, watching that young halutza Sarah. Hannah did not care who he fucked. But she cared that he could not concentrate on Ruth.

"You did? Where?" Hannah asked.

David looked at her as though seeing her for the first time. "What?"

"Salam? The doll?"

"Oh," he said, deflated. "I don't know."

It was some other lost peace he was remembering.

Later, though, he came to Hannah where she was arranging the garden tools, a job that had been waiting since they'd arrived at the new place but which all the halutzim had found reason to ignore. He was carrying a play by David Pinsky, and she found herself choking with frustration that somehow, with everything that was unfolding around them, he was finding time to read. He sat down and patted the earth beside him; she sat. He passed her the book. She held it in her lap. "I was just with Ruth," he said.

A long silence hung between them. They heard someone shouting, and another voice shouting in reply.

"What do you think?" he asked finally.

Hannah touched the play in her lap, the paper thin and smooth like the pages of a prayer book. "I think we should do it," she said.

She was forcing the words up and out. It was the right thing. But she could still feel Ruth's body in her arms, could smell the stink from the gangrene and picture her daughter trying so hard to be brave, and she began to cry. She reached out to hold David's hand.

"Remember, with Igor . . ." she said, but could not finish her sentence. She didn't have to. David had been there. He had been the one to hold Igor down while Meyer used the saw. "It saved his life," David said.

"He was never the same, though."

David nodded. "You're right," he said. And then, "I can't do it."

Hannah thought of everything Ruth had already been through, the loneliness her girl had borne, and knew that she could not choose to inflict on her a single extra dose of pain.

"Thank you," she said.

"For what?"

"For saying no," she said.

David squeezed her hand. She thought he might sit with her a while, and found that she wanted him to. But she could not stand the possibility of being rejected, so she didn't ask. She got up and gave him back the play.

"Enjoy your reading," she said, and part of her even meant it. He had worked so hard and had such terrible luck.

CHAPTER 33

*H*ANNAH LAY DOWN BESIDE HER GIRL. Ruth had removed her own clothes in her fever, and was naked. Hannah curled herself around the back of her, as though she could take her daughter's body back inside her, where it would be safe.

Hannah had not expected the ferocity of motherly love, how it felt like a pain she could never be rid of. She had been prepared to love her child but not to want to serve her; and she had not known that serving her child would be the most intense pleasure, that in serving the child she was also serving herself. And she had not known that this did not end with babyhood, that the gnawing only increased with time. It was a hunger that needed feeding. As the child grew older the hunger to be close to her strengthened, as did the regret over not having held her in the Baby House those early nights. The days of abandonment she could never get back.

And now her child was regressing. Bit by bit, the milestones Ruth had conquered were being drawn back into the darkness.

"Bubala," Hannah whispered.

"Yes?"

"Are you awake?"

"Yes."

"I love you, Ruth."

"I love you too, Imma."

Hannah held her breath.

"Where am I going?" Ruth asked.

She wanted to pretend she did not know what the girl meant. But now was when Ruth needed her most. To tell the truth.

"You're going into the earth, bubala." Hannah's face was wet with tears.

"Will it be dark there?"

"No. It will be light."

"Will Saba be there?"

"He will."

"And Savta?"

"She will."

"And Sakina?"

"Yes, my love. Yes."

But deep down, Hannah still masked the truth from herself. She entertained the idea that the terrible doctor who had dared to fall ill the moment he'd arrived would rally. He would rise from the dead like the Messiah the nuns in Tiberias believed in, and administer a miraculous cure. Somewhere even deeper inside, Hannah knew this wasn't true but she also knew she could not live without her child. And the one truth eclipsed the other and did not let the first one exist.

Ruth would get better.

Ruth said something and Hannah rolled over to hear her.

"I want Salam," the girl cried weakly. "I want Salam. Please bring Salam."

Hannah had wedged a bedpan under Ruth and she now

heard urine trickling into it. She smelt the feces, dark and loose like death, slipping from her daughter's body.

She wriggled back from Ruth and reached for a Tel Aviv newspaper she had cut into squares. She separated her daughter's labia and wiped the small vulva and then separated the cheeks of Ruth's anus and wiped the smears of feces away. As she wiped, more came out, a great flood of shit that contained strings of mucous and smears of darker oil that reeked of illness. Hannah's hand was covered in diarrhea; she wiped it and went back to wiping her daughter's behind. There was no decision to not be repulsed, only matter-of-factness. The feces might be Ruth's or might be her own, there was no difference.

Now Ruth's body expelled a great flood, and she gave a little cry, and convulsed. Hannah remembered the convulsions of birth, her powerlessness against their pain, and knew that this was what Ruth was feeling. Her little body was being thrown onto the beach; it drifted out slowly with the tide until a great wave roused her and threw her again, with full force, back to the living. She was like a tiny mouse in the jaws of some great carnivore. It tossed her up in the air and caught her in its teeth. It tossed her again. Next her back would break. Next it would swallow her.

There was something animal rising up in Hannah too. She changed Ruth's clothes and wrapped her in a light linen sheet. It looked like a winding sheet for the dead—this did not escape her—but she was following some primitive instinct. She would turn everyone else away. What was happening was private; it was not of the human world. She had the urge to lick her baby's body clean. She saw how humans had designed rituals to comfort themselves and how those rituals were empty when it came to the howl of the universe. She would dig a hole with her hands and lie down inside it and bring her daughter with her. She would make a womb in the belly of the earth and they would both return to it together.

The smell from Ruth's leg was beyond comprehension. Maybe she and David had been wrong about the amputation? She could tie Ruth down and use the axe while the child slept. If she had known what had been coming next she would have done it. But it still would have been too late.

As though she had heard her mother's thoughts, Ruth screamed out in protest. Hannah pulled her daughter's tiny shoulders closer.

"Bubala?" she asked.

But there was no answer.

The infection had spread through Ruth's blood. Hannah knew this without knowing how.

At some point after this—Hannah could no longer tell when—Thin Rivka came to be with her; the beautiful nurse Esther would be of no help. Ruth fell into unconsciousness, her forehead burning like a coal. Putrid black liquid trickled from her anus. Hannah got a bucket and filled it from the river and placed compress after compress on her small forehead. At midnight, Rivka made Hannah sleep. Hannah did not remember closing her eyes, or the few hours that passed until she woke. The moon was spilling around them from the open slash in the tent. Hannah got up. Her joints were stiff and when she straightened her knees she felt like a very old woman. The woman she would shortly become.

There was a sound from Ruth's cot, a sound that delivered the news that would change the rest of her life. It was a sound that someone alive makes, but in it was the seed of the unliving. Its existence contained its opposite. The act of crossing the dirt floor to Ruth's body contained the same dichotomy, the going and the not going, the desire to see and the desperate need to not see. Equal parts propulsion and repulsion. Hannah knew that she was crossing a line between life and death, after which her own being alive would never be the same. She did not want to cross that line; she had to cross it. It was like seeing something mangled and furry in the tractor blades. Like the contractions that had led to Ruth's birth: the magnitude of the agony that came and came, but to deny it was the same as denying life. Only going through the pain would take you through the pain.

CHAPTER 34

*T*HE LOCUSTS HAD COME, just as in the Bible. "The Lord brought an east wind on the land all that day, and all that night; and when it was morning . . ." They came in a dark cloud, filling a corner of the sky over Kinneret as the sun rose. By breakfast, the entire sky was black. The halutzim had been told this would happen—it was Allah's way, Youssef had said, to build and destroy and rebuild again—but at Kinneret they had not believed it. They thought they were invincible.

David and Yitzhak and Menachem and Reuven had run into the fields with pots, empty kerosene cans, wooden spoons from the kitchen, banging and screaming and trying to scare off the locusts. They had landed on the crops, on each vegetable in the garden, on every surface of living land. The air was filled with the high buzz of their chewing. Hannah, alongside Rivka and Lenka and Gaby, had raced into the arbour. The women slapped their skirts against the trunks of trees as though they were on fire. Every once in a while the sheet of locusts that covered the ground lifted at the corner, like the edge of a paper being pulled back, but then it settled again and the insects recommenced their gnawing. The halutzim, in the end, could do nothing but watch as their whole year was devoured in the sideways jaws.

After, a silence lay on the land. There was not a blade of grass or a kernel of wheat to be seen. In the weeks that followed the halutzim grew hungry, quickly depleting their reserves, for despite knowing this day would come they had not properly prepared. The famine spread quickly, to the cities as well, and soon merchants from the markets came on horseback to beg for whatever scraps the pioneers might sell.

The Arab fields had been equally decimated. After all the arguing over the land, its destruction was without borders.

It was into this wasteland that Sakina had stumbled. The child had been looking for food. It was an unusual thing for any Arab to do—they were proud, and did not want to be dependent on the Jews in any way. But Anisa had another child who was sick with the kadachat. The little boy needed nourishment or he would die. Sakina had been sent to ask, an ambassador of peace.

Ruth had seen the girl and run out to greet her. The Jewish children did not often play with the Arab children, but these two knew each other and had always had something of a friendship. For Ruth, there was something compelling about another little girl. She spent her days with the Angel Gabriel, and Mikhal and Noam, and did not especially enjoy Susan.

"Salaam," Ruth knew to say to Sakina, and Sakina knew to say back, "Shalom."

The girl had brought her doll. Ruth's eyes widened. She was in love already.

Hannah saw that Sakina had also been sent with a jar of Anisa's cold mint tea. She knew that resources were scarce, and that this gift meant something would be requested in return. But she

wanted to delay the transaction for a moment. She wanted to give
the girls some time to play.

"Are you thirsty, chabibti?" Hannah had asked Sakina, and
the girl's impossibly long, dark eyelashes lifted, and the eyes
brightened. Sakina said yes.

There was a pail of dirty water by the barn, for the livestock.
Specks of pollen and dust floated in it, and it had a greenish tinge.
Sakina looked at the pail.

"From there?" she asked.

Hannah saw the child had been taught not to presume, had
been taught to know her place.

"Oh no!" Hannah told her. "That's for the animals. Let's all
have some of your mother's cool tea."

Hannah took the jar from the girl and went to get glasses so
they could all have a drink. She would look for some cookies too.
She would make a little picnic.

Later, after the drink, came the part Hannah could not understand. The two girls must have gone into the barn. David said he
had stumbled on Sakina hiding behind the stacks of grain. He had
thought someone was stealing their food.

Hadn't he seen Ruth? Hannah asked.

David nodded yes, but then he quickly changed his story. He
had been defending himself. He had thought it was Youssef hiding in the haystack, waiting to get his revenge.

"Revenge for what?" Hannah had asked. Was there another
crime she did not know about? Youssef had only ever been kind
to them.

David said, "Revenge for being here," and Hannah saw that
her husband would never really trust anyone. And that deep down
he also could not trust himself.

She vividly recalled how a bulls' eye of blood widened on

Sakina's dress. David had exactly hit his mark. Hannah was surprised there hadn't been more blood, but Sakina had been a tidy girl, and she had behaved in death as she had in life. It was Ruth who was a mess, crying over the body of her friend with a ferocity Hannah could barely stand to recall, and then falling into a numb kind of stupor, after which she seemed to forget she had been there at all. She asked Hannah about the event over and over at first, as though to make it something unknown, to grant herself an innocence that should have been hers all along.

But soon the only thing she could remember was the doll, and she went around calling its name plaintively, "Salam, Salam, Salam."

And so it was that Sakina was released, like the rest who followed her. Like Old Avraham and Dr. Lowen, both of whom died of loneliness and broken hearts, and like Dov, whose burns also got infected, and who succumbed to his wounds almost without protest.

David would never have admitted relief, but his secret—one of them—had gone with Dov to the grave. One mistake, at least, he would not be held to account for.

CHAPTER 35

*H*ANNAH HELD RUTH. There was still sweat on the child's brow. Time was not real. It was flexible, malleable. Hannah needed only to reverse the current, to travel upstream for thirty seconds. Flowing in two directions was the least of time's tricks—something to which I could have attested. But Ruth, in her arms, didn't move. There was a sound high in the corner of the tent. Hannah spotted the dot, almost imperceptible against the darkness, spiralling its way down. A housefly. It landed on Ruth's leg and started to feed.

Something split Hannah open: a swift slash that sliced her wide. She held Ruth's body and rocked back and forth.

"Bubala, bubala, bubala," she said.

At a certain point she looked up and found the halutzim around her. She realized she would never know their names. David was there too. He was shivering, yellow-eyed, and she saw he had again refused to take the quinine. One day he would die of the fever.

He said something; she didn't hear.

He said something again.

But Hannah's head was bent over Ruth, sounds coming from her mouth, and silence rising off Ruth like the blackest eternity.

David was repeating himself. "Stop it," he was saying.

Hannah looked up at him. His cheeks were sunken, his cheekbones sharp like two exclamation marks.

"Stop it," he said again.

"Leave me alone," Hannah said.

"I have something to tell you," David said. "I'm having another child."

The words passed through Hannah like air through an open door. Ruth's skin was cooler now. The little wings of her shoulder blades were rigid, frozen in place.

"What do you mean?" Hannah asked.

"We are here to make a new world," David said.

She looked at him, uncomprehending.

"A new world is coming," David said. "Sarah is pregnant."

Hannah blinked, looking around like a newborn. The moon leaked its milk. David's news attached itself to the small body she was holding; it was news she could stand the pain of, whereas the first pain was clearly going to kill her. Someone was sliding a thin blade under her fingernails. In some frozen Siberian prison, she heard the clank of the metal door being closed.

"Pardon?" she said.

"Sarah. A new child will be born."

Hannah knew at once this child would be a girl.

A kind of insanity came over her then, a high, frantic rage made of terror and longing and resentment.

Sarah? The pretty milkmaid. The one with the red sleeves.

Did they think this new girl would replace Ruth?

A lone violin note spread out over the hills. Across the field, the fiddler Zeruvabel chose to raise his bow to his instrument and play.

It was Esther who finally led Hannah away from the body. Thin Rivka had tried and Yitzhak had tried but the Angel Gabriel was still on this earth and Hannah could not bear to be touched by a parent. Rivka and Yitzhak were the only two in this new place who could understand the potential of this grief, and she knew that if she went close to them, she herself would be forced to understand too. She kicked at them; she hit them. Rivka with the bump above her waist for everyone to see.

Hannah needed a stranger, and Esther, the nurse, stepped in. The girl took Hannah by the elbow; hours had passed and the corpse was cold, but Hannah still clung to it, refusing. The first wave of hysteria had moved through her; there was a moment of respite. She could feel the next one, rising behind her, casting its long shadow.

"I'm so sorry," Esther said. "Zekher tzadik livrakha."

Hannah barely heard her.

"The doctor's suggestion didn't work," Esther said. She was stating a fact, not asking a question, but the words struck Hannah as if she were a tuning fork. She lifted her head.

"What suggestion?" she asked.

These were her first words in several hours, and when she spoke she tasted blood from biting her own tongue.

Esther looked at her, and Hannah saw the girl's pixie cut short around her ears. She looked like a child herself.

"Oh," Esther said. "Nothing."

But something in the statement made Hannah persist.

"What suggestion?" she asked again.

Esther kept her eyes forward, and her arm linked tightly through Hannah's.

"Nothing," she said, again.

"Esther," Hannah sobbed, putting force behind the name.

"Okay," the girl said. "It was early research. Dr. Lowen's. Didn't he tell you?"

"He didn't tell me anything."

Tears came down Hannah's face and she brushed them away.

"He doesn't have faith in himself," Esther said. "But the study was good. The results were good."

"I have no idea what you're talking about," Hannah said.

"The mould."

Esther ran her hand through her short hair; it stood on end. Hannah could see she was trying to remember. "He told me that he told David's wife. With the brown curly hair, and the red sleeves."

Hannah thought of the red roses embroidered by Shoshanna on the shirt that had seemed to come to her again and again from Ida in the laundry. She thought of the red dress that David had let Sarah keep.

The doctor had meant Sarah. The doctor thought Sarah was David's wife.

"What does the mould do?" Hannah asked, slowly.

"We don't know."

Hannah let out a sob of desperation. "What? Tell me."

Hadassah's face crumpled. "The wound. The infection. The mould might . . . there is some evidence suggesting . . ."

She didn't need to finish her sentence.

Ruth was dead. Hannah would kill herself too.

No. It was someone else who was to die.

From where I am now, I can see the randomness of the universe, the billion variables winging their way through the cosmos in an infinite number of combinations. Sometimes a mystery is momentarily pulled back, only to be swallowed up again in oblivion. As far back as the Ancient Greeks, mould had been used to treat infection. In 1920, two Belgians had observed that bacterial growth was inhibited by a fungal contamination in a staphylococcus culture. They published a paper that was largely ignored. Penicillium wasn't understood until much later.

Dr. Lowen was on to something. But the conditions weren't ready yet. It is unlikely what he thought he knew would have saved Ruth. And yes, he'd tried to tell me, but only half-heartedly, and I had tried to tell David. We were both unable to understand the importance of what he knew. And soon the doctor would die. It would take another decade and countless deaths before this truth was again revealed.

After a while, Hannah returned to her tent. Esther had been instructed to stay with Hannah, but she was overcome by exhaustion and emotion, and wanted the refuge of Shoshanna's arms. When Hannah said she needed to go back just for a moment, to be alone, Esther agreed.

Ruth's body had been taken away. The tent was like a vacated stage, the actors gone home, a few props scattered around. Hannah threw herself on Ruth's pallet. It still smelled like her daughter, sweat and urine and milk and rot. She cried for a very long time. Then she got up. She knew exactly where to look. Her body told her where. She felt around under David's mattress and found something right away. Her hand grasped the object. But it wasn't the gun. It was softer. Looser. She pulled it out tentatively. It was Salam.

If Hannah had stayed with the grief that overtook her then she would surely have died. The pull to action saved her. She felt her body moving, walking briskly out into the night, the doll clutched to her side. The stars were stab wounds on the soft underbelly of sky. The doctor had told two people about something that could have saved Ruth. David, and Sarah. She would kill one of them. Whoever she reached first.

David was gone, it didn't matter where. But I was in my tent, alone, with the gun that Hannah had been looking for. I had taken it, thinking it might protect me. Maybe I should have taken Salam instead.

What I would have given for a doll like that when I was a girl.

What I would have given for a mother who loved me like Hannah loved Ruth.

Hannah's curls were tousled, like she had been in a fight. Her eyes were wild.

"Ruth is dead," she said to me. As though I didn't already know.

For a moment I thought she was coming to me for comfort; I opened my arms. I would hold her.

This was, after all, the thing I actually wanted.

But Hannah's eyes went to my stomach and I knew, at once, that she knew. "You're pregnant," Hannah said.

"David told me," she said, in case there was any question.

A chill washed over me. In that moment, I wanted to rip the child from my womb, to give it to her if that would have helped. I could see the pain I had caused her, and remorse came over me. It was like nothing I had experienced before. How had I been unable to see?

"Did you think your child would replace my lost children?" Hannah asked.

I did not understand what she meant by children; she'd only had one child. Ruth.

Then something else crossed her face: terrible anger.

"You knew about the mould but you didn't tell me. You wanted her to die."

"The mould?" I said. What did she mean? Those half-mad ramblings of the doctor?

Hannah's teeth were clenched, her fists clenched, her cheeks bright red.

"I'm sorry," I said, for her rage was monumental, even if I did not understand it.

"My Ruthie," she said. "My baby . . ."

And she started to cry again, wracking sobs that bent her over with her hands on her knees, gasping like she had run a very long race.

"The mould," she said again. "What if it had worked?" She looked up at me, beseeching. "Why didn't you tell?"

It dawned on me that I had made a terrible mistake. Not one terrible mistake, but two. I had become pregnant. And I had failed to see what was important.

"I don't know what you're talking about," I said, but this was only half true. And then I saw that I shouldn't have said it. I saw her eyes land on the gun. I dove for it, but she was faster. She held it in the air in front of her, pointed not at my heart or my brain but at my belly.

"I'm pregnant," I reminded her. And again I'd made the wrong gamble.

"There won't be any babies," she said. "To replace my Ruth."

The last thing I saw was the pleasure this gave her. I was glad for her. In my small way.

CHAPTER 36

*W*HEN RUTH WAS A BABY she had fallen ill with croup. The wet, barking cough kept the other children up; Liora had sent her with Hannah and David to sleep between them in their bed, in their own tent. The child had suffered, and it had been the happiest two nights of Hannah's life. To have the little body wedged between them, the heat off her like an ember. Hannah had been assigned baby Mikhol to nurse, and she loved him, in a way, but when her own child turned her small mouth toward Hannah's breast it was something else that cleaved open within her. The tiny mouth latched on and sucked and sucked and the milk poured out of her like the milk of the gods. The place where Hannah had torn giving birth had almost healed, but she felt the wound open again and the blood begin to come, like all the fluids of motherhood were releasing themselves at once. She knew how to do this. Nobody had to show her. She had held the small rump of her baby in one hand, lying on her side, and had looked up and seen David watching them both with a kind of love she had not known before.

David was alone in the tent when Hannah returned there now. "Where's Ruth?" she asked, as if she might now awake from the nightmare.

"They took her body," he said. There were tears streaming from his eyes.

"You didn't," she said.

"Didn't what? Let them take her?"

Hannah herself didn't know what she was referring to. She looked down at her hands, half expecting to see them clutching Salam. Instead, she saw the gun.

She saw David seeing it too.

"You didn't," he said.

Hannah smiled.

"You underestimate me," she said.

In the beginning there was light. God parted the waters and honey poured forth. The plants and the animals rose, one by one, as if God was touching Her wand upon the emptiness. Here, and here, and here. She was the God of blood and semen, the God of tears. All the prickly shrubs and all the flamboyant birds and beasts appeared at Her command.

The look on David's face when he understood was like drapes briefly parted; then they fell back and he again looked impassive and cool. In that exact moment the kadachat left him. The fever was gone, and the jaundice, and the insanity that had accompanied them.

Something outside their tent summoned David and Hannah. They walked out into the gloaming. There was a strange light at edge of the horizon; as they watched, it arranged itself into the shape of flames.

"The Arabs," David said. But it was not the Arabs, or the Jews. It was me.

I would not die so easily.

"The crops," David said. But he didn't move.

"You killed Sarah," he said then to his wife, not looking at her, his eyes ahead.

"And you killed our daughter," Hannah replied.

"Now they'll send us away," David said.

But they both knew there was nowhere else to be sent. They were here, children of Eretz Yisrael, killers both.

"Maybe . . ." he said.

"What?" she asked.

"How will they know?" he asked.

He, too, did not want to be exiled again, and forced to wander in the desert for the rest of his days.

Hannah nodded, her eyes forward. An uneasy truce came over them. They were silent in its shadow.

Who would they say had killed me?

They would say I killed myself.

Now I've told you my story; you are the ones who know the truth. I wait to be released, to go where the others went. To be released, though, will not change my past. I can see that from here.

When I was a child my mother was ill. Nobody told me this, but I knew. I understood, too, that this was her excuse not to touch me. She lay in bed like a skeleton and did not invite me to crawl in beside her. What I would have given to breathe her in close up, even if it was the sour smell of old milk, of apples gone to turpentine. But even in death she would not have me. I still don't know why. To be a mother is its own kind of madness.

After Hannah killed me, I rose up into the mountains. I could see the fire burning at the edge of the wheat, and behind it, far below, Levi and Ida. They came out, the first to help, unshakeable in their belief in themselves and their purpose. There was a line between them, unseen to the human eye, but to me it was vibrating palpably. The flames had risen to make a murky half-day, a glow in which lies and truth were obscured. But Levi and Ida were happy. They had been through so many different deaths, and new life was coming to find them. I was so glad for my old friend.

Levi was running, a pail of water in his hands, but he could have run faster; he was letting Ida keep up and run by his side.

Soon, Ida would be pregnant. Her baby would be the first born to the new pioneers. She would be wrapped in Esther's intricate lace shawl, as Shoshanna had foreseen. And everywhere she toddled she would carry with her the doll called Salam.

Levi turned to Ida; he said something in her ear. From a hundred metres away, where she was standing with David, Hannah saw the girl smile.

Who can say what sets us each alight?

Ida and Levi moved forward together, united in purpose. But Hannah and David stayed where they were. The fire was necessary. They stood apart from each other, not touching, letting it burn.

ACKNOWLEDGEMENTS

What a great privilege it is to be able to thank the following:

My beloved editor Lynn Henry.

My agent Martha Webb, my publicist Sharon Klein, and everyone at Penguin Random House in Toronto. Mary-Anne Harrington and everyone at Headline in London.

Degan Davis, my first and best reader. Ayelet Tsabari and Danila Botha for astute and constructive feedback from an Israeli perspective.

The Chalmers Arts Fellowship for sending me to Israel.

The Canada Council for the Arts, The Ontario Arts Council and the Toronto Arts Council for funding that allowed me to write. The MacDowell Colony for the most productive residency I have ever experienced.

Ilana Bernstein, the wonderful archivist at Kibbutz Ein Harod, and Dr Judy Henn for translating archival material and reading an early draft. Tsafrira Shahan for sharing her academic research on women and mothering in the early kibbutz movement. Sonya Teece for transcription assistance.

The novels of the late Meyer Levin—*Yehuda* and *The Settlers* in particular—for informing this book on many levels. *Gideon's Spring* by Zerubavel Gilead and Dorothea Krook. *My Promised Land* by Ari Shavit.

My parents and sister.

My tribe of incredibly powerful and sustaining women friends.

Ayala, my bubala.

Eric. CWFTF.

ALISON PICK was the 2002 Bronwen Wallace Award winner for the most promising young writer in Canada. She has published two acclaimed volumes of poetry, and her first novel, *The Sweet Edge* (2005), was a *Globe and Mail* "Best Book." Her second novel, the bestselling *Far to Go* (2010), was nominated for the Man Booker Prize, won the Canadian Jewish Award for Fiction, and was named a "Top Ten of 2010" book by the *Toronto Star* and *NOW Magazine*. It was also published internationally to acclaim. Her memoir, *Between Gods*, was also published internationally, was a finalist for the BC National Award for Non-Fiction, and was a *Globe and Mail* "Best Book" of 2014.

A NOTE ABOUT THE TYPE

Strangers with the Same Dreams is set in Joanna, designed in 1930 by Eric Gill and released by the Monotype Corporation in 1937. Based on the classic typeface Granjon, and reminiscent of Gill's earlier designs for the faces Perpetua and Cockerel, Joanna is, as he described it, "a book face free from all fancy business."